A GOOD
INDIAN WIFE

A GOOD
INDIAN WIFE

A NOVEL

Anne Cherian

W. W. NORTON & COMPANY

NEW YORK • LONDON

For information about permission to reproduce selections from this book,
write to Permissions, W. W. Norton & Company, Inc.,
500 Fifth Avenue, New York, NY 10110

For information about special discounts for bulk purchases,
please contact W. W. Norton Special Sales at
specialsales@wwnorton.com or 800-233-4830

Manufacturing by The Haddon Craftsmen, Inc.
Book design by Kristen Bearse
Production manager: Anna Oler

Library of Congress Cataloging-in-Publication Data

Cherian, Anne.
A good Indian wife : a novel / Anne Cherian. — 1st ed.
        p. cm.
ISBN 978-0-393-06523-7
1. Anesthesiologists—Fiction. 2. San Francisco (Calif.)—Fiction.
3. India—Fiction. 4. Arranged marriage—Fiction.
5. Culture conflict—Fiction. I. Title.
PS3603.H476G63
813'.6—dc22   2008006168

W. W. Norton & Company, Inc.
500 Fifth Avenue, New York, N.Y. 10110
www.wwnorton.com

W. W. Norton & Company Ltd.
Castle House, 75/76 Wells Street, London W1T 3QT

1 2 3 4 5 6 7 8 9 0

The awful daring of a moment's surrender
Which an age of prudence can never retract
By this, and this only, we have existed

—T. S. ELIOT

The Waste Land, Part V

· ONE ·

THE TICKET AND THE AEROGRAM arrived on the same day. The cleaning crew had placed the mail in a neat pile on the kitchen counter. As always, the condo looked spotless and the lingering sharpness of Pine Sol reminded Neel of the hospital.

He checked the date and route of the ticket—June 16, San Francisco to Frankfurt to Bombay—and put it into his "Going to India" drawer. It held leftover hundred-rupee notes from the previous trip, a handful of light aluminum coins, and the Indian passport he kept meaning to throw away. He had an American one now, and for the first time needed a visa to enter India.

With no hesitation he crumpled his mother's letter into a ball and shot it into the garbage. She would be furious that her hard work was going unread. But after receiving these weekly missiles for the past several months, he knew the contents by heart. She always began with the nagging, "When you are coming back?" Was he really, really going to let Grandfather die without seeing him? Then, after the usual fussing paragraph, "You are sure you are eating the correct foods? Do you get enough of sleep?" she devoted the rest of the thin paper to her real reason for writing. Marriage. Girls. Or, as she put it, "suitable wife material."

On his last trip, three years ago, he had refused to see any of the prospective brides she arranged for him. After a week of shrill and rheumy words, of asking the Gods why they had given her such a difficult son, she was forced to suffer the embarrassment of cancelling visits to those eager families. "I'm so, so sorry, but my son, well, you know how they are changing once they are going to Ahmerica. He is saying he is too young to marry." She would not be able to use that excuse now. He was thirty-five, and as she kept warning, almost out of the "most eligible" bracket.

Neel wanted to throw away the ticket, too, but knew he could not put off the trip. Grandfather had gotten sick last month, and though his mother was vague about the details, she kept repeating that Tattappa did not have long to live.

Did Tattappa know Mummy was up to her old tricks again? Neel was surprised that Tattappa wasn't joining her in trying to maneuver him into an arranged marriage. After all, Neel was the only grandson to carry on the name of their old, well-respected family. According to Tattappa, who had heard the story from his grandfather, the Sarath family traced their beginnings to a tiny kingdom from the days when India, not forcibly yoked by the British, was a jigsaw, each piece the hereditary playground of a thousand kings. When Neel was young, he loved hearing about their first known ancestor, who married the king's daughter and grew to prominence as an exceptionally gifted prime minister. For the past four hundred years the Saraths had added to the "good name" of the family by marrying their own kind, Iyengars, the best of all South Indian Hindus, coveted for their light skin and intelligence. The girls were matched with Indian Civil Service officers, captains in the army, men comfortably perched on the upper crust of Indian society, and climbing ever higher. And the men wed fair beauties like his mother.

Tattappa seemed to understand that Neel had made a new life for himself as Dr. Neel Sarath, anesthesiologist, and now, American citizen. Or perhaps he didn't want to select another bride, having already chosen Mummy for his own son. Mummy, however, clearly wanted the privilege of picking her own daughter-in-law. That first envelope had taken him by surprise. He hadn't expected the cascade of audition shots that slipped through his fingers and littered the floor. The smiling faces were perfectly aware that a set of strange male eyes would be judging them. This, he knew, was the best they could look. The iridescent colors of brand-new silk sarees framed the bottom of the photographs, though always the main focus was the face itself, lightened by whitening powder, lips flush with lipstick. All the eyes looked alike, large and dark. Neel did a double take at the final picture: a girl with two braids hanging down her ears. Was this one young or just unaware that girls of a certain age switched over to one braid? Then he recalled seeing a snapshot of a young Mummy, two fat braids that got cut off by the camera but which, she liked to brag, went all the way to her knees. Mummy had gone on to list the girls; each one fair (therefore pretty) and from an established family. She wanted him to marry someone like her.

Since change was slow in a small, out-of-the-way Indian town, she could easily find him such a wife. Neel had made light of the Freudian inversion with his friends. "I'm not like you guys," he joked. "I don't have a mother complex. My mom has a son complex and wants *me* to marry *her*." Even the names remained the same. Vijaylaxmi, Jayanti, Anusaya, predictable syllables that were unpronounceable jaw breakers in America. Like their grandmothers, the girls believed in the potency of coconut oil, which they dutifully smoothed on their hair every morning to lengthen already long strands. Nimble fingers used identical Mother-taught knots to weave thick jasmine ropes that they entwined into black braids. The sudden disappearance of the starry, perfumed flowers when they got their period, or "monthly," as they called it, was a signal for Neel and his teenage friends to tease the girls. "Tomato chutney, tomato chutney," they shouted. But the girls never responded, and only the bold ones looked back, irises glowing darker from the homemade kajal they carefully applied every day.

Raised for marriage, they learned the subtle differences between masala pastes, knew how to cut cabbage finer than a grater, and practiced decorating the front path of the house with kolum for the yearly ceremonies that marked the seasons. The one adjustment to modern life was college, where parents encouraged them to take easy courses, complacent that the purpose of a degree was to secure a husband, not a job.

Neel only knew them from afar, since "good" Indian girls never talked to boys after the magical—menstrual, he realized later on— age of twelve. He would be surprised if they had any ambition beyond that of luring the prescribed husband and bearing children, preferably sons. Like his mother, they would *ai ai yoo* in horror at bikinis, not admitting that sarees also showed skin. The "bad" girls were the ones who passed along dirty jokes, calling them "nonvegetarian" because of the flesh content. "Why did the ant climb up the king's leg?" they whispered softly, but loud enough for those nearby to know that something vulgar was being voiced. "To attend the royal ball." A trill of giggles greeted this, though, if pressed, no one would be able to say what—sexually or even physically—a ball was. But mostly these were simple girls, who looked forward to imitating their mothers: gossiping, grumbling about the servants, and spattering kitchen walls with the oil from dosas and sambar.

He didn't want his life to be changed—or challenged—by them. He wasn't a traditional Indian man, who sought out an I'll-cook-the-meals-and-bear-the-children wife. His college friends back home were content to marry women who replicated their parents' lives. But from a very young age Neel had wanted to get away, had yearned for a whole other way of being. As a teenager he had even made up a year-by-year plan with goals: Go to America for college, become a doctor by twenty-eight, marry the woman of his choice. He had always known that an arranged marriage with its parent-picked wife and life was not for him.

Caroline, with her sun-filled, silky hair, was nothing like those girls of his youth. She too wore kajal, but hers was a dark blue eye pencil that emphasized the sapphire color of her eyes. "Like Princess Diana," she told him. Her white body, paler still in the torso, was a smorgasbord of fragrances—mint in her mouth, perfume between her breasts; even her stockings gave off the musky aroma of lavender. The one time she wore his T-shirt, he didn't wash it for weeks, wanting to hold on to that enticing mixture of perfume and sex. She was as seductively mysterious as the various unguents, powders, and vials cluttering her makeup bag.

They had just started going out when he went to India the last time. She drove him to the airport and kissed him again and again, oblivious to the stares they were attracting. Neel saw the older Indian immigrants tighten their lips with disapproval, but thrilled to such an uninhibited, Western send-off. Yet he deliberately refrained from telling his family anything about her. Their relationship was uncertain, she was American, and, if that wasn't enough to give his mother a heart attack, Caroline Kempner was a secretary.

His mother would fall to the floor from shock. "A secretary? Why for a secretary? I can get for you a nice doctor like yourself, an engineer, even a First-Class First Bachelor of Arts girl from a fine, fine family, and you want a secretary?"

Like many status-conscious Iyengars, she looked down on secretaries. He could hear her censure. "They are stupid men who like to sit on a chair all the time and Anglo-Indian girls like that one in your father's office." Mummy had never hidden her dislike for Miss Rosario, whose grandfather had been a train driver, making decent wages in this "grace and favor" position the British kept for the Anglo-Indian population they had created through intermarriage. All during the days of the Raj, the Anglos benefited from their tenuous "I'm half/quarter/eighth white" connection to the British. But any claim to superiority vanished with Independence, and, abandoned in India, the Anglos had only one advantage: the English language. Many Anglo girls, Miss Rosario among them, became secretaries and worked closely with men. Such proximity to the opposite sex gave women like his mother another reason to dislike them.

Whenever Mummy visited Father's office, she treated Miss Rosario like a servant, seen but not acknowledged. Neel, however, was fascinated by the short-haired woman, who always wore frocks. Once he had stared at her middle, finally asking in confusion: "Do you have a stomach?" Miss Rosario laughed and said, "Yes, it is right here," pointing to her belt. "I just don't expose it like your mama, who wears a saree."

The regard—and money—given to American secretaries had nudged Neel into respecting them. The department secretary at Stanford had been a premed student who got married and put off going back to school. Still, there were many moments when he wished Caroline was a fellow doctor, or at least a college graduate. He was well aware that their relationship was Indian-inappropriate. But most days he was too busy to think or do anything about it. It was like the annoying hum of a hovering mosquito, landing with a sharp sting only when he wondered why he hadn't met the right woman, or like now, when his mother showed herself, stern-faced with ancient traditions and expectations.

But there was no need to think of Mummy right now. There was still time to enjoy his life. To stock the fridge with steaks and burgers, to drink ice-cold beer by the six-pack, to sleep in the nude. In India there would be no meat, no closed doors, no time to relax in front of the TV. Tattappa refused to buy a set, saying the box contained too many wires and would anyway stop working with the first monsoons. When Neel went home, everything would be crowded, the house from visitors come to see him, and his stomach from the oily snacks—murku, vada—and elaborate meals his mother insisted on preparing, because that was how she showed him love.

Just envisioning the small brick house he had grown up in made him appreciate his sparsely furnished condo. His mother would be upset at the secondhand pieces. "You are poor?" she would worry, not understanding that in America it was possible to find the very rich stooped over at yard sales. When he bought the condo two years ago, he decided to let the furnishings wait till he could afford the best, like the wraparound Bose stereo system and his car. That's what he told everyone. In truth he was waiting for the day when a wife, with her knowledge of French and Italian antiques, could use her eye to find just the right pieces at auctions and estate sales. He wanted a partner who would fill in the gaps that someone not born and raised in America inevitably encountered. He could study magazines and take classes, but remained confounded by the difference between kitsch and classy, and knew only that he didn't want a home filled with the large wooden elephants and badly made inlay tables that so many stores claimed were authentic Indian items.

He put on some Mozart and opened the biography of Picasso. The phone rang.

"How come I have to hear important things from the hospital grape cluster?"

Neel tilted the phone so the voice booming through it wouldn't hurt his ears. Sanjay always assumed that his Indian accent meant he didn't have to introduce himself. And the fact that they had known each other since Stanford days made him feel he could ask Neel almost anything.

"And just what has the grapevine been distilling?"

"You take two weeks' notice, you tell everyone you are going to India, and you don't inform me? Is it because I am the only one brave enough to ask if you are going to get married?"

Neel felt his irritation turn to anger. Sanjay Bannerji had gotten engaged to tall, beautiful Oona the same time that Savannah had rejected him, breaking up their cozy foursome in college. Now, living with a wife who called him "darling," and enjoying Decembers wreathed with Christmas spirit, Sanjay was assuming that Neel was headed to India, tail between his legs, for an arranged marriage.

Neel tried to dispel his resentment with a joke. "You mean to say you didn't receive the wedding invitation? Looks like the famous American postal system is becoming like the Indian one."

"The Indian Pinching System, you mean." Sanjay laughed. "But seriously, why the sudden trip? Everything thik-thak at home?"

"Thought I'd check up on my grandfather."

"He's sick?"

"Tattappa's been unwell for a while. I just thought it was time to see him."

"But not time to get married?"

"I'm waiting for you to arrange that, remember?"

"As soon as you give me my fee, you stingy anesthesiologist," Sanjay said.

"You pediatricians are pathetic," Neel lobbed back, relieved to be on familiar terrain again.

He had barely replaced the receiver when it rang again.

"Hi, sweetie. Did you get the ticket?"

"Yes, it came today," he replied, uncomfortably aware that he could not call Caroline "sweetie" with the same ease. He always underwent this strained moment of relinquishing the anesthesiologist—the man she called Dr. Sarath at work—and turning into her lover. At the hospital he kept his distance (his way of ensuring their relationship remained a secret), using "Caroline" when necessary. She, however, never seemed to have any difficulty with their dual lives.

He remembered that she had researched the airlines and booked his flight. "Thanks again for taking care of it for me." He tried to sound sincere, but couldn't help thinking that while a girlfriend might do this, many secretaries routinely booked tickets as part of their job. She had been equally helpful when he bought the condo, meeting with the real estate agent when he was in surgery.

"Of course I'd do it for you. Why don't you come over?"

"I don't know. I have to call India." Annoyed at the thought of the long trip, he wasn't in the mood to see her. He didn't want to see a dying Tattappa either, but would regret not going. Tattappa, his parents, the whole town, expected it of him. In India it was always family above self, with no one considering his difficulties.

"I'm going to miss you."

"I'm going to miss being here, too," he said lightly, so she wouldn't be upset that he hadn't answered in kind.

There was a small pause, then Caroline asked, "You don't remember what day it is, do you?"

"Your birthday," he said immediately, and then, "No, we celebrated that last month." She had casually mentioned her birthday for weeks beforehand, and he had ignored her hints about a diamond ring, giving her an angora sweater instead. What Hallmark-inspired holiday, Valentine's Day or Secretary's Day—American celebrations that continued to elude him—had he forgotten this time? "I give up. What day is it?"

"It's our third anniversary. How about Chinese take-out from our usual place?"

Picasso wasn't a good enough excuse, and she wouldn't understand his anxieties about the upcoming trip. Most Americans had one fixed definition of India: they conjured up a mystical country rife with swamis or, like Caroline, a dirty Third World slum over-populated with beggars and exotic diseases. Only another immigrant like Sanjay could understand the tug two countries made on the heart. "Okay. Why don't you call in the order and I'll pick it up." As he said it, he realized he was hungry.

"I'll be waiting with open arms."

"What about your legs?" would have been his response back in their salad days. Now he wondered how soon he could leave after dinner. He still had to call Mummy and tell her this trip was specifically to see Grandfather, not girls. He didn't want Father's older sister, Aunty Vimla, running around town telling people he was coming back to get married. When he did marry, it would be to a woman he loved and respected. And he would choose her.

He took the long route to Caroline's apartment, rolling down the windows to mitigate the aroma of ginger, garlic, soy sauce, that kept escaping from the cartons of food like little genies. Fog softened the glare of the street lights and the night air carried the scent of sea and gardens. The roses, terraces of hanging rosemary, lemon trees in full bloom, stirred his senses. He recalled the nights when he had raced over, desperate to see Caroline, smell her, touch her. Now he imagined her undressed, the soft pink of her soles, the deeper pink of her nipples, the blond hair that highlighted the dark. His foot pressed down on the accelerator, the needle swung to the right, houses rushed by in a blur, and in a few minutes he was in front of her apartment building.

He sprinted up the stairs, two at a time, trying not to tilt the stack of boxes. He noticed that some eggplant sauce had seeped out and had just dipped his finger into its oil-dark luster when she opened the door to his ring.

· TWO ·

"AKKA'S GETTING MARRIED, Akka's getting married," Kila lisped, spinning around her mother like a satellite moon and stealing glances at Leila.

"Kila, sit down," Amma ordered, pushing her glasses back on her nose. "You are giving me a headache. And do not go bothering your big sister. It is virry bad luck to mention marriage." Their mother was the most superstitious member of the family, with rules for almost everything. Hands could not be linked behind heads. Shoes had to face the same way. If you forgot something after leaving the house, you had to sit down on a chair before going out the door a second time. Her three daughters had given up trying to make her see logic and just did whatever it was she insisted would save them from bad karma.

"Akka says it's 'very,' Amma, not 'virry.'" Kila was at the age when she enjoyed correcting her mother. Mrs. Krishnan had not studied English, so her words and grammar were often twisted with the intonations of her birth language. But since her daughters had gone to an English medium school, and even dreamed in this new language, she was forced to use it more often than she liked. They usually hopped between their two languages, but Kila always called Leila "Akka," older sister, and her parents "Amma" and "Appa," no matter what they were speaking.

"Virry, very, it is all the same for me. Just to sit down, please." Amma pointed to an empty cane chair. The sitting room had the best furniture in the house and was usually off limits to Kila.

She took advantage of this rare opportunity and, ignoring her mother, jumped straight onto the sofa with its square, starched cushions. Leila sat at one end in the Lotus position, the children's story she was writing draped across her knees so the words were hidden from Amma. Leila let everyone assume that she needed the quiet of the sitting room to prepare for class. But instead of reading *Othello* (she was teaching the tragedies), she composed rhymed stories about cats.

Amma considered writing a waste of time. She would never understand that the stories helped Leila pass the months and years as she waited in vain for her parents to provide her with a husband.

Kila grinned and stuck out her tongue, turning away from her mother. Leila smiled and ruffled her baby sister's hair. She adored Kila, the change-of-life baby no one had expected, and whose arrival eight years ago had thrilled Leila as much as it embarrassed their sister, Indira. Indy, all legs and no bra at sixteen, was mortified that Amma and Appa still "did it," while Leila, at twenty-two, silently applauded her parents—though neither knew exactly what "it" entailed. Leila took over caring for the snappy-eyed Akila—promptly shortened to Kila—giving her oil massages, singing lullabies, teaching her the alphabet.

Kila squirmed out of her sister's reach. "It's hot, Akka," she complained.

The summer heat, sticky, oppressive, unyielding, had settled into every corner of the house. The prickly haze hovered above the coffee table and the low display cabinet containing the few artifacts Appa had brought back from his one trip to London. Even the flies had given into slugdom, bodies plopped on the window ledge, easy targets for Kila's killer aim. Amma had finished cooking by seven in the morning, but every room felt like the kitchen. The windows were shut tight and the fan turned to the highest speed. But the blades whirled ineffectively. Outside, the unrelenting sun cooked the discarded vegetable peels, softened yellow-ripe guavas into various stages of decomposition, and hardened the refuse, human and animal, that studded the sides of the road. All these odors, along with the trail left by the man who sold saltfish from a bicycle, tried to invade houses through the thin cracks that ants used so successfully. People sweated without moving a muscle, and tap water ran tepid. It was the sort of morning when everyone tried to stay indoors, hiding from the heat and praying for the monsoons to break. Only servants, vegetable vendors, and those on a mission, like Mrs. Vimla Rajan, braved the sun and the stinging asphalt.

"It's ice cream weather," Kila shouted, showing two missing front teeth. "Don't you think so, Indy?" She jiggled Indy's arm, then quickly moved away when she realized that she had irritated her sister. Indy had followed Amma into the sitting room, but brought along the newspaper, which she concentrated on while trying to ignore the conversation she knew would soon enough involve her.

"No one is to go out today," Amma said firmly. "It is too-hot-to-go-out weather. And how many times must I tell you those ice cream wallahs use dirty water? Enough, Kila, you must to finish your homework. You have school tomorrow."

"I want Akka to help me." Kila clutched Leila's hand and tried to pull her off the sofa.

Leila gently disengaged her fingers and felt her stomach tighten with anxiety. Amma was all set to discuss Mrs. Rajan's visit. Mrs. Rajan had married her four children very well and was now preparing to do the same for her brother's only son. Every family needed a go-between to arrange marriages, and Mrs. Rajan had the right credentials: tenacity, a long memory, and numerous connections. This morning she had surprised Amma, walking up the front steps like a Grand Duchess, orange-flowered umbrella clashing with her motai pink checked saree. She had accepted a cup of coffee from Leila and then shooed her away from the sitting room, announcing, "I have some virry virry important bizzness to tell to your mummy."

Amma was the staunch optimist of the family, getting excited every time Leila received a marriage proposal, forgetting all the ones that had fallen through in the last ten years. But one by one the boys Amma had tried so hard to capture married into families that bought them what they wanted. And the boys of today— even the so-so ones—kept adding to their demands. Their brides had to come from a good family, be fair-skinned, educated, and most important, bring a large dowry. Leila's qualifications fell very short on the last item since Appa's accident in the steel factory had injured his leg, keeping him from working these past fifteen years. Her own salary as a college teacher was minimal, and barely increased the dowry Amma had begun saving for years ago. Three dowries for three girls was a challenge even without the problem of inflation. Leila had noticed that recently Amma was more anxious to buy sarees, as if new clothes offset a meager dowry. Prospective grooms were not stupid, however. They quickly looked past Leila's silken finery and married women who brought them lakhs of rupees and luxury items such as scooters, cars, and refrigerators.

Leila didn't know whether to be grateful or irritated that Amma persisted in the mad belief that she, a thirty-year-old with only six thin gold bangles when other girls had treasure chests filled with the precious 24-carat metal, could get a good husband. But Amma was no different from the other mothers who viewed their female issues as obligations from the moment they were born. Leila had seen mothers spend hours smoothing the noses of infant daughters into straight, aesthetically pleasing lines; others began keeping an eye out for a son-in-law as soon as their girls reached puberty.

Leila had no idea that as Amma tried to fulfill her duty, she moved back and forth between blaming herself and blaming Leila for her failure. For years Amma had quietly worried that Leila had grown too tall. She was five feet six when most girls had the delicacy to stop at five feet. Amma knew the height came from her side, for her father had been a giant at six feet two. How many men had not approached Leila because they were shorter than she? Amma would never know, and she carried their nameless bodies on her shoulders, never mentioning that she felt responsible for her daughter's desperate situation.

Leila blamed only herself. She had grown too tall, and every proposal had been withdrawn because of her behavior. Daughters were not meant simply to desire marriage; they were supposed to do everything in their power to help their mothers bring it about. It was in the realm of the second expectation that Leila had failed Amma—and herself. That her brief lapse with the man-whose-name-was-never-mentioned had happened more than ten years ago was irrelevant, as far as Amma's elephant memory was concerned. Though Leila often grumbled about her mother's authoritarian ways, she could do nothing but succumb. She had gone behind Amma's back one time, and that had given her mother the right to make sure that from then on, Leila did the right thing. *Have you been a* good *girl?* It had been years since Leila stopped reading the A. A. Milne poem to Kila because it reminded her too much of Amma. "Leila, be good," Amma said so often that sometimes Leila thought her name was Leila Begood.

"Kila, you will please to go now and do your homework by yourself. Leila, you must to pay attention," Amma commanded as soon as Kila left the room. "Indira, put that paper away." Amma used the ends of her pallao to wipe the sweat off her glasses.

Indy reluctantly gave up solving the chess problem and folded the newspaper. In the humidity, her hair stuck out like a halo and she constantly fought its waywardness, hands smoothing the serrated mess, trying to flatten it against her head. Now the two sisters grimaced at each other.

"Mrs. Rajan herself came this morning. Her nephew is coming from Ahmerica in two weeks and the family wants for him to see you," Amma told Leila triumphantly. She emphasized that the request came directly from the boy's family.

"What is he, a fourth-time-tried-but-failed PhD?" Indy inquired sarcastically. The last proposal was from a man living in Dallas who had failed to get his Physical Therapy license for the fourth time. He had kept Amma and Leila on tenterhooks for a week. Amma went to the Temple every day, making pujas so he would say yes. Leila prayed silently that he would not. Indy sided with Leila. She could not picture Leila, with her fish-shaped eyes, even pomegranate teeth, and soft, straight hair, married to a man with cratered skin who made smacking sounds when chewing his food. Leila *did* want to marry; she just didn't want to be ashamed of her husband. She wasn't like some girls who didn't care who they married as long as they acquired the "Mrs." label. But she knew that if the man agreed, Amma would force her into the marriage. Afterwards, the sisters had laughed in relief at his put-on American accent and cowboy hat that had got stuck in their low, narrow doorway.

"Indira, please, just because of only one man. No, no, Mrs. Rajan's nephew is a doctor. He came first in his class from some virry good college. Sanford, Sunford, something like that. He owns his own house, a big one, in a virry good locality, and Mrs. Rajan says he works for some famous-famous hospital in San Frahncisco."

"So what's wrong with him?" Indy asked.

"Amma, do they know we can't afford a dowry?" Leila asked at the same time.

Amma glared at Indira. "There is nothing at all wrong with him.

You will to see for yourself. I saw him at Raju's wedding. That was what, three years ago? He is tall and virry handsome."

"Amma, you haven't answered my question," Leila said. She was tired of men who assumed that her family, once rich but now only "good," could somehow still come up with the requisite rupees.

"Yes, yes, Leila, the family knows our situation. Mrs. Rajan came out herself and said they do not want a dowry. They want only a good girl. Her doctor nephew makes enough of money. Why does he need Indian rupees?"

"When is this to be?" Leila asked, resigned to yet another rejection. She wondered why the Saraths wanted their son to see her. Men from America were the ultimate sons-in-law, fought over by the mothers of every nubile girl. She had always assumed she would be part of that group of desirable girls, a logical progression for someone popular in school and college. She had been known as pretty and clever, admired because the Anglo-Indian girls asked her to help them write love letters to their boyfriends, imitated because she often wore her straight hair in fashions that were almost Western. But once even the ugly girls got married, she had become the object of whispered conversations. People cruelly—and correctly—deduced she taught English only because she wasn't married. Everyone knew that colleges hired single women as cheap labor. Most girls' colleges had a constellation of aging, anxious women who had been forced to make teaching their career because the "Mrs." career, the one they really wanted, had bypassed them.

"He is to come next Sunday. Only two days after he arrives," Amma said with great satisfaction.

Leila was surprised that she was one of the first girls lined up for his viewing pleasure. Some families showed their foreign-living sons more than a hundred girls, with the most important ones appearing early in the parade. She knew this doctor would see many girls before choosing a bride. One of Appa's distant relatives—a PhD candidate in New York—had met eighty girls, and in the end was so confused that he married the last one he saw.

Leila thought she had been born in the wrong century. At one time—the good old days, she and Indy joked—women received dowries and even chose their husbands. Kings used to hold lavish Swayamvaras for their daughters, and on the appointed day, royal scions came from all over to win the hand of the princess. Occasionally there were prowess tests, but usually the princess walked down the row of hopeful princes, considering them one by one, finally indicating the husband of her choice by placing a garland around his neck. Leila often wished she were in that position. She would have been able to walk right past the man from Calcutta instead of being rejected immediately. "I like my wife to be more plummy," he had said, ending both hope and conversation. "Plummy" had stumped Amma, until Indy explained the rude man had meant plump. For the next two weeks Leila was forced to hide all the food Amma tried to make her eat until things went back to normal.

"We shall to buy a new saree," Amma announced.

"Amma, I don't think we can afford—" Leila started, but Amma cut her off. "It has been a few months since you bought one. We shall to go shopping tomorrow."

Leila felt a future fight seed itself inside her. She refused to dress for certain failure. She didn't want to spend her money to sit on a chair and be judged by strange eyes.

"You didn't tell us his name, Amma," Indy said.

"No? It is Suneel, Suneel Sarath."

"Suneel Sarath," Indy tested the name. "Akka, you can call him SS."

"What is so funny?" Amma asked, her antennae going up immediately. Amma's radar for detecting bad words in English had been alert ever since she intuited that Leila should not be teaching Indy the song: *Spell it with an F, a U, a C, and a K. What does it spell? Fuck!* She had reacted the same way when Leila brought home the phrases "Up yours" and "Balls" that were casually exchanged by anyone who was someone in college.

"You want for me to wash your mouth?" Amma used to threaten.

Leila didn't. But she also didn't want to be left out, so she simply switched to numbers, adding up the letters of the words she wasn't allowed to say. Amma could only stand by in frustration as "Forty-six" and "One hundred and thirty-five" were bandied about by both sisters.

"SS," like numbers, could stand for anything.

"Hmmph." Amma knew she had missed something, but was too excited to care. As she left the room, she repeated, "We shall to buy a saree tomorrow."

"Nazi," Leila said softly, then fell to laughing again with Indy.

The laughter covered the hope that streaked through her like the bright tail of a comet. Maybe this time she would be lucky. A doctor from America. The last decent proposal had come five years ago. Leila now thought of the short, naturalized British citizen as just another sharp point in the ascetic bed of nails she was beginning to believe might be her destiny. Yet everything had started out so auspiciously. The two sets of parents shared numerous acquaintances and Leila had talked to him for a whole hour, during which a chance remark led to the discovery that they both enjoyed reading the Brontë sisters. He had visited the Brontë Parsonage in Haworth and raised her hopes by suggesting that she, too, would be charmed by the quaint town, with its cobbled streets. So Leila was not too worried when they didn't hear from him the first day. She even convinced herself that he was too short to be accepted by anyone else. By the second day it was more difficult to hold on to the hope that he liked her. But, she consoled herself, he had confessed to jet lag, laughing about the dark circles under his eyes. When the third morning dawned, she woke with the certain knowledge that he had chosen elsewhere.

Still, when the rejection came, she cried for days. Indy, sweet, kind Indy, had declared her hatred for Mr. British. "Imagine living with a people we kicked out of our country. There will be others," she whispered. But Leila knew that "good catches" had so many choices they never settled for a dowryless bride.

Mr. British was only an engineer. On credentials alone, this doctor was more impressive. And he lived in a country that was the number one destination for Indians. It was a proposal worth the long and despairing wait.

If it worked out.

· THREE ·

NEEL GOT HIS FIRST TASTE OF India in Frankfurt as he waited to board the plane for the final leg to Bombay. There were Indians everywhere. He had forgotten that brown came in so many hues and textures—fleshy, hirsute, pale, dark—that now surrounded him in the waiting area. His ear caught phrases of languages he had not heard in years. Malayalam—"*Ivede va*," yelled at a little boy who was scampering down the corridor. Bengali—"*Jol khabo, na*," as a young girl handed a bottle of water to an elderly woman. Only the announcer's German told him where he was.

Wanting to make an unapproachable impression, Neel set out a stack of articles as soon as he took the window seat he had requested. He deliberately did not make eye contact with the man across the aisle. Neel had long practice—almost in one glance—at decoding travelers and recognized Mr. Rolex as a fellow Non-Resident Indian who would want to launch into a "clubby" conversation. The couple in front were an unlikely match made possible by America: The fat, balding man had parlayed his foreign status to acquire a pretty wife who would never have considered him had he held the same job in India. The old woman beside Neel would probably need help during the flight, something he found himself doing on every trip now that so many Indians lived in America and were visited by elderly parents who did not speak English.

"Oh, no," he sighed when he heard a crying child—an Indian couple proudly taking their progeny home to be admired and doted upon. The parents were equally loud and Neel could hear every word of their conversation with Mr. Rolex. He had been mistaken, after all; they were an Indian-American couple, the dark-haired wife of Italian origin. And they were returning for good. "Harry has lived in my country, so now it's my turn," the woman said enthusiastically. "That's just one reason," husband Hari said. "It is difficult to be neither fish nor fowl in America, and I told Lisa our daughter will be more accepted back home. I mean, when the British came, our kings greeted them with open arms. America is not such a welcoming country." Mr. Rolex agreed, but Neel thought the man was a simpleton. After that he concentrated on the articles, relieved that neither-fish-nor-fowl proved to be quiet, sleeping till touchdown in Bombay.

About twenty hours later, he stepped off the tiny Indian Airlines plane he had boarded at Bombay and was immediately embraced by the heat. It clung to him like the suit he wore to go deep-sea diving, both familiar and uncomfortable. Airport workers unloaded luggage on the grass-and-weed, dog-gambolled strip that served as the runway. The sun didn't seem to affect them as they laughed and tossed the baggage: cardboard boxes tied with string, suitcases with oddly shaped bulges, each well plastered with the owner's name and address.

Neel heard his name and turned to see Mummy, her high noon yellow saree blending in with the crowd of brightly dressed people. She was waving, shouting, "Suneel, Suneel!" He was so used to his one-syllable American name that for a moment he did not respond to the sing-song Indian word; then he waved and indicated the carousel.

There was only one ancient, creaking carousel in the airport whose grandiose, multi-syllable name (after a freedom fighter or politician, no one could agree) belied its small size. Until he went to America, Neel thought all airports were composed of one building equipped to handle two flights a day.

The slow-moving girders unloaded his bag last. At least it wasn't lost.

He walked toward his mother, wanting to kiss her hello, but knowing that would embarrass her. Instead, he asked, "Have you been standing for a long time?" His plane had been delayed for two hours in Bombay because of the rains, and there were no chairs in the tiny waiting area.

"No problem, no problem." Her face was all teeth from smiling.

He was chastened by her cheerfulness. Rested from having slept during the Indian Airlines flight, he was still peeved at the assortment of inconveniences that had hampered him from the moment he arrived in Bombay. Cafeteria closed. Just one window—with a long line—to exchange money. A taxi strike, which meant taking an open, jolting, smelly auto from the international to the national airport. Yet she, who had risen at dawn to make the five-hour trip to the airport, was too happy to care about simple annoyances like standing and waiting.

Crammed in the backseat of the car that couldn't accommodate his legs, he half-listened to her excited words. Each was careful not to bring up the topic they were most concerned about: girls and Tattappa's health.

His mother talked rapidly, making up for the time spent apart. The steel factory had built a large auditorium for his old school. His father was on the organizing committee for collecting money to enlarge the Temple. Neel rolled up the window, preferring the heat to the brown dust that already glazed his shoes and clothes. He wished the car was air-conditioned as sweat gathered behind his knees and puddled into his socks. They drove through small villages where thatched-roof huts were surrounded by a sea of red—chilies drying in the sun, his mother reminded him. "Nowadays some people are even putting paddy on the roadside. They want the cars to clean off the husk. Then they are getting angry if there is any problem," his mother's voice rose in outrage. Water buffaloes humped together in the muddy rivers. Monkeys screeched from trees. They had to stop for ten minutes until a peacock finally dragged its cumbersome tail across the road.

In a few hours the horizon changed from trees to rows of cement buildings. The driver slowed down as the car approached their town and Neel peered out his window as if it were a giant TV screen. Women coolies glided by, easily balancing precarious towers of bricks on their heads. Hawkers stood behind old wooden carts frying samosas, aloo chops, and vadas, and the smell of stale oil and flour wafted into the car. Big red buses rolled by, their color forever stained by the black fumes escaping from exhaust pipes. Neel could make out the agile conductor moving up and down the aisle. These men had amazing memories. Even in a packed bus, they knew who got on at what stop and always calculated the right amount for the ride. If only he could recall diseases and cures with as much accuracy and ease.

Male coolies, muscles popped out clearly, pushed carts heavy with wooden boxes. Four family members sprouted like fingers from one scooter. Gaunt rickshaw drivers made illegal shortcuts, almost causing accidents. He had forgotten that driving had few rules in India. It was first come, first go, with greater use of the horn than the brakes. When he was young, he used to beg his father to let him press the horn on their scooter.

As they made the once-familiar turns, Neel's worries about Tattappa increased. He leaned forward with all the intensity and fear of his younger self when the red brick house came into view. He was Tattappa's boy. Tattappa had raised him while Father spent long hours in the steel factory and Mummy supervised the kitchen work or visited friends.

The car stopped and Neel saw Tattappa stand up from his customary cane chair on the verandah, looking no closer to death than he had three years ago. After the last telephone conversation with Mummy, Neel thought he would find his grandfather in bed, able only to suck in soft rice and water. But there he was, chest bare as usual, a lungi tied around his teak brown waist. His gray hair was thinner and his shoulders more wrinkled and stooped, but the arms that embraced Neel were as strong as ever.

No one noticed Neel's surprise. Tattappa, Father, Aunty Vimla clustered around him, excited and talking all at once. Mummy ordered the servant girl to bring coffee immediately and ushered Neel into the sitting room.

Neel had not felt this angry in years. He knew he should not have believed his mother. She would do anything—lie, exaggerate, even pretend that Tattappa was dying—to bring him back within marriage distance. But far away in America he couldn't be sure that Tattappa wasn't really sick, and he never imagined that she would go so far as to tempt the Gods with such a flagrant lie.

He was livid that he had been duped and that Tattappa had gone along with it. The old man was too humble to ask Neel to make the trip just to see him, but he had not hesitated to collaborate with Mummy. Such inconsistencies drove Neel crazy and were part of the reason he kept his San Francisco life so separate.

He knew it wasn't the right time, but the words formed themselves inside his mouth. "Tattappa, I thought you were very sick?" Neel didn't bother to keep the accusation out of his voice.

"Sick?" Tattappa blinked, eyes enlarged and a little watery behind his thick glasses.

"Yes, Mummy wrote that you were very sick. Practically dying." He glanced over at his mother, but she was busy pouring coffee into cups that he remembered were only brought out on important occasions.

"Aaah yes, yes, that is also true. Every day I am getting closer to dying. So. So it is good that you are home."

"Let us not talk of sad things." Mummy handed Neel a cup, smiling, looking at her sister-in-law for confirmation.

"On your virry first day home we must only talk of happy happy things," Aunty Vimla agreed, slurping her coffee loudly.

Neel winced at the sound of air rushing in to replace the words in her gossipy mouth. Her shrill voice had constantly ruined Neel's youthful achievements by comparing everything he did to her son, Ashok, even though she never showed them any proof, like report cards. She merely "hmmphed" that Neel's first place was good, but the marks were not up to Ashok's standards. During his last visit, she had bragged about the nice wife she had found for Ashok, telling Neel that if he didn't hurry up all the good girls would be taken. Now that Ashok and his sisters were all married, she had come here with her sanctimonious words to interfere in his life. She had always used her authoritative role as Father's older sister to bully Mummy and belittle Neel. No one admonished her, not Father, who for some strange reason had always been intimidated by his sister, nor Grandfather, who doted on his only daughter because Aunty Vimla looked like her mother.

"What—happy things—do you want to talk about, Aunty?" He now knew what she was up to. It wasn't just Mummy and Tattappa; Aunty Vimla had joined the campaign to get him married. But she had lost any power over him long before he got into Stanford's medical school and Ashok, who had applied the year before to the MBA program, received a thin, polite rejection letter. "Stupid stupid school," Aunty Vimla dismissed the California university. "It is better for Ashok to stay here. India is good enough for us, so why not for him?"

Aunty Vimla took another loud sip of coffee. "Oh, any happy thing is okay okay with me. You look virry handsome, virry good. But I am sure everyone in Ahmerica is telling you that also."

"Right now I'm so jet-lagged I don't know whether I'm standing or sitting."

"You are definitely sitting." Aunty Vimla laughed. "Just to keep on sitting. We will all take virry good care of you."

"Yes, that is correct," his mother agreed, nervously rearranging her saree pallao.

Aunty Vimla said, "Your grandfather"—she glanced at Tattappa and quickly added—"and your mummy and daddy, we would all like to see you married. So, with your mummy's help, I have made some good arrangements for you. First-class girls. You have simply to sit and see them. Then if one is to your liking, you simply sit and get married. Simple."

"Thanks for your concern, Aunty, but I came to see Tattappa, not a girl." Even if he had wanted an arranged marriage, he wouldn't give her the satisfaction of ensuring he got a girl inferior to Ashok's wife.

"You can see both, your grandfather and the girls, why not? Other boys, they are doing it all the time."

"Suneel, it will make us virry happy to see you married," Mummy said. "Don't you agree?" She turned to Tattappa.

"Ah yes, that is true. But Suneel has also to be happy." Tattappa patted Neel's thigh.

"I'm happy as I am. I'm not getting married, and that's final. Let's not talk about this any longer. Please." Yet he knew his polite American words would remain foreign to their ears and not change anything.

"But what shall I tell all those families?" Aunty Vimla lamented aloud. "I have already promised that you will see their daughters."

"Frankly, Aunty, I don't care what you tell them. Perhaps you should tell them the truth. That you made the promises without consulting me."

"See, Appa, how badly he is talking to me," Aunty Vimla complained to Tattappa. "And I am only trying to help him."

"Suneel, don't be so angry," Tattappa said. "You know that we are only wanting the best for you. Your aunty and mummy have been working virry hard, arranging some virry good girls for you to see."

"I told Mummy I didn't want to see any girls. Or did she forget to tell you that?"

"She made that mention to me," Aunty Vimla readily acknowledged before Tattappa could respond. "But we mummys always know what is best for our children."

"I've got to get out of here." Neel stood up, determined to put a stop to their haranguing. If only Tattappa would talk on the telephone. But he refused to, so everything had to go through Mummy, since Father, too, disliked the ringing instrument.

Even Tattappa looked surprised. But Neel was too angry to care. If he could change his ticket easily, he would take the next flight back to San Francisco. To a life that he controlled. Unfortunately, everything in India took a long time—except arrangements for marriages.

"Suneel, wait for me." Tattappa hurried out the gate after him while Mummy cried, "Where are you going?" and Aunty Vimla, struggling to get her girth out of the chair, half-lifted it before sitting down again in defeat.

ALL THE WEIGHTLESSNESS, the fatigue that had settled on his skin like a rash, vanished as soon as he left the house. He was full of energy. If he were in San Francisco, he'd head straight to the health club. Right to the punching bag that swung in the air, the hit-without-telling cure for daily frustrations. Instead, he kept walking until he reached the edge of the old basketball court. One of the posts looked like the Leaning Tower of Pisa. The hard earth of the court had been gouged out in places by the rain. Neel looked around for a ball. He wanted to slam the black and white sphere into the basket as if it were Aunty Vimla's face. But there was no ball anywhere, and the rusted hoops bent downward, the bits of net torn and dirty.

He was home. In an environment where he felt loved and comfortable in a way not possible in the United States. And yet, he no longer fit in. He loved living in America, but knew that there, too, he didn't quite fit in. It was the classic immigrant dilemma.

Tattappa came up behind him. "Suneel, brings back some virry good times." Tattappa smiled at the memories.

Fourteen-year-old Neel used to meet the team here every morning for practice. He was the captain ("That is only because you are so tall," Aunty Vimla said to put down Neel's talent), and Tattappa, an old-time basketball player himself, never missed a practice. Neel had played so many championship games on this dirt rectangle that served as a court. He couldn't picture himself in the baggy navy blue uniform, could not recall how many games his team had won, but remembered the ritual he always performed before free throws. Bounce the ball three times slowly before taking aim at the basket. Had he always made the baskets? Probably not. Such a silly little ritual, he thought now.

In the last year of high school, all the seniors met here at night. Tattappa had no idea that Neel used to sneak out of the house to smoke forbidden cigarettes with his friends. The strong, cheap Charminar tips glowed contraband red in the dark as the sixteen-year-olds dreamed their futures aloud. College, girls, jobs, marriage. Neel yearned to travel: Paris, London, New York. Drive a fast car. Fly a plane. Have the best stereo equipment. Gamble in casinos reckless about winning or losing. When the others spoke of marrying India's current Bollywood heartthrob, he pictured himself with a blond-haired wife with Elizabeth Taylor's violet eyes. Mark's mother had eyes that color and she was the prettiest woman he had ever seen. Blond, blue-eyed Mark Krueger had become his best friend and introduced him to the wonders of the Western world during the one magical year the family lived in their town. Neel never forgot their best-friend days, though Mark and his parents had returned to the United States many years earlier.

During the three years it took to get their undergraduate degree, the group fell apart as marriage claimed its members. Neel remembered the first to succumb: handlebar-mustached Mohan, his voice permanently hoarse from smoking, with an affinity for numbers first manifested when he counted to a thousand before his third birthday. How they tormented him. Mohan had just announced his engagement, a little shamefaced because he had sworn not to give in to his parents' pushing until he finished his master's degree. Everyone ragged him, and Neel coined a ditty on the spot that the others picked up and began chanting:

> *What is wrahng? She is strahng*
> *She is nice, her hair has no lice*
> *She is fine, quite divine;*
> *Her skin is very light,*
> *So Mohan said, "Ahl right."*

Parents always win in the end, Neel could hear Mohan's voice genuflect to filial obligation.

"Suneel, Suneel," Tattappa said placatingly.

"Tattappa, they didn't even have the decency to wait a few days before starting in on me." Indians were like that, but he wasn't an India resident anymore.

"You know how our women can be. But they are not bad. Only a little pushy."

"The pushy part I can handle, I think. But Mummy lied to me.

She told me you were ill. That's the main reason I came home. It wasn't easy for me to get leave at such short notice."

Tattappa didn't say anything for a few minutes. "She is only virry worried for your future. You know in India it is our thinking that everyone should get married. It is not like Ahmerica, where many people don't care about families."

"But she lied to me about you."

"No, no, Suneel, my sickness is not a lie. I asked your mummy to say I was only a little weak because I wanted to tell you myself. The doctor has found some cancer." Tattappa shrugged his shoulders, the gesture indicating he had placed himself in God's hands. "A little here, a little there. Six months they have given me."

Neel forgot Mummy, his anger, the fear that somehow he would be coerced into marrying while at home. All he could think of was Tattappa reciting long passages from the *Ramayana*. Telling him how a British bullet had blasted off his little finger during the fight for Independence. Cheering Neel on at every basketball game. When asthma racked Neel's knobbly young body, only Tattappa's presence had brought comfort.

"Let's get another opinion. I'll fly you to the States. We'll get the best oncologist to check you."

"Calm down, Suneel, you will only to make yourself sick," Tattappa said. "Your father is virry much like you. He took me to another doctor and that one also did the same exam, poking this way, taking this tissue. Paah! A waste of time. He gave the virry same diagnosis."

"Can't they operate?" Neel asked, though he knew the answer.

"No. Six months, and if all the days are like today, then I shall to be happy. My grandson is home."

"Tattappa, I'd like to talk to your doctors, make sure you are getting the best treatment. And following orders." He remembered Mummy telling him that Tattappa was being difficult.

"You can talk to the doctor, why not? But right now he has gone home to his village to see his father. You see, everyone is going to their families."

They turned back, Neel dragging his feet as if that would some-how slow Tattappa's cancer.

"Suneel, we have left your mummy virry upset. Maybe you can see some of the girls they have arranged for you. Only to make peace in the house while you are with us."

"Please, not you, too, Tattappa. You know I don't want an arranged marriage."

"You have never come out and said it, but yes, that I know. But also it is not good to live alone for too long and I am only a little worried that you are not yet married."

That makes two of us, Neel wanted to say, but he could not sud-denly confide his personal life and desires to Tattappa. They had never discussed marriage, not even during the last disastrous visit when Mummy went around the house with a teary, defeated face. Now, surprisingly, Tattappa was implying that he would accept any bride Neel brought home.

"So you wouldn't mind if I married an American?" Neel tested Tattappa's prejudice.

"It is not a question of minding or not minding. It is simply bet-ter to marry one's own kind."

For some years now Neel had analyzed the reasons why he had not met his "own kind" in America. Not a girl Tattappa would consider suitable, but the sort of women his colleagues married. One by one his former classmates at Stanford—Sanjay, Brendan, Victor—had walked down the aisle with a wife who was pretty, well educated, and whose family, seated in the front pew, exuded wealth and power. In their designer wedding gowns and profes-sionally sculpted hair, they had just the sort of pedigree Neel longed for in a partner. Tattappa would neither have understood nor accepted a daughter-in-law named Savannah. "Ahmerican?" he could hear Tattappa shout. "We are Indians. Did I fight away the British only to have my own family spoiled with the blood of a white fahrinner?"

Now Neel said, "By 'one's own kind' you of course mean a nice Iyengar girl."

Tattappa ignored the statement. "Suneel, if you had someone in Ahmerica, you would definitely have made that mention to me. So why not just see one of our girls? I am not asking for you to marry her."

"Tattappa, you know how it is here. If I see a girl, Mummy will expect me to marry her."

"No, Suneel, even your mummy cannot force you to marry against your wish. Just it will make her happy that at least she is trying her best for you. There will be no fights, no sadness in the house."

He was using his illness to blackmail Neel into submission. A sick man needing peace. Neel decided to change tactics. "I don't think that's right. Not just for me but also for the *girl*." He stressed the last word, hoping Tattappa would note his kindness. "She won't know I'm using her to get Mummy off my back."

"Nowadays girls know that not every boy who sees them will want to marry them. So there is no need for you to worry for that little reason."

"Even if I were to agree—and I'm not saying yes," Neel clarified, "Mummy said she and Aunty Vimla have lined up lots of girls. Which one would I see?"

"That is a good point. I am not sure who all they have arranged. Ah, but now I remember. There is this one girl. She is a little on the old side. And the poor parents, they don't have the money for a dowry. Why don't you go see her?"

"Why would you want me to see someone like that?" Neel

couldn't believe that Tattappa was behaving like Aunty Vimla. He was a doctor. From America. He could command the best girl not just in their town, but from the Iyengar community anywhere in the world.

"Because then if you say no, it will not be a problem. Everyone will understand."

NEEL CLOSED THE BATHROOM DOOR behind him, thankful to get away from the living room where Aunty Vimla and Mummy thought they were planning his future. The last two hours had resurrected the short list of women in his past. Should he have told Tattappa about Caroline? He had never even mentioned Savannah, the girl he so desperately wanted to marry, and whose rejection had left him afraid to approach any woman for years. Time was an effective Band-Aid and he no longer cringed at his youthful, romantic foolishness: Playing with her ring finger to try and figure out the right measurements, planning to slip the diamond into a flute of champagne, practicing asking her to marry him.

Savannah Sibley. It was strange to think of her while standing in this spare, practical bathroom. The white porcelain did not rise up to form a comfortable toilet seat, but curved, peanut-shaped, around a hole in the floor. There was no inviting tub to soak in and no shower with a hundred spouts to massage a tired body. Just a leaky faucet that spurted water into a faded blue bucket. Bathing was a big production in India that began long before one entered the bathroom. He had to turn on the small hot water geyser, wait until it heated, then fill the undersize bucket with hot and then cold water to get the temperature right. Bending to get the water was the hardest part for a tall man like Neel. The mug that hooked onto the side of the bucket held so little water it required three pourings before he could begin to soap himself.

Savannah had never known this side of him. He had told her about Mark Krueger, the American boy whose father was the biggest big shot in the steel factory. "Darling," the violet-eyed mother called Mark and his father. She gave them glasses of Tang, so much tastier than the lime juice his mother made, and introduced him to canned peaches, a flavor he did not know how to explain to Tattappa. In those days, America was the faraway land made closer only by powders and cans bursting with flavor.

He had seen Savannah at a party, his bones melting even before he heard her speak. Silvery hair that glistened with every head movement, dark blue eyes—and smart enough to get into Stanford, where she was studying French. She was the type of woman he had dreamed of meeting and marrying. Determined to have her, Neel approached her as he would an exam. During his life he had acquired the confidence that if you applied yourself well, you would get the grade you desired. What he hadn't accounted for was how society, her deb-strutting, white-columned Southern society and upbringing, could hamper his hard work. There was an ironical symmetry in their families, a clash of colors that prohibited mingling. Her parents, preeminent Southerners, had met him with a series of polite, pointed questions—Hindu? Indian?—forcing him to consider the brownness, and limitations, of his own face, albeit Stanford-educated, the doctor tag within year's reach. Tattappa, too, would have looked at Savannah's pale skin and found it lacking.

The year with Savannah had been a series of revelations. It proved that a white girlfriend was more advantageous than an American passport. One allowed you entry to countries without a visa; the other moved you up the social ladder. But Tattappa would not be able to comprehend that. He had never left India, felt too persecuted by the British to trust a white person. He didn't understand the difficulty of living in a country whose welcoming

Statue of Liberty ushered one inside without promising equality. Neel had presumed that when he went to America he was simply moving countries, but staying in the same echelon of the educated upper class. The experience with Savannah's parents taught him otherwise, but didn't make him want to return home. If anything, it cemented his desire to become as American as possible, and that included finding the elusive white wife.

He wished there *was* someone whose picture he could show to Tattappa and say, "I'm going to marry her. Period." He was fed up with his married colleagues asking him how he had "escaped." He was tired of laughing and giving the same trite answer.

The relationship with Savannah had been his only serious one at Stanford, and when he started at the hospital he kept away from the smiles and interested eyes of the nurses.

Caroline pursued him, and in a weak moment, he permitted himself to succumb to her brazenness and beauty. Sure it would never last, given their differences, he had gone out with her. Weeks went by, years accumulated, and somehow he never took a step to end it. He told Caroline they should keep their private life a secret because it could have professional repercussions. But in truth he was ashamed of being seen with her, a mere secretary with a high school education. He did enjoy her California chic and felt proud of the way other men looked at her. No one could accuse them of fitting the profile of one typical mixed couple: handsome Indian man, blowzy and ill-kempt white woman. He just wished she were more like the women his friends had married. He wanted to marry up, not sideways, and certainly not down.

Now he was cornered by his own inability to produce a girl and by Mummy's scheming. He had the oppressive sense that India was stalking him with its customs and expectations. Even the bathroom walls felt like they were enveloping him, repackaging him into the young boy who had been trained to listen to his elders. But he wasn't that boy anymore. He was a successful anesthesiologist who managed his own career and life.

It was as if he had never left India. The sinuous crack in the tile had always looked like a dead snake. Ubiquitous spiders embroidered the corner of the ceiling in a variety of patterns. The paint on the doorway was still peeling in a steady, diagonal slant. He had always disliked the sweet, feminine aroma of the sandalwood soap on his skin, and recoiled from the dark ring of mud and God knows what else around the edges of the floor. He wished India were more like America. Even if the cleaning crew did not come every week, his condo never got this dirty.

Last trip he had brought back some Comet and asked the servant to scrub the bathroom. But within half a day the floor had acquired its regular patina of dirt. It was always like that.

No matter how hard he tried to bring America here, India inevitably asserted itself.

· FOUR ·

BOTH LEILA AND NEEL WON a victory the Sunday they unwillingly met each other.

On Saturday, Neel's mother said she couldn't understand why he didn't want to meet a twenty-year-old girl, a recent graduate in English. When he heard the girl's age, he exploded. "For God's sake, I'm thirty-five." His mother quickly said, "Amita's parents, they do not mind."

"I don't care about them. I mind. I told you, I'm only going to see one girl. And I refuse to see someone who is so young. I'll see the older one."

Muttering under her breath that America had made him "virry difficult," Mummy asked Aunty Vimla to phone Amita's parents. And grumbling under his breath, Neel deliberately put on a suit the next day. Tattappa suggested he wear a kurta pajama, but in spite of the heat, Neel opted for a light gray pinstripe. He had to assert his independence, show that he wasn't giving in entirely.

Leila regretted the thinning silk of the saree. Should she have allowed Amma to buy her a new one? For a week they had battled, high-pitched words giving way to sullen silences that made meals awkward for the whole family.

But Leila did not care. She knew this America-returned doctor was going to marry elsewhere. Right after Mrs. Rajan's visit, they had heard through the servant grapevine that Suneel was also going to see Amita. Petite Amita with hair that flowed down to her knees. Even Indy, who generally did not envy people, was jealous of Amita's straight, silky hair. Leila had taught Amita the previous year and knew that her parents were rich enough to own two cars and employ four servants. Most families, even relatively poor ones like theirs, had one servant, but four was a mark of great wealth. Then there was Amita's beauty, which had achieved a legendary status ever since a talent scout suggested she try for the Miss India pageant. Amita had refused. Naturally. No good girl from a good family would compromise herself by taking part in something so public. Instead, the story became her crowning glory. Leila knew who was going to win this doctor pageant and wished that Amma could, for once, see the situation for what it was.

"Why have you to be so stubborn, Leila?" Amma shouted.

"Amma, why do you insist I always do everything your way?"

Leila's words immediately conjured up Janni. Tousle-haired, joking Janni. He was the uninvited guest, never seen, never spoken of, but whose absence was the stick used to "straighten" Leila out. Amma would never forget or forgive her daughter for shaming the family.

"I have a saree," Leila said quickly, wanting to purge the specter from the room.

"An old saree," Amma countered. "For seeing such a good man you want to be wearing an old saree?"

Leila was relieved Amma was talking instead of shouting. "The green one is not that old, Amma."

"Old is old," Amma said, her face set.

"It's good enough." Leila decided to be blunt. "You know he is going to say yes to Amita."

"You know, you know." Amma shook her fist. "You know how I have suffered all these years? So many people asking why for you are not married? And now I bring you a good man and you, you . . ."

Leila, too, had heard women ask, "So, Mrs. Krishnan, when is your fair and beautiful Leila going to make you a mother-in-law?"

In the silence Leila could hear Kila playing house with her one doll. "You have to make coffee every morning for your husband . . ." Indy was ironing their saree blouses for tomorrow, body tense from the fight she could clearly hear.

"I shall to go out and buy the saree by myself," Amma threatened.

"Go," Leila challenged her mother. "See if I care. See if I wear it."

She didn't want to add a Suneel saree to her collection. All her silk sarees, the good, going-out ones, bore the memory of rejection; she knew her wardrobe by the men who had not wanted to marry her. She had to put a stop to it, even if Amma persisted in the mad belief that every new proposal was a real possibility.

In the end Kila needed a new school uniform and Amma dropped the talk of a saree, though the disapproving look never left her face.

So Leila had dressed for this morning's sit-and-be-seen in a peacock green saree almost a year old.

The doorbell chimed. He had arrived.

Soon Leila would take out the coffee tray. To meet him, and also to show that her legs were in walking condition. In the old days, girls suffering from polio waited decorously in the sitting room to avoid walking, and thus married unsuspecting men. No one took chances like that anymore. Girls were like cows, their pedigrees discussed openly and parts checked out.

Kila rushed into their bedroom, face alive with what she had just seen.

"They are all of them here. Are you ready, Akka?"

"She's ready," Indy replied for Leila. "Did you see him?"

"Yes." Kila turned her attention to what really mattered. "Akka, can you save some samosas for me?" Kila loved the fried snacks, but today Amma had not allowed her to have any. She wasn't sure how many members of the Sarath family were coming, and didn't want to run short.

The samosas reminded Leila she was hungry and she hoped her stomach would not disgrace her by singing loudly. But she had been unable to eat any breakfast and had surreptitiously fed the cat her dosa under the table.

"Kila, don't be such a pig." Indy yanked one of her sister's braids. "What does he look like?"

"Handsome. He's all dressed up."

"Dressed up?" Leila immediately felt drab. The green color was still vibrant, making a nice contrast with the pink border, but the sheen and crispness that give a brand-new saree its fullness were long gone. For a moment she regretted fighting Amma.

But it wasn't just pride that had made her oppose even Appa, who ordered her to "Stop back-answering your mother, and go buy a saree so we can finally get some peace in the house." It was hope, the feeling that emerged only in the dark of night when everything seemed both possible and impossible. And with hope had appeared the absurd notion that if this time the answer was going to be different, then she had to make certain the occasion itself was different. A whole procession of new sarees had brought her rejections, so an old one might change her luck. This was probably the last best proposal she would ever have and behind her unconcern she desperately wanted it to work. It was only a matter of time before she was set aside, "not even dusted while I sit on the shelf," she said self-deprecatingly, and Indy the one brought out for potential grooms.

Kila turned to Leila. "Yes, he's wearing a suit. And I could smell him from where I was peeping behind the window. What do you call it when men wear perfume, Akka?"

"Fe-men-ine." Indy wrinkled her nose at Leila. They both thought men who wore aftershave were a little affected. After encountering numerous men whose artificial body scent reflected a changed mind-set, the sisters had decided that clean smelling equals clean thinking.

"Cologne, Kila," Leila answered, trying to gain composure by thinking of something other than Suneel. His name had reverberated in her mind all night. Suneel. Suneel. She had even tried out Leila Sarath, until she realized it was bad luck to do that. "It's not perfume. They put it on after they shave."

"Then how come you and Indy don't put it on?"

"Because we shave our legs, not our faces, you stupid." Indy gave Kila a little push.

Amma appeared at the door and wagged her index finger. Leila rose to follow. Their earlier anger had evaporated, replaced by uncertainty and a hope that momentarily united them. They both wanted the same thing.

"Akka, don't forget about the samosas," Kila whispered, as Leila walked past her.

"Remember he is nervous, too," Indy rushed her words. "If he makes you uncomfortable, just picture him with a lota."

Men crouching beside water-filled lotas had amused them since their first train ride to Appa's village. It helped alleviate the boredom of the trip, and broke up the monotony of the endless graph of emerald rice shoots spiked by the hairpin silhouette of workers. They would peer through the bars of the bogey window, searching for the village men and their telltale brass pots that glinted in the early morning sunshine. The train never bothered the line of villagers, who kept talking amongst themselves, sometimes waving, as if going to the bathroom was a social occasion.

But this time Leila couldn't giggle at the memory of the "scatological society."

Even before she entered the sitting room, Leila heard Mrs. Rajan: "The new-style sofas are not at all comfortable. I like these old kind. Virry clever of Mrs. Krishnan not to make the change."

It was impossible to make a rich impression at the exact moment their poverty was being touted as good judgment. Why had Mrs. Rajan brought the proposal if she meant to tarnish it even before it had a chance?

Leila and Neel didn't look at each other for the first five minutes.

Leila served coffee to his parents. She concentrated on the milky brew. As she poured the hot liquid, she smelled the faraway, sweet aroma of America, and heard the "r" sounds in his accented words.

Neel focused on the father. He had visited Britain and surprised Neel by really knowing his way around London. As they spoke of Cleopatra's Needle and the mummy in the British Museum, he saw the bright green material that swayed this way and that, occasionally leaving his range of vision.

"So, Suneel, you have anything to say for yourself?" Aunty Vimla's voice broke the fence Neel had erected. Now he had to look at the girl. Acknowledge her presence. Say something.

He took refuge in being American.

"Hello," he said, as he stood and extended his hand. "I'm Neel. How do you do?" His words came out with the full roundness of a California accent, not the clipped speech that many Americans assumed came from a British education. This was the first time he heard himself sounding like an American. People in India said he did, but he always thought his accent had an English polish to it. When he first got to Stanford, he enjoyed telling his classmates that the British had stolen their accents from India.

Her grasp was surprisingly strong and she looked him straight in the eyes.

"I'm Leila." She let go of his hand, but still felt embraced by his aftershave. Leila wanted to add something, but her mind refused to cooperate. Disconcerted, she looked down and saw the shining curves of his shoes. All she could think of was telling Indy that a man's foot indicated the size of his penis. Sitting on the bed they had laughed, but now she felt tongue-tied. Everyone was looking at her and she could not even raise her eyes from the spot that had brought on that humiliating thought.

Her bent head annoyed Neel. What sort of girl had Tattappa suggested he see? He didn't find shyness an endearing quality and now it only made a strained situation worse. Was this all he was worth? An aging thirty-year-old in an old saree? Living in a small house, a father without a job, a mother so eager to please she kept offering him samosa after samosa?

Aunty Vimla had gone on and on about how Mrs. Krishnan made the tastiest samosas in town. They smelled delicious, but God knows how many grams of fat were in the deep-fried triangles. Yet there were only so many times he could refuse and be considered polite. As he bit into the spicy potato mixture, he glanced at the girl and tried to figure out how he could make this painless for both of them. If only he could leave right now.

But he was trapped. Trapped in their best room with its best furniture, including the glass-fronted cabinet filled with the requisite Walkie-Talkie doll. Mr. Krishnan had doubtless brought it back from England and everyone had probably seen the foreign marvel walk and talk just once before it was put away.

And he was trapped by the best intentions of his family.

He couldn't blame them entirely. He had walked into this house of his own volition. His precise, anesthesiologist's mind, adept at making correct decisions, had gone over every detail last night. He hadn't chosen his field at random. He was the doctor of exactitude, the one who researched the situation thoroughly, knowing that even a fraction too much or too little could cause complications. He had lived his life this way, so this new episode didn't pose too great a challenge. The plan was simple: Get ready in the morning, be polite but uninterested in the girl, then return home and reread one of the many letters Caroline had written him. Clever of old Tattappa to recommend he see this girl because she had been rejected before. Her family would not, could not, expect otherwise from him. His pride would have preferred the young English graduate his mother kept saying was beautiful, but wealthy parents invariably had great expectations. Once he stepped into their large house they would own him, demand explanations why he didn't want to marry their precious daughter. The Krishnans could only ply him with food, not questions.

As he looked down at the girl's glossy hair, last night's well-thought-out strategy lost its clarity. He hadn't once considered the possibility that he might be nervous. Sweat rolled down his underarms and his neck itched. The suit was hot. He should have worn a kurta. He was reacting like his college friends, who told of suddenly uncoordinated fingers, legs bolted to the ground, coffee cups falling in a febrile dance of "Will she, won't she?" But those men had *wanted* to marry the girls they were seeing. Had he really imagined this would be easy twelve hours ago? That he could saunter in and out like this was a restaurant? Was he crazy? Indian crazy. The phrase was reverberating in his head when he heard Tattappa's voice. "Suneel, why do not the two of you go outside? These are mahdern times. Go, go, walk, talk."

He was trapped again. It was like his first downhill skiing lesson. Every instinct told him to lean back, but the only way down was to lean forward. He had bought into this lesson and the only way out was to follow Tattappa's suggestion—and the girl.

Leila preceded him out of the room, determined to make up for her earlier nervousness. She wanted him to think highly of her. She wanted him to like her enough to say yes. On paper he had all the credentials she aspired to in a husband—a doctor from abroad and, in that swift meeting of faces, handsome. Skin shaved clean of beard or mustache, a square jaw, and a cleft in the cheek. He exuded success and confidence, all the more alluring because he lived in America. Most of her college friends had longed to marry men from abroad. A foreign address added greatly to one's status, even if that country was Indonesia or Malaysia, so close on the map and in culture. This Suneel, with the MD behind his good looks and a house in San Francisco, was a man she would be proud to call her husband.

"Do you mind if we just stay in the garden?" she asked as soon as they stepped off the verandah. If they walked on the road all the neighbors, and not just the Nandis who lived next door, would see them and ask questions afterwards.

Neel took in the tiny patch of stubbly lawn. "Sure," he agreed. The smaller the garden, the shorter the walk, the sooner he was out of here. Anticipating the worst, he was surprised both by her well-spoken English and her looks. Somehow he had equated her age, and her previous rejections, with ugly and a bad accent. She was fair, with light brown eyes that tilted slightly at the corners, and spoke as if English were her only language. She was also taller than the average Indian girl and he noticed again that she hadn't oiled her hair. The black strands shimmered in the sun as he followed her.

He searched for a topic of conversation. But what could he possibly say to a girl who had spent all her life in a small town? They had lost any commonality by age twelve. Caroline and he at least had the hospital to chat about. He glanced sideways at the girl. She was holding her saree so it didn't drag on the muddy ground. He was just about to comment on the weather when she spoke.

"Is your name Suneel or—?" Leila left the blank, not sure if she had heard his introduction correctly.

The question was unexpected. She was starting the conversation and making it seem like an interview. He wondered if she was one of those demure-on-the-outside but in-control-on-the-inside women. Westerners thought Indian women, with their shy smiles and silent ways, were docile, but he knew better. Mummy had probably taken charge as soon as she married Father. In company, she always acted the part of the deferring wife. Neel, however, knew the truth and disliked the duplicity. The household key ring was tucked into her saree at the waist and, like the old Indian joke, another ring was attached to Father's nose. Where she led, he followed.

"It's Neel. I changed my name shortly after I got to Stanford. Americans find it easier to pronounce than Suneel." His name hadn't been butchered; the idea of changing it to mark his new life had come from a classmate.

"So you created your own Ellis Island?" Leila was happy to have this chance to show her knowledge of America.

"What?" Neel looked at the low cement wall separating this garden from the next one.

Leila wondered if she had mispronounced Ellis. "It's the small island near New York City where immigrants used to stop. And every time officials could not understand the names, they simply changed them."

"Of course," Neel responded. So she knew a little American history, this English teacher.

He looked remote and irritated, and Leila wished she could take back her comment. Perhaps he was touchy because people always commented on the change? More and more Indians were returning home with abbreviated, Western versions of names that had distinguished their families for generations.

The pattern Neel had been staring at revealed itself: cow dung patties slapped against the cement wall, the fingerprint indentations visible even from this distance. He recoiled from the fetid odor of drying dung that reached out toward them. What sort of family permitted such germ emanation near their house? This would never happen in America.

A fly circled him slowly, loud and taunting. Neel stopped, gaze fixed on the dung-drunk, hovering body, willing it to disappear. It must have come from one of the cow dung patties and he didn't want it near him.

Leila watched the man watch the fly. She had noticed the look on his face when he saw the drying rounds of cow dung their servant Heera used as fuel. Although it never bothered her, she wished Heera had not chosen today to plaster the wall. The dung was fresh and gleamed a sticky brown. His mother's servant probably did the same thing, but Neel-Suneel must have forgotten this. She knew from friends who had married men living abroad that foreign places had a way of making Indians look down on their own country. Just last year Mr. and Mrs. Pillai who lived on the next road, had installed screens on all their doors and windows. Their daughter refused to bring her children from England without that protection. That she herself had played barefoot in the rains and eaten cart food that bore the imprint of a hundred flies was never mentioned. Within six months the screens had rusted and formed holes, though the Pillais kept them on, to be fixed before the next visit.

The fly hung in the air, flaunting its brilliant colors, daring Neel to take a step forward.

Leila knew their meeting was over, and with it, her chance to be his wife. There was no getting away from the cow dung. Besides, he did not want to talk and had obviously made up his mind. Amita, the uncrowned Miss India, was going to win. The best she could do was get it over with as quickly as possible. "I think it likes your aftershave. Flies are drawn toward sweet smells. We can go back," she said, and turned before he could reply.

Leila could feel her footsteps dragging from disappointment.

Once again Neel found himself following her, but this time he was thinking that his earlier assessment might be wrong. She wasn't shy and didn't mind expressing herself.

They approached the front steps without talking.

He's definitely going to say no, Leila thought, and everyone is going to know that because we're returning so quickly.

As they climbed up the steps, a furry ball flung itself at Leila. Neel was startled and took a step back, sliding on the wet cement and almost falling.

"ET!" Leila bent down to stroke the cat. This was her baby, the kitten she had found abandoned outside the college cafeteria. Kila claimed that Leila loved ET more than anyone else. If only she could pick up the purring bundle and run to her room. Hide from the questioning eyes just beyond the front door. Instead Leila said, "ET, are you waiting for your old friend the sparrow again? You know you'll never catch that bird."

Now it was Neel's turn to query her. "ET?" he asked. "Since when have cats been extraterrestrial?"

"Her real name is Elizabeth Taylor," Leila clarified, "but we call her ET for short." Leila picked up the cat so Neel could look at the pointed, gamine face. "See, she has one blue eye and one green eye, and everybody kept saying she was ugly. So I gave her the name of a beautiful woman."

As if sensing their interest in her, ET slowly and deliberately opened her pink mouth wide and yawned.

So it was that when Leila's mother and Mrs. Rajan peeped out the window, they saw the pair laughing.

· FIVE ·

"A HONEYMOON IS FUNTAHSTIC, YAAR," Ashok said during the dinner his wife, Smita, had spent hours preparing for Neel.

Lunch and dinner invitations started pouring in as soon as Aunty Vimla's megaphone mouth broadcast Neel's engagement. Neel didn't know they had so many relatives, or relatics, as he privately named the toothy backslappers. Uncles, aunties, cousins, all laid claim to his time, wanting to congratulate and feed him. They meant well, but he could not get over the feeling that each house was another reminder that in India there is no choice. Things are what they are. If a bus is late, don't try and fix the system, just wait for it. If the flour from the ration shop is full of worms, don't return it. It just means that all the flour has worms, so spread it out in the sun until the worms crawl away and die. You have to accept things.

He was to accept his engagement and eat with a happy face in all these houses that were so eager to fête him. He didn't really want the array of vegetables, spicy sambar afloat with drumsticks, and always rice and curds to cool the stomach at the end of the meal. But he had no idea how to change his situation, and so made a pretense of acceptance and smiled till his facial muscles hurt.

He even attempted to put on a show at Ashok's house. Neel had never liked his cousin's superior attitude, and now Ashok parachuted into their youth, when he had always floated above, acting cocky. This time it was because Ashok had married first—and clearly, to a girl far superior to Leila.

"I tell you, Suneel, you simply have to take a honeymoon. Smita and I went to Singapore. Of course we did not leave the hotel room too often," he winked at Neel, "but we did do some little shopping."

Neel politely praised the blue-flowered china (from Japan), the thick glassware (from Taiwan), and Smita even brought out some of the sarees they had purchased. He watched the proud parade with a stoic smile. No one in America opened their cupboards in a display of show and share.

The much-ballyhooed honeymoon surprised Neel. When he was a boy, newlyweds didn't waste money on hotels and eating out. But according to Ashok, a small class of Indians, equivalent to American yuppies, *had* progressed. Neel just hadn't been around to witness it.

"Why not go to Australia?" Ashok recommended. "From there it is easy to take a yakht to New Zealand."

It took Neel a second to realize his cousin meant a yacht. "Australia? It's much too far," Neel declined. Ashok was just like Aunty Vimla, insistent as only Indian relatives know how to be. He was not content to suggest an idea; he had to complete it with an itinerary. Neel didn't want to go on a honeymoon. He just wanted to get back to the States—and Caroline. He thought of her constantly, and had even tried calling, but the operator could only patch him to Bombay, at which point he heard, "I'm sorry, sir, but the lines they are down. Must be from the monsoon. You must please to try again."

"Too far," Ashok scoffed. "You sound just like an old man. Anyway, Australia is on the way to America."

"I'm not sure what atlas you've been looking at, but, at any rate, I've already been there. I gave a paper at a conference in Sydney two years ago." He dangled the tidbit, wondering if Ashok would surprise him and change course.

"Maybe you have seen Australia," Ashok ignored the last sentence. "But I am quite sure, in fact, hundred percent positive, that

Leila has not." He looked at Neel's parents and proclaimed, "I think my younger cousin Suneel has become old-fashioned living in America. We are more modern here in India."

Neel resisted hitting Ashok, who was as pleased with himself as if he were a thoroughbred. Yet all he had was an MBA from XLRI, an American-style college in North India, a desk job with a company headquartered in England, and a wife who was fair, MA-tried-but-failed, from a rich family that had sent them on the "funtahstic" honeymoon. When they were young, Ashok had capitalized on the three-year age difference to strut the part of Mr. Know-It-All. Not anymore. Now everyone except he and Aunty Vimla realized that Neel had surpassed him. Neel didn't even know why he was having this ridiculous conversation.

He wouldn't be in this boxy, overstuffed living room but for Aunty Vimla. He would be confirming his ticket to the United States instead of requesting a change as he had this morning. A week ago, he had gone to bed an American ("I'll be polite when I go see the girl tomorrow") and had woken up an Indian ("I have to marry her because otherwise it will ruin the family name?").

Now Aunty Vimla was behaving as if she knew him better than anyone else, ordering Smita to pour Neel more coffee he didn't want. "Our Suneel misses our cahffee in Ahmerica. My daughter-in-law makes the virry best. No ahrdinary milk. She only uses condensed milk. You must to tell your Leila that."

Mrs. Krishnan, too, had added a liberal swig of condensed milk to the coffee Leila served him that confusing morning. His teeth were aching from the unaccustomed sugar when they finally left the small house that didn't want to let go of him. Aunty Vimla, one step behind Neel, couldn't wait to leave the garden before panting, "So, did you like her? Did you like her?"

Afraid the Krishnan parents, smiling anxiously from the verandah, could hear them, he responded, "Fine, she was fine."

"I told you," Aunty Vimla stated loudly, "I only have first-class girls for you. So there is nothing wrong with her?"

There was nothing obviously wrong with the girl, except for her age and the fact that she represented an arranged marriage. She was pretty, fair, and spoke excellent English. He knew she was somewhere in that house, wondering about his answer. But perhaps he had made that clear to her.

Neel pushed open the wrought-iron gate. It creaked forward reluctantly, only moving wider when he pressed his foot on the bottom rung. The idiot driver had parked the car down the road and was sitting under a tree, smoking a cigarette. He hurriedly stubbed it out and started the engine when he saw them emerge. "Aunty, I told you. She's fine."

"Not too tall?"

"No, not too tall."

"Ah, that is because you are also tall. How could I forget? Mr. Basketball Team Captain. Good, good. I told you she will to be extremely virry fine."

"Mrs. Rajan, your umbrella." Mrs. Krishnan waved the flowery plastic that burst open in her hands. "So sorry, so sorry," she apologized as her husband helped her close the bright orange umbrella.

"Not to worry, even if it is broken, our Suneel will bring me another one from Ahmerica. You wait there. I will come and get it. Appa"—Aunty Vimla turned to Tattappa—"maybe I will stay a little more time?"

"It is okay with me. Suneel, what do you have to say?"

Neel was delighted to get rid of Aunty Vimla. If she was this obnoxious outside the car, she would be much worse during the ride home. He had seen the girl and now wanted to enjoy the peace it had procured him. She was probably staying behind to vacuum off the last of the samosas. She wouldn't, couldn't tell the Krishnans anything without talking to him first. "Sure, Aunty can stay. As long as she has a ride back to her place," he added politely, in case he sounded too eager to be rid of her.

"Don't you worry anything about me. Everything will be okay. You will see."

What Neel did see one hour later was an even more animated Aunty Vimla, her spittle dotting the Stanford T-shirt he had changed into. She had come flying into the house, breathless, so eager to report her latest handiwork that the words came out in bursts of one syllable: "They have a-greed to the match, Ap-pa." That one sentence brought a big smile to Tattappa's face. He congratulated Neel, who immediately demanded, "What are you talking about?"

"You said the girl was fine." Aunty Vimla beat her index finger in the air. "You said it. They heard you. So I made the arrangements with her family."

"I'm not getting married!"

"They have accepted it. Now only you are telling me you do not want to marry her? No, no, I cannot allow that."

Dabbing the wet stains off his T-shirt, Neel thought she looked like a blowfish, cheeks swollen in outrage. "Tattappa, please tell Aunty to calm down. I never said I would marry the girl."

"Ah, but you did not say you did not want to marry her. I asked you. I asked you right in front of their house, and you did not say that," Aunty Vimla reiterated, her voice gaining in volume.

"What did you expect me to say after that brief meeting? And with her parents within hearing distance? This is ridiculous. We leave you behind to get your umbrella and you go ahead and get me engaged? Without even talking to me about it? Tattappa, please tell Aunty to go and undo the mess she has just created."

"Suneel," Tattappa shook his head. "That is not possible. Your aunty has already given the word of our family."

"Tattappa, I never gave my word that I wanted to marry this girl."

"Your aunty gave you the chance to say there was something wrong with the girl. But you said she was fine. I asked you if Aunty should stay behind. Surely you knew the meaning of that?"

"No, I did not. I just thought Aunty wanted to eat some more samosas." He could not control his nasty tone.

"But this was not a visit, Suneel. It was to see a girl. And afterwards you have to tell the girl's family what the boy thinks."

"I assumed we would discuss my answer—which you already knew, Tattappa—when we got home."

"Yes, yes, that is the way it is sometimes. But not when your aunty is staying behind. That is a sure sign of our interest."

"Our interest? What's 'our' about this, suddenly? It's my life. My decision."

"My this, my that." Aunty Vimla narrowed her eyes. "Mr. Ahmerica you are suddenly. How can you be forgetting our customs so quickly?"

"Tattappa, are you telling me I have to get married now?"

"Surely yes. Otherwise our family name will be shamed. Your aunty has already given our word. It is like a vow. How can we go back on it?"

"I'll tell you how. I'll go there right now and tell them it's all been a mistake. She's too tall, she's too old, and she doesn't have a dowry. Isn't that what you told me when you suggested I see her?"

"Yes, I was giving to you all the reasons why you may wish not to marry her. But you never said any such things to your aunty. I was virry much surprised. Then I was thinking that maybe you liked the girl."

"It is done." Aunty Vimla patted a handkerchief on her sweating face. "The marriage is to be in fourteen days."

"Not my marriage, Aunty. Ashok is your son and he had to listen to you. But I don't have to." Neel could have throttled the pleased look out of Aunty Vimla's face. He started out the door.

"Where are you going?" His mother spoke for the first time.

Mummy had never taken up for him in the old days and he couldn't expect her to now. Tradition meant she had to bow to her older sister-in-law, and though she could lead Father around, she never interfered with Aunty Vimla. Father, as usual, was keeping himself out of the fight, just sitting in his chair. Neel thought his eyes were sympathetic, felt that he wanted to say something, but years of capitulation had castrated his ability to express his opinions. "I'm going to the Krishnans. To tell them that Aunty Vimla made a mistake."

Neel didn't know Aunty Vimla could move so fast. She catapulted her two hundred and twenty pounds out of the chair, and only stopped when they were face-to-face. "You will not to use my name like that," she hissed. "I have done for you a big favor and you are going to spoil my good name?"

Neel knew Aunty Vimla had only done herself a big favor. She wanted him to marry Leila to increase the worth of her own daughter-in-law. She was making a fuss about her good name to ensure that he didn't get a good girl. "Fine. I'll tell them that *I* don't want to marry the girl. Frankly, I don't care what I say just as long as I get out of this."

He had one foot on the verandah when Aunty Vimla screamed: "Appa!" Neel swung around to see his grandfather fall to the floor. The next hour was a mixture of wringing hands and worried faces staring down at a hospital bed. He never went to the Krishnans.

Now here he was, seven days later, sitting in his cousin's house holding a cup of sweet coffee he didn't want, while a sick Tattappa recovered in bed.

"No thank you," he said firmly. "I don't want more coffee."

He placed the cup on the side table, right under Aunty Vimla's offended eyes. Too bad it would go to waste. But he had to take some control over his life.

He felt as if he had metamorphosed into a character from Kafka's novel. One day he was Dr. Neel Sarath, a man whose only obligation was work, who ate beef when he wanted to and spent nights with a white woman outside the bounds of marriage. The next day, without his permission, he had been forced back into his discarded skin. He was Suneel once again—grandson, son, nephew, consummate Indian male. People he didn't recognize thumped his back in congratulations, proffering unsolicited advice, demanding more and more of him. Suddenly he was both the most important person and, conversely, the one least respected.

Giving in to that initial guilt shove had created a buffet of other obligations. His afternoons and evenings were a blur of faces and food. He didn't bother asking his mother their destination. He simply got into the car, smiled at people he didn't know, and ate with his fingers because Mummy would keep apologizing to their host if he asked for a fork. Just yesterday he had reluctantly agreed to bare-chest himself and wear the traditional white silk veshti for the wedding ceremony.

Now Mr. Honeymoon was building another obstacle in the race Aunty Vimla had signed him up for. Everybody, he was assured, would consider him an out-of-date miser if he didn't take Leila somewhere. He was America-returned. People expected him to want a honeymoon.

Aunty Vimla, Mummy, Ashok, Smita—he didn't need to hear their voices to know what they were saying. His pulse beat in time to their rapid, go, go, go words. Nags, the lot of them.

"Suneel," Aunty Vimla kept up the pestering, "I simply cannot understand why you are refusing to make a nice honeymoon."

It was the thought of getting away from her, from the hopelessness and anger, from the manic preparations and winking eyes, that decided Neel. He gave the locale as much deliberation as he had given his decision to see Leila. He wasn't about to ratify the bogus marriage by going to an Indian equivalent of Hawaii. When his friends in the United States began getting married and sailing away to Maui, Mexico, the Bahamas, they had openly envied Neel's easy access to India, for them an exotic honeymoon spot. But he thought it boring and backward, and never imagined that one day he would pick an Indian town for his honeymoon. If a fortune-teller had predicted the events of the past week, he would have laughed and demanded his money back.

When he finally settled on a place, Ashok immediately found fault.

"Ooty? Ooty?" Ashok repeated, voice high with astonishment. "It's for school kids, yaar. When I went there, it still only had one cheapo Chinese restaurant. If you want to stay in India, why not at least go to the Lake Palace in Udaipur? Now that is a very fine, very first-class hotel."

Neel had never been to Ooty, and as a young boy had yearned to study in any one of its prestigious boarding schools. But though he had begged and pleaded, Tattappa told him they simply could not afford the tuition. It was for rich people and diplomats who wanted to send their children to Indian schools that weren't too "Indian." Now he was a rich man who could easily afford this one-time summer haven of Indian kings.

Ooty had been home to the Todas long before the British carved it into a resort. They dotted the hills with tea estates where Englishwomen, the so-called grass widows, gratefully spent the summers while their husbands remained on active duty in the hot plains below. Until the 1970s it was still possible to see old Britishers, ghostly remnants of the Raj, tapping their canes along the streets. Like so many cities, Ooty had reclaimed its old name:

Udhagamandalam. The king was long gone, but his palace was open to the public, and boating on the large lake was still the main activity.

He did not discuss the honeymoon with Leila. He did not discuss anything with her. There was no time for the two of them to meet, what with the wedding taking place two weeks after their only meeting. He was relieved not to see her. The closest he came to her were Aunty Vimla's reports of activities in the Krishnan household. He had no interest in those, either. What did he care that the family had decided to hold the wedding and reception in their garden? He had not lived in America so long that he could not decipher the underlying meaning: the Krishnans did not have the money for a hotel. He retained a vague recollection of the house and garden and hoped there would be no cow dung patties on the wall. He barely remembered Leila.

Knowing he could not put it off any longer, he cabled the hospital to inform them he was extending his trip. Sanjay would know what that meant. Would Caroline, too, guess that he was returning a married man? Would she realize, though, that that would be the only change?

Relatives began descending a week before the wedding and he had to give up his bedroom. He suggested putting them up in a hotel, but no one would hear of that. It was Indian hospitality over American common sense. It gave his mother more work, but she did not mind. She was anyway collapsing from the sheer happiness of preparing for his wedding.

She had become an unexpected ally since Tattappa's fall, the only one in the family who didn't blame him. Even Father had told Neel that if he'd behaved in a proper way it wouldn't have happened. That fateful day had become a tragedy of interlocking mishaps, with Neel at the center of every episode, but the final act belonged to Tattappa.

He remembered being riveted by Aunty Vimla's close-faced anger even as he tried to distance himself from her spouting, shouting mouth. Anxious to get away from her, he strode toward the verandah. His back was to the living room and he couldn't see Tattappa hurrying to come between his daughter and his grandson. Aunty Vimla, eyes like Cerberus, turned and tried to catch her father, but was too late. Tattappa hit his knee against an end table and fell to the floor.

The room went from screaming anger to deafening silence. Aunty Vimla was the first to move. "Appa, Appa!" Her screams were heard by the neighbors as she extended her arms in front of her father, guarding him against Neel.

"You," she accused Neel, "you are the cause of this! Go, go away now before you make more damage."

"I am a doctor, Aunty. Let me check him."

"First you make him fall, then you want to see what you have done. Go and get a taxi," she ordered her brother. "Appa must go to the hospital."

Tattappa lay like a question mark on the cold mosaic. His chest rose and fell heavily, as if he had just run a marathon. Neel walked around Aunty Vimla and her protestations and took his grandfather's pulse, checking the thin body for broken bones.

"He hasn't broken anything," he told his mother. "Where's Father? We should get Tattappa to bed."

"Your father went to get a taxi." Amma stood by fearfully, twisting and untwisting an edge of her pallao.

It was obvious they didn't need him. He was a son of the house and a doctor, but they had managed without him for years. Everyone knew what to do, had done this before. When his father returned, Neel simply followed orders, and sat quietly in the taxi as they drove to the hospital, where Father again took charge. It was an Indian hospital, perplexing Neel with its endless head nods and use of connections to avoid waiting, but Father knew his way around. Neel didn't even ask to speak to the doctor. He sat in the waiting area, trying to ignore Aunty Vimla's histrionic sobs.

They kept Tattappa in the hospital overnight. As Neel had said, there were no broken bones or cracked ribs. The doctor wanted him to stay, "Just in case only, only for observation and the family's peace of mind."

Neel dropped all talk of going to the Krishnans. The wedding plans went on. Tattappa insisted on that. Aunty Vimla, who visited her father every day, body stuffed into a chair by his side, agreed. It would be bad luck to change the date.

Two days before the wedding, as relatives stowed their suitcases under his bed, Neel moved into Tattappa's room. He removed Caroline's letters from the side pocket of the suitcase. They carried her scent—Chanel No. 5—and her words. "Sweetie." She was the only person who had given him an affectionate nickname. Savannah had only ever called him Neel or, sometimes, Neely. He remembered the exact moment when Caroline began using the endearment, and how he had played the message over and over again, just to hear those two syllables. To his ear they carried the promise of the life he wanted. He wasn't Father, who didn't mind that Mummy called him "Suneel's father," or Ashok, who enjoyed being called "My hubby." He hid the packet of condoms—handed to him by a grinning Ashok—among his toiletries. His mother was already talking about coming to the States to assist with the birth of their first child. She acted as if he *wanted* to get married.

Tattappa seemed to think that as well. He had recovered enough to confer with various priests who came to the house carrying big charts. Tattappa wanted to ensure that each aspect of the wedding was conducted at the auspicious time. Everyone agreed that it was a great effort on his part. The fall had tired him, "made his cancer worse," Aunty Vimla claimed, and he usually slept most of the day.

As much as Neel disliked the endless round of lunches and teas, he was relieved that the invitations kept him away from Aunty, who had grown into her role as the allegory of accusation.

The morning before the wedding, Tattappa said, "Suneel, this marriage, I know it is not exactly to your liking. But of one thing I am sure. She is a virry good girl." Neel could hear his mother in the kitchen, the clink of stainless-steel glasses she was filling with coffee. "I know, I know," Tattappa continued, "I said many things earlier. And they are all true. So, she is a little old. So? I think that will only make her a better wife for you. Our young girls when they go to Ahmerica can become a little uppity. Tell me, you have nothing to say?"

Neel shook his head. It was too late to say, "I don't want to marry her." It had been too late from the beginning. How could he ever explain this to his colleagues? "Get out, man," he could hear them say. "This is the eighties. It's not the Middle Ages. It's total bullshit." But they hadn't been raised in this house, with its small altar in the dining room, the curtained, open doors that defied privacy, the windows that let in the rain and kept out Western ideas. They wouldn't understand that bullshit *was* important in India, that if he said the word, he would be reminded that it was used as fuel to cook food and to fertilize the land.

He wasn't even sure how he had got himself in this position. His ignorance—and arrogance—perhaps. He had never been to see a prospective bride before. Like Sanjay, he had only heard of men who went home for a vacation and returned with a wife. He had seen them on the plane, the shiny polyester suits their only nod to being in America. They ordered the vegetarian meal and preferred speaking with the male attendants. Neel had always dismissed them as idiots who gave India and Indians a bad name. He wasn't one of those men straitlaced into following tradition. And yet here he was. When he was young, the boy who pointed a finger in accusation at another was always taunted that three of his own fingers pointed back at him. Now he was the idiot, sitting on a hard mattress, unable to say what was really on his mind.

"So you did not get a dowry like Ashok. No matter. The Gods have given you enough of money. Many people do not know that I, too, did not get a dowry from your grandmother." Tattappa paused. "Suneel, it is the family and the girl that is important. I have been watching this girl, Leila, for many years now. She is virry much like your grandmother and I think will be a good daughter to our house."

His mother brought in the coffee. She kept forgetting that he drank his black and sugarless and he was getting used to the tastes of his childhood again.

As soon as she left, Tattappa lowered his voice. "I have spoken to the priest. He has picked July 24 as the ahspicious day. So. Of course you are mahdern and do not have to wait, but I wanted for you to know."

Tattappa was delicately referring to the traditional night of consummation, "the" night, Neel and his teenage friends had called it. Some boys bragged that they had peeped through keyholes and watched as their newly married cousins, sisters, brothers, "did it." Ashok had already confided that no one followed the priest's precept. It wasn't like the old days when child brides and grooms needed time to mature.

This was something he hadn't even thought about when he yielded to their joint pressure and said, "Yes, I'll marry her." Now Tattappa was informing him of what else was expected of him. Thank God no one could force their way into his bedroom.

· SIX ·

"ARE YOU GOING TO THE MOON, AKKA?" Kila asked Leila, her brown eyes narrowed with worry.

"Don't be stupid, Kila," Indy snapped. "Akka is going to Ooty." They were sitting on the back steps of the kitchen, eating the last of the spinach pakoras Amma had fried for their four o'clock snack.

"Ooty! Can I come, Akka?" Kila asked immediately.

"Amma told you a hundred million times at least that you can't go. Why must you be so irritating?" Indy struggled to keep from crying. She had prayed all these years for Akka to get a good husband, and now did not know how she would manage life without her. Ooty was the first step in the journey Akka was to make without her.

Kila ignored Indy, and pulled at Leila's hand.

"Aunty Vimla said the sweet is very expensive. Can you save some for me?"

"What sweet?" Leila was confused.

"The sweet in the hotel."

"Oh, Kila, you mean suite. It's a room in a hotel." Leila and Indy burst out laughing.

Kila, pleased to have caused the merriment, asked, "Will you bring me back something?"

"If Mohammed can't go to the mountain, then Ooty shall come to Kila. What would you like me to bring?" Leila ruffled Kila's curls.

"Ice cream!" Kila promptly shouted her favorite food.

"I'll try," she promised, "but it may melt."

Such light moments were rare, for with the wedding taking place so soon, the household was dominated by work. Leila wished there was time to enjoy her engagement, to tell all those pitying friends, "Yes, I'm marrying a doctor." Pause. "From America." It was like standing first in class all over again. She would say it modestly, though. She didn't want to jeopardize her good luck by appearing proud. From the time they were young, Amma had never missed a chance to tell them the warning story of Lord Krishna and the gopis.

"Our own Lord Krishna was playing on the riverbank with the cowherds' wives one day. But the silly gopis, instead of only being happy, became virry proud. So what did Krishna do? He disappeared in front of their eyes so that in the future they would never be proud in that way again."

It wasn't just Amma's stories; Leila also knew from teaching her students about hubris that good fortune could easily vanish. Faustus, Tamurlaine, Macbeth, they all had risen, only to ride the wheel to the bottom.

Yet in spite of her newfound joy, she often felt uneasy—and afraid. Now that the main event, the marriage, was arranged, she fretted. She worried that Suneel would find her lacking once they reached San Francisco. She didn't know him and he wasn't making any effort to see her. She recalled every moment of their meeting, and had imagined him coming to their house, her fiancé now. They would walk down Main Road side by side, in full view of the townspeople. Surely he would take her to the best restaurant, the Chinese one that had opened ten years ago and which she had visited just once. She would see again the deep cleft in his cheek, learn a little about his tastes, ask him about America. He was probably as busy as she was, but most grooms from abroad visited their future spouses at least once before the wedding. It was one of the major distinctions between marrying a man who had remained in India and one who had experienced the West.

Leila could not tell Amma her fears. Amma assumed that her daughter was as delighted as she. The smile on her face reminded Leila of the permanent pleated skirt she used to wear when she was ten years old. No matter how she sat or where she laid the skirt, the pleats never got disarranged. Amma was ecstatic because she had performed her duty as a mother beyond even her own expectations. None of her friends had an American doctor for a son-in-law.

Indy, as always, understood Leila's apprehension. A week after the engagement, they crouched under the pale yellow mosquito net on Leila's bed, speaking in whispers so as not to waken Kila, who slept just a few breaths away, one foot sticking out from under her counterpane. The sisters didn't look at each other, but talked as they watched the fireflies pirouette around the dark room. On. Off. On. Off.

"It is the same moon in America," Indy said, consoling herself as much as her sister. She had spent every night in this room with Leila. Soon they would be parted by waters—and a husband.

"America. I never thought I would actually live there." That one sentence carried a lifetime of longing. Like so many others Leila, too, had dreamed of a better life in America. America—not Europe or Australia—was the place they aspired to. It wasn't famine or unemployment that drove their desire. It was the movies, the sheer openness of a country that had also rid itself of the British and seemed friendlier to foreigners. American lore had even trickled down to their servant. When Heera heard that Leila was going to live in America, she assured her that all the roads were paved with gold. There was that much money there.

Indy noticed that Leila had said "live," not "visit."

"Now maybe Amma will let you come there to study." Leila pulled her legs into the Lotus position and turned toward Indy.

It was a comforting thought, but Indy knew that Leila or no Leila, Amma would never let her go to America as a single woman.

"I told you everything would work out okay." Indy kept rolling a corner of the striped counterpane.

"Oh Indy, you were like me. You just hoped." Leila thought of the green silk morning Suneel had come to see her and how Mrs. Rajan had walked back up the steps and they had all known his answer.

But Indy wasn't thinking of Suneel. Her thoughts were in the past. "I meant Janni. No one knew—"

"The doctor knew." Leila interrupted, her heart jackhammering at the remembered incident. She recalled the surgeon's face in the hospital, more shocked than concerned.

"He was Appa's cousin. He would never tell anyone." Indy's conviction came from her own integrity.

"Maybe he did tell someone. Maybe that was why all those proposals fell through. They were afraid that I would do it again."

"What rubbish." Indy's voice was shrill. "The other proposals were wrong for you. You were waiting for Suneel."

"You really think so?"

"Of course."

"Do you think he will still like me in America?" The illusional safety of the dark allowed Leila to ask this question, the one she worried over every night, as if it were a rosary bead.

"Is it the same moon in America? If he likes you enough to marry you in India, of course he will like you even better in America."

THE NEXT DAY WAS another cyclone of activity, Amma yoking everyone in the household to the various wedding preparations. Leila never even got a chance to sit down. "I feel like Mrs. Porter and her daughter," she sighed, "except that I don't have time to soak my feet in soda water."

"You and your poetry," Indy teased, eyes shiny with unshed tears. "I never thought I would actually miss it."

Along with Amma and Indy, Leila searched through all the shops, even the ones tucked in narrow alleys, for sarees. Aware that the wedding was expensive, Leila protested she didn't need too many, but Amma was not about to send her to "Ahmerica, where all the girls show their legs and what-not," without a proper wardrobe. Leila hoped that she would be one of those what-not girls soon. But she didn't tell Amma, who years ago had forbidden Leila to wear pants. As a teenager, Leila had borrowed Appa's shirt and tie to wear with her blue denims, and Amma had scolded her for days. "Shameful girl, going out in men's clothes. No other girl does this. Why must you be so . . . so . . . ." The other girls thought it fashionable, but not Amma. A week later, when Leila couldn't find the denims, Amma claimed the dhobi must have lost them.

Now Amma only reluctantly allowed her to add a few salwar kameezes to the growing saree collection. Even though the kurta covered her midriff, reaching almost to her ankles, and each pant leg was so wide it was difficult to tell they were two, Amma felt the North Indian garment was more risqué than a saree. So Leila dutifully accompanied Amma to the bazaar, hurrying from shop to shop to shop. Saree Niketan, Queen of all Sarees; the shops had different names, but each had the same crisp aroma of new cloth.

Benares silk, shot silk, raw silk, Tanjavoor silk. The bright colors and materials that slipped between her fingers confused Leila. But not Amma, who took off her glasses and peered at the material to check for flaws, carrying home the packets with pride and determination. When the shop owners learned Leila was "States bound," they insisted she buy the "Sunday-Monday" saree. "It is the best of buys, madam," the buck-toothed shopkeeper assured them. "All of our ladies living in abroad are liking it. You see, can to wear on both sides. Two sarees for the price of one." He held up the yellow saree and then quickly turned it around to show the pink on the other side.

The longest search was for the wedding saree. After exhausting the supplies in all the major stores, they went to a tiny shop Mrs. Rajan had told them about. Anticipating a good sale, the shopkeeper gave them complimentary lime juice, and unfurled rows of neatly folded wedding sarees for Leila's approval. Every possible combination of red and blue, the traditional colors for a wedding saree, were spread out on the counter. The latest fashion was narrow blue borders, but Leila thought it would make her look even taller. She also didn't like the large gold dots sprinkled all over the red body of the saree.

"I want something simple, not so heavy."

"Simple simply not good for wedding saree," the old man shook his balding head. "Better you keep that for home saree. For wedding you must to look like peacock."

Amma agreed. People judged wealth and status by the bride's saree and jewels. She couldn't give Leila as much gold jewelry as she would have liked, but they could afford an obviously ostentatious saree. Amma pointed to a Kanjeepuram saree, purplish-red, interlaced throughout with gold thread.

"Amma, I'll disappear under all that weight," Leila protested. "Not to mention a sex change to become a peacock," she whispered to Indy, who giggled.

"This saree virry fine," the old man spread it out completely. "Not to worry about weight. You will hundred percent not to feel heaviness on wedding day."

In the end, Leila got her way. The red saree she chose for the most important event in her life had a wide blue-and-gold border and scattered throughout the red body were thumbsize almond-shaped designs, the thin gold thread ensuring it wasn't too heavy.

"The almond is good luck, for sure," Amma said. "But it is so light." She tested the weight of the material. "Still and all, if this is what you really like, Leila—"

The old man folded the saree disapprovingly and said, "Okay, madam. But tomorrow you come back and buy the other saree. Is much more better."

Since she had disappointed Amma, Leila allowed her mother to choose the reception saree. Many brides saw the reception as an opportunity to make either a fashion or a wealth statement. Leila didn't care what she wore. By then she would be Mrs. Suneel Sarath and she didn't have to impress anyone. But remembering the first and only time she had met her future husband, Leila stipulated that the color be green.

She continued to worry quietly that Suneel wasn't coming to see her. Everyone knew stories of America returnees who were coerced into marriage, and the fear that he might be one of those heavy-footed ones was never far from her thoughts. She knew his grandfather had been in the hospital, but she also heard from Smita that Neel was going out for lunches and teas almost every day. Couldn't he find the time to stop by, even for a few minutes?

Smita had become the daily visitor Leila hoped Suneel would be. She never told them when she was coming, just showed up in the mornings, or, if they weren't home, in the early evenings. After all, she constantly told Leila, they were going to be cousin sisters-in-law and Ashok and Suneel were very close to each other.

Leila and Indy didn't trust her sudden friendship.

"Did you hear what I heard?" Smita announced one morning.

"What?" Leila was irritated. Smita had just looked over her jewelry and pronounced the bangles "so old-fashioned, I wonder if our Suneel will like them." It had upset Amma, who decided then and there to have them melted and reworked into the latest style. Amma had begun to treat Suneel like a god who has to be constantly pleased. But Leila liked the leaf design and also thought it was a waste of Appa's hard-saved money.

"About the fight. My servant girl told me. That same morning Suneel came to see you and his grandfather became so sick. A big fight in their house."

Leila's fears felt like a necklace, choking her throat so she could not say any words. She looked at Smita.

"A big, big one," Smita repeated. "My mother-in-law had to settle it. She is very good at making the peace."

"So, what was it about?" Indy demanded. Smita was implying that SS was just another foreign returnee who was being forced to marry, and Indy didn't like it. Leila was worried enough already without this idiot adding her ten-paisa bit.

"Don't know. It was in English so the servant could not understand."

"So then why are you telling us this?" Indy was angry.

"Maybe you know?"

"Maybe you should ask your mother-in-law before opening your mouth and telling us these stories."

"Don't be like this, Indira. I am only trying to help."

Smita's insinuations followed Leila to the gold shop. It didn't help that Amma kept bringing up Smita's name.

"It is a virry good idea to make your bangles look like new. Smita also did the same when she married," Amma said as they entered the shop, which reeked of betel nut. The old man's teeth were red from years of chewing and every few minutes he expertly aimed a stream of spittle into a stainless-steel glass.

"Ah, it is our virry own Leila. Keeping yourself bizzy before the wedding?" Mrs. Rajan's wide girth appeared in the doorway, blocking all the light. "You must do a virry good job for her," she ordered the goldsmith. "She is coming into my family."

Smita smiled uncomfortably behind Mrs. Rajan. She didn't

say anything, swinging the half-full bags back and forth as she waited for her mother-in-law to move on. But Mrs. Rajan was in no hurry.

"My father is a little only improved. Suneel sits with him every morning. A good good boy. Ahmerica has not spoiled him in any way. I told him to come and see you," she nodded at Leila, "but he is bizzy bizzy meeting all our many relatives. He is saying there is plenty of time to be with you in Ahmerica." She laughed.

"We will miss Leila." Amma enjoyed the luxury of saying those words.

"Such happiness she is going to. I should not even say this"— Mrs. Rajan motioned them closer—"but Suneel's mother, she wanted for him to see another girl, many other girls. But he refused. You see, I had told him our Leila is a first-class girl. He saw her and was happy. So, no more girls. No Amita. But his mother, she made a fight. I had to stop it. Anyway, now all is settled. Soon you will be in our family." She pinched Leila's cheek.

"We heard about the fight." Leila glanced at Smita.

"But how? How?"

"Servants," Leila said. "You know how they like to gossip."

"Stupid stupid servants. They always get everything mixed up. Never listen to them. Now you know the truth. You were his first-class first choice."

Leila wanted to run after Mrs. Rajan and thank her. Her fears were being carted off by the figure that now waddled down the road.

She laughed more than was warranted when Indy whispered, "Too bad there's no Talk Marathon at the Olympics. Mrs. Rajan would win the gold medal."

Leila's imagination was entering the happiness Mrs. Rajan said awaited her. She would be with Suneel, and they would eat at candlelit restaurants, spend the weekend painting a room, and walk in the park holding hands just like couples did in American films.

———

THE WEDDING INVITATIONS WERE hurriedly printed on plain white squares. Every evening the three girls, along with cousins and friends, wrote addresses and licked stamps. But according to tradition, certain people had to be invited by a family member. Otherwise they would be insulted, would make a big fuss about not attending the wedding, and a relationship would be severed. So Appa set out early in the mornings and returned late at night. Sometimes he didn't go to more than four houses because people insisted he stay for lunch, tea, dinner. They were being polite, but were also curious about this remarkable match.

Meanwhile, the Krishnan house was inundated with relatives come to witness the miracle wedding. Cousins four times removed arrived with their children, bearing all types of food. Bags of new rice, strings of coconuts, tins of chuklis; the kitchen began to look like a storeroom. Families slept in every possible space, body to body, and people ate meals in shifts. No one used plates, they just spread a banana leaf on the floor and ate whatever had been prepared.

Two days before the wedding, a woman came to decorate Leila's hands and feet with henna. A bride without henna was like a wedding gown without a veil. Indy thought the red color was "bloody awful, I don't know why brides have to look like Dracula." She grinned, then made a scary face. "I vant to eat your blood." She pretended to choke Leila, who screamed and collapsed on the bed laughing, as Kila, too, joined in the vampire game. But this time Leila didn't agree with her sister.

"I shall bloody well look the part," Leila faked a British accent. "You, my dear, might not like it, but I happen to think red is the color of life. Do you concur, Watson?" she asked Kila, who nodded vigorously.

Kila was fascinated by the henna woman, who was a walking advertisement of her handiwork. Designs of mangoes, flowers, almonds, took up every inch of her arms and she had clearly put henna on her hair, for the chignon curled atop her head looked like a dollop of ketchup. She was so fat that rolls of flesh jiggled between her blouse and saree. When she saw Kila staring at the large gap between her two front teeth, she laughed and said, "It means I am virry rich."

Indy looked at Leila and mouthed, "In fat."

As the woman mixed the green powder with oil and tea water, she told them of other brides she had painted.

"One time I remember, this poor bride was crying so much she could not stop shaking. Tell me, how could I do a good job? Poor thing didn't want to marry the man." She bent and whispered in Leila's ear, "Secretly in love with the neighbor boy, you know. But he was an Iyer, so, nothing to do, she must to marry the Iyengar boy her parents chose."

The woman outlined the soles of Leila's feet, and when she saw the wedding saree, made small almond designs on her palms.

"You must to let it dry for minimum four hours, otherwise the color, it will not be nicely bright," she ordered as she left.

Forced to sit still, Leila watched her mother's sister decorate the floor of the verandah. Squatting on her haunches, saree bunched up between her legs, Aunty Latha put down a series of dots, carefully joining them in patterns that went back centuries. The art of housebound women, Indy had dismissed the kolum designs when she refused to learn how to draw them. Leila used to help Amma, usually during festivals, but their patterns were never this elaborate and intricate. Today, Aunty Latha etched the cobweblike design on every step as well as the mud pathway. White, for good luck, and also to let passersby know this was a wedding house. Would Suneel want her to do this in America?

Leila hoped not, because in a week she would have exhausted her designs.

As the sun kept setting toward the wedding day, Leila felt a calm she had not expected. Even the nosy relatives didn't bother her. She got used to people traipsing through her room, peeping into open suitcases that were quickly filling up.

"You are taking such a heavy tava to Ahmerica?" One aunty lifted the iron skillet.

Amma had bought household necessities she was sure America did not have, like dosa tavas, idli makers, and thin white cotton towels that were perfect to wrap around wet hair because they soaked up water and dried quickly.

On his daughter's last night as Leila Krishnan, Appa limped into the room without saying a word and gently pressed her face into his chest. Standing in the circle of his arms, she breathed in the smell of Lifebuoy soap, familiar from her childhood. He had never used any aftershave. When she was Kila's age, they used to read the newspaper together. But once she got her monthly he stopped any physical contact. It had been that long since he had touched her.

Trying not to cry, Leila continued packing until Amma beckoned her into the kitchen, ordering Indy and Kila to stay in the bedroom. The two younger girls were not used to being left out and Amma seemed a little anxious. Leila wondered if the reception was costing more than they had anticipated.

No one else was in the kitchen. A pile of banana leaves lay on the counter, and the yogurt pot was covered for the night. Three glasses stood near the kerosene stove, where milk rose to a boil. Amma kept her eyes on the foaming white liquid as she explained that the priest had chosen July 24 as the night Leila was to begin her wifely duties. Relieved her task was over, Amma lifted off the silky skin and poured the milk into the glasses.

Leila remembered that Amma had been just as peremptory—and oblique—when discussing her first period. The two of them had gone shopping, and in the short gap between the rice shop and the police station Amma explained that women bled every month, discreetly touching the box of sanitary towels they had just purchased. Still, that first period had been a shock and Leila had thought she was dying. But instead of asking Amma, she read books and talked to friends bold enough to give her information about their "chums," as they called their menstruation.

Now, hearing about the night she was to lose her virginity made her so nervous she almost dropped the glasses of milk.

"Be careful, Leila," Amma cautioned.

The thought of being close to Suneel excited her. She had waited thirty years for this. She had never even kissed anyone. She had sat beside Janni, and talked to him for hours, but that was all. No man had ever touched her hair, played with her earlobes, stroked the length of her body the way men did in the romance novels she and Indy still read. These boy-meets-girl-but-something-goes-wrong novels were the closest she and other girls came to knowing what happens in bedrooms, since neither mothers nor teachers divulged such information. Men cup breasts in their large hands. Kiss a girl all over her quivering face, deliberately avoiding her lips until she can't stand it any longer and their lips lock. Most tantalizingly, they show desire by pressing their male hardness against her thighs. Leila trembled, recalling the way lovers looked at each other in the movies. Kila was of the age when she said *"chee!"* during every romantic scene, but Leila strained her eyes, trying to learn. An Anglo-Indian senior in school had taught some of the girls to recite *Donald Duck/Went to fuck/Got it stuck/Cried, "I'm out of luck."* Leila had taught Indy in turn, though neither of them understood it.

What if by this time tomorrow night she knew what it meant?

· SEVEN ·

THE WEDDING DAY FOUND ITS WAY to dawn with no sign of rain. Leila woke to her mother's hands gently pressing into her shoulder. It was time to bathe, and the auspicious hour was now, before sunrise, when only the naked road lights cast a dull, scratchy yellow over the uneven asphalt. The other houses were darkly quiet. No chirping of awakening birds, just a guard dog barking far away.

In high school, every exam day had begun with Amma waking her up very early in the morning. Amma would quickly make a cup of coffee, and Leila would study the last portions of chemistry, physics, history, between sips of the sweet brew that was meant to keep her awake.

Now Leila stood silently in the bathroom, uncomfortable about the upcoming ritual. She could barely remember the last time Amma had bathed her. For a moment she wanted to crawl back into Amma's womb, wanted to forget that this was the last time they would do something so intimate together. Then Amma filled the bucket and motioned her to sit on the little wooden stool.

Leila shivered as Amma poured a mug of cold water over her. The long saree petticoat and sleeveless blouse, "the Indian nightie," Indy called it, clung to her body. The paste of turmeric and sandalwood felt warm as Amma's fingers kneaded her skin. Inch by inch, every part of her was covered. Amma lifted the petticoat discreetly to reach her thighs.

This was the bath of brides, destined to leave her skin a faint, glowing yellow, her body perfumed like burning incense. Only now was she ready to put on the special nine-yard wedding saree, and she walked into her bedroom, where Indy, Aunty Latha, and the others waited.

Most sarees are six yards long, and on warm evenings servants often walked back and forth in twos, drying the rectangular material between them so they would not need to spend money on the ironing man. Leila had worn sarees since her sixteenth birthday, and was used to wrapping them, shroudlike, as Indy liked to say.

But this one, three yards longer than ordinary sarees, kept going around and around, adding bulk to her slim hips.

"I look fat." She stared in distress at her reflection as Amma draped the pallao over her left shoulder. She also felt she looked old. At another time she would have joked that since she was probably the oldest bride in their town, it was fitting that she wear a saree, the oldest national costume in the world. But it was too close to the truth, and so she concentrated on how the folds of silk fell from her waist to the floor.

"No, Akka, you look beautiful. The color really suits you." Indy kneeled down to fan out the pleats. Usually Leila did the same for Indy, but today was different.

"Now you sit and we will to decorate your face," Aunty Latha said, taking over from Amma.

Leila felt the cold touch of gold as delicate strands of the shining, 24-carat metal framed her hairline, falling in a gentle curve to her ears. A thick gold chain was pinned to the middle of her head, completely covering her parting. Earrings shaped like open umbrellas dangled, almost to her shoulders, their weight pulling at her lobes. Aunty Latha clipped on a diamond-studded nose ring "to bring your husband plenty of good luck," and slipped gold bangles, interspersed with glass ones, over her wrists. Most of the jewels had been borrowed from relatives eager to help, with Aunty Latha contributing the nose ring.

"You must to be virry virry careful when he removes the bangles tonight," Aunty Latha warned. "If the glass breaks, you may get hurt." Everybody laughed, and briefly, Leila felt a thrill at the upcoming night.

Aunty Latha's warm breath was sharp with the scent of cardamom as she bent over Leila's face to paint the red dots. One by one, the same size and shape, they went on in a line above her eyebrows. Black kajal to outline her fish-shaped eyes. A finger dab of rouge on her cheeks, and finally, red lipstick. Her face was ready.

Amma took charge of her hair, weaving it tightly into one long plait that reached Leila's waist. A rope of champa and jasmine flowers embraced the braid so that no black strands showed. When the last flower was in place, Kila proclaimed, "You look like a princess, Akka," and Amma corrected her immediately. "She looks to me just like a queen."

Leila felt sweat dampen the sleeves of her new silk blouse, and wished she didn't have to dress so early. She perched on the couch in the sitting room, a painting in red and gold that the guests came to view and comment upon as if she were not present.

She tried to distract herself by reciting Eliot, *The Chair she sat in, like a burnished throne,* but was too nervous to recollect the lines.

Indy stood beside her, trying to look happy on this, their last day together as sisters without husbands.

"She looks virry calm, don't you think?" Leila didn't know many of the faces peering into hers. Amma seemed to have invited anyone they had ever known.

"Look, she's even wearing golden slippers!" a little girl exclaimed, her voice full of wonder.

"So lucky that it is not raining."

"The white flowers look nice against her hair, no?" The woman who said that was fussing with the flowers in her own daughter's hair. Leila recognized the dull slant to the girl's body and felt the determination in the mother's hands. How many times had Amma dressed her and taken her to weddings so people could see her? This poor girl, too, stood quietly as her mother rearranged her in the hope of attracting the eye of some prospective groom or mother-in-law. Leila wished she could whisper confidence and confidences in the girl's ear, tell her, "It will all work out. Look at me."

The men didn't come inside the house. They paced outside, near the bright orange shamiana, filling the air with smoke and discussions of promotions and new hires.

"I heard some naughty, naughty children say they are going to hide the groom's shoes," a woman's voice came from behind Leila.

Lelia wondered if Kila was one of the naughty ones. Kila had been excited at the prospect of this pre-wedding game. Someone—always a child—on the bride's side would hide the shoes that the groom took off before entering the shamiana. Harmless fun, it was meant to bring the two families together. It was also a quest for money; the groom's shoes remained hidden till a barter was agreed upon. She hoped Suneel would recompense Kila with at least a hundred rupees. It was cheap for him, just over three dollars. If she had a chance she'd tell Kila to ask Suneel for a mate, thus doubling the money.

Smita rushed in with the news that Suneel had arrived. He was in the marriage mandapam, directly in front of the priest, with Ashok seated behind to help.

Leila heard only that Suneel was outside. The rest of the words, the people heating the room with their curiosity, were lost to her. He had come! The wedding was actually going to take place. Suddenly she felt frail and faint, and didn't think her legs would carry her into the garden where he sat waiting.

But when that long walk began, she had the support of her two aunties, and a druglike composure that gave her an even gait. She thought of Rajput queens who were drugged for the walk to their husband's funeral bier. Leila had seen artists' renderings of the tragic events. The queen sitting on a high pile of wood, her husband's head on her lap, surrounded by flames that burned the dead body and turned the living one into a satee, a virtuous woman. A handprint on the palace wall, a lacy signature made by henna, was all that remained of these poor queens.

She shook these unlucky thoughts from her head. She had to think happy thoughts or no thoughts at all. When she entered the shamiana, a hush descended on the crowd.

ASHOK HAD INSISTED ON ACCOMPANYING NEEL, who didn't know how he could refuse without being rude. Tattappa had wanted to be the one escorting Neel, but he was still weak and in bed.

All the way in the car, Ashok fussed. Every time Neel shifted, Ashok gave a warning "Hey, hey!" Just to shut him up, Neel tried to keep still. He had never been comfortable about exposing his torso and now that feeling was compounded by the constant worry that the veshti tied around his waist would fall off. He had not been allowed the security of a belt. "Shameful," Mummy had remonstrated. The sandalwood paste that striated his forehead, arms, chest, even his stomach, reminded him of patients being prepped for operations. But they always signed consent forms.

Even in the marriage mandapam, an area set apart at the front of the shamiana, Ashok kept up a running commentary. But now at least Neel was sitting in front of Ashok, and no longer had to hold his breath at the pungent blend of cigarette and coffee fumes. The priest, an old man with skin that looked like cracked eggshells, had a surprisingly loud voice. His nonstop chanting, the heat, the sickly sweet incense, the smoke from the sacred fire, suffocated Neel. He could barely breathe, and as he kept his face lowered, he watched how the beads of sweat fell off his forehead and onto the veshti, the damp circles growing larger.

Neel had not sat cross-legged even as a child and now his whole body hurt. He tried to get comfortable, but it was impossible. His spine curved into a C and he didn't know what to do with his hands. Should he place them on his knees? Leave them hanging at his sides? He knew people were staring at him. He felt as if he were staring at himself. What was he doing here? His breathing quickened. His chest seemed to swell like a balloon. He was going to hyperventilate. That would stop the wedding. Or would it not?

The silence rolled into the mandapam like a tsunami wave, with Ashok and the priest being the last to relinquish speech. It was a sign that she was now approaching. He forgot about his lungs and sat stiffly, staring straight ahead at the tiny altar with the fire and the sticks of incense. He remembered how his friends had turned around for that first sight and proudly watched their frothy Aphrodites come closer. One had even blurted "I do" before the priest finished asking the question.

Encased in the red saree, Leila looked down at the orange-yellow garland of marigolds she was holding, past which she could see her toes. Amma had repeatedly told her to keep her eyes on her feet. Leila had planned to look up, not caring that people would gossip she was a bold bride, but now that earlier resolve didn't even occur to her.

She knew she had arrived at the mandapam by the scent of Neel's aftershave. Had she really thought aftershave was feminine? She was sitting so close to him their knees touched. Was she too close? Would the priest ask her to move? She had seen the slim, gray-haired man perform many pujas from a distance. Now he was just a few feet away, and she watched as he poured ghee into the fire. Immediately the air was filled with the sound of sibilants. *Shhhhh*, the fire whispered that this was a sacred occasion, and then the flames danced back to their normal rhythm.

Leila took a quick peek when she exchanged garlands with

Suneel, looking down immediately when their eyes met. The garland he placed around her neck was so long it bunched up in her lap. She lifted it carefully when she stood up. She bent her head and Suneel tied the mangalsutra around her neck.

Then the priest motioned them forward. He took an edge of Leila's saree and prepared to tie it to Neel's veshti with a knot. But his old, trembling hands had difficulty doing this part that he had performed a thousand times, and people began snickering. Unknown hands threw rice, and when the knot was finally tied, everyone clapped their hands, as if the electricity in the theatre had come back and the movie was playing again. Leila followed Suneel around the fire, her eyes riveted on her henna-edged feet. "I'm married, I'm married," she thought, the words almost lifting her feet off the ground.

Neel wanted to shout, "I refuse to marry this girl I don't know." But Hindu wedding ceremonies don't have the out offered by Christian priests. Once he was in front of the fire, there was just one route—around it, on a slow walk that bound him to this unknown woman forever. The Hindu priests were clever. They tied the couple twice, once with the mangalsutra, and then by knotting their garments together.

Aunty Vimla bustled over, two bright orange laddoos in her hands.

Aunty Vimla forced one into Neel's mouth. "For sweetness in your life together," she said.

Leila ate her laddoo and prayed, "I hope my life with him will always be sweet."

Neel took a bite and almost choked. Standing just out of touching distance, surrounded by relatives and friends, was a beaming Tattappa. He looked radiant, as if he was the bridegroom. Neel tried to catch his grandfather's eyes, tried to figure out how Tattappa, who had complained of leg and chest pains just this morning, could suddenly become so well.

· EIGHT ·

"BYE-BYE! DON'T FORGET TO BRING ME some ice cream!" Kila shouted, jumping up and down on the white kolum, her new blue shoes destroying Aunty Latha's careful pattern. But everyone was too excited to notice or scold her.

The guests rushed to the road to watch Leila and Neel drive off on their honeymoon. The reception was to be held the evening after the happy couple returned from Ooty. Grandmothers grumbled amongst themselves that it wasn't proper; there wasn't even a tasty lunch to gossip over. Gray heads shook their disapproval—couples were supposed to spend the first night in the bride's house. Then they could go away. The younger generation, however, envied Leila. Anything Western was better than doing things the Indian way.

Awkwardness swaddled Leila. She wasn't used to sitting so close to a man—or in a car. She looked down at the shiny red vinyl lining, pumped up with foam even at the edges, so different from the sagging seats in buses. Outside the window, life continued as always: a stray dog licked at some garbage, a bicyclist saved his strength by holding onto the side of an auto rickshaw, and a group of teenage boys raced between honking vehicles to get to the other side. A bus drew up alongside. The number 100, she noticed.

It was the bus she used to take to college. She had so enjoyed the freedom of doing something on her own. Indy still took the rickshaw to the convent school and Kila had not yet been born. Amma made Leila promise to sit on the women's side only, and never even approach the back row, which stretched across the width of the bus and was unisex. But like the other girls she kept giving herself reasons—a fallen book, a slipping saree pallao—to look at the men sitting just across the aisle, so close and yet so forbidden.

Then one summer morning the bus was like the inside of a hot samosa, teeming, steaming with people. Leila could barely get on, and when she did, was pressed between two boys. She was stuck, like a piece of carbon paper, forced to bear their delighted imprints.

"Leila," a male voice called from behind. She didn't turn. Couldn't, anyway. However did this man know her name?

"Leila, come take my seat."

She still didn't respond until a woman's voice said, "*Aiyoo*, you in the red saree. This nice boy is giving up his seat for you. Come sit with us in the back."

"Thanks," Leila mumbled, as she slid between two housewives and their bags of vegetables.

"It's Janni." He was standing in front of her now, swaying as the bus made a turn. "You don't remember?"

She remembered him as a little boy who joined his sisters when they all played together. His family lived in a small brick house on the next road. A family of Muslims who ate goat meat. His mother always wore a black chador and hardly ever came outside. But all that didn't matter when they were children. Every evening they played "Seven Sisters" and "Gulli Danda." But then one day they just stopped playing together. Now here he was, his head almost touching the roof of the bus.

After that, she began looking for his wide smile and the black hair that bounced off his forehead. Started hoping there would be no empty seats on the women's side. They never spoke, only smiled and looked away quickly. Within two weeks he was saving the space beside him. The first time she went straight to the back row without even looking for a seat, her mind couldn't concentrate all day. She kept smelling his closeness. Thinking of the shirt he was wearing. Remembering again how the black hair peeped out from under the cuffs. Did the other people on the bus know what was going on? Would it get back to Amma? But the more she sat beside him, the less frightened she became of getting caught.

Sometimes they whispered.

"Pretty saree."

"I have a test. Wish me good luck."

The car went over a pothole and Leila slid across the seat, her arm touching Neel. Her husband. Why was she thinking of the old days when her new life was just beginning? Why couldn't she simply enjoy her changed circumstances, the mangalsutra around her neck, his American T-shirt that she would soon be putting away in their shared almirah, this car, so luxuriantly empty with just the two of them. Their honeymoon car. Indy had wanted to write "Just Married" across the back but didn't want to anger the rental company. Instead, she had tucked a small note into the bumper with those two words.

Leila glanced up at Neel, so close beside her, but he did not take his eyes off the road. Today she had a right to sit beside him, yet the permission seemed to create a distance. A little guilty that she had been thinking of Janni, she moved away, pressing herself against the door, the shiny metal of the curved handle cold against her ribs. They were husband and wife. This man, whose mahogany brown fingers were casually wrapped around the wheel, was bound to her forever. Everything, including her name, was different. He was responsible for the way people looked at her, with awe and jealousy. This morning Amma had placed a black dot on Leila's scalp to ward off the evil eye. It was usually put on babies, but Amma wasn't taking any chances. Good luck was finally visiting Leila and Amma wanted it to stay.

A few weeks ago, Neel had been sitting beside his mother in just such a car, jet-lagged, not listening to her chatter as he anxiously wondered about Tattappa's health. Now Neel saw the laughing, salubrious face of his grandfather on every cyclist, rickshaw driver, and pedestrian he drove past—with an unwanted wife in the passenger seat.

Tattappa had kept Neel in India, within marriage distance of the girl Tattappa liked. He knew that Neel was fully prepared to jeopardize the Sarath name to get out of the marriage. So the Master Manipulator had staged a fall. Did Tattappa even *have* cancer? Or had he made up the story about his doctor going home to the village to keep Neel from learning the truth? He was naive, foolish, to have trusted his family. To them he was not Dr. Sarath, only the son who didn't know what was good for him. He had put them first by coming home and the irony was that they had put him first by arranging this marriage. He had walked into it with his eyes open. But his eyes had been open too long in the West and by the time he adjusted his vision to India, it was too late.

Now he was driving on the wrong side of the street as he steered the car toward a honeymoon he didn't want. All the rage and impotence of those first days of knowing he would have to get married had given way to obsessing over actual events. Which was the initial mistake? Had he missed an opportunity to get out of the marriage? He drove methodically, automatically, like one of those robots shown in safe car ads.

As the minutes ticked by, and large fields took the place of town buildings, Leila began to fret at Neel's silence. She had wondered endlessly about this very moment when they would be alone, starting their life together.

"Are you all right?" Neel finally asked.

His question startled her. She had gotten used to smelling him, not hearing him.

"I'm okay, thank you," she lied, not knowing how to tell her husband she needed to use the bathroom.

She said it like an Indian—"tank you"—and to Neel the mispronunciation made her even more alien. He had practiced saying "Thank you" for weeks when he first arrived at Stanford.

"Shall we make a restroom stop?" he asked.

"Darling, I need to take a leak," he would have said to the wife he wanted. Now he had to be stilted, obtuse, almost formal. He hated it. Why had this happened to him? Ashok had told him that Prakash had upset his family by marrying a French girl. A blond-haired, blue-eyed girl, taller than Prakash, Ashok had given the details with amazement in his voice. Lucky, lucky Prakash. How had he done it?

Leila's fears fell away at the solicitous question. It was magic, pure magic. In the Mills & Boon romances she had devoured since high school, the authors invariably portrayed a scene where the man reads his lover's mind. Leila's favorite stories were about young English au pairs who are forced into arranged marriages with handsome Greek men. The predictable plots began with the required reluctance of both parties to the marriage, though midway through, after fights and scenes of cultural misunderstanding, everything changes. By the end they are madly in love, often with a baby on the way. In her relief—and happiness—that life was following fiction, Leila said, "Yes, Suneel."

"I'd rather you called me Neel," he stated flatly.

His words made her shrink even more against the car door. They were just married and she had already irritated him.

They didn't speak again. Even if she had wanted to say something, she didn't want to risk disturbing him, especially as they drove up the steep mountainous road with its dangerous U-turns.

This was the first time she was going somewhere other than Appa's village, so she tried to enjoy the unfamiliar landscape. The trees grew taller and thinner, dark green mangoes giving way to light pines, and the air became so cool they rolled up the windows. They crossed a narrow river and she wanted to point out the wild elephant taking a bath, but didn't say anything.

IT WAS NIGHT WHEN THEY finally reached the hotel and she stood by in pride and bafflement as he handled everything. She had never stayed in a hotel before and Neel had booked them into a five-star one. The Mughaloid red stone structure had minarets and crescent balconies. The staff were courteous and stiff in gold braid uniforms, as though they were attending a maharajah. The doorman practically touched their feet as he ushered them inside.

The cock-eyed concierge grew even more obsequious when he heard Neel's American accent. "On your honeymoon, sir?"

Leila smiled shyly at the man, pleased he had guessed correctly.

Neel took the proffered room key and snapped, "No, we're not." He couldn't comprehend why Indians couldn't mind their own business. Relatives, shopkeepers, brand-new acquaintances, everyone asked personal questions as if it was their right to know such things.

Neel waited impatiently for the elevator to arrive.

"Why did you lie to him?" Leila asked when they got in.

"I dislike people fussing," Neel said, surprised by her question. "Don't you?"

Not wanting to disagree, she kept silent.

Their suite was enormous, and Leila went to the window, trying to see the lake that the concierge said was visible from their room.

"Do you want to unpack while I stretch my legs?" Neel asked. He desperately wanted to get away from her, from the hotel, the bed.

Leila thought a stroll under the full moon would be romantic, but was grateful for his considerateness. She set about preparing herself for him, her mind a patchwork quilt of information stitched together from romantic films and novels. Love scenes were never shown in Indian films, and the foreign ones only had those bits not cut by the censor board. Now their suggestiveness seemed even more alluring. Men tugging at a saree. A bride shyly turning away only to have her husband pull her closer.

Leila bathed and rubbed perfume between her breasts. If she had married a man living in India, they would be at home, the room decorated with fresh garlands, the bed strewn with flower petals. She would be aware of the rest of the family, just a wall away. She shook the creases out of her nightie, relieved that they would have privacy for this very private act. The nightie was long and white, printed all over with little red hearts, an extravagance she had insisted upon, going against Amma, who thought Leila ought to sleep in a saree. But most of her friends had made nighties for their weddings. A conspiratorial Smita had shown her the almost transparent one she had bought in Singapore.

Leila lay under the covers, listening for footsteps outside the door. A giggle gurgled to the surface, breaking out into a smile. Here she was in Kila's "sweet" and it *was* expensive—and huge. And it had a purpose. This morning a former schoolmate had whispered, "He could play Rhett Butler or Heathcliff. He's so handsome!" Her skin tingled as she imagined Neel walking in the door, coming straight to the bed and taking her in his arms. She could not imagine what a lip-to-lip contact would feel like. Did one have to practice not to get the noses in the way? Was it possible to do something wrong? Science books explained the parts of the body, not their passionate actions. She remembered the size of his shoes and wondered how a penis looked.

When they were young, Indy and she had long discussions about the male physique. *Vasco da Gama/Went to the drama/Without his pajama/To show his banana*, they chanted behind Amma's back. One day they even tried to sneak a look at the *Kama Sutra*. While Indy distracted the owner of the bookshop, Leila rushed to find the book of love. "What did you see? What did you see?" Indy couldn't wait to ask as they left the shop. "Nothing. It was covered in plastic. We would have to buy one in order to look inside," Leila said, knowing that the shopkeeper would never sell a sex book to unmarried women. Mills & Boon novels were seductive, not instructive, and her married friends hoarded their new knowledge like Brahmin priests who maintained the magic of ceremonies by refusing to share age-old Sutra secrets with lower-caste Hindus.

She hoped she would not disappoint him and tried to still her own disappointment. What was keeping him?

When Neel returned, he said quietly, without looking at her, "Why don't I sleep on the little bed tonight? I think we are both tired and need our rest."

He locked himself in the bathroom, thankful for the hot showers in five-star hotels. He stood under the water for a long time, remembering Caroline and how she had kissed this part, caressed the other, licked and loved him, her blond hair soft and fine and sparkly. He had never desired her this much, not even in the beginning of their relationship when they made love all the time and everywhere, against the fridge, on the dining-room table, in the shower. Just one day with Leila and he regretted having insisted Caroline be a closet girlfriend. Why hadn't he married her? Who cared about degrees? He had enough for both of them. Why had he refused her invitation to meet her parents in Wisconsin last Christmas? He was stupid, stupid, still afraid of rejection, still seeing Savannah's parents in his mind's eye, not giving Caroline's family a chance.

He would make it up to her, continue seeing her when he returned to San Francisco. He leaned against the wall, suffused with longing, his body quivering, his head spinning a little from the heat. He pictured her white perfection, seducing himself into physical communion with her. When he finally got out of the shower, his heart was beating madly, and he was so spent he had to sit on the edge of the bathtub.

He took his time brushing his teeth and flossing. He wanted Leila to fall asleep so he could pass by the bed quickly, without having to talk, make an excuse as to why he wasn't approaching her bed.

Leila could not sleep. She wished he were beside her. She wanted to experience sex, longed to be initiated into womanhood, finally to partake in the whispered conversations between married women. She had not expected he would be traditional enough to follow the priest's recommendation. She had the desire, but not the courage, to go to his bed. And even if she did slide in beside him, she had no idea what to do.

This morning Smita had smiled and whispered, "Tonight, huh?" Leila could make out his long form and wondered how he could sleep. The nightie felt unfamiliar, but her tears were not. She had cried herself to sleep so many times before, but had not expected to do so on her wedding night.

When Leila awoke the next day she was surprised that she had slept—and that she felt rested. Where was he? She looked around the room, filled with pale morning light despite the thick, dark curtains she had drawn together the night before. He had slept on the other bed. Had he gone?

Neel heard her stirring and decided he should get up. His legs ached from being curled up all night on the child-size mattress. It seemed to him that every time he fell asleep, a lump in the mattress or a strange dream woke him. His face, especially his eyes, felt heavy from lack of sleep.

Leila's heart beat rapidly when she heard him, almost bursting out of her when his pajama-clad body appeared. He was still here. She smiled, her lips keeping their curve even when their eyes met. She didn't want to stare, and looked away. But her mind whirred with questions. Had his eye been like that yesterday or had something happened in the middle of the night? Was this how he really looked?

"Goo morning," Neel mumbled. "I'll go wash up," he started toward the bathroom, "if that's all right with you?"

"What the hell?" He didn't know he had said the words aloud till he heard them, the sound echoing slightly in the cavelike bathroom. He peered at his left eye. No wonder his eyes felt heavy. There was a large bump on the upper lid. How had he got a sty overnight? He never got sties. Neel shook the marbled counter in anger. It was this damn country. He had stayed here too long. His previous trips were always for ten days or maximum, two weeks. Now this had happened. It wasn't the usual foreigner complaint of Delhi belly, it was worse. As he soaked the hand towel in hot water to make a compress, he hoped the sty would disappear by the time he left for the States.

"I must have developed a sudden sty overnight," he felt compelled to explain when he finally came out of the bathroom.

"Oh," Leila responded, thinking thank God, it isn't a permanent condition. For a while she had wondered if she had simply not noticed his eye in their two emotional, life-changing meetings. Now she took a closer look. "I don't think it's a sty. It looks like a spider's lick."

"Spiders don't *lick.*"

"I know. It's what we say when something like this happens in the night."

93

"You've had this before?"

"My sister Kila did. A tiny creature must have bitten you, but Appa likes to say it's the spider."

"How long before it goes away?" Neel wondered which tiny creature in this land of infinitesimal critters had got to him last night. This, too, in a five-star hotel.

"It depends on your body." Leila found that suddenly she was no longer shy or shamefaced around him. "It could go by this evening or maybe tomorrow."

"Let's hope it's this evening," Neel said, relieved at her answer.

THE CONCIERGE ASSURED THEM it was a perfect Ooty day: "Lovely blue sky, very fine sun." He suggested a walk around the lake, and Neel agreed, glad that the sunglasses would cover up his eye.

A rush of wings flew past. "Two for joy," Leila said spontaneously, pointing to the mynah birds now sitting on a bush.

"What?" His response was automatic, the one he always used when he wasn't listening. He wished he were yelling at his family instead of walking beside her. Tattappa, Mummy, and Aunty Vimla, the three Machiavellis, had a lot to answer for. They might think themselves invincible, but he belonged to the same family. Surely, if anyone could find a way out of this marriage, it would be he.

"It's what we said as children. Don't you remember? One for sorrow, two for joy, and so on." She wanted to get close to him, and words were the only way she knew how.

"Boys didn't do that."

"It's even the title of a book by Rumer Godden, *One for Sorrow, Two for Joy*."

As the last word left her lips, she realized that nervousness had made her confuse the title *Five for Sorrow, Ten for Joy* with the childish saying. She was wondering if she should correct herself, when he said "I've never heard of Rumer Godden."

He didn't read fiction. But then she didn't know that. She didn't know anything about him. "I keep forgetting you taught English. What is your favorite book?" His question was perfunctory, just this side of polite.

"The *Oxford English Dictionary.*" She was too shy to tell him that the last time the same question had been asked, she was a finalist in the Freshman Beauty Pageant. It was one of the rituals of attending college, and an occasion for the seniors to tease the newcomers as they walked across the stage. Afterwards, her classmates congratulated her on the clever answer, making her wonder whether she had won more for her brains than her looks.

Leila had hoped to impress him with her answer. When he didn't respond, embarrassment quickened her pace. White rose bushes had encroached upon the dirt pathway, narrowing it to the width of one walker. She gathered her saree folds close, so the silk wouldn't get caught in the thorns.

"*Minngaaoo.*"

She stopped. Under a trellis of green leaves was a thin, clock-eyed kitten. Leila kneeled down immediately and began calling to it. The calico turned its gramophone ear toward her voice, but started a backward, on pointe, walk. She reached toward it, her fingers signing there was no reason for it to be afraid. "Come here," she whispered. But in its short life the kitten had learned not to trust people and ran away.

Leila watched the reddish-black fur disappear and straightened up from her crouch. But something stayed her and she almost fell to the ground. Her pallao. She hadn't wrapped it around her when she leaned toward the kitten and now the end was spread across the rose bush, an army of thin thorns marching through the blue silk.

She could hear Neel breathing behind her as she tried to lift off the material. But her hands couldn't reach that far to the left and she stood still. Should she ask him for help?

"Here, let me do it." Neel wanted to yank it off the bush. He stepped closer and her bare midriff pressed into his arm. Her waist was so slender his hands could span it and then some. The pallao wasn't shielding her blouse and he could see her upturned, pointed breasts. She had a figure like the sculptures of Indian women in temples, with big and small curves in all the right places. He had always thought the ancient sculptors had vivid imaginations; no woman could have that kind of a body.

His hand moved toward her. He was just about to touch her when he jerked his arm away, a thorn piercing his finger.

"Did you get hurt?"

"Nothing serious." He sucked the drop of red that shimmered on his skin in a viscous dance. What was he thinking? Thank God she hadn't been able to see anything. He took a quick step back and this time concentrated on freeing the silk.

THAT NIGHT, THEY ATE AT THE restaurant in the hotel. It was small and dark, with oversized menus featuring oversized prices. It was also full and they were lucky to get a table.

"Do you know what you would like?" Neel asked, taking his sunglasses off for the first time that day and settling deeper into the corner seat he had deliberately chosen. He wanted to get the meal over with as soon as possible. He was feeling more and more uncomfortable with her. It wasn't anything in particular. It was just that she was there, beside him, in his face, as Caroline used to say of the patients who annoyed her. So far they had found nothing to talk about, as if every topic had a built-in virus that killed discussion.

"Yes." Leila scanned the menu desperately. These were the foods Mills & Boon heroines ordered when eating with their lovers. Spaghetti in Bolognese sauce, veal cacciatore, pasta primavera. Thankfully, the menu became Indian: tandoori chicken, curried prawns, pork vindaaloo, but that still didn't help a vegetarian. At the bottom she found chana batura and ordered it.

"One chana batura for the lady?" Leila wondered if the waiter was being snide or if she was imagining a tone in his voice. It was amazing how Indians scorned those Indians who were not cognizant of Western ways.

"Sir, what can I get you?"

"I'll have the Beef Stroganoff with a salad, oil and vinegar dressing, light on the oil, please."

Leila was as mystified as if Neel had spoken another language. Unused to his accent and words, she only understood that he had ordered beef. He ate *beef*. Leila knew that many Indians, even Iyengars, were no longer strict vegetarians. Amma cooked eggs and they all drank milk. She was getting used to some of her friends eating chicken, but no one she knew ate beef.

She was just about to ask if he also ate pork and mutton when the couple at the next table greeted them.

Neel had noticed the two foreigners when they entered the restaurant and immediately wondered where they were from.

Leila had only seen foreigners from afar, and now this couple was sitting so close she could see the blue veins on their arms. The man with his dark hair and eyes looked like a fair Indian, except that no Indian she knew would go out to a fancy restaurant in a crumpled shirt. The woman's hair was cut short like a boy's, and her face was white, with dark spots all over it. Freckles, Leila realized, and wondered why so many books said they were cute.

Neel soon found common ground with the American couple. He felt revived. Cynthia and Harold were familiar. He treated people like them every day. Stood behind their carts at the grocery store. Sped past their cars on the freeways. They were part of his life in a way Leila wasn't.

At the same time he felt the stirrings of the exact feeling he had experienced the first time he saw Mark's mother with her unfamiliar violet eyes, and from that initial moment had wanted to impress the woman with the white, mysterious face. He never reacted this way to Indian women. They were easy to figure out and posed no challenge. Now, too, that force took over and Neel felt compelled to impress Cynthia.

Leila had never heard Neel speak so much. He was full of information for the couple, who had vacationed in San Francisco a few years earlier. Golden Gate Park, Chinatown, Sausalito, talk of her future home swirled around her. "Did you know *Alcatraz* means 'pelican' in Spanish?"

"We must be boring you," Cynthia said to Leila as they paused while the waiter brought the food.

"No, no, I'm enjoying hearing you. Really, I'm learning a lot."

Their eyes were on Leila. She was uncomfortably aware that they had picked up their forks and knives. She had never eaten chana batura with anything but her fingers. At home they used spoons only for ice cream or payasam, the coconut milk pudding Amma made for birthdays and festivals. Her hands were on the spoon when she remembered Josephine, the Anglo-Indian teacher, telling them how she had eaten an entire meal with a fork and spoon. Since such utensils were not in anyone's kitchen, the teachers had merely said, "Wow," impressed with her ability. "You don't understand," she had gone on. "A fork and *spoon*. I was supposed to eat with a fork and a knife. Ever tried to cut meat with a spoon?" Now Leila reached for the stainless-steel fork and knife, trying to make it look like she had used them all her life.

"I just love your saree," Cynthia said. "Isn't it gorgeous, Harold?"

"Yes it is. Why don't we get you one, honey?"

Cynthia pointed to the small red pottu Leila had pasted on that morning. She had begun wearing them when she got her first monthly and would only stop if she became a widow.

"Is it a decoration or is there some religious significance?" she asked Leila.

"Some people say it represents the third eye of Shiva, and others—" Leila stopped when she heard Neel.

"That's just old people talk. It's all a moneymaking device. Gimmicky. They started out with plain red dots and now you can get them in any color and shape."

"I think Cyn would look lovely in a bright purple one." Harold stroked her cheek and then covered her hand with his.

Leila noticed he could not stop touching Cynthia.

"Are you also . . . that is to say, you are on your honeymoon?" Leila asked, sure of the answer.

Their laughter was unexpected. "No, we're not married," Cynthia said. "But we've been living together for years."

Leila stared at Cynthia. No one she knew would ever confess to such behavior, but then, no good girl would sleep with a man outside of marriage. She kept staring at the other woman, as if immorality were as visible as a pottu. But aside from the tight dress that showed her nipples, Cynthia didn't look different from other women.

"I'd like to get married," Harold said. "Cyn's the one who is still making up her mind."

Cynthia said, "It pays to be careful. No matter what anyone says, women lose if things don't work out."

"Cyn's a feminist." Harold raised his wineglass. "And long may she reign."

"I take it you two are married," Cynthia said.

"Yes, ma'am, we are." Neel's voice was forcefully jovial. "I am a taken man."

"Was it an arranged marriage?" Cynthia asked. "We've heard of them, but do they still happen?"

Neel immediately felt like the two-headed snake he had read about in the Steinhart Aquarium. How many moments like these awaited him in San Francisco? It was bad enough to have an arranged marriage. But it was almost more humiliating to have to explain it to Americans.

"Aren't all marriages arranged in heaven?" he joked.

"Well, tell us, was your marriage arranged?" Cynthia asked again.

"From across a crowded room," Neel began after a brief pause. He had to make up a story. "She was pouring tea, looking very serene and domestic. I glanced up at her and couldn't take my eyes away. I don't think she noticed me." He laughed. "Anyway, before the first cuppa was cold, bam! That was it."

"Love at first sight." Cynthia sighed. "How marvelous. Did you also fall in love right away?" she asked Leila.

"Probably not," Neel said quickly. "But she's not about to say that in front of me." He smiled at Leila.

Leila's lips widened in response as their faces mirrored each other. It was like the line from Donne's poem: *Our eye-beams twisted, and did thread/Our eyes upon one double string.* She had always taught her students that it was a painful image. It wasn't, she wanted to tell them. It was an erotic joining, a very visible coming together without physically being together.

Neel hoped she didn't think he was serious. My God, even she couldn't be that naive.

"You are one lucky man, Neel. Your wife is a knockout." Harold turned toward Leila. "I think Indian women are gorgeous. Their eyes. Their skin. Their hair, hmmm. I love the way you talk, it's so musical."

Leila wasn't sure how to respond. Indians never made personal remarks, unless the woman had chosen a public career such as a model or an actress. She looked down, inwardly pleased, unable to stop smiling. That her speech was musical confused her. She knew she didn't sing well. In school the music teacher used to give her a passing mark without letting her sing. What could Harold mean?

"I think Harold wanted to come to India just to see the women," Cynthia said, laughing. "We almost didn't get here. It was a major pain to get a visa. You would have thought we were planning to steal the Taj Mahal, the trouble they gave us at the Indian Consulate."

"And people told us it's difficult getting to America," Harold said indignantly.

Neel didn't listen to the rest of the conversation. He wanted to reach across the table and kiss this woman with the broad Baltimore accent. She had shown him an exit on the dangerous slope he was speeding down with no hope of getting off. He couldn't believe he hadn't thought of it himself.

And the best part was he could blame America. The United States was making it almost impossible for Indians to get visas. It affected everyone: students who had received full scholarships, tourists, even brides. The visa problem wasn't just a loophole, it was a giant void that would bury Leila forever in India. Even Aunty Vimla, the Great Aunty of Interference, wouldn't be able to do anything about it.

He'd leave Leila behind with Tattappa. Tattappa said she reminded him of Grandmother. Well, Tattappa could have her. Indian men did it all the time. Most of the workers in the Middle East lived like bachelors while their wives stayed behind in India. And going to the Gulf was much easier than getting to the States. Once he got home he'd delay the paperwork, do whatever was necessary to keep her in India till the divorce.

In four days he would be on the plane to San Francisco. Alone. What had happened in India would remain in India.

"YOU WERE RIGHT," NEEL SAID the next morning. "That spider's lick is gone." It was as if his plan from last night had taken over and now, even the annoying sty had disappeared.

It was nice of him to use her words. "Spiders don't *lick*," Leila copied him, accent and all.

Neel burst out laughing. He hadn't expected the mimicking, just a thank-you or a silent shake of the head. "I see I'll have to watch what I'm saying around you."

"What shall we do today?" Leila felt emboldened to ask.

"Anything you want." Neel was magnanimous. She had told him his eye would return to normal soon and very soon his life, too, would return to normal. He could give her this last day in Ooty.

"How good are you with your hands?" Leila asked.

Was she getting at something? No, it had to be an innocent question. "Can you be a little more specific?"

"Do you want to row a boat or throw a stone?"

"Hmm. Can you swim?"

"No."

"Then it's the stone stuff, since I can't be responsible for your safety in the water."

Neel didn't admit it, but he was intrigued by her suggestion. He wondered if it was some ancient bowling game.

It turned out that the stone was the central attraction in the recreated Toda village. The small thatch huts were scattered on the hillside, and as the guide explained, anthropologists were not sure of the Todas' origins. Some believed they were indigenous Indians, others that they came from Africa, given their facial features. They certainly had strange rituals. The heavy stone was a test given to suitors who demonstrated their strength, or ability to look after a girl, by hurling it as far as possible. It was a Marriage Olympics, the guide joked, with the man who threw the stone the farthest getting the girl.

"Anyone would like to try?" the guide asked.

A couple of foreigners went for the challenge, clapped on by their partners. A lanky Australian got into the spirit of things, groaning when he picked up the stone and then kneeling at his wife's feet, begging her to take him even though the stone had barely cleared a yard.

Leila glanced at Neel, but he shook his head. It wasn't for him. His family had already put him through one ancient ritual.

Leila sensed that Neel wasn't enjoying the outing and wished they had gone boating instead. Then maybe they could have talked instead of following a guide. The tour included a visit to a botanical garden, but once they got there, Neel wandered off with his camera. He returned just in time to board the bus, explaining that he had got absorbed taking pictures of the various flowers.

As they left Ooty, Leila felt as though nothing had changed during the two days of their honeymoon. Once again she sat on the far side of the seat, wondering why he wasn't talking to her. What would their family think of this silence? She had always imagined couples returning with a secret closeness that everyone easily recognized. Perhaps Neel was a quiet person? Then she recalled his animation the previous night. He might not be telling her stories about San Francisco, but at least she was learning things about her husband.

Neel knew he had to plan out the days carefully until his departure. This time he wasn't going to be unprepared. First off, he would suggest that she go to her home. He'd tell everyone he wanted to spend time with Tattappa. He could hear Aunty Vimla simpering and saying, "There will be plenty of time for the bride and groom in Ahmerica. Our Suneel loves his grandfather virry much." Too bad he wouldn't be able to see her face when she grasped the fact that she had been bested.

He didn't realize he was driving so fast till he came to a curve and had to brake before swerving past the large Tata truck that had stalled in the middle of the street. The driver, who was changing a tire, shouted something at them.

"I'm sorry about that. I'll slow down. Can't have an accident now." Not when he was just about to get rid of her. She smiled and something in her eyes stayed him for a moment. Had she guessed his plan? No, she couldn't have. She was just a simple girl from a small town.

He did, however, feel sorry for her. It wasn't her fault that she was part of Aunty Vimla's crazy proposal for Neel's life. As a well-raised Indian girl, she was waiting for him to initiate things. Her upbringing did not permit her to think of a divorce. No, she had no idea what he was planning.

The least he could do was ensure she suffered as little damage as possible. He'd make certain everyone knew she was still a virgin. That way she could get married again. He'd give her enough money when the divorce came through to make her even more attractive to other men. He was positive she would get another husband. She was fine, really. Pretty, well spoken, unobtrusive. It was just that *he* didn't want her. In fact, if he managed it correctly, he need never see her again.

· NINE ·

LEILA STARED AT THE CLOSED DOOR. Neel was gone, leaving her in this cold flat with the smell of unfamiliar flowers she had only seen in books.

Nothing had gone right after they left Immigration and entered America. Once outside, she had immediately looked for some soil. She wanted to touch the earth and ask for its blessings with her first footsteps in San Francisco. She walked a few paces behind him, looking for a gleam of brown. But all she saw was an endless expanse of concrete and asphalt, as if America was hiding that which had made it so rich.

"Come on." Neel urged her into the taxi and she reluctantly abandoned the search, fretting that this was not a good start to her new life. She had been on the long-jump team in school and before every turn had always taken the time to quickly touch the ground and then her forehead. Even the Catholic girls on the team had done it.

The taxi driver asked question after question about India. Drivers back home never spoke to their customers and if they did know English, it was a word here and there, a sentence thickly accented and corroded with grammatical mistakes. This taxi smelled of stale cigarette smoke and the man's half-chewed fingernails were black with dirt. She wished Neel would tell her where she was and what she was seeing. Tall buildings outlined with white lights, like the tiny earthen lamps people lit during the Festival of Divali, except that these did not flicker in the evening air. Billboards advertising strange products like Bacardi. Soundless cars speeding by in the wrong direction. Large green signs with the destinations written in white: Civic Center (the spelling making her look twice); Fell Street; and the only one she already knew, Golden Gate Bridge. She missed the putt-putt of auto rickshaws inserting themselves between vehicles, the drone of large red buses, the constant honking; she missed understanding what was around her.

"Nice neighborhood," the driver commented when they stopped. "Bet you don't get much crime here."

"That's right." Neel smiled for the first time since getting on the plane in India. He enjoyed living in Pacific Heights. It was one of the better areas of San Francisco and he had never seen another Indian in the neighborhood. The Indians who could afford the price preferred to live in the suburbs in their version of the American dream, which was large houses with swimming pools.

Leila was still looking for some soil, determined to have an auspicious beginning, when Neel opened the glass door of a tall building. Once again she reluctantly abandoned her search and followed him into the foyer with its flowery sofa and wall-to-wall mirror, waiting while he pressed the UP arrow for the lift.

Leila recalled Mrs. Rajan saying he owned a house. The lift was old, even by Indian standards, with a grille door that had to be pulled twice before it closed.

Neel didn't know whether he wanted her to hurry up and get into the elevator or stay in the lobby forever. He only knew that he hadn't thought she would be here, in this building, on her way up to his condo.

But while he had been ticking off the slow, interminable honeymoon hours, constantly telling himself he would soon be rid of her presence, his family had been bribing their way through the visa loophole he had relied on. Which family member could he blame this time?

On the drive back from Ooty he had been almost jubilant, relieved that this ordeal was finally ending. He had even thought that if people made a fuss, he would stay in her house, do whatever was necessary, just as long as he could get back to San Francisco alone.

His plan had started off fine. Everyone seemed pleased that he wanted to be with Tattappa and the only time he saw Leila was at the reception. It had begun miserably, with rain leaking through the shamiana, and Neel feeling like an idiot on the stage that had been erected so all the guests could see them clearly. He didn't even get to eat, because people kept coming up to talk to them. But most of the irritation left when he reminded himself that this was the final scene, almost the end of the play. He uncled and auntied all the elders, permitted strangers to hug him, even smiled at the man who said, "Today you have got for yourself a rare pearl."

It all went smoothly till the very end, when Aunty Vimla bustled over, almost knocking over a flower pot. She ceremoniously handed him the envelope and he put it on the table, assuming it was money.

"Open it, open it," Aunty Vimla insisted surprisingly, for usually no one checked gift money. "It is for you and your Leila."

Three workers were dismantling the shamiana, careful not to knock into the stack of empty tables and chairs. The caterers were cleaning up, some sweeping the ground, others gathering glasses. Only the family remained, and they were the ones who now surrounded him.

He glanced at Leila, the bemused look on her face a copy of his feelings.

"It is not what you think. No money. It is a present from all your immediate family, your Tattappa and your mummy and daddy. And me also." She was so pleased she almost snatched back the white rectangle to open it herself.

The thin slips of paper were clipped together. Typed in red letters was the route: India to Frankfurt to San Francisco. "I already have my ticket." Neel was baffled.

"Ah, ah. This is not for you. It is for your wife. How can she go with you to Ahmerica without a ticket?"

"But, but . . ."

"It is a good good surprise, yes? See, anything and everything is possible. Now you will not be alone in Ahmerica." Aunty Vimla clasped her hands together.

They had out-thought him once again. Favors must have been called in, money exchanged; even the priest had been complicit, altering the marriage license to the year before. That they could pull it off made as much sense as the ticket in his hand. He was stuck.

Leila's parents were beaming and she herself looked happy. Only the two sisters began crying, the younger one hiding her face in Leila's saree till the mother picked her up and went back to the house.

Neel tried to make excuses ("I need to get the condo ready") and gave reasons ("Doesn't Leila need to stay until the college can get a replacement?"), but nobody listened. They had done all this—even risked getting caught—just for him, they kept repeating.

When had they realized that he meant to leave Leila in India?

The elevator shuddered to a stop on the third floor. Neel rolled their bags to a door marked "303" in brass letters. "I always take my shoes off," he said as they stepped inside. Leila's "Of course" was swallowed by his American explanation, "I haven't got round to buying carpets and I'd like to protect the floors." As if he wore shoes inside his parents' house, she thought.

Leila's feet instinctively arched away from the cold wood while her mind began filling with questions as she examined the large room. It was almost empty, with a sickly sweet smell. A sofa and a coffee table stood in front of the fireplace. Long black wires linked speakers in every direction. In the middle, as if it had been lifted from a still life painting, was a white vase containing a riotous mass of flowers. The source of the smell. Leila walked toward the centerpiece, hoping this was all a joke. That the envelope prominently displayed above the flowers would contain the answer to her main question. Whose flat was this? It must belong to one of Neel's friends. He was teasing her. Soon they would go to the large house he owned.

Before she reached the vase, Neel grabbed the envelope, glanced at it, and said, "It's for me."

Leila continued looking at him.

"From the office," he finally said. "To welcome me back. And you," he added. He saw his whole life in front of him with Leila asking questions he didn't want to answer.

How soon could he get away from here? She was still staring at him, waiting for him to take charge. He'd show her the condo. It's what he did with every visitor.

Leila followed, rubbing her arms to keep warm, as he opened the cupboard containing the stacked washer and dryer, then stood at the window as he pointed out the sea he called the Bay.

"The view is even better during the day. Unless it's foggy," he said. "Those twinkling lights are the Golden Gate Bridge and that flashing one is Alcatraz."

So this was what he had been talking about in Ooty. An island named Pelican. And there was the famous bridge, set off in lights. It was as if all the roads, too, were paved with lights. Not the gold that Heera had told her to expect. But nothing was what she had expected. The road in America had dropped her off at a small, underfurnished flat.

As soon as the tour was over, Leila locked herself in the guest bathroom and held onto the edge of the basin.

What sort of mess had she gotten into? Her hands shook, and her heart thudded so loudly she was sure Neel could hear it. Had he lied about anything else beside this small flat? Was he really a doctor or had the Saraths just said that? Appa hadn't checked up on Neel, the way most fathers did when they married daughters to men living abroad. They only had two weeks before the wedding, but even with more time, there was no one they knew who could verify Neel's life in America. Neel had not spoken much about himself. His aunty had claimed he lived in a house. His aunty had said Neel was rich and wouldn't accept a dowry even if they could afford one. In their small town it was usually the poor who lived in flats, boxed in on all sides by other families. But even they had furniture.

Tears splattered onto her hands, changing the color and texture of skin that had dried out on the plane. What could she do? She was married to him.

She had to accept it. Just as she had accepted the flaw in her wedding saree, the one Indy had found after they brought it home. A small swathe of color different from the rest. The shopkeeper would never take it back. He would claim they had done something to it. "At least it can be hidden in the pleats. We can arrange it so it will not show," Amma had placated them.

Would she also have to arrange herself as the wife of a liar? Everyone knew of at least one girl who married a man claiming to be a lawyer, pharmacist, engineer in America, only to discover upon arriving that her husband was a waiter or a taxi driver and that she had to get a job to made ends meet. For all of them, the horror had begun when they arrived at their new home. One man rented a small room in a house—"my house," he had told his bride back in India. To make the lie worse, he expected her to clean it in exchange for a lower rent. Leila had even heard of a man who left behind his American wife, married one in India, and then disappeared with her jewels. At least Neel had not wanted her gold. She had left it behind for Indy when he told her most people in America did not wear 24-carat gold.

She looked at her red eyes in the mirror. She hadn't even cried when saying good-bye to Indy. Kila had clung to her, weeping uncontrollably, hot tears and snot smeared all over Leila's new salwar kameez.

She felt as if she were neither living nor dead and knew nothing.

Water. She needed to wash her face, be calm before going out to confront him. She turned on the hot water tap. Nothing happened. It was the same with the cold water tap. There was no soap, no towel. Was he too poor to afford that? She wiped her face with the edge of her kameez and opened the door.

"I turned off the water in this bathroom when I left." Neel walked past her without giving her a chance to say anything. "Why don't you use the other one while I get this going?"

It had to be his bathroom because it smelled like she was standing inside his aftershave bottle. She washed her face carefully, suddenly aware of her hunger. She had not been able to eat the food on the plane, drinking juice instead.

"I think I'll go to the grocery store. There's nothing in the fridge and you must be starving. Any particular juice you like?" Neel slipped into his shoes, thinking of Caroline, hoping she was in her apartment.

This could have been another moment of mind-reading magic, Leila thought through her misery.

"Anything is okay," Leila said, though she really wanted to cry and scream at the same time.

The marvelous life she had dreamed of was dismantling even before it started. Amma and Appa would be shocked and upset, but it was *her* life that was ruined. Even if the man lies and cheats, it is always the woman who suffers. Cynthia was right. But in India, the suffering infected the entire family. Her failure meant that Indy and Kila would be considered problems by potential grooms, as if failure were a gene. Should she accept her fate for their sake? Maybe she was just imagining things. Was she not thinking properly because she was so hungry? She *had* picked the wrong conclusion that first morning in Ooty. But one look around the virtually empty flat told her that even though her mind may not be working at its full capacity, her eyes were not betraying her. No wonder he had kept his distance before and after the wedding. Had he been afraid that she would somehow find out the truth? His lies were by convenient omission. But they were still lies.

"See you in a bit. Make yourself at home," he said, and left.

Home. It was her first night in America and she was alone in a cold flat. Her footsteps echoed loudly and the wooden floor creaked in places. When would Neel return? She had to talk to him.

· TEN ·

"YOU BASTARD! YOU FUCKING BASTARD! I hate you, I hate you. How could you do this to me?" It was on the tip of her tongue to call him "Brown shit," but she held back.

Neel stared in amazement. She had never used such words before. And they kept pouring out of her pink lips. After leaving Leila in the condo and rushing over to see her, he had expected kisses, not curses.

"You prick. You lied to me. Why didn't you tell me? Dickhead. Asshole. Jerk!"

At the last word Caroline curled up into a fetal position on the sofa and continued sobbing.

Neel didn't go to her. He was completely baffled. How did she know about the marriage? He had not mentioned it in the telegram, using the enigmatic "unavoidably delayed" instead.

Someone must have told her after she took the flowers to the condo, letting herself in with the emergency key he kept at the office. He had wanted to thank her for the bouquet and the note. *Until our tulips meet again. Love, Caroline.* In the very beginning of their relationship he had once sent her tulips with just those words.

"I came here as soon as I could to tell you myself. To explain."

She looked at him from between matted lashes. "Bastard. Go home. Go fuck your wife. Your *wife*! How could you do this?" In one brief trip to see a dying grandfather, the three years she had put into their relationship had been reduced to nothing by a woman he didn't even know.

Suddenly, Neel knew what to do. He went over to the sofa and held her tightly. Soon her protests grew halfhearted and she stopped crying.

"It's okay, it's okay. Everything is going to be all right," he promised in a soothing voice. "Shh, shh. Tell me, how did you find out?"

"Sanjay told us." She sniffed and blew her nose. "He, he thought you were at the hospital today and wanted to congratulate you."

Neel remembered that Sanjay's brother was Ashok's co-worker. Indians were obsessed with other people's lives. Even in America they bored into his, like tenacious termites.

"Sweetie," he stroked her hair, "I'm sorry you had to find out from Sanjay. Let me explain, all right? Just listen."

He could see her face settle into understanding with his every word. His own voice convinced him beyond any doubt that he wanted to keep their relationship. It proved that nothing had changed, that he wasn't really married. And that was of paramount importance to him.

"So you see, I did it because of my grandfather," he said.

"I can't imagine my pappy forcing me to get married." Caroline touched Neel's face. It was going to be all right. It wasn't as if he had reunited with his childhood sweetheart and rediscovered their youthful passion. Poor Neel had been forced into a marriage he didn't want. She would get her doctor after all.

"Your family isn't Indian. It's pretty common there. Emotional blackmail. Pronouncements like, 'Do this or I will die.'"

"I guess Sanjay's grandparents are different."

"No, not at all. When Sanjay announced he was going to marry Oona, his mother warned him it would kill his grandfather. Sanjay's grandfather also fought to get rid of the English. His mother didn't speak to Sanjay for a year."

"I didn't know that. Wow! Poor Sanjay." She didn't understand

Indian customs. She only knew she wanted to be Neel's wife. In spite of her parents and brother, in spite of Neel's reluctance, she wanted him. He was Indian, but he was a doctor—and that was much better than the bartender fiancé she had left behind in the Midwest.

"Sanjay doesn't like to talk about it. And anyway, his grandfather died shortly after the wedding," Neel exaggerated. The grandfather had actually come around and even met Oona before dying three years later.

"Ouch."

"Yes, I'd hate to have that on my conscience."

"But sweetheart, sweetie, what happens now?"

"We carry on as before. May our two lips meet again and again." Neel kissed her.

Her mouth opened and he pulled her closer in relief. He had worried that she wouldn't understand his sudden marriage, but she was wonderful, wonderful. His gratitude eased into a thankful love and now he regretted all the times he had been mean to her. Insisting on taking separate cars to restaurants when they risked eating out. Letting people believe he was single. Refusing to visit her family.

She had been so sweet last Christmas, saying she didn't want him spending the holidays alone. Her parents had invited him to come home with her. They were from Wisconsin, "bad cheese country," she called it. She had been born in France while her father was in the army, before he inherited the family farm. But Neel hadn't wanted to chance walking into another bad experience.

Caroline hadn't told him much about her parents, but he instinctively didn't trust them. If Savannah's well-traveled parents had dismissed him, he was sure that Caroline's parents, even with a European touch, had kept their smug insularity.

"Did you like the flowers?" She smiled up at him, wishing her face wasn't puffy from crying.

"I loved them."

"And I love you, love you, love you."

Neel believed her. She probably also liked the idea of being with a doctor. Neel understood that. He, too, had wanted to marry up.

"Caroline, I'm exhausted—" he began, but she interrupted him.

Her hand traveled down his torso, lightly, just the way she knew he liked it. "No talking now. Let me take care of you."

· ELEVEN ·

ALONE, FRIGHTENED, INCREASINGLY COLD and hungry, Leila stood by the window and stared into the dark. Even the night sky seemed different in America, obstructed by skyscrapers and lightened by the glare of unfamiliar road lamps. The smell of the blue and pink flowers was suffocating. She wanted to open the window but that would let in the chill air.

She lost hope that Neel had played a trick on her, that he would come back and they could start their life. As she watched the red taillights of passing cars, she realized that he really had gone to the shop, and really did live in this tiny flat.

She wished she could call Amma and Appa to come rescue her. But that would be admitting defeat—again. Besides, they had married her off and expected her to stay put. They would offer no comforting words, just a firm, "You must to stay with Suneel."

Who was this man her parents had married her to? She had to find out, had to know why he and his parents had done this to her. Mrs. Rajan had lied. "Our Suneel has a fine fine house in Ahmerica," she had boasted. Was the family so desperate to get Neel married they made up success stories about him? What was wrong with him that they were trying to cover up? Was that why he never saw another girl? It was all so confusing. She thought of home, the road on which the Saraths lived, their big red house with the mango tree next to the gate. No one had ever said anything mean about Neel's mother. She had an honest reputation. His grandfather, especially, was well respected both in the steel factory and in the community.

She began searching through the flat, starting with the two piles of letters on the coffee table. Colored advertisements; a huge envelope declaring Neel Sarath a possible winner of $1 million; and near the bottom, a *Stanford Magazine* addressed to Dr. Neel Sarath.

He *was* a doctor. He hadn't lied about that. Relief weakened her legs and she sank onto the sofa, only to feel the springs cave in under her. What kind of doctor was he if he was too poor to afford a good sofa? This was a red cloth one, with a large brown stain on one side, both arms pockmarked from plucking.

Leila wondered how sweet, nice Tattappa would react in this situation. But he wasn't a woman. He had always had power, the automatic right of a male. Amma would be shocked at her behavior. She would expect Leila to sit and wait. Do nothing, be demure. But she had been demure enough for ten lives.

There was just one promising place to look: Neel's desk, a large rectangle protected by thick glass. He was very organized, the central drawer neatly divided into sections by plastic containers. One for pencils, pens, another for stamps. Leila saw his Indian passport and checked the date of his birth. It was correct.

Only when she investigated the file drawer did she begin to learn about this man whose name was now hers. Telephone bills, Visa card bills, gas and electricity bills—he saved everything according to the month. She looked through them, thinking, "I'll divorce him. I won't stay with him. I won't let Amma force me. I don't care if people talk. I'm not like the others. I can't accept that it is my fate." The desk was nestled between two bookcases, the volumes arranged by subject. Most of them were medical books, but she saw that he had a complete edition of Shakespeare. At another time it would have made her happy. Not now. Warm, large tears fell on her hands as she bent down to look at the next file.

She was spurred on by the clock. What if he returned and found her at his desk? Would he hit her, throw her out of the house? Smita had told them of a girl whose husband used her arms as an ashtray, stubbing out his cigarettes on her skin. He belonged to a good family but had gone crazy in America. Leila was afraid of what Suneel might be capable of.

There was no one she could turn to in America. Certainly not her former classmates, who lived in big houses in Pittsburgh and Houston. They would feign sympathy, but would be the first to broadcast yet another "poor Leila" story.

In a file marked LETTERS, she thumbed though a sheaf of blue, yellow, pink-colored papers, some with flowers, others with big, intertwined hearts. *Darling Neel*, the two words waltzed around the room like lovers. Each love letter was signed, *Your Savannah*. Her fingers trembling so she could hardly turn the pages, she read a few. Tahoe, Mendocino, Carmel—they had visited many places together. The last one was dated eight years ago. She thought: "I'm not the only one with a Janni in my background." Then she worried that he could still be in love with Savannah. But surely too many years had gone by. She put away the letters, convincing herself they didn't mean anything.

The next file was marked CONDO. She did not know what that meant, but opened it anyway and saw a flyer with a prominent picture of the building. Under the picture was information on the flat, except that it was called a condo. There was a map of San Francisco showing the various neighborhoods, with descriptions noting crime rates and the average household incomes. According to the literature, some flats, condos, like Neel's—theirs—were more expensive than houses. Another paper was titled "Comps," with addresses and prices of condos close by. This was why the taxi driver said they live in a good area. They did, even though it was not an area of houses.

Leila noticed a square piece of paper on the floor. As she bent to pick it up, she saw that it was a photograph of a blond woman. Just the face, lips smiling, blue eyes well delineated in deeper blue, skin as white as a lychee. Was this Savannah? There was no name on the other side. Only the message: *Love you madly*. The girl's face, her eyes, the hair curved into her jaw, made Leila uneasy. Jealousy drove away her earlier fears. It was one thing to say *she* would leave *him*; now she faced the fact that he might want to be with another woman. But Neel had known this blond girl a long time ago. In eight years, many things could happen. One could get a PhD and one could forget a person. There was no reason to be jealous.

That was Neel's past; she was Neel's future. He had come back to India to marry and had chosen her. But where had the picture fallen from? She knew she should not have snooped around the flat. Amma always said she acted before she thought. Now Neel would know she had been looking through his things. Hoping, crossing her fingers, that it came from the letter file, she put it back and promised herself she would never do such a thing again.

The desktop held a small black tray with stones arranged in a pattern on sand. Sand was a type of mud, she reasoned. She touched it with her finger and brought it to her forehead. There— she had blessed herself. Everything was working out, just in unexpected ways.

She sat on the desk chair, only to jump up. A shrill pealing echoed in the room. It sounded again and her eyes followed the unusual tone. The phone. It rang again, like a cat mewing for its food. Should she pick it up? What if it was this woman Savannah? Could it be Neel?

The voice that boomed through the receiver was male and Indian. It was Sanjay Bannerji, one of Neel's friends, calling to congratulate them.

He laughed when she told him where Neel had gone.

"Good God, shopping at this time of night! I always told him not to keep a bare fridge. Your husband is a male Mother Hubbard. It's a good thing you took pity and married him. Now at least he won't come back to an empty condo or an empty fridge."

The Indian accent and acceptance calmed Leila. Neel must have told people about their marriage. Now Sanjay was even inviting them to dinner.

"I will set it up with Neel. We have to celebrate this wonderful news," he insisted.

She had panicked. It was going to be all right. When Neel finally returned that night, the raw, desperate feeling raging inside her was gone, replaced by fatigue and shame. But she could not look him in the eye. As she watched him put a frozen pizza in the oven, she wished she wasn't starting her married life with so many secrets between them.

· TWELVE ·

LEILA STEPPED OUT INTO the cool but sunny afternoon, a red Kashmiri shawl embroidered with flowers wrapped around her shoulders. She had been living with this misleading weather for ten days, but was still surprised that the bright rays did not warm her skin. Just beyond, on the horizon, the sun transformed the Bay into a show of loose diamonds so dazzling she could hardly look at it.

A brisk breeze rustled the aerogram and she tightened her hold. She was going to post it herself. She didn't trust the postman to actually pick up the letter if she left it in their lobby as Neel had instructed. She was used to postmen who did as they pleased, sometimes not coming at all, other times keeping interesting-looking envelopes that might contain photographs.

She had passed a postbox on her daily walks and recognized it from American films. Still, it baffled her the first time she went to post a letter. She circled the arched, metal box, looking for a hole like the slit mouths of the red postboxes back home. All she saw was blue, blue, blue. She stared at it, but the metal crouched, humped in silence. Finally, just when she was about to admit defeat, she saw the handle hidden beneath the top curve which pulled down to create the opening.

This was already her second letter home. She had so much to tell them, wanted so much for them to share in her wonderment, starting with that initial impression of San Francisco in the day-light. The wide, cement pavements uncrowded with people; the low, long cars that transformed the road into a flashing rainbow; the picture-postcard buildings in perfect condition. Most had no gardens at all, she noticed with surprise, while those that did were bright with the thick lawns and flowers she had read about in books. No fruit trees anywhere, just tall trees that occasionally grew right out of the pavement. One house had a long row of rosemary and she gazed at the purple flowers, marveling at the cascading profusion. There was the bell-like sound of the telephone, the milk carton that opened only on one side, the hot water that flowed all day. The fat newspaper, fatter yet on Sundays, the taste of nectarine juice, the Brobdignagian eggs. The packaged foods amazed her both by their variety and the amount of typed information. Kila would have loved to play with the empty strawberry baskets.

Leila wished her letter could be like the scratch and sniff advertisements in American magazines so her family could experience the myriad flavors of America.

Kila, I have not yet been to an ice cream parlor but when I go, I promise to tell you the exact number of flavors they have here. Her father would want to hear about the house. She didn't explain it was a flat, knowing Appa would not understand. *There are two bedrooms and also two bathrooms. We are situated on the side of a steep hill and at night I can hear the cars roar up with great acceleration. San Francisco is like Rome except that instead of seven hills it must have been built on a hundred!* She told Indy, who had such trouble with her long braid, about hair products. *There is a whole shelf of shampoos for different kinds of hair. I bought a bottle of Pantene, the same one Smita brought back from Singapore, and it is really very good. I am getting quite addicted to the TV. There are more than fifty channels and on Sunday they even have an Indian program. I saw an interesting documentary about the Bengal tiger. It was made by foreigners (naturally!) but they did have some Indians in it.*

She didn't know what to tell Amma about Neel and their life in

America. Amma would never ask about the auspicious night, but Leila felt its absence in every sentence she wrote. Would Amma guess that nothing had happened yet? Would Amma blame her? Maybe Amma would tell Leila she was silly to keep hoping that Neel would touch her before the night chosen by the priest—tonight. In a little less than twelve hours she was going to do more than sleep beside Neel.

Amma would definitely be interested in Neel's friends, and whether Leila had enough sarees to wear to all the dinners. She fully expected that Leila and Neel would receive invitations from their neighbors, like all newlyweds in India. She would not be able to comprehend that Leila hadn't even met anyone in the building. People smiled when passing each other in the hallway, but didn't say anything. Their pink, voiceless lips told Leila how far she had moved from the Nandis—the Nosy Nandis, Indy's sobriquet for their neighbors—who constantly peered across the separating wall or came over to drink tea and gossip.

Leila was happy that she could write of Sanjay's invitation. *Tonight we are having dinner at the house of Suneel's friend, an Indian doctor.*

The end of the letter was specially for Indy: *I miss our evening walks and have started taking short ones around the neighborhood. The hill is good exercise and when I am standing at the top I can see the ocean and know that everyone I love is on the other side.*

The walks were her way of absorbing their neighborhood—and America. She let go of the aerogram and heard it drop. In about a week their postman, wiry, Prince Charles–eared Doreswamy, would ride by on his rickety cycle, ring the bell, and hand it to Amma. Unless Indy rushed to the gate first.

Leila took another route back to the condo, an address she knew by heart, along with the long phone number. These small remembrances were her victories, tangible proof that she was settling into wife-life. She already had a daily routine and woke with Neel. She had fantasized that their mornings would be a mixture of American romance and Indian food. But so far the dosa tava and branched idli maker remained in their original boxes. Neel never kissed her "Good morning" like the husbands in films. He didn't even want coffee or tea, showering quickly and leaving. When she offered to make him a hot lunch, he refused, saying, "I usually grab something from the cafeteria. It's much easier." He didn't want her to cook for him. He wanted her to take this time to adjust to America.

It wasn't just the outside world—the sharp needles of the fir trees, the sloping roofs of houses, the expansive celadon sea jaunty with sailing craft—that thrilled and excited her. She also began using gadgets she hadn't known existed. Housework was hard work back home. Everything—laundry, floors, grinding, cleaning the pots and pans that got black from the kerosene stove— was done by hand. The first time she used the vacuum cleaner, it began making a clanking sound. If only she could run over to the neighbors and ask for help. But their doors were firmly shut, like those in hotels. So she waited till Neel returned. "I think I broke it," she blurted as soon as he opened the door. Afterwards she laughed in relief when Neel showed her the penny that had been sucked into the rectangular box.

The washer/dryer gave her particular pleasure, and not just because the clothes washed themselves, unlike at home, where Heera pounded their sarees on the floor of the bathroom and then hung them to dry on a line in the garden. Leila's fingers trembled every time she touched Neel's underwear. The tiny bits of white material were erotic. She loved to fold them neatly as they came out of the dryer, warm and fresh-smelling. The triangles with their wide elastic bands and slit openings affirmed that she was married and had a right to know that Neel wore size 34.

Sometimes she still caught herself trying to turn on the light switches the Indian way, downward. But she no longer looked for the familiar blades of the ceiling fan. San Francisco had air-conditioned weather. Even the wood floors were cold, so she drank endless cups of hot tea and wore socks.

But mostly her days were long hours spent waiting for Neel to return home. And she often spent the evenings like she spent her days, alone. He told her that the work ethic in America was very different from India. No afternoon siestas, and few early evenings.

He tried to help, buying a guidebook on San Francisco and suggesting she follow its day trips to Fisherman's Wharf, Alcatraz, Muir Woods. She imagined a forest tall with trees, the ground covered with mushrooms. Every Rice-A-Roni ad on TV made her want to ride a cable car. But nothing in her upbringing had prepared her to sightsee alone. Appa always accompanied Amma, and girls never walked anywhere unescorted. It was considered too daring, an invitation for ruffians to yell bad words and make obscene gestures. So she kept waiting for Neel to show her their new city.

Then yesterday he had called at noon to say he would be back past midnight. And suddenly the seconds and minutes and hours were like the face of the clock she was staring at, predictable and slow-moving. On the spur of the moment, she picked up the guidebook. All these days she had stood on various hills and looked over at the bluffs of Marin, the towers of the Golden Gate Bridge, marveling that she was in San Francisco, that she didn't need to get permission to go out, that these sights belonged to her as much as to anyone else in the city.

She decided to walk to Union Square, where Neel had taken her to shop on their only outing together. She knew it would please him. He wanted her to be more American and women in America went everywhere alone. According to the TV, they even took holidays by themselves.

Union Square itself was a scruffy grass patch hemmed in by buildings. She was surrounded by the skins and smells of America, amidst people who looked as if they belonged on the pages of magazines, with coordinated clothes and shoes and handbags. Even the very old women resembled faded fashion sketches. She was glad she had worn her new salwar kameez.

Glad, until she noticed that people were staring at her. It wasn't like home, where bold young men let their eyes linger over a few parts of the female body. Here even the young girls seemed to be looking at her. Was it her outfit? She *was* the only one wearing bright red silk. The tailor had made the pants too long and they hung over her shoes. The black border of the kameez was complemented by the dupatta around her neck. She had started the walk wearing the dupatta Indian-style, draped across her shoulders, the two ends lifting lightly off her back with every step. But the wind kept whipping it in different directions, so she twisted it around her neck, bringing both ends to the front, her hands holding them in place.

"That's a beautiful costume." A gray-haired woman touched Leila's shoulder. "My daughter and I are wondering, is it a sarai?"

The light turned green and a crowd of people carried her across, separating her from the duo. Leila was amused at the woman's mispronunciation. She had also never thought of her clothes as a costume. When they reached the other side, the daughter spoke before Leila could respond. "It's silk, isn't it? Such gorgeous material."

"Yes, it's a salwar kameez, not a saree."

"Well, we just wanted you to know it's beautiful. And so are you."

After that, Leila didn't look away from people's eyes. They weren't judging her; their glances were curious and admiring. Amma would be unhappy that she didn't wear sarees every day, but the weather was too cold, even for thick silk ones. Salwar kameezes were the next best things to the pants she planned to add to her wardrobe, and more suitable for walking.

She stopped in at Gump's, not knowing what to expect from such a funny-sounding name, and, like Alice, fell into enchantment with the glassware. "Hand-blown," the labels said, and she imagined an old man blowing see-through perfection somewhere in Sweden. Every country was within grasp in America. Furniture from Japan and Indonesia, baubles from France, delicate crystal from Italy. On a shelf by itself was a bud vase, tall and slim, with the words *How do I love thee? Let me count the ways*. The vase was as exquisite as the line of poetry. She wanted to buy it for Neel, but she didn't have the money.

She also didn't have the right feelings for him. She loved him because she was married to him and couples were supposed to love each other. But she didn't love him the way girls loved their husbands and lovers in romance novels.

Yet Neel never seemed to be far from her thoughts, more so in Union Square. The place symbolized her new life; it was to the Macy's here that Neel had taken her shopping. That was a week ago, but she remembered every moment, playing it over and over again, like the ads on TV.

He'd called unexpectedly and given her ten minutes to get ready. She quickly drew on kajal, combed her hair, changed into a new yellow saree, and was waiting downstairs when the car pulled up.

She had never seen such a luxurious shop. The different levels reminded Leila of tiered wedding cakes, each one beautifully presented and decorated. The small tables slippery with silky, lacy underwear, glass counters aromatic with perfumes in small and giant bottles, hats hanging on pegs, hangers draped with ready-to-wear clothes that filled her eyes with so much color she thought she was going blind, all were bewildering and seductive. But there was no time to browse. They only had an hour, Neel's lunchtime. He was giving it up for her.

Her head moving like the windshield wipers of his car, she followed as he strode through the labyrinth of clothes.

His question, "What do you want?" was as inviting—and confusing—as the different TV channels. Leila chose a brown pants suit, knowing that the color would look good on her. The smooth material followed the shape of her body. She felt as powerful as the Gods and Goddesses who transformed themselves in a moment.

She kept staring at herself, wondering what Amma would make of her reflection. But even Amma would not be able to say anything to the son-in-law who was buying this outfit. Neel. He was waiting to see the new girl in the mirror. She parted the curtains of the changing room and sauntered out like a model. This was how she had walked on stage to receive the crown when she won the beauty queen title in college. He didn't say anything, just looked at her for a long time.

"We'll take it," he told the sales lady. Leila was relieved and pleased. He also bought her a pair of closed shoes. When she stepped into the soft black leather her toes felt warm, as if his fingers were clasping her foot.

Leila had worn those shoes to post the letter. She looked down at them, still mystified by her hidden toes. She had only worn slippers in India. And tonight, for the dinner at Sanjay's house, Neel had asked her to wear the new pants suit. She wanted to look beautiful and make him proud in front of his friends. Neel had not said much about them, only that Sanjay Bannerji was an Indian doctor married to Oona, an American woman. Leila had never met a mixed couple.

She hurried to the flat, laying out the pants suit that still smelled of the shop, still bore the touch of his hand. Neel had warned her that unlike Indians, Americans don't expect their guests to be late.

She would miss the comfort of Indian Stretchable Time, miss the freedom to arrive two hours past the invitation and still be considered polite.

She brushed her hair and felt it light and soft around her face. Neel had asked her to loosen her hair that day in the shop. Her forehead looked bare without the pottu, but it didn't suit a Western outfit. A special outfit, a special night.

Tonight wasn't going to be like Ooty when she hadn't even known if Neel planned to follow tradition. She had been thinking of this evening for days. She dabbed perfume on her wrists and sprayed some between her breasts. The brief brush of cold hardened her nipples as she imagined what awaited her after the dinner.

· THIRTEEN ·

"WHY DIDN'T YOU TELL ME YOU were taking her to Sanjay's tonight?" Caroline demanded.

"It's not important." Neel played it down. "Just an obligation." It was absurd of Caroline to be upset over something he himself didn't want to do.

The reception area was unexpectedly deserted, but they kept their voices low from habit.

"What do you mean, an obligation?"

"Sanjay felt obliged to invite us and I felt obliged to accept." Neel looked down at the patient's chart.

Caroline persisted, determined to reestablish her rights. "Why on earth would he feel obligated to invite you and—her?" Caroline didn't want to know "her" name.

"It's an Indian tradition. Inviting couples." He wished someone would come by and interrupt them.

"You mean newlyweds, don't you?" she sneered. "Gosh, I had no idea you were *so* into following Indian traditions. Aside from having—what did you call it?—an arranged marriage."

Caroline knew Neel liked the distance between himself and India. When he first came to the hospital, all the single women had tried for him. One by one they moved on, but not before discussing the mysterious Dr. Sarath. Juanita was sure he hadn't responded to her because she was too reminiscent of Indian women. Dark-haired Fiona, who had had a similar experience with a Middle Eastern intern, was convinced the doctor wanted a blonde decorating his arm. When Caroline finally got him to go out with her, she sensed what had drawn him in, getting confirmation after the concert they attended on his birthday.

She had surprised him with tickets to an Ali Akbar Khan concert. His mother only listened to South Indian classical music and Neel had never heard of Khan, who belonged to the North Indian school. Expecting to be bored, he was surprised to find himself enjoying every moment of the performance, but during the interval had felt out of place in the motley group of expatriates and wide-eyed Indian wannabees. Halfway around the world, he was surrounded by sarees (the Indians wearing the over-bright ones, the Caucasians looking like slightly better versions of Hare Krishna singers) and ornate slippers patently wrong for San Francisco's chilly evening air. His discomfort must have been obvious, because Caroline never suggested another Indian event.

Yet he had started out being very proud of India. In his first weeks at Stanford he had actually liked it when people praised his English. But he quickly grew tired of the compliment and of the ridiculous questions people kept asking him. India was very hot, wasn't it? They forgot about the Himalayas and the monsoons. Aren't all Indians vegetarians? They were shocked that he ate steak. Do Indians meditate every morning? They clearly didn't believe him when Neel said he had never done so. And then there were the embarrassing questions about the population problem, the bride burnings, and arranged marriages.

Indians think all Americans are rich and drive new cars, he told his roommate, who had come to Stanford on a scholarship and, like Neel, had to budget his money carefully. But Steven just shook his head, laughing that anyone would believe poverty could escape an entire nation and its people. So one day, after two blond girls asked Neel if anyone kept count of the dead bodies floating down the river in Benares, he created his "I'm just from there, I don't know all the answers" persona.

He had thought briefly of resurrecting India's past glory, when this fat finger of land, jutting into the sea, had given birth to men and ideas still looked upon with wonder. But Americans couldn't even pronounce the two great epics, the *Ramayana* and the *Mahabharata*. No one really cared that Panini had written the first grammar, and the decimal point was too small to brag about.

He also didn't like it that he had to dig into history to find the patriotic feelings that welled up so readily in Americans. He often thought that he had either been born in the wrong country or the wrong century. Tattappa always said, "Born right after Independence, you are a virry lucky boy." But Neel thought that was precisely when India began producing more men than ideas. The men of ideas left the country in an ongoing exodus the media referred to as "the brain drain." He had been among them. If a man is his passport, Neel Sarath was no longer Indian.

Sanjay continued to ask him to join the various Indian associations that kept springing up in nearby Silicon Valley, children of the brain drain. But after living in America almost a third of his life, Neel didn't want to become part of an India club, where some members would embrace him just because he was an Iyengar. He enjoyed meeting the diverse nationalities in the Bay Area, the women who spoke their minds, the men who sought out new sports to excel in. It had been that easy accessibility, as well as the sense of limitless possibility, that made him sign up for tennis, scuba classes, flying lessons. In the past few years he had grown so accustomed to being with whites that sometimes the brown face in the mirror surprised him.

"Anyway," he sidestepped Caroline's reference to his arranged marriage, "you know I can't take you to dinner."

"Don't think I'm good enough for your doctor friends?" Caroline raised her voice. "Let me tell—"

Neel interrupted her, "What I meant was, Sanjay's wife only cooks Indian food." He didn't want another fight about why they didn't socialize together.

Caroline vehemently disliked Indian food. The few times they went out she invariably chose a French restaurant, ordering in French, which pleased the waiter—and impressed Neel.

"But isn't he married to an American?" Caroline dug through her purse.

"Yes, Oona is from Maine." He felt the sickly familiar embrace of jealousy. Sanjay, that short, belly-bulging Bengali Babu, had managed to attract an elegant, tall Stanford graduate who came from East Coast money. Her parents owned a vacation home in Aspen, and though Sanjay went there every winter, he was not interested in learning how to ski. Neel, who had saved up to take advantage of Stanford's outdoor programs, loved the challenge of black diamond slopes, but didn't have the luxury of talking about "the family cabin."

"You don't even like Indian food!" Caroline said.

He never suggested going to Indian restaurants with Caroline, preferring the anonymity of Western restaurants. She didn't know that he did in fact miss the flavors of spicy chicken curry, cool raita sprinkled with roasted cumin seed powder, green cabbage speckled with chilies and coconut.

Oona cooked Indian food not because it was fashionable to experiment with exotic cuisine, but because she genuinely wanted to learn everything about her husband's world. She was almost more traditional than an Indian bride. How would Oona react to Caroline, who considered herself French? Neel often wondered.

Having unwittingly compared the two women, Neel was overcome by the deficiencies he invariably associated with Caroline.

"Oona is a good cook," he defended the other blonde. "She went to a lot of trouble to learn, using cookbooks and attending classes. I'm sure the dinner will be excellent." Sanjay was lucky because his home life was both foreign and familiar. In the early days of his marriage, Sanjay had made some noises about their differences. He never denied that he had gained a wonderful wife. He just said that in a love marriage like his, he had also lost something—the range of shared experiences one could build upon. Neel thought that Oona was busy correcting that loss.

Neel picked up his pen and prepared to leave.

"Sweetie, I'm not criticizing her cooking." Caroline took the pen out of his hand, surprised by his response. His enjoyment of Western food was another advantage for her. Why was he annoyed? She didn't want him to leave feeling that way. She leaned forward so that the neck of her blouse dipped forward. It was a trick she had learned in high school. Sex was like makeup. Learn to use it, and it enhanced your natural charms.

Her sexual boldness continued to surprise Neel. On their first date she had invited him up for coffee and then excused herself. Neel assumed she was using the bathroom. He was fiddling with the receiver when she walked in stark naked.

Now, too, he reacted immediately and shifted uncomfortably.

"See you tonight?" She smiled.

"How about now?" They never risked making love in the hospital, but Neel could visualize her white ass bent over the operating table, legs spread apart on a vacant bed. He swallowed, his Adam's apple bobbing up and down.

"I'm ready," Caroline responded immediately, glad that he desired her. He had to keep desiring her. "I'm not wearing any panties." She had recently read that many French women didn't bother with underwear.

Neel pictured the blond triangle, as excruciatingly inviting as his first sight that night when she slid up against him, her white body smooth and hairless. She had tiny "baby coconut" breasts, with the pinkest of nipples.

"I was just kidding. This is a hospital," he said, trying to look stern.

"Oops, sorry, Doctor. I thought you were bold and daring." She shook her head so that her hair cascaded around her face.

Gold. The color never ceased to fascinate him. Oona said she wanted their children to look exactly like Sanjay. A loving tribute— but ultimately foolish, Neel thought. Much better to be born white in America. Then their children would never have to worry about glass ceilings and rude comments.

Neel moved behind the counter and put his hand under the short black skirt, touching the bare skin, her thigh warm. She shivered. His hand moved up slowly, his fingers gradually approaching that junction of all men's beginnings.

"Sweetie, you aren't sleeping with—her—are you?" Caroline pressed his hand between her legs. The question had burned inside her ever since his return, with visions of Neel and the unknown woman in the condo she had never spent the night in. But she had waited for the right moment to ask it.

"What do you think?" He began to explore her.

"I don't know. You tell me." Caroline willed him to say no. What would she do if he was sleeping with both of them?

"My grandfather asked me to marry her. Not sleep with her." He could hear Tattappa saying, "Suneel, I have spoken to the priest. He has picked July 24 as the ahspicious day." Today was July 24. The mood was broken. He jammed his hand into his pocket.

"Do you know what I'm thinking about right now?" Caroline felt his withdrawal and moved against him. "It's big and it's hard," she paused coyly. "And it's on my bedside table." When Neel didn't respond, she said, "The *Kama Sutra*."

He loved the way she mispronounced the word. He had bought her the large edition for Christmas and she had proclaimed it the perfect book since she didn't need to read it. The pictures were enough.

"I knew there was a reason I was born double-jointed. *Double your pleasure, double your fun*," she sang, bending her fingers so they looked like claws.

Neel laughed, then saw Patrick Connery from the OB/GYN unit coming toward them and quickly reached for his clipboard. Caroline busied herself with the schedule.

"Neel, how's married life?" Patrick asked.

"Fine, fine." Neel moved away from Caroline. "How are the twins?"

"Noisy. When do we get to meet the new Mrs. Sarath? I've got all these stories about you I want to tell her."

"That's reason enough to keep you far away from her. You'll get me into more trouble than I'm in already." Neel swung into step beside Patrick. Patrick was yet another colleague who wanted to meet Leila. How long could he keep putting people off?

He wished he could cancel the dinner tonight, send Leila back to India and pretend the trip to see Tattappa had never happened. He wanted the complications of his old life, not this new one of juggling two households and two women. Leila wasn't demanding, but she was there. Which meant food in the fridge, explanations about the tiniest details of life in America, and invitations like this evening.

Oona had probably prompted that call. Why was she was so keen to adapt to the Indian way of life while living in America? She was taking Bengali lessons. And classical Indian dancing, Sanjay told him proudly. An oxymoron, Neel thought immediately, a tall, blond woman performing Bharat Natyam steps in a silk saree. Then he remembered Leila coming out of the dressing room at Macy's.

The pant suit had transformed her, but she wore it like it was someone else's clothes. A few of the other customers stopped and stared, making him think that perhaps he was right. Her face was too Indian for the outfit. "Her eyes are made for dancing," Tattappa had said, referring to the intricate eye movements in Bharat Natyam and Kathak. Leila looked better when Neel asked her to let her hair down. The loose black strands framed her face, giving her the look of a love child from the sixties.

He hoped she would remember to wear it down tonight. This was their first social outing and he was nervous that she might do or say something to embarrass him. He hadn't acted as a couple since the days with Savannah and wasn't used to others judging him by who he was with. At least Leila spoke English fluently and her knowledge of poets and novelists—if she brought them into the conversation—would be impressive.

He had forgotten to ask if there was some food she didn't eat. Sanjay, no doubt prompted by Oona, had kept asking him. He had finally said no, just to placate Sanjay.

It didn't matter, however. Even though he didn't know Leila, he could count on the fact that she was Indian enough never to draw attention to herself by revealing that the food was not to her taste.

· FOURTEEN ·

THE HOUSE WAS PART OF A new development and looked exactly like the others in the cul-de-sac, cream-colored, red-roofed ("Our Stanford connection," Sanjay maintained), with an emerging garden in front. Yellow and purple pansies that Sanjay grew because you could eat them, like the marigolds back home, lined both sides of the walkway, and grapelike wisteria clustered around the porch pillar. Across the street children played jump rope on the pavement, their voices carrying in the evening air.

Leila lost part of her nervousness when Sanjay opened the door, hands joined in the age-old Indian greeting. "Namaste, Didi," he bowed, and the typical Bengali face and accent gave her the illusion of familiarity.

Neel took a deep breath to contain his irritation. Sanjay *would* call Leila "Didi—Big Sister," trying to transform America into India.

The sharp aroma of mustard oil reminded Leila of meals cooked by their Bengali neighbor, Mrs. Nandi. Sanjay could have been one of Aunty Nandi's sons, except that he was wearing jeans, not kurta pajama, and standing behind him was his wife, tall, white, and very blond.

For a moment Leila was paralyzed, could barely breathe. Was it Savannah? Had Neel not married Savannah because she had married his friend?

Sanjay stepped aside and the porch light illuminated the long hair and smiling face of his wife. It wasn't the face from the photograph. Leila took a deep breath. She had been more anxious about those letters and the picture than she realized.

"Welcome to America. I'm Oona." She stepped forward and held out her hand. Oona didn't kiss Leila. Sanjay had explained that Indians don't like strangers touching them, and Oona had said their "Namaste" seemed so formal and distancing. "Germ-free," Sanjay corrected her.

Leila smiled in return and felt her hand warmed by the blond woman's clasp.

Neel kissed Oona's cheek, then handed her two bottles of wine, red and white. "Your husband didn't know what marvels you were concocting tonight so I took the liberty of bringing one of each."

Leila hadn't known they were bringing anything. At home a gift like this would be considered insulting, an indication that the host could not afford wine.

"Oh Neel, how sweet of you. You shouldn't have," Oona said, while Sanjay promptly joked, "*Arre, arre*, why do you think I invited him? He knows all about wine and has expensive taste, which suits me very well. Come on in. Look who else is here."

"Bob, Shanti," Neel greeted them. "Good to see you," though he had not expected anyone else to be there.

Leila took in the other couple, mixed like Sanjay and Oona, but with the sexes reversed. She had never seen anyone with red hair before, except Archie in comic books. In real life the effect was clownlike. Bob's six feet five exaggerated the comedic look and reduced his wife to a midget.

"Shanti, Bob, this is Neel's wife. Leila Didi, this is Shanti, who is anything but *shant*," Sanjay teased. "She talks, talks, talks, and because she is an editor is always correcting my grammar. Bob works with me in pediatrics. Top floor of the hospital, which means we are the best doctors."

They went into a living room that was a mosaic of India and

America. Oona pointed out that the leather sofa (their first purchase after marriage) set off their dual heritage: her grandmother's hand-knit afghan on the back and a maroon Kashmiri carpet on the floor. The mantelpiece held wedding and family pictures, black and white for the Indian side, color for Oona's parents. Sanjay suggested a quick tour of the house, "to make you comfortable," showing her the bathroom with its pale blue seashell wallpaper, the piano room where Oona practiced her dance steps, even the wreaths his wife brought out for the different seasons. "I keep telling her the Bay Area only has foggy weather," Sanjay said in mock despair.

It was the first American house Leila had been in and she took careful notes: the bouquet of dried flowers on the piano, the large art book on the coffee table, the collection of pastel-colored shell-shaped soaps in the bathroom that matched the wallpaper.

The kitchen cupboard best delineated the dividing strands of their braided lives. One shelf had Western spices only, marjoram, thyme, oregano, names Sanjay usually mispronounced, though he liked to say "dill weed" at any opportunity. Oona had naively assumed Indians didn't smoke dope, so was surprised to learn that Sanjay had been high on ganja all through his college years in Calcutta, becoming a serious student only in Stanford. Indian spices, some store-bought, others made by Sanjay's mother, filled another shelf, and beneath that were the bottles of pickles, garlic, mango, chili, carrot, bitter melon, all so spicy Oona never touched them.

"So," Shanti looked at Leila as she sat down on the black leather sofa, "you're the lucky one who finally snagged Mr. Bachelor here."

"Snagged?" Leila bypassed the "lucky," not wanting to be proud, and concentrated on the bit she did not understand. How could a broken thread refer to her? Shanti looked like an Indian but dressed like an American, and her accent was equally confusing, caught between the two countries.

"She means married," Oona explained, coming to sit beside her. "Shanti's been bugging Neel about it for years."

"He *was* the odd one out in our small group of marrieds," Shanti said.

"Still is." Sanjay laughed. "We two married phirangis. He married a nice girl from back home. Not that you aren't nice, my lovely wife." He winked at Oona.

"What was that marriage theory of yours, Sanjay?" Shanti asked.

"Which one?" Oona raised her eyebrows and sighed.

"About how one chooses one's partner."

"Do we have to hear this?" Neel said. He had not chosen his partner and didn't want to hear theories from those who had.

"I'd like to hear it," Leila spoke up, wanting to be part of the group.

"Arre, marriage is too mysterious for theories," Sanjay explained. "I think I just said that here in America we Indians are funny creatures. We either marry the exact opposite of ourselves, like Shanti and I did, or we go back and marry the girl next door."

"That sounds mutually exclusive," Shanti said. "I don't remember it quite like that."

"That's because I change my theories all the time. As I said, marriage is mysterious, which follows because weddings are so mysterious. Speaking of which, I still don't know why you had to go and get married behind our backs." Sanjay shook his head, the glasses and bottle clinking in his hands.

"Champagne?" Neel stood up to help. "Are we celebrating the imminent arrival of a new generation of Bannerjis?" he deliberately asked. About a year ago Sanjay had told him that Oona wanted to start a family but that he wasn't ready. Neel had listened, amazed and envious. Savannah hadn't wanted to marry him and here Sanjay was putting up a fuss even though Oona didn't mind taking the chance that their babies might be brown. He hadn't said anything then, and now wondered if this was still troublesome or if they had resolved the issue.

"No news on that front as yet, though we're working on it," Oona said, smiling at Sanjay. "We're toasting your marriage, of course. You do drink champagne, don't you?" she turned to Leila.

Leila nodded. She had never tasted champagne before, but was sure she would like it. The very word evoked romance. Candle-light. Trysts. Love. In Mills & Boon novels, couples were always drinking champagne. Neel had taken the bottle from Sanjay and was turning the wire carefully, holding the neck away from him. He was relaxed, confident. This was the Neel she had seen that night in Ooty when they shared a table with Cynthia and Harold. He was so different from Sanjay. If someone blinked Sanjay into Calcutta, he would fit right in. Sanjay had not lost any of his Indi-anisms in the long journey over. Leila could not take her eyes off her husband, this man whose very foreignness made him exciting. She thought of the night ahead and wished they could leave right now. Shanti was right. She *was* lucky to have "snagged" him, the handsomest man in the room.

"Cham-pug-knee," Sanjay deliberately spoke as if he were a vil-lager who read English like Hindi, sound for sound.

Neel cringed. That old joke again. Sanjay could be incredibly childish sometimes. He acted the same way when he told other doctors that his favorite weekend getaway was "Yos-a-might." But Oona enjoyed his sense of humor. She smiled up at him as he poured her a flute full of golden bubbles.

They all raised their glasses and Sanjay said, "I was going to bring out a small piece of toast, for the toast. But . . . no matter. To my new Didi Leila and her husband Neel. May all your troubles be little ones."

Another old Indian joke. "On the contrary," Neel said smoothly, "may all *your* troubles be little ones," though he knew the punch was gone.

Oona laughed. "I'll drink to that."

"So Leila," Shanti asked from across the room, "how do you like living in America so far?"

"I like it very much," Leila responded immediately. "I always wanted to come here." She could say it easily now because she was here.

"Just like me and ten million other Indians. I remember when I first arrived." Sanjay pushed back the recliner until his feet were level with his knees. "I stood at a street corner counting the cars. My God, there were so many different types. About three cars stopped and the drivers asked if I wanted a ride."

"Oh no, what did you tell them?" Shanti asked.

"I told them, 'Thank you very much but what is this thing with so many wheels? In India we are still using only the cow and the cart.'" Sanjay exaggerated the Indian accent, bobbing his head sideways. "Then I blew my nose on the street and did the 'whack-thoo' bit." He mimed spitting.

"You know, Sanjay, it's people like you who give Indians a bad reputation," Shanti said, her voice stern.

"Arre, don't be so serious. I just said, 'No, thank you,' very politely and continued watching the cars—with my mouth open." Sanjay laughed.

"Honey," Bob reminded his wife, "you did a pretty good job of giving Indians a bad reputation yourself."

"What do you mean?"

"Remember the warranties?"

"What's this? What's this?" Sanjay asked.

"Now that I have your full attention." Bob smiled. "Well, we'd received the usual assortment of kitchen appliances for our wedding and I came home one evening to find Shanti throwing away all the warranties. She said they were useless. No one would honor them."

"But I was new here," Shanti defended herself. "I didn't know how different things are in America. In India, no one takes anything back."

"Now of course my wife is the queen of returns." Bob laughed. "It's gotten so bad I refuse to go shopping with her most of the time." Shanti hit him playfully. "Ouch! You know I'm only kidding." He pulled her against him so they took up just one half of the loveseat.

"That's Shanti for you," Neel said. "Give her an inch and she'll make a long mile out of it."

"As if you didn't return your car," Shanti scoffed.

"That was an entirely different situation," Neel clarified, carefully balancing his drink on the armrest of the wing chair. "It was a brand-new Porsche with a defective motor. They're lucky I didn't sue them."

"Do you still have the BMW or did you finally sell it?" Shanti asked.

Neel had given it to Caroline. "Parking one car in San Francisco is bad enough. I decided to stick with the Porsche."

"You'll have to get a car for Leila," Shanti said. "You aren't going to be one of those ghastly Indian husbands who leaves his wife at home all day, are you?"

"You forgot pregnant and barefoot," Neel joked, then added more seriously, "She's going to be working, so yes, she'll need a car."

Leila stared at him. A job? Didn't he make enough money as a doctor?

Shanti spoke before Leila could respond. "Neel, you've become such an American. It took me a while—oh, six months at least—to adjust to this crazy, work, work, work country. You can't expect

Leila to step into a marriage, a new city, *and* a new job. Unless that's what you want," she belatedly said to Leila.

"In a few months, yes, I think I will start looking for a job."

Neel was relieved to hear this. She *had* to work and become independent, otherwise he would be stuck with her forever. As soon as she was making some money, they could separate and start divorce proceedings. She could even return to India if she wanted. But she would probably stay here, where divorcées were not looked down on. He wouldn't feel so bad if she was doing well on her own.

"Take your time," Shanti advised. "Don't let living here pressure you into working. I waited till I found something I really liked. Until then I lived the good life: sitting around at home, visiting, watching TV. Just like India."

"We must have lived in different Indias," Leila said. "I taught for the past eight years, and we don't have a TV." She had assumed she'd paid her dues, that being married to a doctor meant never having to work again. She had imagined herself busy raising children.

"I wish we didn't have a TV growing up," Oona said. "So many wasted hours. Tell me, Leila is such a beautiful name, so lilting. Does it have a special meaning?"

"I don't know. My mother was reading the Leila-Majnun story—it's like *Romeo and Juliet*—just before I was born and liked the name." Amma must not have realized it was a Muslim story, or maybe she hadn't seen the need to be traditional when young. Leila had always been pleased she wasn't a Meera or an Asha. Every now and then a really fair baby would grow up to be Pinky, and sisters were often rhymed, Sindhu and Bindu, Maya and Chaaya. From a very young age Leila had delighted in her unusual name and its difference from the more common Leela. When a teacher said she was being silly, since both names had almost the same pronuncia-tion, Leila pointed out how the letter "r" changed fiend to friend. "As far as I know, Leila doesn't have a meaning like your name does," Leila said, thinking of Una in Spenser's *Faerie Queene.*

"You are the second person who thinks I was named for the Lady of Truth," Oona said delightedly. "But I'm sorry to say my story is more pedestrian. It's Irish, like Charlie Chaplin's wife, with two o's."

"Enough of these tales," Sanjay announced. "I want the real story of your marriage. No Indian censorship allowed." He looked directly at Leila. "I can see why Neel said yes to marrying you. After all, you are very fair and beautiful. But whatever possessed you to marry this joker?"

He roared with laughter, and everyone joined in. Leila looked over at Neel. Which of her truths should she tell them? That Neel was the first man to say yes to her? That Amma would not have allowed her to say no? That she had liked him?

She opted for a light American answer. "He liked my cat and I thought any man who likes cats would make a good husband."

She looked over toward Neel. It was the first time she had turned to him for something. He knew the incident and could complete it for her, tell them what he had told the couple in Ooty.

Neel picked up: "You should have seen that cat. Ugly and thin. Lee calls it Elizabeth Taylor to make up for its lack of beauty."

"That's a sweet story." Oona was enchanted. "But I'm confused. Neel, aren't you allergic to cats?"

Allergic? Leila had never heard of anyone being allergic to cats. Neel had even petted ET. Poor, sweet little ET, who gave sandpaper kisses and whose breath carried the smell of the sea, even though she was a vegetarian and had never eaten fish. Leila missed ET so much she talked to every cat she saw during her walks. She had asked Neel if they could get a kitten, but the building did not allow animals.

"Yes, I am allergic to cats," Neel acknowledged. "But it wasn't around very long."

"Long enough to trap poor Leila here," Sanjay responded.

"I thought it was women who trapped men." Bob smiled at Shanti.

"As usual you've got it wrong," Shanti parried. "Back in the cave days, men used to go hunting and trapping. You, my dear, hunted me all the way to India."

"I wouldn't have, honey, if you hadn't laid the trap by being so beautiful."

Neel watched as Bob gallantly raised his wife's hand and kissed it. Bob was one of those foreigners who finds every Indian woman irresistible. The kindest adjective Neel could associate with Shanti was homely. She was intelligent and well-read, but contrary to Bob's doting eyes, she was no beauty.

Leila considered Shanti's skin and widening figure. Shanti was lucky. Bob was so obviously in love with her it was clear he didn't care that she was "black," as Amma would say. If Leila was the same color as Shanti, she would still be unmarried.

"Speaking of traps, has Neel taken you up in the plane yet?" Shanti asked Leila.

Leila recalled the trip to America, the restless hours strapped in the small seat, the food she had been unable to eat, the endless bed of clouds that made a lie out of Wordsworth's *I wandered lonely as a cloud.*

"Yes," she said, thinking it a strange question. Didn't everyone come over on a plane?

Neel shifted uncomfortably. Leila had misunderstood Shanti. It was moments like this that he had been dreading. Caroline was the only woman passenger in the Cessna 172 he enjoyed flying most weekends. "Shanti's making fun of me," he told Leila. "She's always carping that it's dangerous to fly small planes, warning me it's a death trap."

Leila waited for him to say more. He flew a plane? Why hadn't he told her? Was she going to learn to fly? She could become the Indian Beryl Markham, a writer *and* aviatrix. Excitement vied with the embarrassment of being wrong in front of so many people. "Not yet." She looked at Shanti. "I thought you meant the trip from India." The words faded and her face grew hot.

"We're still waiting for you to give us a ride," Oona reminded Neel.

"Any time you want to go." Neel smiled. He was lucky that the other two partners had such busy schedules they didn't have much time for flying even at weekends.

"You've been saying that ever since you bought that plane," Sanjay complained. "I am your oldest friend in America and all I hear about are your weekends in Sonoma and Monterey. You haven't even given me a bird's-eye view of the bridge."

"You two have known each other since medical school, right?" Shanti asked.

"I met Neel even before I met Oona. I knew him when all he did was study and chew gum."

"That's all he did?" Shanti raised her eyebrows.

"That's all he did that I can talk about." Sanjay clarified. "Oh, how I remember his chewing, chewing, chewing. I thought he would turn into a cow."

"Lies, sheer lies," Neel denied. "We hung out some, but then he met Oona, and the next thing I knew he was off to the East Coast to ask her hand in marriage. Why her parents gave their permission to this fellow is still beyond me." He had forgotten how he used to chew gum when he first came to Stanford. He'd been satisfying a craving that began as a boy when his American friend Mark had given him bubble gum one day. Just one stick of gum, just one day when he had lorded it over Ashok, who gazed in amazement at the bubbles coming out of Neel's mouth. But the memory had followed him all the way over the ocean, only being cancelled out by endless packets of gum.

"What's not to like?" Sanjay stood up and patted his chest. "Besides, I countered all their arguments with great intelligence."

"Darling, my parents didn't give you a hard time," Oona protested. "Or did they? I wasn't in the room, remember?"

"Your father wasn't too bad. You mother was worried I might take on a few more wives. When I explained that I was a Hindu, not Muslim, she wanted to know if our children would grow up worshipping cows."

"Did this really happen or are you putting us on?" Shanti wondered.

"Oona's parents were concerned that I was a Hindu. Boston Brahmin was one thing, Hindu another. I told them I was born a Hindu, but found too many holes in any faith to be religious. If I were Catholic, I couldn't believe that the Virgin gave birth. I'm a doctor, after all. And as for the reincarnation that my parents so blindly accept, I die and can return as a dog? Though, of course, it doesn't make much difference in this dog-eat-dog world. . ."

"Sanjay, you are such a, such a . . . " Shanti struggled to find the right word as the others laughed.

"Sensitive man?" Sanjay suggested. "True, true. If I wasn't, I would have started laughing in church during the Easter service I attended with Oona's family when the preacher talked about Jesus entering Jerusalem on a donkey and I kept thinking, say ass, man, say ass."

"Sanjay, darling, that's enough," Oona said firmly. "Dinner," she announced. "And Neel, I put the cashews to the side of the biryani."

"Thanks, I appreciate that."

"You do carry medication with you, don't you?" Oona asked.

"I keep it in the car," Neel responded.

"You're definitely becoming American." Sanjay slapped Neel on the back. "Most Indians don't have allergies. Especially to nuts, for God's sake. But it's a good thing you have the medication with you. We were at a party where this chap ate just one pistachio and it got so bad he couldn't even inject himself. Someone else had to do it."

"Don't worry about me. I'm very careful about what I eat." Neel dismissed their concern. "Your biryani always turns out great, Oona, but I've been looking forward to the beef curry."

Vegetable biryani was spread out on a platter, slices of green, yellow, purple amidst the fluffy rice, the entire streaked with saffron in an "S" shape, as if Oona had tried to make it in their honor, Leila thought. The table was covered with food—crisp, fried lady fingers, potatoes and beans, shredded carrots, the orange flecked with the black dots of mustard seeds, and in the corner, an assortment of pickles.

"No meat today, Neel," Oona said, ushering him to a chair. "I wasn't sure if Leila was a carnivore and decided on a cruelty-free meal."

"I'm sure vegetables don't like being plucked. And what's beef if not chewed-up grass?" Neel responded.

"Vegetables aren't alive in the same way animals are," Oona said, not wanting to tackle the other argument. She had never known Neel to be belligerent before.

"Who says that? A rubber tree bleeds when it's tapped. Besides, Lee doesn't mind if we eat meat, do you, Lee." The question came out as a statement. He knew she would agree.

"Are you Leila or Lee?" Oona wanted this discussion to end. It wasn't like Neel to make a fuss. Was he suffering from post-wedding nerves?

"I'm Leila," she said automatically. He had never called her Lee before. Leila had looked forward to changing her surname, not the name she had responded to since she was a baby. Neel had shortened his, but that had been his choice.

He seemed so irritable, aloof, and she was beginning to get angry with him. Then she wondered if he, too, was thinking of the night ahead. She looked at his face, directly across from hers. Was it possible that he was nervous?

"Please, everyone, eat up. I promise you this rabbit food is very tasty." Sanjay opened a bottle of wine.

"I assumed all Indians were vegetarian until I met Sanjay. And when I met Neel, I realized how wrong I was! But I guessed correctly with you, right?" Oona asked Leila.

"My whole family is," Leila said. "And so is . . ." she was going to say Neel's family when he cut her off.

"Lee, can you pass me the okra, please?" He pointed to the dark green lady fingers in case she didn't know their American name. Neel didn't want her discussing his family. She hardly knew them.

Neel was addressing *her*. Lee, Didi, she had accumulated two new names in one evening.

"Arre, here comes Mr. America with okra," Sanjay taunted. "And see, he's even eating with a fork. What's wrong with the original one?" He lifted his fingers.

"Nothing, I'm sure," Neel responded. "I simply prefer a fork." He cringed at the sight of turmeric-stained fingernails and the odor of curry powder that clung to one's hand hours after the meal. Forks had been invented for a reason. Like gloves. He always used gloves when peeling garlic and had taught Caroline to do the same.

"But the food tastes better when you use your fingers. Oona, we are surrounded by Americans. We are the only true Indians here."

NEEL SUPPRESSED AN URGE to drop Leila off at the condo and go immediately to Caroline's. He compensated by having a shower. He hadn't realized how much he would dislike being coupled with her. She just didn't fit in. If only, if only . . . he refused to complete the thought. Yes, he had made his bed. But he didn't have to lie in it—and he didn't have to like it. Bits of the evening's conversation, the look in Shanti's eyes, came and went through his mind as he washed his body, his hair, even under his fingernails.

Who would have thought, during their Stanford days, that Sanjay's relationship would be the one to work out? While Neel did his best to rise up to Savannah's standards, Sanjay liked to say that he had to slow down for Oona to catch up with him.

At least Sanjay *had* encountered some problems with Oona's parents. But it hadn't lasted and Sanjay had got what he wanted, while his own quest had been unsuccessful. He was so used to getting what he set his mind on that Savannah's rejection blindsided him. That was the moment he realized that the number three on his list was not going to be easy to check off. Anyone could go back to India and get married, even a taxi driver. Had his desire for a non-Indian wife started with Mark's mother, with her short hair and perfumed dresses? Sanjay had reminded Neel of all that tonight, along with the bubble gum.

LEILA LEFT THINKING it was a most confusing, un-Indian gathering. Back home it was easy to categorize people—rich, poor, modern, old-fashioned, upper or lower class—and then deal with them accordingly. America seemed to have done away with such useful demarcations. This evening, everyone was uniformly courteous (she had never heard so many "thank-you's" and "please's") and Oona, especially, was kind. Even Sanjay had grown progressively more American as the hours wore on. He was consistently polite like an American, even though he joked like an Indian, using "Arre" instead of "Hey," and the combination was disconcerting.

She had wanted more than anything to shine and make Neel proud. She had envisioned making witty comments and being so intelligent that everyone would think Neel was lucky to be married to her.

Curled into the side of the bed, Leila smelled the perfume she had sprayed on with such hope. This was supposed to have been a wonderful dinner at which she sparkled, followed by a romantic drive home and then their coming together in the bedroom. But Neel had not said a word the whole way back in the car. This was worse than the first night in Ooty. What was he thinking?

She felt confused and hurt. Had he forgotten about tonight or did he just not want her? Should she remind him or would he think her ill-raised? If only she had the courage to touch him, to cover his face with kisses. But she was intimidated by his silence and her ignorance. This marriage, and Neel, were perplexing. All along, she had assumed the difficult part was capturing a husband. Her friends had made the transition seem as natural as motherhood, but she was discovering that being a wife wasn't as simple as learning to open a milk carton. If she made a mistake, she still managed to pour the milk.

Amma's voice reverberated in her head. "Leila, it must to be your fault. It must to be because you have stopped fasting. You must keep the fast. Not for a good husband. That I have given you. But to be a good wife."

Amma was right. It must be her fault. For years men had rejected her and now it was happening again.

Unbidden, she saw again the photo of the blond girl, the different hues of the love letters. Maybe Neel wanted a more American wife. He had become quite American.

So could she.

SANJAY AND OONA HURRIEDLY did the dishes before rushing upstairs to "play God," as Sanjay put it, "and you, my believing wife, can pray to God that we conceive a healthy child." As he put the champagne bottle in the recycling bin, Sanjay thought that finally, finally, Neel was finished with Caroline.

"Did you like Leila?" he asked.

"Very much. I'd been worried we'd have to entertain that blond bimbo he's been seeing."

"Caroline? No, I never thought he'd marry her, for God's sake. But I was beginning to wonder when he'd give her up."

"Well, she's out of the picture now. Wonder how she took it." Oona wasn't really interested, her mind on the ovulation test she had done that morning.

"Oh, she'll probably find another intern or doctor. She only went out with Neel because of his money."

"Oh, Sanjay, how can you say that?"

"I knew she was a gold digger the moment I saw her. You think everyone is like you. But people don't just come in different colors, you know." Sanjay held up a champagne flute to check the glass for streak marks. "I never thought Neel would return with a desi wife, but I think Leila will be good for him. He needs someone stable."

Oona agreed. Savannah had been so sweet at Stanford, but had changed her mind in Atlanta. Oona and Sanjay had been planning a surprise engagement party when Neel returned alone. "We broke up," was all he said. No mention of the diamond ring Oona had helped him select, no details of what had happened. After that, Neel didn't date for a long time. Oona knew he had been badly hurt, but she also knew he had picked the wrong girl. Anyone looking at Savannah could have told him she was waiting for her mirror image: a blond-haired, blue-eyed, trust fund husband. Certainly not an Indian who was working his way to the top.

Now Oona said, "Neel's a lovely man, but quite complex and difficult. Do you think Leila will be able to cope?"

"Yes, if I know Indian women. They look wishy-washy, but they have steel insides."

"Are you just saying that because she comes from a steel town?" Oona knew her husband's penchant for jokes and puns.

"Ha, ha! That's a good one. But no, that steel has nothing to do with the steel I'm talking about. Remember how Grandfather cut me off when we got engaged? Grandmother pretended to go along, but she was the one who sent us your wedding saree. Took a lot of courage, but she did it because she knew Grandfather was wrong. South Indian women are notorious for being even more steel-boned than North Indians. Why do you think I married a nice, pliable American girl?" he teased.

"To have children?" she reminded him.

"Oh my God, let's go before my sperm forget how to swim up the American channel."

"Darling," Oona admonished, smiling.

"At your service." He ushered her into the bedroom.

SHANTI HAD BEGUN ANALYZING the new addition to their group the minute Neel and Leila walked in. She had pegged Leila immediately—and, surprised by Neel's hasty marriage, was further surprised by his choice of wife. She had assumed he would return with a fluffy airhead Indian version of that ridiculous secretary he'd been seeing for years. Neel had no idea she knew, but Oona had let it slip one afternoon when Shanti pondered aloud why such a handsome and charming man wasn't dating or married. Shanti had noticed Caroline at hospital parties. Who could miss it? But she had never thought her Neel's type of woman.

She was relieved to see that Leila didn't call attention to herself by talking loudly and dressing in clothes one size too small. Leila was the product of a small Indian town: good family, well educated, shy without being withdrawn—with a mixture of confidence and modesty that Shanti recognized as her own pre-America self. Both of them had married late and each had to contend with an obvious handicap. For Shanti it had been color, for Leila height. India's overpopulation made it an unforgiving country. People demanded perfection, especially from girls. Shanti smiled, thinking that here, Leila would be considered of normal height. And pretty in a way not appreciated in India, where fair skin was more important than high cheekbones and a silky complexion.

She looked down at the freckled, sleeping face of her husband. He was a good man, this giant who had taken her away from a life of pitied spinsterhood. But like most good men, he wore blinders, and Shanti knew he hadn't understood any of the uncomfortable moments she had noticed. Bob was used to American openness and could not decipher Indian subtleties. During their wedding reception in Bombay, an aunt had piled his plate with hot pickles. Bob thought it was her way of welcoming him, of introducing him to Indian food, and refused to believe that the sweet old lady was actually making fun of him. But Shanti knew her aunt was waiting to see Bob spit out the chili-hot pieces of mango so she could point to his reddening face and cackle.

They had had completely different reactions to Neel's marriage. Shanti was aghast, while Bob smiled and said, "Good for him." He reminded her that many Indians did the same thing. But Shanti

knew that Neel was not like other Indians. He had made the delib-
erate decision to shed the past, which inevitably, like a plugged-up
leak, would show itself again.

Shanti was aware that Neel responded to Oona in a way he
never did to her. She had long suspected he had a white fetish, but
it didn't bother her. After all, Bob had an Asian fetish. His first
wife had been from Sri Lanka.

Bob had been eager to introduce her to Sanjay from the moment
he joined the hospital. Shanti had met a few other mixed couples
and automatically assumed that Bob's pediatrician colleague was
like some of the other Indian men married to foreigners. They
were the ones who, uncomfortable in their own skin, wanted a
white wife to fit in better. Not any white wife but a blond, blue-
eyed wonder they could show off. Sanjay, however, was just Sanjay. He wasn't the type to keep bringing attention to his white wife,
whether it was to remark on the amount of sunscreen needed for
a visit to his parents or to sigh that all Indian cooking had to be
done on the outside barbecue since his better half wasn't used to
the smell of curry. As Sanjay said, he would have married Oona
even if she was purple.

Neel had misunderstood and responded, of course, purple is
the color of majesty, and you would try for a princess. But Shanti
understood what Sanjay was saying. He had not gone looking for
love. It had happened and the object happened to be American.

Neel was very different. He was smooth, charming, and had
made a dedicated effort to become his new passport. She would
never have predicted an arranged marriage for him. Why *had* Neel
married Leila? Was it pressure? Certainly not love. He must have
succumbed to his family, which stunned Shanti. He was a strange
one, and now this latest action had rendered him completely
inexplicable.

Leila, of course, had married him because he was a doctor

from America. No doubt she believed she loved him, or at the very least, was happy to be married to him. Like most Indian girls, her romantic ideas came from Hindi movies. Shanti hadn't watched one in years, but she remembered how those lengthy love stories, in which everyone burst into song, were typically implausible. Like others in the audience, she too left her reason behind when buying a ticket. Still, there was something thrilling about watching love—deep, all-encompassing love—unfold from a glance. The predictable happy endings were what every Indian bride expected and wanted.

Would Leila be able to cope, so naive, so far away from her family and the social structures that had molded that very innocence? She would have to change; they all did. Soon Leila's convent school accent would lose the light dusting of her mother tongue, and by the time she had children, she would be giving them a bath, not even conscious that she wasn't pronouncing it the Indian way, "baahth." Shanti hadn't only begun believing in warranties; she had also given up the Indian belief that marriages have lifetime warranties. There were no such social certainties in the United States. Leila would have to fight if she wanted things to work out. Shanti thought she had detected that fight in her. For a brief moment she had seen the anger darken Leila's eyes when Neel called her Lee.

· FIFTEEN ·

TRANSFIXED BY THE COMMOTION of sounds and smells, Leila almost walked past the shop, in spite of the books piled outside the door. This was what she missed in pristine Pacific Heights, where it was possible to go for whole blocks without seeing another pedestrian. But here, all around her, was India, magically transported to Clement Street. Cars honked at those drivers parked in the middle of the road, their hazard lights blinking insolently, while others swerved quickly to take a just-vacated space. Children dripped ice cream on the sidewalk. Old women staggered, pulled down by heavy grocery bags filled with Indian vegetables she did not see in their local supermarket. The very air was spiced with the flavors of Asian restaurants—Chinese, Thai, Cambodian, Malaysian, Korean. The frying onions and garlic smelled like the open-air food carts back home, and the range of skin colors made her feel at one with the others.

Leila had wanted to visit this bookshop after reading about it in her guidebook. Since the dinner at Sanjay's two weeks ago, the guidebook had become her friend. If she could not get close to her husband, at least she could behave like an American and get to know her new city.

The immigrant flavor of the street was a bonus she hadn't expected. She was further delighted to find that the shop itself was another corner of India, with handwritten signs, and paperbacks heaped any which way on the tables and jammed onto shelves. For years she had resented the hours spent preparing lectures, wanting to be with a husband, feeling humiliated that Amma treated her like a child precisely because she wasn't married. Now, with no deadlines and no one to monitor her movements, she missed that other life.

She glanced at the best sellers, turned the large, glossy pages of a few art books, then made straight for the literature section. The first thing she noticed was someone carrying a tooled-leather bag with its signature Shantiniketan design. Could she be Indian? Leila edged closer, wishing the aisle were better lighted. Suddenly the dark-haired girl glanced up. Large brown eyes looked into her own and Leila smiled, partly to cover the embarrassment of being caught in the act of staring.

In that second Leila thought how Shanti and Oona had said they would love to get together but had yet to call her, and felt again the loneliness of her solitary walks. She passed people who looked friendly, their white faces lifted in a polite smile, but they were neither familiar nor approachable.

"Your bag, it's from Shantiniketan, no?"

"It's from India."

The accent was unexpected, and bewildering. Leila had assumed the milky tea complexion meant the girl was just like her, an Indian living in America. But the words sounded as if they came from the TV.

"Oh," Leila did not want to say that Shantiniketan, the school started by Rabindranath Tagore, *was* in India.

"You're from India, aren't you?"

"Yes."

"I thought I recognized the accent."

"And I thought I recognized your face."

"What do you mean?"

"As Indian."

"Well, my parents are from there. But I was born here."

"It's strange. When I close my eyes, you are American; when I open them, you are Indian."

"No one's ever accused me of changing in the blink of an eye before. I'm Rekha." She smiled.

"I'm Leila. If you are not in a hurry, maybe we could have a cup of chai, I mean tea?" Leila suggested spontaneously.

"Sure. Why not? A warm idea on a cold day."

Leila had never been to a café before. The long list of teas and coffees was as perplexing as the array of clothes in Macy's. She was used to the limited choice of her college cafeteria, which served either regular tea or masala chai. She ordered orange pekoe tea, intrigued by the idea of something fruity in her cup, while Rekha asked for a giant cappuccino.

The tea, when it came, looked just like tea. But when she tasted it, Leila realized it had no sugar and sprinkled in two packets.

"Here, have some tea with your sugar," Rekha teased, handing her a bunch of sugar packets from the next table.

Leila laughed and emptied a third packet into her cup. "I like my tea very sweet." She had missed the camaraderie of women, particularly her sister, and this was the next best thing to sitting on the bed with Indy.

Leila was bemused by this girl who pronounced her name "Rikka." Her face could be seen on any Indian road, yet the incessant hand gestures, the choice of words, the tilt of the head, were totally foreign to Leila. As was the conversation. They had just met, and yet Rekha didn't mind sharing details of her life that most Indians would consider too personal to tell anyone, much less a stranger.

"I used to teach in a small private school in Annapolis, but decided to get a journalism degree at Berkeley. Thought I'd meet some men, you know."

"So you are a writer too?" She hadn't meant to put herself in the question, and hoped Rekha didn't notice.

"I'm leaning toward TV, but we do have lots of writing assignments. You're a writer then?"

Leila hesitated. The children's stories seemed trite beside Rekha's graduate work and ambitions.

"Yes. I write cat stories for children. But it's really a hobby."

Rekha was amazed to discover she was interested in talking to a bona fide, old world Indian. Leila, with her British "a's" and soundless "r's," was so different from her parents and their friends. They were embarrassing. The men matched striped shirts with plaid trousers and the women looked like samosas, huge rolls of fat distorting the graceful lines of the sarees they insisted on wearing. Their conversation revolved around two issues: glorifying India and recommending the children get "First-Class marks" in school. They refused to speak English inside the house and didn't care when shopkeepers, Girl Scouts selling cookies, even the plumber, couldn't understand them. She had been so scrupulous about separating herself that at age thirty, she had never met a young Indian.

"You actually had an arranged marriage?" Rekha was incredulous. "My parents have tried to get me to have one, but I either change the subject or leave the room. In fact, my mom just wrote me about some guy. Let's see if I can find the letter." Rekha rummaged through her bag, taking out a few books before unfolding it: "*Rekha, your father has heard of this fine boy with a very good family. He came from Delhi two years ago and is studying English at the University of Florida. So you have some things in common. Can we arrange for him to contact you?* Absolutely not, is what I always say. But do they listen? Absolutely not," Rekha put away the letter. "I guess you didn't mind?"

"That's how most Indians get married." It felt strange to explain an arranged marriage. In India, love marriages had to be defended. Parents were not above locking girls in their room until they came to their senses.

"No dating? Going to the movies? Dinner?"

"Oh, no, never."

"You mean to tell me no one in India has boyfriends?"

"Maybe a few girls do. But they are the racy ones." They were also the ones who got bad reputations that were painfully resurrected with every marriage proposal.

"And of course you weren't racy?" Rekha smiled at the choice of word.

Leila hesitated, thinking about Janni. No one in her new life need know about him. "My mother would kill me if I even said hello to a boy. She'd say that I had brought disgrace to my family and no one would marry me or my sisters." She could almost hear Amma's words, and sitting so far away in a country where couples lived together and kissed in public, it sounded almost silly.

"I bet my mom wanted to kill me lots of times, even though I was one of the last girls in my class to date. I couldn't talk to her about it, so I'd sneak out after they went to bed. Got caught once or twice, but that was nothing compared to making the cheerleading team. When my mom saw me in the short skirt, she practically yanked it off me."

"You just kept doing all that?"

"I had to live my life. We were the only Indian family in our town, the only ones in school. I wanted to fit in, be part of the group."

"But now everything is okay with your parents?"

"Well, yes. I don't live with them, which makes it easier. Though they still call me on Friday nights to check if I'm home."

When Leila looked puzzled, Rekha explained, "Friday is big date night."

Leila didn't respond. Friday nights she usually oiled and washed her hair. "End of the week grime," Indy used to say. Saturday had been the only day of possibility. And she had grabbed her chance.

It had started with the notes. Pages torn from an exercise book that Janni passed to her as they sat together on the bus. She hid them inside her textbooks to read over and over again, sometimes right under Amma's eyes as she turned to the chapters she was supposed to be studying. *Will you come see a film with me?* That single line, written in Janni's sloping handwriting, filled her with delight and fear. She wanted to see a film, any film, with him, but she also knew it was the wrong thing to do. Good girls didn't go out with boys. Conversely, good boys didn't put girls in the position of having to say yes or no. Plus he was a Muslim and she was Iyengar, which elevated the wrong to a taboo.

But it was just a film. And she kept convincing herself that these were modern times. The Hindu Muslim killings had happened before she was born, during Independence, and were something she knew only because they were in her history book. People were getting less strict all the time, with some Iyengars marrying Iyers.

So, on the appointed Saturday, she told Amma a lie. She didn't tell Indy anything. It was her first secret from her sister. Indy was too young to understand, too innocent to keep it from Amma. Leila wore the nicest saree she could without raising Amma's suspicion and met Janni in front of the cinema.

The film played for the others; she was only aware of sitting in the dark with a man. Janni leaned back, crossing his legs so that an ankle nested against her saree. It was the closest she had come to touching any man and she hoped he could not hear her heart.

"Leila, come with me at once." She hadn't noticed the limping figure patrolling the aisle with the relentlessness of a searchlight. Suddenly Appa was looking down at her, pulling her by the hand. Janni and she stood up together.

"Shhh," people whispered.

"Even our expensive seats have noisy people," a woman grumbled.

They stumbled out of the dark into the sunlit lobby. It was empty, Leila noted gratefully. She didn't look at either man, just stared at the floor.

"Uncle, let me explain," Janni pleaded.

"You. You leave my daughter alone or I will break your legs," Appa threatened. "I never want to see you near her again. Understand?"

Appa and she struggled home under one umbrella, the rain plastering her saree all along her left side. Amma was waiting at the front door, her open-mouthed fury making Leila shiver far more than the wetness that had crept into her bones.

"Weren't you frightened to marry a stranger?" Rekha interrupted Leila's thoughts.

Jolted back to the present, to Neel, Leila responded, "But it wasn't as if he was a complete stranger. My parents knew his background, his family, and we saw each other before the wedding."

"Didn't you want to know him better before committing yourself to him?"

"I had no choice. That is the way things are done."

"And now you're a doctor's wife. I guess there must be something to arranged marriages. At least you don't have to bother with the whole dating game. You're really quite lucky," Rekha mused. Perhaps her mother wasn't all wrong. It was so difficult to meet men, and it seemed as if all the good ones were either commitment-shy or gay. Then there were those who were taken. Like Tim. When she first met Tim he told her he was married, but unhappy and considering divorce. They had been going out for the past six months, and Rekha was getting tired of only being allowed to call him at the office.

Sitting across from a possible friend, Leila permitted herself to feel like the lucky bride. Even in America, Neel was regarded as a good catch. She chose not to remember that she hardly saw him.

He worked late almost every evening and went flying on the weekends. He never asked her to join him and she didn't want to force herself on him. The TV was her companion, with movies, animal programs, cooking shows, and news taking the place of Appa's snores and Kila's excited screams. There was no Indy to talk to and gain strength from, just the long hours between sleep.

The empty nights embarrassed her. Amma had told her about the night, July 24, but hadn't told her what to expect or what to do if nothing happened. So every night she edged a little closer to him, and every Monday she fasted, hoping that soon life would be different. She spent her days walking around San Francisco, looking through the newspaper for a job, trying to enjoy all this time she suddenly had, so different from her busy teaching days.

"No, no, I'm sure you are much luckier." Leila adopted the Indian approach of never acknowledging good fortune. "You must have many boyfriends."

"Just one and he's in the doghouse."

"Doghouse?" Leila pictured a man in a tiny, red-roofed house with Snoopy sitting on top.

"I'm mad at him. We had a date last night and he cancelled on me. I'm just back from vacation and he can't make the time to see me?"

"Oh." Rekha seemed to expect her to say something, but this was beyond Leila's limited experience.

"He told me it was to see his divorce lawyer. But I've heard that excuse before, and now I'm wondering if he is ever going to get divorced or if he's just stringing me along."

Leila was not used to people being so frank about their private lives. Her friends hid problems and pretended everything was wonderful. Bad news usually came from the mouths of servants. When Nalini returned unexpectedly from Malaysia, it was the servant girl who announced that the husband had sent her back. That was five years ago and still no one knew the real story. There was no talk of anything scandalous like a divorce, though some whispered the husband wanted one and Nalini, of course, did not. It was bad enough to be back home at her parents' house, but getting a divorce would spoil any marriage prospects for her younger sisters. Boys were never affected. Even a mad mother or a drunk father would not stop a man from finding a bride.

"Do you believe in a woman's intuition?" Rekha asked.

She had intuited that Neel didn't want an arranged marriage that first meeting. Leila thought for a second before saying, "Yes. I don't think intuitions lie."

"Well, in that case I ought to break up with him. Mine tells me he's never going to get that divorce."

All the time they sipped their tea Leila had assumed that Rekha, so pretty and sure of herself, must naturally belong to the group of lucky women for whom things always work out. They buy a white metal bangle and it turns out to be silver. They lose something only to find it the next day. She had always wanted to be a Rekha. Now it was more than the tea that warmed her. Other people had problems, too.

"I've got to run," Rekha exclaimed, looking at her watch. "I'd love to see you again. Would you like to exchange phone numbers?"

Rekha rushed off, Leila's rounded handwriting tucked into her bag.

Leila walked home, bolstered by Rekha's promise to meet next week. For the first time in her life, she had met someone entirely on her own. All her friends back home had been pre-selected—by her school, their background, or her parents. Amma would never permit Leila to befriend a woman who was going out with a married man.

Just a few months ago in Ooty, Leila had been shocked to learn that Cynthia was living in sin with Harold. But in America, Leila could see Rekha without the judgmental, codified glare of Indian eyes. She liked her. Rekha was honest and intelligent, and it would be nice to have someone to ring or invite over for tea.

Everything looked brighter—the sky, the vivid lobelias, even the black asphalt, and the cars that never seemed to wear it down.

· SIXTEEN ·

NEEL SORTED THE MAIL. Advertisements, three bills, and a letter from his mother. He set it aside for Leila. She answered the letters, which now arrived every other week, no doubt still penned in minuscule handwriting to get maximum use of the aerogram. Leila had also taken over the housekeeping and he'd been happy to have the cleaning crew return the key. As far as he knew, they had not stolen or broken anything—unlike so many of Mummy's servants, who were caught and immediately sacked—but he was never comfortable that they came and went while he was at the hospital.

Where *was* Leila? He'd assumed she would be waiting for him, as usual. Irritated, he paid the bills and just as he finished, the door opened.

"Oh, you are home already." The long walk had set Leila's heart beating, but now her pulse raced for other reasons. He looked dignified and handsome in the dark blue suit, so different from Appa, who wore lungis at home. Rekha wasn't able to meet with her Tim and here she was with Neel. He wasn't another woman's husband but her husband, come home early.

"Yes. I thought I'd take you shopping for some interview clothes, but now the stores will be packed and parking will be a nightmare."

"I'm sorry," Leila said, though her blood still surged. The day kept growing more wonderful. "I went to Clement Street today and met somebody."

"Who?" Neel asked immediately, dreading that it might be someone she knew from India.

"A girl named Rekha. She's very nice. An Indian who was born here."

"What did you do? Just go up and say hello?"

"No, of course not. We met in a bookshop."

"It's bookstore in America," he automatically corrected.

"I know. But it's bookshop in India. She goes to school at Berkeley."

"Hmm. I got accepted there for engineering."

"She is studying journalism."

"Oh, another of those people who will stay in school forever."

"She used to teach in a school for some years," Leila defended her new friend. Neel's corrections and assumptions were spoiling her good mood. Who was he to say what Rekha should do?

"I don't understand why people can't decide what they want to do when they're young. Everyone in America seems to be going back to school." Except Caroline. He had asked her to take advantage of the hospital's tuition remission program, but she maintained that work and their relationship kept her busy. It bothered him that she didn't want to better herself, but wanted to get it secondhand, from a man.

"She's my age and studying to be in television."

Neel shrugged. What did he care about this unknown woman? "What's for dinner?"

"Shall I prepare pasta primavera?"

"You know how to make that?"

"Yes, they showed it on a cooking program."

"Actually, I'd prefer some Indian food tonight. Is that all right?"

"Of course it is," Leila said, happy again. It was the first time he had asked her to do something for him. And it made her feel like a wife. Tonight, she would cook a meal fit for a king. A vegetarian king. She was getting used to the pulpy feel of chicken when cutting it, but invariably felt like Lady Macbeth afterwards, washing her hands again and again.

Dinner took hours to prepare in India, even with the help of Indy and their servant Heera. Indy must have taken over her job of cleaning the rice, sitting on the kitchen step, looking for black and white stones before whisking away the chaff. In America, Leila pressed a button on the blender and within a minute the blades whirled the masala into a fine paste. Poor Heera spent hours at the masala stone, her strong arms pushing the granite rolling pin back and forth, back and forth, until all the lumps disappeared. "See," she'd slap the yellowish red spice paste on a plate. "And I used very little water." She took such pride in her work.

Cooking had been an occasion for laughter and conversation, tasting and the stealing of tidbits. She wished Neel would keep her company, but he was watching the news.

She set the long grains of rice to soak for twenty minutes and began chopping the vegetables. The cauliflower and scallions were the simplest to prepare. As soon as the tiny black mustard seeds popped, she spooned in the cream-colored urad dal, scallions, turmeric, and salt. She fried them for a few seconds and then added the cauliflower and hot water.

She loved the knobbly fenugreek seeds that gave the potatoes and eggplant its punch, though their odor was very strong. The vegetables sizzled in the cast-iron pan, absorbing the coriander, cumin, chili, and turmeric. For the raita she used a trick Aunty Nandi claimed removed the bitterness from the cucumber. She sliced off the ends, and rubbed the cut part with the pieces until a white froth, the bitterness, seeped out. Only then did she grate it, squeezing out the water before spooning in a mixture of yogurt and sour cream. Just before serving it she sifted on some paprika for taste, color, and decoration.

In an hour, the kitchen only looked American. Spices suffused the air, almost masking the musky aroma of basmati rice. Leila remembered her Hindi teacher explaining that *bas* meant "smell." It was the rice of kings, and only the rich could afford it in India.

All the Mughal emperors had eaten basmati rice mixed with saffron and cashew nuts. But Leila served it plain. She didn't keep any nuts in the house because of Neel, though cashews, expensive in India, were a luxury she would have enjoyed indulging in here.

Neel ate quickly, fork moving regularly from plate to mouth. Leila felt as invisible as Shakuntala, but she wasn't a simple forest maiden who had married a king. She could not let him ignore her like this. *Speak to me. Why do you never speak? Speak.*

"Rekha invited me to visit her in Berkeley." This was the wonderful nugget from today's expedition. She wanted him to know that Rekha liked her enough to proffer an invitation. She was making friends.

"You should go. It's a beautiful campus."

"Is Mills College close to Berkeley?"

"Not too far. It's in Oakland. Why?"

"Indy applied there and won a scholarship. But Amma would not allow her to take it, even though it's a girl's college."

"Tough break. What was it in?"

"Maths."

"Math," Neel again corrected her. "She must be pretty good to have been accepted."

Leila ignored the correction. "I think she's like a computer. That's why I made her apply. I wrote for the application and even filled it out for her. If we had been married then, I'm sure Amma would have allowed her to come." Leila had been the one to fight with Amma, while Indy just sat on the bed and cried. It had always been that way with them. They could fight for each other, but not for themselves.

Neel stared at Leila from across the table. In the lamplight her eyes glowed, the color and shape of almonds. Sanjay had told him Leila was beautiful. He wondered why she hadn't married earlier. She was fair, pretty, and so well raised she never insisted on anything, never complained.

"Do you want to study here?" he asked her. An American degree would give her a better advantage in the job market.

"I never thought of it."

"It will get you out of the house, you'll meet people," he urged her.

He was just like Amma, wanting her to do his bidding. "I saw some creative writing classes that looked interesting," she said.

"Now that's the one thing I definitely don't understand about America. How can one possibly teach people to be creative? The British don't offer such ridiculous courses. Shakespeare never went to college."

"Shakespeare attended grammar school," she pointed out. But Neel did have a point. She didn't need to take a class in writing children's stories. She just had to be more disciplined.

"Grammar school. That's different. Here it's all about making money. There are classes for everything. Just ask Oona. She'll tell you about some strange classes. Flirting, for example."

"When shall we invite Sanjay and Oona for dinner?" Amma had always reciprocated within a few weeks, making a meal that was better than the one served them.

Never, Neel wanted to say. Sanjay's invitation was now the breeding ground of another which would lead to yet another. He had to put a stop to it before they became a cozy foursome. He was about to say so when the phone rang.

Caroline, Neel thought, hurriedly reaching for the receiver, thinking that she was so used to calling him on the phone she must have forgotten to use the pager.

But Leila had already turned, and he watched her answer it, wondering what she would say, what Caroline would do.

"Yes, he's here." She handed him the receiver.

Neel kept his face impassive, wondering how it would look if he took the call in the study.

"The hospital," she continued, her voice resigned. Just when things were going so well.

"Nah, I wasn't playing hard to get," Neel joked, relieved to hear the male voice at the other end. "Forgot to change the battery in the pager. I'll leave immediately." He hung up.

Couldn't the hospital do without him just this one evening? Leila wished as he put on his coat.

"Neel," she began uncertainly.

"What?" He was already at the front door.

"Nothing. I hope it's not too serious. At the hospital."

Inexplicably, he was glad that he didn't have to lie. He *was* going to the hospital, where a particularly vicious strain of flu had laid up so many doctors others did double shifts or came in at all hours of the night. Leila didn't seem to mind his long absences and sudden returns. His mother didn't like being alone at night. If Tattappa and Father had to be away, she stayed in Neel's room till they returned. He turned to look at Leila. She looked so brave, so alone, so . . . lovely. His hand missed the doorknob and hit the wood.

"Ouch." He shook it back and forth.

"It helps if you rub it." Leila wondered that he didn't know that simple, effective remedy.

His left hand massaged the spot clumsily.

"Faster," Leila instructed.

"I'm right-handed, remember? Here, can you?" Neel held out his hand.

Their eyes met. Leila didn't drop her gaze as she stepped forward and, using both sets of fingers, gently but firmly warmed the bruise.

She smelled fragrant, a scent he couldn't place. Not of Indian food at all. Her skin was like milk chocolate, the long lashes fluttering against her cheeks. A swathe of hair swung free from behind one ear and brushed his wrist.

Immediately, Leila gathered the loose strands and moved away. "Better?"

"Much. Thanks." Neel was still trying to figure out the scent, hoping she hadn't seen the goose bumps from that quick flick of hair.

He opened the door. "Incidentally, dinner was very good. Thanks."

She didn't want his thanks. She needed him here, wanted him to tell the hospital to call another doctor. But she had been brought up on stories of women who had waited. Parvati had spent years worshipping at the feet of Shiva, the three-eyed God of Destruction, until he opened his eye and noticed her. Shakuntala, too, had waited, even raising her son on her own until the king returned to get her.

Leila stood at the window and looked down, watching his taillights glow smaller and smaller.

She had enjoyed the dinner and wished she hadn't wasted those few minutes being annoyed at him. They spent little enough time together; but the more she saw him, the more she liked him—his sharp mind, the way he wore his clothes, his maleness so evident in the hairs on his arms, the cleft on his cheek that she longed to touch.

But Neel kept himself busy being a doctor and she didn't know how to bring him to her side. All she knew was that she had to do something for herself while she waited for them to become a unit.

Avoiding the sinkhole in the couch, she picked up the loose pages on which she brought a gray-haired cat called Annigma to life.

When her father loses his glasses, Annigma turns into a detective and asks other creatures to help her find them, including a bird called Margot. It was the last two lines that needed reworking.

Margot the Magpie cocked her head to one side, shook the well-groomed feathers, and replied:

> *"I look for shiny little things*
> *Which afterwards I flaunt*
> *Like silver pens or golden rings*
> *That no one seems to want.*
> *I saw those glasses once before*
> *Upon your Father's face.*
> *I'd never take them, don't you know*
> *Stealing's a disgrace."*

As Leila pondered how to fix the last two lines, she read on.

Annigma sighed with disappointment. If Margot said she hadn't taken the glasses, then she didn't have them. No one Annigma knew said things that weren't true.

· SEVENTEEN ·

CAROLINE GAVE SHORT ANSWERS the rest of the workday. "Yes," "No," "Maybe." It didn't matter who she was talking to, specialists, patients; she was too angry and hurt to give a damn.

On the drive home she cut in front of an old lady, almost getting into a fender bender with the long blue Pontiac. "You shouldn't be on the road, you old grandmother you," she muttered and gunned her BMW.

She wasn't in the mood to cook, still upset over the argument with Neel. All she had in the fridge was a packet of hot dogs. She slathered on mustard, mayo, and ate them plain, without bread. Neel didn't like hot dogs. He preferred sausages, especially when she boiled them in beer. She had taught him that, introduced him to all the wonderful aspects of her world. And how was he repaying her? He was going to the conference in Reno without her.

She had heard that Sanjay was taking his wife; what if Neel decided to do the same? Were Indian women insistent? She didn't know, and at times like these, not knowing frightened her.

"You better not take her," Caroline had warned. "It's our special place. I want to go with you." Once every few months they flew to Reno in Neel's plane. Neel was a different person there, freer— less anxious about being seen together. And she enjoyed winning money. Or losing. Neel never minded.

"You know you can't go," he said flatly.

"I'll stay in the room the whole time if necessary. But I don't want her there."

Instead of placating her, he had turned on his heel and left.

Two days of dishes were piled in the sink and suddenly Caroline couldn't stand the clutter any longer. She put on her latex gloves and began cleaning the kitchen. It was what she always did when she was miserable—like after a breakup.

But she wasn't breaking up with Neel. No, this time things were going to go her way.

She hadn't realized how difficult it was to date a married man. Once the shock of his marriage wore off, she decided to bide her time until he got divorced. They would carry on as before, as Neel promised, until his crazy grandfather died. Meanwhile, if she didn't talk about the wife, or ask about her, she wouldn't exist. But now Neel might be taking the wife to Reno. And the wife could, legitimately, go.

The phone rang.

It had to be Neel. He was calling to tell her he was sorry.

As always, her mother began talking even before Caroline put the receiver to her ear.

". . . and he's doing fine."

"Something wrong with Pop?" The doctor had advised a change in diet after Pop's heart attack last year. But Pop loved his meat and beer too much to give them up.

"No, love, Pop's fine. He's over the moon same as me. It's Cathy. The baby came a little early, an eight-pound boy. But they're both doing well."

Cathy's first four were girls, and everyone was excited about her finally having a son. The two sisters had been close as teenagers, but Cathy married her sweetheart straight out of high school and began having babies. In those days, Caroline, voted "Most Likely to Have Her Name in Lights," had pitied her sister. Stuck on the small farm her husband had inherited, eating, giving birth, eating, giving birth, till her body looked like a haystack. But Cathy had a husband who loved her and five—five—children who would look after her. She would never be alone.

"Give Cath my best. What's the baby's name?"

"Tristan. She was going to name it after Pop, but you know how he's been saving that for your son."

"I know, Ma." Ten-year-old Caroline had made that promise and he had taken her seriously.

"When are we going to meet this doctor of yours?"

"Soon. He's busy."

"So you keep saying. But even doctors must get vacation time?"

"Ma, we'd need at least two weeks to come out there. Anyway, he's taking me to Reno this weekend. In his plane."

"Send us a picture this time. I'll show it to Bonnie next door. She thinks only millionaires have planes."

They had never even seen a picture of Neel and only knew him as "Your doctor in California." They bragged about the doctor part. "Bring him home so he can see how real Americans live." Pop had insisted she invite him last Christmas, threatening to call the hospital. "He's coming," she kept telling them, though Neel, thank God, had refused to accompany her.

Her best friend, Natalie, said she was playing a dangerous game. When was she going to tell her family he was Indian? "After we're married," Caroline always stated, to which Natalie responded, "You think that's going to make it all right?"

Perhaps not. But it would make it a done deal. In France, her parents had been suspicious of "the Frogs," hardly ever leaving the base, refusing to learn the language. They still called blacks "niggers" inside the house and as far as Caroline knew had never met an Indian, certainly not socially.

No one in the family had married out. She recalled how Aunt Bessie had carried on when Cousin Laura dated a Jewish man.

Laura was a dummy. She had brought him home for a Fourth of July barbecue and the poor man hadn't lasted the evening. The family refused to give him a chance, just ignored him completely. Caroline was the only one who tried talking to him. Living in California had changed her even more, but she was well aware that the family remained the same.

Now her mother was asking her, "Reno. You wouldn't be going there to get married, would you? It would break Pop's heart not to walk you down the aisle."

"And Cathy's. She wants to be maid of honor."

"You'd better get on it, then. I know I told you not to make Cathy's mistake, getting pregnant right out of school. But you didn't have to wait this long. You sure your doctor is going to make an honest woman of you?"

"I keep telling you, the men here are different. They need more time."

That's what she told Natalie, too. Natalie didn't trust Neel and couldn't understand why Caroline wanted a man who went to see his dying grandfather and returned with a wife. She rolled her eyes every time Caroline insisted, "He's working on the divorce. Just give him a little breathing space."

Caroline listened to the loud voice over the mouthpiece. "Men are the same everywhere. If he's thinking so much, maybe you should go ahead and get pregnant. It's now or never for you. Besides, it'll give him something real to think about."

"Ma!" Ma would never have said something like this five, ten, years ago. But now she, like Caroline, was getting desperate. She merely wanted Caroline to have what she had: a husband and family.

"Just something for you to think about when you're in Reno. Make a nice playmate for Tristan."

· EIGHTEEN ·

THE PHONE RANG FOR THE FOURTH TIME. Shanti had called to say an Indian writer was giving a reading, did she want to go? and Neel to announce he would be home late. Then it was Rekha, changing the time of their meeting to four o'clock that afternoon. As Amma always said, when the monsoons finally came, they made you forget the dry, cracked earth of summer.

"Am I catching you at a bad time?" Oona asked.

"Oh, I'm very busy," Leila joked. "I was just about to practice the rope trick. I wanted to see if those Indian fakirs were fakes."

Oona laughed. "It's last minute, but the judge rescheduled a hearing so I unexpectedly have the day off. I'd love to come see you."

It was just like being back home, Leila thought contentedly, as she cleaned and cooked. People dropped in all the time, often staying for a meal. She ran around the rooms with the vacuum cleaner, and made sure the bathroom was guest-ready, as she and Indy termed it.

"Namaste." Oona handed Leila a package. "A belated wedding present." This was her first visit to the condo she knew Neel was so proud of, though he never said so. But she'd thought Sanjay was joking when he told her it was practically unfurnished.

"Thank you so much." Leila held the silver-papered box awkwardly. She didn't know whether to open it or put it away.

"It's a great view," Oona said from the window. "You can almost reach out and touch Angel Island. What a perfect day to see the bridge. We don't get anything like this in the South Bay."

"Yes, it's nice," Leila said vaguely. She didn't understand why Americans were so crazy about a view. It wasn't as if people sat by their windows looking out all the time. "Shall we go to the kitchen? I'm making some pakoras." She wanted to usher Oona out of the living room as quickly as possible. The large empty space and the sagging couch embarrassed her.

"What a charming place," Oona admired the high ceilings and moldings. "When was it built?"

"I really have no idea. Neel knows all that." Lately, Leila had begun seeing their home as Neel's condo. He didn't want her to change anything, and point-blank refused to buy more furniture. "I want to get some good stuff at auctions," he said, but when she found out about a few, he was too busy to go.

"Will you have some tea?" She placed the gift on the counter, then picked it up again when Oona said, "If it's tea you're making, you may want to open that."

Leila didn't have to feign her delight when the paper fell away. "A kettle! And it whistles like a train," she read the print on the box. "Thank you."

"I'm glad you like it. I have one just like that and use it all the time. Sanjay approves of it because the spout is lined with twenty-four-carat gold. He calls it the real stuff, unlike the fourteen- and eighteen-carat gold that's more typical here. I had no idea Indians cared so much for gold."

"Yes, we Indians love our gold. Some rich girls even wear gold anklets, though I've never heard of gold on a teakettle. My mother will be amazed." Leila filled the shining kettle.

"I never drank so much tea as when Sanjay and I went to India. Tell me, did the British take the tea habit from India—steal it, my husband would claim—or was it the other way around?"

"You know, I have no idea. I come from the south where people drink coffee. Though in my house we also drink a lot of tea."

"What is 'tea' in Hindi? I've forgotten?"

"Chai. And in my college we'd say 'Who's aye for a chai?' Any time was a good time for a chai break."

Leila put spoonsful of chickpea batter mixed with green onions, spinach, and cumin powder into the hot oil.

Oona took a deep breath. "It reminds me of Sanjay's mother's cooking. She used to serve the most delicious meals. I'd heard of people losing weight in India but I came back about ten pounds heavier. "

"She must be a good cook. I'm not very good, you know," Leila quickly disclaimed, using Amma's words. She liked the way Oona pronounced "Sanjay," as if she were beginning to say "sand" instead of "sun."

"I'm sure you're a very good cook. Or cooker, as I heard someone say in India. Sanjay says English is the strangest language. Bake, baker, garden, gardener, but no cooker for cook." They both laughed. "Oh, that smells delicious. I wanted to learn how to cook, but Sanjay's mother refused to let me do anything."

"She sounds just like my mother." Leila smiled, thinking of Amma bustling around, taking charge of everything. The girls could help by cleaning the rice or grating the coconut, but only she stood in front of the kerosene stove, converting vegetables into curries.

"Do you miss your family and friends?" Oona asked.

Leila thought of ET jumping onto her shoulder and meowing into her ear, the daily comb battle with Kila's fusilli hair, helping Indy decide which saree to wear and then arranging the pleats.

"Yes. Especially my sister," she said.

"You're so brave, Leila. Having an arranged marriage, coming to the United States and then settling in with no trouble." Oona thought how most Americans she knew would have had a nervous breakdown. Here there were support groups for every variety of angst and couches for those who wanted one-on-one attention.

"But that was expected of me. You are the one who is brave. After all, you married a foreigner."

Oona's obvious love for India drew Leila toward the white woman. Neel never talked about home, hardly ever asked about his mother's letters. Perhaps it was because he wanted her to adjust to America. Yesterday he had suggested she cut her hair. "You'll look more modern when you go for job interviews."

"I never consciously thought of Sanjay being a foreigner until we went to India. Then I felt like a foreigner, which in turn made him seem alien."

"I don't understand?"

"Oh, it was all the customs I didn't know. We had our first major fight in India. We had gone to his cousin's house for tea and I was so full from lunch at another person's house that when they brought around the tray of sweets, I couldn't eat any. Sanjay was livid at me for slighting his cousin. I didn't know it was rude and reflected badly both on Sanjay and his cousin, who had made the sweets herself."

"Oh yes, you have to eat when you go to people's houses or they will be insulted. Do you fight here?" The words left her mouth before she realized it was a Nosy Nandi question.

"Sure. Not all the time, but there are cultural issues that crop up every now and then, aside from your everyday please-put-the-ice-cream-back-in-the-freezer. Tell me, how are *you* coping with the cultural differences?"

"Not too bad." Leila poured milk into the tea, and watched the dark brew turn a soft sparrow brown. She didn't find America hard to decipher; all she had to do was read the ubiquitous paperwork that was attached to every product. Neel was the problem. She kept learning things about him—he clipped his nails every week, he didn't like pepper in his food—but they weren't a unit. He never asked her a simple question like: "What did you do today?"

She wished she could ask Oona if her expectations of marriage were unreasonable. But Amma had raised her to be very careful not just about what she said but who she voiced it to. Leila had grown up amongst aunties who extracted unhappiness even when it wasn't there. If a bride said she wanted to wait a while before having children, it was automatically assumed she could not get pregnant. Leila couldn't be absolutely sure Oona wasn't like the aunties. She hadn't learned to decode Americans the way she did Indians.

"What do you do with your time?"

"I joined the library so I've been catching up on my reading. And next week I start driving lessons, after which I'll begin looking for work." She refrained from saying, "I write." Oona might make much of it and Leila wanted to surprise Neel. She had finished the Annigma story and had already done some research in the library on agents and publishers.

"Oh, the luxury of not having a job. Poor Sanjay! He comes home ready to play and I have briefs to read and arguments to prepare. Where has Neel been taking you in the evenings?"

"I think Neel is making up for the time he was in India. He works almost every evening."

"Really? I guess anesthesiologists have it rougher than pediatricians. The last time Sanjay worked late was, oh, over two months ago. Poor you. Anyway, you should see more of Neel in Reno."

"Reno?"

"Didn't Neel tell you? That's where the annual medical conference is being held this year. I'm taking a few days off and we plan to drive there. Neel, of course, will probably fly up. You are coming, aren't you?"

"I don't know. Maybe Neel won't want to go."

"He always goes to those conferences. Sanjay's not too crazy about them, but it's for their CME credits. It's great for us women. We get to gamble and hang out while they attend boring talks."

"Gamble? I thought Reno was for quick divorces?"

"No, Reno is getting to be more and more like Las Vegas, with everything from easy slot machines to craps tables. And fabulous buffets. We'll have a great time, I promise you. Why don't you and Neel come up with us? Our car can easily fit two more."

"That's very nice of you. But really, I can't say anything for sure without talking to Neel."

"I just remembered Sanjay saying that he is on a panel with Neel. Which means he is going, so you, of course, are going, too."

"But Neel might not want to take me." The words were difficult to say. Oona didn't know she hadn't even been in the plane yet.

"Of course Neel will want you to go with him. You're his wife."

Leila held that phrase to her chest like a hot water bottle. She had recently begun to doubt it. But Oona was correct. She *was* Mrs. Sarath.

BY THE TIME OONA LEFT, it was past three-thirty and Leila set off immediately to meet Rekha. Every walk still contained the thrill that she was on concrete instead of sending up small squalls of mud. The cold air that pricked tears out of her eyes was so different from the sticky warmth back home. She shook her head. She had to stop thinking of India as home. This was her home now and she was beginning to own it. Just last week the painters had finished with the apartment building across the road. The old cream was gone, replaced by pale blue, but she would always know that original color.

Tall apartment buildings, stuck together, gave way to houses, and she saw people weeding gardens, gathering leaves into piles, snipping flowers whose blooms had faded. A dog walker picked up the pile just deposited by a golden retriever, though the odor still lingered. She increased her pace. She had looked up the address on the map and been fooled by the distance. Places always looked closer on paper.

The café was almost empty and she chose a corner seat. The herb tea smelled deliciously familiar, the cardamom evoking Amma's Sunday-only biryani. Indy used to call it the culinary obstacle course because of the cardamom, cloves, and round, fat peppercorns in the biryani. The rest of the family would have finished eating, and there was Indy, slowly, painstakingly picking through the rice because she didn't want to bite into one of the spices.

"Sorry I'm late." Rekha was out of breath. She considered punctuality a crucial difference between Indians like her parents, who were habitually late, and Americans.

"Hi. I was a little late myself. I was actually afraid you might have left."

"Oh I'd never do that. Just give me a sec and I'll get something to drink. I'm dying for some brew."

Leila watched Rekha. She was so confident, chatting with the man behind the counter, dropping coins into a tip jar labeled "Counter Intelligence." It was obvious that things came easily to her. Including Tim. She had told Leila on the phone that their relationship was "back on track."

"Leila, I've been thinking a lot about you ever since we met and I've had a brilliant idea!" Rekha vigorously dissolved the powdered cocoa in her cappuccino. "Well, actually, I have to give Tim some of the credit. I was telling him about you and it suddenly occurred to us that I should do my MA thesis on arranged marriages. Concentrating on the woman's perspective, naturally. What do you think?"

"I never did a thesis, just exams, so I don't know what that means."

"Oh, a thesis is just a long paper. At our school it's anywhere from thirty to sixty pages. Most students do it toward the end of their second year. But I thought I'd get a head start. And use your know-how, if you don't mind?"

"But I don't know much." An arranged marriage was something one lived, not something one studied, like bugs or Shakespeare. At the same time she felt a rush of pride and beneath it, the thought that Neel would be impressed. Her pride stalled. It would also mean that she would have to talk about him and their marriage.

"You know a whole lot more than me. For instance, how do couples agree to marry each other after a short meeting? I mean, what was it like for you and your husband?"

Leila went back to that Sunday of uncertainty and hope, when she had thought the old green saree would somehow make Neel say yes. Now that everything had worked out, her superstitious insistence seemed absurd.

"I think we both liked the idea of an arranged marriage. And we trusted our parents to find us a suitable partner."

"Whoa! That's a whole lot of trust."

"But that's the way it is in India. We have complete faith in our parents."

"What if the parents are wrong?"

"But how can that be? They want the best for their children."

"So-ooo. Tell me, did the two of you like each other right away?"

"We liked each other," Leila echoed softly. She felt shy to elaborate. Everyone had said how Neel must have really liked her because his aunt had come back up the stairs even before they left their compound and because he refused to see other girls. But if Neel had liked her so much, why did she feel like they were two strangers in a train compartment? Polite, but uncomfortable about being in the same space.

"Was it love at first sight?" Rekha teased.

"I don't know about that." Neel had said that in Ooty and she had believed him. Since then she had heard him be American suave many times. "Maybe." Her discomfort increased. "It's a very charged meeting because everyone knows it will end in marriage or rejection." Hers, finally, had been marriage. She felt again the absolute thrill when she saw Neel's father the next morning with a big smile on his face. Leila had served him coffee (sweetened with the condensed milk Kila had not managed to finish), all the while thinking that he was now her father too.

"That would be intense. But how do parents go about choosing someone?"

"They match education, social standing, and of course, religion. If a couple is like-minded there is a better chance for the marriage to work out. But you know, people do it even here in America. The radio advertisement for Perfect Strings always says that the singles who join are professional and music lovers."

"I know we have video dating services, even dinners for singles. But here it's a question of getting people who want to marry into the same place so they can check each other out. It's up to the individuals. Parents never get involved."

"In India, parents have always been present. Maybe because in the old days of joint families it was important for everyone to get along. Of course it was most important for the boy and girl to like each other."

"But what if the boy and girl," here Rekha smiled, "don't get along after they marry?"

"I don't know. I don't know any couples who are like that." She crossed her fingers as she said it. A childhood leftover, though Indy always said fingers couldn't cross out the lie in a lie.

"That's amazing. No divorce?"

"Not in our town. But I think divorce is becoming common in big cities like Bombay. It's considered fashionable, people daring to follow a Western idea."

"The things we Americans export." Rekha shook her head. "But there must be couples in your town who are unhappy. What do they do?"

"I suppose they have to live with their fate. A divorce is too shameful, not just for the girl—I mean woman—but for her whole family."

"That's it right there! The angle for my thesis. Here women *can* get divorced. There's no social stigma since almost half of all marriages go kaput. I'll have to research women's shelters, see if they get any Indians coming in." Rekha thought ahead to where she would find such women. "So in India the women just stay put?"

"Sometimes the wife will be sent back to her home. But usually the family will not keep her. It's expensive and shameful." Leila remembered Amma saying that Nalini was lucky her parents were letting her stay home instead of forcing her to return to Malaysia.

"Are those the women who get burned?"

"Oh no. Those are usually from the lower class. And it's not because the boy, man, is unhappy with his wife. It's because of dowry. His family will demand more money, which they need to marry off their daughters. If they don't get it, they pour kerosene on the girl, burn her, and then he gets another bride. And another dowry. But I've only read about such cases in the newspaper. We've never had it happen in our town."

"I had the impression it happened all over India."

"No, not at all. That's just the media blowing things out of proportion. Before I came to San Francisco I thought I'd see people dying of AIDS everywhere."

Rekha took a sip of coffee. "I know this is kind of personal, but remember, I want to be a journalist, and am always on a quest."

Leila felt her heart beat faster. What question was she going to have to answer?

"Did you give a dowry?"

She smiled in relief. Rekha hadn't asked about their first nights and days together. How could she tell Rekha that it was the same as now, except that then Neel used his grandfather as an excuse and here in America he used his work?

"No. Neel didn't want one." She was too embarrassed to say her family didn't have the money.

"Is that unusual?"

"Yes, though there are modern men who realize the girl is her own dowry. You know, of course, that in the old days men were the ones who gave dowries. But then it became the women. Maybe it will change again and stop completely."

"I certainly hope so. And I'm happy you married an enlightened man. Though I suspect he fell in love with you immediately. You're just too bashful to say so. You tell him I said he's a lucky man."

Leila just smiled and wondered what Amma would make of that order. "I brought you my children's story."

"'*Annigma, the Cat Who Loved to Solve Puzzles.*' What does the name mean?"

"It's from the Greek, for 'riddle.'"

"Oh, clever. Thanks. I look forward to reading it."

"Rekha, is it very difficult to get admission into Berkeley?"

"Usually. Why?"

"I was thinking of doing another MA degree."

"Another one? So you can be a MaMa before you become a mother?" Rekha smiled.

"Very funny. No, I used to teach in India, but I'd like to do something different. New country, new career."

"What did you teach?"

"English literature."

"In school?"

"In a college."

"Wow. You never told me that. So many of the women in my mother's generation don't have careers. Yours is pretty impressive."

"It was nothing, really. Just a job till I got married."

"Just a job!" Rekha snorted. "You know how difficult it is to get jobs like that over here? The competition is way fierce."

"Maybe it's easier in India because girls' colleges like to hire women. And then we usually teach till we get married."

"What do you want to study now?"

"Creative writing."

"I think it's part of the English Department. And yes, it's difficult to get into that department," she warned.

"What else can I do with my education and experience?"

"How about volunteering? The YWCA is always looking for English teachers. These would be young immigrant kids, Chinese, Vietnamese, who need help learning basic skills. It's not Shakespeare, but they could really use you."

"I'm a little tired of teaching all those dead authors. It would be a nice change to help young children. That way I can also begin to understand the school system here. Should I just ring, I mean phone, the YWCA?"

"That would be a start."

"Thank you. I'll do it tomorrow."

Yes, Leila thought as she walked home, tomorrow is another day. Maybe she would get a volunteer position. It was a good compromise between what Neel wanted and her own desires. She still didn't understand why he was so eager for her to find a job.

Perhaps Neel would be waiting for her like the last time she met with Rekha. She pictured him in his suit and immediately thought of the nude scene she had seen yesterday in *Romeo and Juliet*. The censor board had cut it in India, just like all love scenes in foreign movies. Leila had seen more naked bodies on the TV screen than the flesh of her own husband. He had been bare-chested at their wedding, but she was too shy to look. He always slept in pajamas, not a lungi like Appa, and kept to his side of the bed.

At every crosswalk she hoped the lights would be green, so she could get home faster to Neel. The green also meant he would be home waiting for her. It was a game she had devised to enliven her walks, letting the outside world decide her future. The first three lights were red. As she waited for the little man to flash, she looked up to the sky to make a wish. But the bright orbs of the street lamps obliterated the stars and only a sliver of moon was visible.

· NINETEEN ·

"SEVEN-SIX-FOUR-TWO Gulf requesting frequency change."

Full of pride, Leila stared at the back of Neel's head, marveling at his expertise.

The radio crackled and a voice floated into their confined space. "Frequency change approved, seven-six-four-two Gulf. Good day and safe flying."

Jake Robson, one of the three co-owners of the four-seater, was flying with them to Reno. He turned around to Leila. "How are you enjoying yourself so far?"

"It's wonderful. But I don't think I want to be Beryl Markham anymore. It's much too complicated to fly a plane."

"Oh, nonsense. You can learn in no time. I'll give you a quick lesson now," Jake offered.

Leila leaned forward eagerly, but Neel's words snapped her into an upright position. "Don't do that. You'll change the trim."

Neel could barely contain his anger. The taxi had been late. He had almost lost the hard copy of his conference paper. And then Jake had decided to join them at the last minute. Neel couldn't refuse Jake, who traveled so much he hardly ever used the plane.

They all heard the big thud at the same time. "I'll go . . ." Jake started to get up but Neel stayed him. "Lee can get it. It's just behind her."

Leila looked back carefully. She didn't want to jeopardize the trim again. Their flight bag was on its side. She found the handle and tried to straighten it.

"Did you get it?" Neel could feel her tugging.

"It's too heavy."

The bag was heavy because of *her,* Neel thought. Inside, nestled between his shirts and pants, were her clothes. There had been no time to buy another overnight bag and the Samsonite was too big. Her things in his luggage. Her body in his bed. Caroline didn't know they slept in the same bed. But it was easier than getting another one. That would be making too loud of a statement, though she must know by now that he hadn't wanted to marry her.

He wished he were going up to Reno alone. But Sanjay and Oona had invited her and it would look bad if Leila drove up with them.

"Don't worry, Lee, I'll do it." Jake smiled at her. "See down there? We're just getting to the mountains."

They looked like papier-mâché mounds, mostly brown, though Leila could see the pointed rise of reddish-green trees. It didn't seem possible that mountains could kill. These looked so harmless, as if the poke of a finger would deflate their swell.

"Lee, this must be yours? It was in the side pocket." Jake handed her a scarf.

Perfume, unfamiliar, like the sugary scent of crushed petals, drifted up from the silk piece Jake put into her hand.

"It's not mine." She had bought suits, pants, sweaters, even jeans, but no accessories. She was still learning about American fashion, and had trouble enough getting a sense of the big items. She doubted she would ever reach the stage of wearing scarves.

"Hey, Jason must have landed a girlfriend." Jake laughed. "Jason's the other owner," he explained to Leila. "We always tease him because he's kind of shy. I'd better leave it here so she can find it again." He tucked the pale blue and pink scarf where he had found it.

Neel realized that Caroline must have left it there last weekend.

He hadn't told her that Leila was going to Reno. She would never understand and what she didn't know couldn't lead to a fight. He'd make it up to her—fly up to Sonoma and surprise her with a mud bath and massage.

When they landed, Jake took off with a friend while Neel hailed a taxi. Everyone seemed to have arrived at the hotel en masse and they found themselves at the end of a long line at the check-in counter. Neel could not understand how big hotels stayed in business with such inefficient workers. Fifteen minutes later, they were still waiting behind six people.

He wanted to scream. Leila was just standing there, not saying or doing anything. He had told her they wouldn't have time together, that even his evenings would be filled with dinner meetings. But she had insisted on accompanying him. "Oona will keep me company," she had stated.

Out of the corner of his eye he saw Patrick approach.

"Neel, hello there. Just get in?" Patrick held out a large pink hand that seemed an extension of his equally large, florid body.

"Patrick," Neel shook the proffered hand. "This is Lee. Lee, Dr. Patrick Connery from OB/GYN."

Leila felt as though someone had snatched the mangalsutra from her neck. She touched the black and gold wedding beads, wondering why Neel had not simply said, "This is Leila, my wife." Or even joked, "This is my worse half, Leila." His mood had not improved after they landed. She should have followed her instincts and stayed in San Francisco. But Oona had convinced her to come, and she had cancelled the appointment at the YWCA, guilty because the woman was going away on vacation and didn't have an opening for another month. A part of her, it was true, had also reacted to Neel's resistance.

She said the words Neel should have. "I'm Mrs. Sarath."

"A pleasure to finally meet you."

"Nice to meet you, too." She felt a little phony using this American phrase, but it was useful. It both said and didn't say anything.

"And how is our country treating you so far?"

Neel tried not to listen as he checked in. But Patrick always spoke as though the world were deaf. The insistent volume of his words and Leila's softer, accented speech grated on his ears. Patrick was going on and on about yoga.

"Mrs. Sarath?" the clerk called. At first Leila didn't connect the "Sairath" with her name, which she though of as "Surruth." Then she turned toward the man. "A message for you."

"It's Shanti," she told Neel, feeling happy for the first time that day. "She wants me to meet her in front of the slot machines. Where would they be?"

Neel pointed her in the right direction and reminded her he would be out for dinner. She had just disappeared from view when Sanjay came around the corner.

"Hey, Neel. Where's Leila?" he asked.

"Where's Oona?" Neel countered. He knew that Sanjay was checking up on him.

First Oona had invited Leila to Reno, then last week Sanjay had cornered Neel in the cafeteria. "Listen, man, you can't just leave Leila in San Francisco."

"She has things to do," Neel said.

"On the weekend? What's the matter with you? You're acting like a bachelor."

"What's the matter with *you*?" Neel hit back. "You're acting like my parents."

"Arre, I'll back off. I was just reminding you that we husbands have responsibilities."

Sanjay could afford to be Mr. Super Husband. He hadn't been foisted with a wife he didn't want. Neel's plan to get rid of Leila by making her independent wasn't going very well. She wasn't looking for a job in any organized fashion and didn't seem interested in learning how to do it the American way. If she kept following this route, he'd be stuck with her forever.

Now Sanjay said, "Oona's up in our room. The drive tired her. Though I was the one driving the whole way. Go figure."

"Women," Neel commiserated, trying to smooth over his earlier words. "Lee's with Shanti. They're probably winning at the slot machines."

"Good. We're having dinner together tomorrow, right? Big buffet, here I come!" He rubbed his stomach.

Sitting in the room by himself, Neel felt defeated. Marriage had a greater reach than he could ever have imagined. He'd thought he could leave Leila at home and continue on with his life, until she got the point and left. But people were forcing him to play the role of husband.

Except for Caroline, who seemed to expect him to compensate for his husband role by being an ever-present boyfriend. She had even refused to make love the other night, angry that he wasn't taking her to Reno.

"THIS IS A WHOLE DIFFERENT AMERICA." Shanti waved her hand, indicating the bright lights and levers. "Want to try your luck?" She jingled the change she'd won.

"Maybe a little later." Leila yearned to get away from the smoke and the desperate look in people's eyes. The atmosphere was palpable with longing. Two years ago, Amma had taken her to see a reputed palmist, and they had waited behind another mother anxious to find out why her daughter was still unmarried. The smelly, walnut-faced man held Leila's hand too long and emitted great sighs between bouts of coughing. "You, my daughter, ah. You will to suffer. Yes, definitely I see that. But you are born under a lucky star. Many many happy things will happen to you. Definitely. So you must not at all worry. In the final everything will come out okay." Amma had beamed until Leila reminded her the words didn't mean anything. He probably said the same to all his clients.

"Go on, try one." Shanti held out a quarter.

Leila popped in the coin and pulled the lever, watching to see what would come up. No match. No cascade of metal as in the machine next to them. "I guess I'm not lucky." She grimaced. For a brief second she had been caught up in the excitement of the colors and the noise and hoped for a win.

"You know what they say," Shanti comforted her, "unlucky in gambling, lucky in love. Speaking of which, where is that handsome husband of yours?" Shanti felt guilty that she hadn't made a greater effort to get to know Leila. But every time she planned to call, something came up. The interference of America, she called it privately, since the pace was so much slower in India and visits were always possible.

"Handsome husband has become Mr. Busy Bee," Leila joked, not wanting Shanti to guess the truth. Indians were so good at looking beneath the words, unlike Americans, who took things at face value.

"He's not going to be busy the whole time, is he?"

"He warned me that he had meetings and what-not. I actually came to see Reno, and to spend some time with you and Oona. That is, if you have the time?"

"Sure I do. But I'll have to talk to Neel about this. He can't bring you here and expect you to play Little Orphan Annie."

If only she could ask Shanti about Neel. Did Shanti know about Savannah? Had there been other girls? During that walk in the garden, right after putting ET down, and knowing he was going to reject her and accept Amita, Leila had asked Neel why he wanted an arranged marriage, implying the obvious: Don't you have an American girlfriend? So many foreign-returned men married to please their parents even though they loved someone else. Neel had shrugged his shoulders and responded, "I didn't wake up one morning and say, 'I want an arranged marriage.' It just seems the logical choice now." After their marriage, she had taken great comfort from his words.

"I suppose he will find some time." Leila smiled.

"Neel's a great guy. And from what Bob tells me, he's a superb anesthesiologist. You may not know this, but it's difficult for anesthesiologists to get jobs these days. Neel had four offers." Shanti focused on Neel the professional. Leila didn't need to know about Caroline. That was in the past, and since most Indians don't date, at least not openly, it would be difficult for Leila to understand.

"I didn't know that." Leila felt a swelling of pride. She was married to a very accomplished man. Everyone wanted him in the operating room. That was why Neel worked so late at night.

"His job really suits him, don't you think? It calls for absolute knowledge of the situation and precision. No mistakes allowed. That's Neel in a nutshell and probably why he's so good. Though he's not the bragging kind. He talks, but not about himself. Or you, for that matter. I just know that you both are from the same town, that you taught in a college and of course that you are very charming and pretty, which is why Neel married you."

Leila looked away, realizing that she would never be able to take any comfort from Shanti. In just a few sentences, Shanti had progressed from Indian to suave American. Shanti would never have tagged on the charming and pretty compliment in India. And what was she *really* saying about Neel? That he was quiet and didn't open up about himself? He did like to talk and joke. But perhaps Shanti was right. Neel could banter around, but even with the others she had never heard him say anything personal.

"You can say thank you, you know." Shanti laughed. "It's something you will have to learn here. People are very free with their compliments and they won't understand if you don't respond."

Leila looked down and played with her napkin. Shanti's forthrightness was even more difficult to take than the compliment. None of her friends in India would have been so bold as to correct her. Now Shanti was almost accusing her of being rude.

"Hey, I didn't mean to make you feel bad. It's just that I went through all that in the beginning. When I met Bob's mother, she took one look at me and said, 'Bob, you never told us you married an Indian princess. She is beautiful!' I had never, ever, been called even pretty, so of course I kept quiet. Then Bob nudged me. I looked up and there were all these smiling faces looking at me, waiting for me to say something. Do you know what I said?"

"No."

"I'm mortified just thinking about it. I hid my chin in my neck and muttered, 'I wish the earth would open up and take me in.'"
Both Shanti and Leila laughed.

"Like Sita."

"Yes, like our famous Mother Sita. Thank God the earth left me alone. Anyway, I don't want you to go through anything like that."

"Thank you. And thank you for the compliment."

"Those two little words, 'thank you,' were another learning experience. Bob kept telling me I wasn't saying them properly. He used to tease me all the time. 'I tink you said tank again.' I finally figured out that in India we never pronounce the 'th' sound. Bob taught me to put my tongue between my teeth," she demonstrated it. She didn't tell Leila that it was only recently that she had started calling her husband "Bahb," and not "Bawb," which the hospital personnel never understood.

"I'll remember that," Leila said, though she thought she had pronounced the word correctly.

She studied Shanti's face: the dark, high forehead, deep-set eyes, and jutting nose. Almost black hands picked up a biscotti, a diamond gleaming on the ring finger. Shanti and she had followed such different paths to America. Shanti acted as if she had gotten everything she wanted in life, including a husband who loved her. That was what made her confident, and Leila felt a daub of envy. Shanti was like Rekha. She hadn't taught students who got married as soon as they graduated and then brought their babies to see her. She never had to sit out endless rejections. Bob was the white knight who had rescued her from all that. Suddenly Leila wanted to know their story.

"How did you meet your husband?"

"Strange coincidence, I always say. I used to have a pen pal when I was in my teens, but you know how it is, after a few years we stopped writing. It must have been, oh, about twenty years later I suddenly received a letter saying her brother was coming to India. Could he look me up? Bob was that brother."

"Your parents didn't mind that you married him?"

"Yes and no. I was almost in my mid-thirties by then and we all assumed I'd never get married. I can't tell you how many men I saw, all of whom rejected me. Then Bob came along. He didn't seem to care about my skin color, so I decided not to care about his. I think my parents were secretly relieved I was finally getting married. Besides, they could at least hold their heads up because he is a doctor. You know how prestige-conscious people are in India." Over the years she had stopped telling people—especially Indians—about Bob's first wife.

"Oh," things began clicking in Leila's brain. "You are almost newly married too, then?"

"Heavens, no. We've been married almost eight years, but thank you for the compliment." Shanti smiled and continued, "Now I can finally thank my mother for not allowing me out in the sun.

She forced me to stay indoors in the summer, not concerned about cancer or wrinkles, mind you, but in case I got darker. I guess you can say I'm aging well." She laughed.

"My mother was the same way. Any time we went out, we had to take an umbrella."

"One of those ugly black ones, right? I tried to tell my mother that black absorbs the heat, but she never listened."

"My sister Indy would also say that, and Amma always replied, 'That's between the sun and the umbrella.'"

"The first time I went back to visit, I took my mother seven different-colored umbrellas, one for each day of the week. It was a joke, but she was thrilled. She still uses them, I think."

"Do you go back often?"

"In the first few years, yes. Now it's not automatically India every time we take our vacation. Anyway, I'm quite different now. More of a feminist, so the whole male-oriented Indian society really gets on my nerves. I can't stand it when my father sits around and expects my mother to serve him. He's retired, but I guess the work of a housewife is never over."

"My parents are like that." Leila wondered why Shanti objected to a woman looking after her husband. "So you don't miss India?"

"No, not really. But whenever we fought during our first years of marriage, I'd pack my bags and threaten to hop on the first plane. It's harder to go back now. It's . . . well, I guess it's just different."

"How?" Leila thought of her classmates who returned as different people. Some had American accents, others claimed they couldn't eat spicy food anymore. She wanted to become more American, but she didn't want to stop being Indian. Was it only a matter of time before she also became that way?

"For one thing, we fly in and out so quickly I get a very superficial sense of Bombay. What shocked me the most during my first visit was how dirty everything was. I'd heard others say it, and had always dismissed them as snobs. So it was odd to be in their shoes."

"You mean the roads, and the buses belching black soot?"

"Those, obviously. But also the five-star hotels. Bob had taken me to the Taj on our first date and I was awed. It was so fancy. The waiters kept filling the teapot and Bob kept pouring, so I kept drinking. I was too shy to go to the bathroom and when we finally left the coffeeshop I was like a giant water balloon, just waiting to burst." Shanti puffed out her cheeks and laughed. "Anyway, we went back there to recapture the good old days and all I saw was the shabby upholstery and the chipped china. You know, nothing was really five-star about the place."

"I guess that won't happen to me. We only have a three-star hotel in our town."

"You'll change," Shanti prophesied. "You won't know it and you may not even want to, but you will change."

Shanti was right. She had already changed. She did things by herself without relying on Neel and it was making her a stronger person.

· TWENTY ·

NEEL READ THE SLIP HANDED TO HIM: *I'm by the pool. Come and see me as soon as your panel is over. Caroline.*

He crumpled it up and stuck it in his pocket. He looked around the room. Nothing had changed. Dr. Ichikawa was still giving his talk, and the audience, like those anywhere, fidgeted, wrote notes, spoke to each other, and occasionally got up and left. Yet everything had changed. What was Caroline doing? Didn't she know it was too dangerous? The place was crawling with doctors from the hospital.

He tried to concentrate on Dr. Ichikawa's remarks. But his mind was churning with fear and anger. He had never liked being out of control. First Leila had forced his hand and now Caroline was waiting for him downstairs. She was crazy to have come here.

He considered leaving her by the pool. Not going down at all. But what if Patrick saw her? Or Sanjay? That would be the worst. And what if she did something more stupid? Right now he didn't put anything past her. His collar felt as damp as his clammy hands.

FIVE FLOORS BELOW the conference room where Neel was leading the discussion, Leila, Shanti, and Oona took the last table that provided an unobstructed view of the pool.

"Don't they feel shy?" Leila looked at the women, all clad in bikinis or skimpy one-piece suits.

"My dear, they work out like crazy just so they can show off."

Oona looked regretfully at her Coke. "I know I should have ordered the diet one."

"But why would they want to show their bodies to strangers?" Amma had forbidden Leila to wear T-shirts from the age of twelve, saying they were indecent. She was slowly getting used to all the bare skin she saw during her walks, but she hadn't even seen Indy in a bra and panties.

"Why does the sun shine?" Shanti quipped. "Because it can."

Oona picked up the menu. "Let's order something. I'm starving."

"But didn't we just have lunch?"

"I'm hungry again. So much for wanting to look like those women." Oona nodded toward the pool. "Hey, isn't that Neel? He must be looking for us. Quick, everyone, wave and get his attention."

Leila had seen Neel for almost a full minute before Oona noticed him. But she hadn't said anything, wondering why he wasn't at the conference. This morning he had told her he would be busy till midnight. Had the panel finished early—was he really looking for her?

Neel searched around the pool. He couldn't find Caroline. Perhaps she had gone, he thought, hope outpacing anger. But no, there she was on one of the bright blue chaises longues. She was in a pair of shorts, one of the few women not in a bathing suit.

He strode past the other bodies without looking at them, his eyes on Caroline. She was gazing into the distance and hadn't noticed him. Should he go before she saw him? Send her a note the way she had sent him one?

"I think he's coming toward us," Oona said.

"Are you sure he sees us?" Shanti asked.

"Who could miss all these flying hands?" Oona continued waving.

Neel stopped in front of Caroline and she stood up.

"Hi." Now that she was seeing him face-to-face Caroline was nervous. His nostrils were flared and the vein on his forehead pulsed. She had never seen him so angry before.

"What are you doing here?"

"What is *she* doing here?" Caroline countered, hurt that he hadn't even greeted her.

"What do you mean?" Neel hedged.

"I know you brought her, Neel, and you promised not to." She was sure now. She had called his home repeatedly, hoping the wife would answer, but after a day, had known that the sick, angry feelings inside her weren't based on neurotic imaginings.

Neel was just about to argue that he hadn't promised any such thing when he realized he would be better off dealing with the issue at hand.

"Caroline, you had no business coming here. What if someone sees us?"

"What if? They'll have to know sooner or later."

"I prefer later and I prefer deciding when and how."

"I think it's time you took my preferences into account."

"Did you come here just to make me angry?"

"No." Caroline almost broke down, "I came here because I love you. Neel, sweetie . . ."

"If you really love me, you'll go back right now."

"Neel, I'm so sad and upset, I just had to see you. I need you to comfort me." The more distant Neel grew, the more she wanted him.

"Caroline, this isn't the place or time for that. I have another panel in fifteen minutes. It's best if you leave right now. I'll take care of the bill."

"I haven't checked in yet."

"Good. Then let's get you a taxi to the airport. We can discuss this in San Francisco."

He turned and saw Oona, Shanti, and Leila. It was like his very first operation—everyone looking, waiting for him to do something. He forced himself to smile. He'd make up some story later on. It was important that Caroline not see them. When she bent to pick up her bag, he half waved and indicated that he was leaving.

Oona and Shanti turned toward each other like bookends, trying to keep to themselves the knowledge they didn't want Leila to guess. Leila didn't look at either of them. She stared down at the tablecloth and counted the packets of sugar. Then she reached for her hair, cut recently to shoulder length, and twisted it into a knot. Suddenly the loose strands felt suffocating.

"Talk about forgetful doctors! Neel must have left something behind so the secretary had to bring it up." Shanti made the excuse, her mind trying to catch up with her eyes.

"You're right." Oona jiggled the ice cube in her glass. "I thought she looked familiar. Sanjay calls her 'Madam Fake' because she insists people pronounce her name the French way, Caroleen."

"Madam Fake." Shanti laughed. "That's a good one."

Leila couldn't speak. She, too, had recognized the woman. This was the girl whose picture Neel kept in his files. It wasn't Savannah. It was a girl named Caroline whom Neel saw every day. Whom he was seeing now instead of coming to his wife.

· TWENTY-ONE ·

THE REST OF THE DAY LEILA SMILED and nodded to Oona and Shanti. If only she could make an excuse and leave. Lie down. Cry. Vomit. Stop her heart from thudding its grief so loudly. Her eyes gave her no respite, constantly replaying the picture of the blonde. Caroline. She knew the woman's name. It wasn't Savannah. That was someone else to worry about.

Oona kept pointing out the sights, her voice as cheerful as a tour operator's. Leila couldn't hear the words and it suddenly occurred to her that Nalini must feel this way all the time. Leila, too, had joined in the chorus of commiseration. "Yes, how terrible that Nalini's husband refuses to send for her from Malaysia." Poor, unwanted Nalini. But it can be worse, she communicated silently with her faraway friend. A husband can prefer another woman.

It shamed her deeply that Oona and Shanti had seen Neel bend over the woman, leave with her, while he just waved to them.

She managed to murmur the right responses and even ate half the plate of food. A few hours ago, she had been excited to be going out to dinner with the two women. Now the restaurant felt claustrophobic, the smell of the food nauseating and the conversation interminable.

Nalini had to put on a face for the hundreds of people who knew her story. Leila only had to do it for two women. But it was physically depleting, and by the time they said good night, she was exhausted, though wide awake.

Alone in the room, she slumped on the edge of the bed, bone-less. Wanting to weep but unable to. Maybe she had already shed all her tears. Cried them internally these past months when Neel had rejected her every night.

She remembered that first, frantic night in America when she kept thinking a divorce was the answer. Such bravado was only possible on a jet-lagged mind—particularly since there was practically nothing to give up. Now everything was different. She had lived with Neel. Thought of him as her husband. They were not intimate in the bedroom, but she had intimate knowledge of him. That he slept on his back, that he snored only when he drank beer, that a long stream of urine was always followed by three short squirts. She had convinced herself that the letters and the picture in his files meant nothing. Kept waiting like Patience on a monument for him to claim her as his wife. Believed that he spent late nights working at the hospital.

When Neel came in at 1:00 a.m., she pretended to be asleep. She did not want to talk to him. If he had something to say, he would have found her by now. He was the one who owed her an answer. She opened her eyes to slits, like ET, and watched him look down at her. Was he going to wake her up? No, he simply turned down the covers and slid in beside her. She tried to sleep, but every attempt was foiled by the poolside tableau.

The image of the white woman in her short shorts was imprinted onto her eyelids. It was as if she had stared at the sun and every blink produced a dark semblance of the yellow disc. Neel waving, Neel leaving with the woman.

The next morning, as Neel put on his tie, he said, "Sorry I couldn't come by yesterday, but I had to rush off to another panel. My secretary, Caroline, was delivering a packet of slides she thought I'd left behind by mistake. As it turned out, I didn't need them." For a second her heart surged with relief. But the way he pronounced the name, Caroleen, his going to meet her when he'd said he was so busy, told Leila he was lying.

He gave the same explanation to the others when they met for breakfast. "She was coming here for the weekend and decided to bring them herself. As I told Patrick, it's a bit much. We both think she's bucking for a raise."

Leila watched him smile, watched the others move their lips like a family of apes. Sanjay made a joke. "The secretary in Pediatrics is just like a child. Her list of Won't Do's is so long, no one has made it to the Will Do part."

She wanted to embarrass him the way he had her. Wanted to tell the others about the photograph, the late nights, the lonely weekends. But even as the words bubbled inside her, she suppressed the volcanic thoughts. She was still too much her mother's daughter. She swallowed her shame and, like the dutiful wife of Amma's expectations, went with Neel to the airport.

Jake had called earlier to say he wouldn't be returning on the plane with them. She gazed out of the side window, not wanting to look at Neel. The smell of flowers was strong. It was Caroline's scarf. Jake had been wrong. The scarf belonged to a cheap woman who wore bright shorts in order to hunt down a married man. Neel was in a talkative mood and pointed out this mountain, that lake. She wanted to choke him with the scarf. Stuff it into his mouth. Make him writhe in pain. She did not know how long she could listen to his polite words. She looked in the side pocket for the scarf, but it was gone. Was she imagining things again, the way she had that first night in America? The scene from yesterday asserted itself in her mind. It had been taking place for sometime now. She had just been too trusting, naive, stupid, to realize it.

She had ignored even the obvious clues: late evenings at the office, nights spent on the other side of the bed while she slept on, a virgin. What manner of man did not want to make love to his wife? Gay, or one involved with another woman. The bouquet of flowers that smelled like the scarf that smelled like Neel did after some of his late nights "at work." And she had been so eager to please him in every way. A beggar.

She remembered a science experiment in one of Indy's psychology textbooks. A frog was put in a pot of water that was gradually heated. The frog could jump out at any time, but the experimenters found, to their surprise, that it never did.

It would be so easy to jump off the plane. To fall like Icarus, to be absorbed by Mother Earth like Sita. But Shanti hadn't wanted that, and neither did she. Not this time. This time she wanted to live. No man was worth dying for.

How was her life going to be in San Francisco with this knowledge eating her insides like acid? What was she going to do when he called to say he would be late?

The answers would come to her. No need to rush them. Ten years ago, but so well remembered it was as if it had happened yesterday, she had suffered the repercussions brought on by thoughtless rushing. This time, she would wait. Not wait for him to act, like she had been doing these past months. She would wait to see how *she* would act.

At this moment she only knew that she wanted to stop him playing the innocent guide. "Suneel," she used his full name deliberately "Jake already told me everything."

Jake had pointed out the mountains below as well as the scarf in the plane. "Where is that scarf? Maybe you should give it to Jason."

She was disappointed when he calmly agreed, "Good idea."

· TWENTY-TWO ·

TWO DAYS AFTER RETURNING FROM RENO, Leila received an aerogram from Indy:

Dear Akka,

I'm sorry I haven't written for so long. It's simply that whenever I get a chance I seem to be writing to Srinivasan. Amma is so excited it makes me nervous just thinking that something may go wrong. I know that everyone is hoping I will have the same luck as you. So far the only similarity is that both men have names beginning with the letter S. Srinivasan Thiruvengaram, ST, and of course Amma got extremely angry when I jokingly referred to him as Sanitary Towel.

It is amazing how much I already know about Sam. That's what his friends in Cambridge call him. He is studying economics and loves to play chess. We send each other chess problems in every letter. He is coming to India in four months especially to see me!!! I am so worried. I know he has already seen my photo, but what if he thinks I'm old when he sees my gray hair? You know how frizzy and awful my hair can look. You were so lucky with your husband. He fell in love with you and didn't want anyone else. . . .

Leila caved into the sofa, her body weightless from fear. Was Sam going to be another Neel? Men who changed their names and their countries were not to be trusted.

She read the letter again. There was some hope that Indy's situation would be different. Amma was allowing her to correspond with Sam. If only Neel and she had corresponded. She may not have found out about Caroline, but she may have been able to read between the lines.

She had merely wondered if he already had someone in his life when they met. Now she knew that someone to be a slim white woman in short shorts. In the last forty-eight hours, Leila had alternated between wanting to kill Neel and wanting to run back to India. She pictured him on the evening news, dead in a car accident; envisioned an earthquake, a large crack on the street that closed over his lying face. Once she even began packing her suitcase, throwing in sarees any which way until in their perfect folds she saw Amma's face. Amma would never want her back, especially now that Indy was almost engaged to Sam.

Had Leila defeated upper-class, educated women like the beautiful Amita only to be supplanted by an American secretary? That brief sighting in the sun tormented her. Where once all blondes looked alike, now a tall one was singular. She wished she had the guts to call the hospital and tell off the French accent. "Leave my husband alone," or, "Don't you know Neel is married?" But it wasn't right to put all the blame on Madam Fake. Neel wasn't behaving as if he was married. Never had, certainly not with her.

Neel didn't mention Caroline's name again, but it was the main refrain in Leila's mind. Caroline was there in the mornings when Neel hurried off to work. She was there when Leila took a walk, averting her face from the flowers she used to admire. Caroline had sent the bouquet. Offices don't send flowers when someone returns from vacation. Caroline was there in the evenings, when Neel phoned, his disembodied voice announcing what she already knew. Alone in the blackness, Leila walked back into that morning by the pool.

Suddenly determined, she picked up the phone and began dialing. Then stopped. She had barely replaced the receiver when it rang from under her fingers. Caroline?

It was Rekha, nervous and quick-voiced over the phone.

"Remember I told you I've begun volunteering at a shelter? Well, I'm here now and there's an Indian woman who doesn't speak English. Looks like her husband has been beating her. Do you think you can come and translate for her?"

"What language does she speak?"

"Indian, I guess."

"We have more than one hundred and sixty languages and none are called Indian."

"Oops! I'd better find out. Be right back."

Leila glanced around the gleaming magazine kitchen with its fancy gadgets, hoping it would be a language she didn't know. She didn't want to listen to another woman's problems.

"It's Hindi," Rekha said.

"I don't know it very well. It was my second language in school."

"You know more than any of us. Can you come right away?"

As she walked toward the shelter, emotions jumbled together in Leila's stomach like aviyal, the curry Amma made with the end-of-the-week vegetables. Her mind constantly analyzed past scenes, which now took on new meanings. Why had she not been alarmed when Oona said Sanjay did not work late? No, puffed up with uxorial pride, she thought Neel was more important than Sanjay. She had made excuse after excuse for him.

Over the last two days she was slowly acknowledging that everything was very wrong. She was like Indy, who had refused to see any white hairs in the mirror though she had begun graying at twenty-one. Only when Indy found one in her comb did she admit her too early maturity. Leila felt as if she were looking at a gray strand that, visible now, was rapidly multiplying. It wasn't right for a husband to leave his wife alone every weekend. It wasn't normal that he didn't want to touch her.

She knew that Neel had followed tradition in allowing his family to choose her. She was so entranced with her changed status she had refused to admit he never wanted the marriage.

She considered her two options: Keep quiet or question him. Indian women were adept at keeping quiet. Maybe that's why there were so few divorces. We absorb, pretend, and soldier on, Leila thought.

Although she was raised to be submissive, she wasn't frightened to confront him. But it would also mean going against Amma's wishes. Amma had arranged a good match and expected Leila to make the best of it, for her own sake and for her sisters as well. Amma always said that the first years of marriage were difficult. She had compared them to the exile Prince Rama endured in the *Ramayana*. Rama had to suffer for fourteen years before returning to his kingdom and throne. Amma herself had begun married life in a joint family, under the control of her mother-in-law. The old lady was a typical product of her time, taunting Amma that she was incapable of bearing sons, even though Appa kept saying that a child's sex was determined by the man. Leila vaguely remembered her grandmother. A shrimp-shaped figure slurping rice and water from twiggy, withered hands. She had died when Leila was seven years old. That was when Amma became happy. Perhaps the same would be true for Leila. Caroline would vanish and she and Neel could begin their life together.

She was so absorbed in her thoughts she almost walked past the shop Rekha had told her to look for. The shelter was somewhere around here.

"Can I help you?"

For a moment she didn't know the man was speaking to her. He looked like a TV star, blond hair lifting in the wind, blue eyes smiling.

"It's okay," Leila stammered, not sure she should be talking to him. In India only low-class men approached women and it was usually with bad intentions.

"You look lost," he insisted, not moving away.

Leila didn't want to ask for directions to the shelter. What if he thought she was going there for herself? But he was waiting, and she said, "I'm looking for the Women's Shelter," adding quickly, "I'm a translator."

"It's across the street from us," he pointed to a yellow building. "The small lettering is difficult to read."

"Thank you." She turned to leave.

"Where are you from?"

Should she answer? "India," she said softly.

"You have a lovely accent and . . . you're very beautiful."

"Oh."

"Nice talking to you." He held out his hand.

"Thank you." She flushed and bit her lips. She had forgotten to place her tongue between her teeth. She took her hand back and stepped onto the asphalt without checking to see if it was safe.

Rekha was waiting for her in the entrance. "Did you find it okay?"

"Yes." Leila could still hear his voice: "You're very beautiful." Neel had never even told her she was pretty. She had forgotten that she *was* pretty. Amma still had the blue "La Belle" sash she had brought home after being crowned Most Beautiful Freshman.

"Anu's waiting down the hall. But first let me introduce you to our director."

Leila followed Rekha into a large office that was green with plants, one corner filled with toys.

"Leila, this is Amy Wong, the director of the shelter. Amy, Leila Sarath."

"Thank you for coming on such short notice."

Amy had the yellow skin and waterfall-straight hair of women who belong to the Scheduled Tribes in Northeast India, except that she sounded just like an American.

"You're welcome," Leila said, though she wasn't sure what they expected of her. She regretted saying yes over the phone. What type of person was this Anu that she took her problems to strangers? Indians hid things, even from other family members.

"Rekha, did you fill Leila in on Anu?"

"I'm just about to." Rekha ushered Leila into the corridor. "Anu came in this morning. The poor thing is terrified and so far we have only been able to give her some tea. It must have taken so much courage to come to us, but we still don't know why she is here. All we've been able to understand is something about her husband and a green card. But as I said over the phone, I suspect her husband has been beating her."

Anu was sitting alone in the room, head bent as if from the weight of her bun, her tiny frame overwhelmed by the chair. One glance at the bright purple salwar kameez told Leila the woman was from North India. She looked tired, but exhibited the watchfulness of an attentive, unsure ET as Leila approached.

"My name is Leila. I'm here to help you," Leila said in Hindi.

Then the woman smiled, showing overlapping front teeth stained with paan.

"It's good you can speak Hindi. I only know a very little English. My good name is Anu."

Leila glanced over at Rekha.

"Ask her why she came here," Rekha prompted.

"Can you tell me why you came here?"

"The policeman gave me this some months ago. So today I showed it to a taxi driver and he brought me here." She handed Leila a white business card folded so many times the address of the shelter was difficult to read.

"What policeman?"

Anu's lips twitched and she didn't answer immediately. She kept her eyes on the cup of tea, which was still full. Leila guessed she was probably too shy to ask for sugar. "My husband was beating me one night and the neighbors called the police. Two very big black men came and they made my husband stop."

"Did you come today because your husband is beating you?"

"No. He has not beaten me for a few weeks. But yesterday he got angry and said he was going to throw me out of the house. It's because we got a letter that his younger brother just had a boy. My husband really wants a son and we only have two daughters. He says I don't have a green card and when he throws me out, they will send me back to India."

Leila remembered when Premila, who lived down the road, had a daughter. Her husband would not even look at the baby. He just told Premila that the next one better be a boy. Premila was lucky. Ten months later she had a son.

"How did you come to America?"

"On the airplane."

"What I mean is, did you come on your husband's green card?"

"I don't know. But my husband is an American," she said with pride.

"How long have you been here?"

"Seven years."

"After five years you too can become a citizen. And your daughters are citizens. You don't have to worry about being sent back to India."

"Are you sure? How do you know?"

"Because my husband is a citizen and I came the same way you did." Anu and she came from opposite ends of India and from entirely different social classes. But in America they were more alike than different.

"If you are sure, then I can go now." Anu stood up.

"She's leaving already?" Rekha asked. "Ask her about the beatings."

Not wanting to delve into another's private misery, but knowing that Rekha expected it of her, Leila asked the nosy American question, "What if he beats you again?"

"I was only afraid they would send me back to India. My parents are very poor and they do not have the money to take me and my two daughters. So if you say that I'm an American, then they can't deport me."

"Do you want to report your husband to the police?"

"No, it will only be worse for me. And for our baby."

"You are pregnant?"

"Yes, and I pray this one is a son."

"Do you know that the sex of your baby is determined by your husband?"

"No. He always tells me it is my fault we have girls. My mother said the same thing. We give birth to the baby, so we must also be responsible for the sex, don't you agree?"

Leila didn't argue. She looked closely at Anu and noticed the red and blue marks on her throat. It looked as if her husband had tried to strangle her last night.

"Where are your children?"

"I kept them at my neighbor's house. My husband is at work and will return only at night."

"Where does he work?"

"At a factory. He doesn't tell me what he does, but it must be important because he works very late."

"Maybe you should try to learn some English," Leila suggested. She wished there was something more she could offer, but didn't want to impose her opinions on Anu. English, however, was the first step to staying in America and ultimately becoming an American. If Anu knew some English, she could have talked to the policemen, and just that small way of standing up to the husband might have improved her life. "There are free classes for that in America." Leila realized that people like Anu needed her more than schoolchildren who had their own class teachers.

"My husband does not like me to go out. He thinks a wife's place is in the house. He also says he knows English, so why do I need to learn?"

"You will need to talk to your children. They will go to English school."

"They already know English. But I talk to them in Hindi."

"I can teach you," Leila offered.

"No, I must not make my husband angry. I have to go now. My children are waiting for me. Thank you. You have given me great peace of mind."

Leila made a brief report to Amy and Rekha.

"So she is going back to her abusive husband?" Rekha was outraged.

"She says it is her duty to stay with him. Her parents married her to him and that's that."

"Why stay with a husband who beats you and says your only worth is to bear sons?"

"We Indians belong to a culture that does not respect a woman without a husband. This way she can hold her head high outside the house, even though she can't do that inside the house. It is better to have a husband, even a bad one, especially if you have children."

"A number of Asian women are raised to feel that way," Amy agreed. "It's going to take time and work to make them realize that they, too, deserve a good life. Divorce is ultimately better for the children because otherwise they repeat the pattern of abuse. Thanks for helping us, Leila, and I insist Rekha treat you to some tea. It's the least we can do. Listening to these stories isn't easy."

"Maybe I can help again," Leila said.

"That would be great! We always need volunteers." Amy gave her a form, asking her to fill it out and return it at her convenience.

At the café Leila wanted to talk about her short story, but Rekha's mind was on Anu.

"This is so depressing. I can't bear to think what that poor woman is going through."

"She probably thinks it's her fate, and as long as she does not trouble her parents she will have some solace." Leila, too, had believed that at one time. It seemed to her that most Indian girls were taught an alphabet that began "A is for Abnegation."

"It really kills me to think that so many Asian—Indian—women, are living versions of Anu's life. I want my thesis to bring attention to the problem and help a few of them at least. First off, Amy says they hardly get any Indian women walking in or calling, and when one does come in, she refuses to talk."

"Anu is so ashamed of her situation she would never divulge more than she has to."

"Really?"

"Yes. I would feel the same way." It was the closest she had come to telling Rekha the truth about her non-marriage.

"How am I going to collect data? If a walk-in like Anu won't tell me her problems, who will?"

"Maybe there is no story."

"How can you say that? You just spoke to this woman."

"Our culture makes it very difficult for people to open up."

"And here in America we spill our guts on national TV. Speaking of which, I'm leaving Tim. I finally realized that he is never going to leave his wife."

Hope, seductive and tantalizing, serenaded Leila. If beautiful, educated Rekha didn't think Tim would leave his wife for her, then Neel would never go to Caroline.

"Why do you say that?"

"For one thing, he still goes back to his wife every night. We sleep together, but he always has to hurry home so she won't suspect anything. I'm such a fool. I initially fell for Tim because I was tired of dating men who were terrified of commitments. I figured he's married, he's not afraid. I never thought he'd want to *stay* married."

Leila assimilated this new information. Neel, too, came home every night.

"But doesn't Tim love you?" Leila worried that Neel's love for Caroline would wipe out any obligation he might feel toward his parents or her.

"He says he does. But I think he loves his assets more. In California, wives get half of everything."

"Even if they divorce within a year of marriage?"

"Yes, I'm pretty sure. But Tim's been married for five years. Yesterday I told him to go back to his wife. I never want to see his married face again." Rekha grimaced. "Pretty pathetic, huh?"

Leila wanted to assuage Rekha's sadness.

"Do you know what your name means?" she asked, for the first time feeling really close to her new friend. They both yearned for out-of-reach men.

"No," Rekha replied. She was grateful she hadn't been saddled with Rashmi. Her younger sister had been forced to make a joke out of her name. "Don't rush me," she'd say. In her teens, Rekha had considered changing her name officially to Rebecca, but had abandoned the idea when her parents said they would not give her any money for college.

"Your name means 'line,'" Leila said. She pointed to Rekha's hands and continued, "Like the fate lines on your palms. Did you know that the lines on your two hands are different? The ones on your left palm are what you are born with, while the ones on the right are what you are going to make of your life."

"Can you read my palm? Now would be a good time to get a glimpse of the future."

"No, I can't do that. But you can do something no one else can. You can change the lines."

"Really, how?" Rekha sounded bemused.

"My father always says that when you can't stop bad or sad things from happening, that is the time to remember you are still in charge of your life. *You* can make it different. Like you did yesterday."

· TWENTY-THREE ·

SANJAY LEFT TWO MESSAGES REMINDING Neel about the annual doctors' get-together on Friday. This year he was in charge of organizing it.

He brought it up again when they ran into each other in the cafeteria.

Neel was avoiding him because he didn't want a lecture about Caroline coming to Reno, but Sanjay only said, "You told Leila, right?"

"Yes," Neel mumbled. "We may not be able to come. I'm on call that night."

"Arre, see this. BYO Pager." Sanjay held up the invitation. "I thought of everything. I even ordered some Indian food. Took good advantage of being in charge. You have to come and help me eat up the tandoori chicken in case these bozos think it's too spicy. It won't look good if there's a lot left over."

The party had been started decades ago by doctors to promote camaraderie amongst themselves. Neel enjoyed going to them, meeting the new doctors and reconnecting with ones he saw only once a year.

This year, however, he was glad to be on call. Reno had made him want to retire from social life permanently. He kept remembering how Oona, Shanti, and Leila had seen him with Caroline. Thank God she had left. But the encounter shook him so much he had kept checking every room he entered to see if she was there.

226

At least she would not be at the barbecue. He only had to worry about Leila.

"Remember the barbecue I told you about? It's tomorrow," Neel told Leila when he returned home.

"Barbecue?" Leila envisaged a deep pit billowing with smoke.

"I thought I left the invitation on the table."

Leila considered his face and the lips that formed those words—lies again. "You told me nothing about any party," she said flatly. She went to the table and quickly sorted through the inch-thick pile of mail yet to be recycled. Catalogs, advertisements, old magazines fell in a colorful cascade from her fingers. "No invitation."

"That's odd," Neel said. "Ah, here it is. It got stuck in this Safeway advertisement. I can pick you up after work if you like. It will be freezing, so remember to wear gloves and a hat."

Leila stared at the bright red 8 by 10 invitation. Had he really left it on the table or had he slipped it in just now? She remembered that first night in the condo, when Caroline's picture fell out and she put it back, worrying that he would know she had gone through his things and so not respect her.

"You don't have to come, you know," Neel said into the quiet.

"I won't, then. It will probably be too cold for me anyway," she said, and left the room, angry at herself for feeling hurt.

Caroline, of course, would be there.

THE NEXT NIGHT, Leila wrestled with her decision. Any moment now the barbecue pit was going to be dug and the coals fired for an evening of fun. She was being ridiculous. Neel clearly didn't want her there; Caroline would be present; so why was she so full of regret?

She turned on the TV and there was Julie Andrews singing *The hills are alive. . .* Even Amma had gone to see Julie Andrews dance on the Alps. The movie felt like an old friend, and every song pushed the barbecue further back—until the blond head of the Baroness appeared. The woman wanted the Captain for all the wrong reasons. Poor Julie Andrews. Forced to watch the ball from the terrace. She loved the Captain, but did she tell him? No, she just let the Baroness lead him away. In Reno, Leila too had done nothing. The glass door had been like a movie screen through which she witnessed her humiliation.

But what if Neel *had* been telling the truth about the slides? What if he *had* brought home the invitation? And if he was an out-and-out liar, she could at the very least force herself between him and Caroline.

It was almost sunset. She hurriedly layered herself in her warmest clothes and rushed outside, ready to flag a taxi the way people did in the movies. None appeared. Just long streams of cars that huffed and puffed at the stop sign like snorting animals.

"Trying for a taxi?" a voice spoke from behind her.

It was an old man she had seen in the lobby of their building.

"You'll have better luck on Broadway. Thattaway," he pointed.

"Thank you." She ran in the direction indicated. Just as she reached the corner, she saw an empty taxi approaching. Feeling like a real American, she hailed it and was pleased when it snaked over beside her.

"Baker Beach," she said, settling into the cushioned seat.

The taxi driver was a young Russian who immediately placed her as Indian. He loved Hindi movies and Leila was amused that he knew so much about Bollywood. She decided it was a good sign for the evening ahead.

The traffic was light and they were there in no time at all. But as the taxi sped off, she was overcome with regret. Now that she was here, she wanted to go home and forget the whole idea. She stood in the dark, surveying the scene on the sand.

People were everywhere—standing, sitting, stretched out on towels, many encircling the four fires. No pit filled with coals, but smoke streaming out of black metal boxes that must be the barbecues. She saw a number of blond heads, but they were too far away for her to make out if Caroline was there. She couldn't see Neel. Had he changed his mind because she had said she wouldn't go?

"Arre, Leila Didi, Neel said you were under the weather." Sanjay came over, a big smile on his face, fingers red from the tandoori chicken he was eating.

"Under the impression that the weather was going to be cold, not freezing." Leila smiled, drawing the shawl closer around her.

"That's why I call it the brr-brr-cue. These crazy Americans like the beach in any weather. Thank God there's no fog this evening. Come stand near the fire. Look, Neel is hogging the one over there. Let's get him to share."

Neel was amongst a group of people. Leila scrutinized them and exhaled with relief when she saw no Caroline. A yellow tint caught her eye and she turned immediately. But it was only Oona, walking quickly toward them.

"I'm so glad you came, Leila. Come, let me introduce you around."

"Arre, why are you doing Neel's job? You stay here and keep me warm. Neel, look who crawled out from under the bad weather."

But before Neel could break away and come to her, Patrick waved his hands and called her. "Come see the twins before they fall asleep."

The welcome, coupled with no sighting of Caroline, loosened any earlier regret. And all her fear vanished with Patrick's next words.

"This is our once-a-year elitism," he explained. "It's only doctors and their spouses, so it's like a big medical family."

NEEL STOPPED IN MIDSENTENCE when Sanjay called to him. What was she doing here?

He joined her, squatting in front of Patrick's twins.

"Your wife's the smart one here," Patrick claimed. "She's the only one so far who can sort out the twins."

"But it's easy," Leila protested. "This one has a very serious, I'm-going-to-be-a-doctor-when-I-grow-up expression and this fellow here is definitely going to join the circus."

"Perish the thought of another doctor in the family." Patrick laughed, while a woman named Arlene said, "I still don't see the difference. You must have a knack for these things."

"They know all sorts of things in India," Patrick's wife announced.

"Yes, like when to quit while ahead." Leila uncurled the baby fingers from her hair and stood up.

"Neel," she finally acknowledged him. "I felt better so I decided to join you."

"Glad to hear that. Something to drink?"

"I'm fine, or how do you say it here in America? I'm good, thanks." Leila smiled and picked up the drink she had placed on the sand.

"Don't believe her," Sanjay joined them. "She's not good." He paused. "She's better than good. To have taken on this joker? She's a real saint."

"There he goes again," Neel sighed. "Putting me down. Come on, I'm a pretty good catch, aren't I?" he questioned the group.

Leila smiled and took another sip of the frothy, bitter drink. She didn't like it, but didn't know how to get rid of it tactfully.

"No one going to stand up for me?" Neel looked chagrined. "You," he pointed at Leila, "have to be on my side."

As he came toward her, Leila asked, "Why? I only married you. I don't have to side with you."

Everyone laughed. She couldn't stop smiling. This was the evening she had hoped for during that dinner at Sanjay and Oona's. She felt liberated—no Caroline to worry about, just these nice people.

"Arre, Leila Didi, Neel is right. You married him. So you're stuck with him."

"Sanjay, you change your mind so quickly, you must have been a chameleon in your past life."

"But in this one I never change color. See? Brown today, brown tomorrow."

"How about brown on the court? They're calling for a game of Husbands versus Wives," Oona said.

"Now *you* get to play against *my* side," Leila teased Neel.

But Neel and Sanjay both decided not to join in, each claiming they had to save their hands for real work.

Standing in one corner of the makeshift volleyball court, she was aware that Neel was watching her. She joined in the laughter and the quest to keep the ball alive, darting here and there, getting balls that others had missed. She could hear Sanjay shout, and once thought she heard Neel yell, "Way to go, Leila!"

The Wives lost, but, as Sanjay said, they had won over everyone at the barbecue.

The evening was coming to an end, and some groups drifted together as others took off.

"The last of the lot." A figure came out of the dark carrying a tray of drinks and Leila followed the others in taking a bottle. It tasted very similar to the previous drink, but was lighter and not as bitter. With every sip the taste got better till she began taking large swigs, like the men were doing.

"Hey, take it easy," Neel said softly.

"I'm doing something wrong?" Leila wondered if she had unwittingly committed a gaffe.

"You're fine. I just think you may want to stay that way. That's beer you're chugging down so rapidly."

"Beer!" Leila was so surprised that the word burst out loudly.

Sanjay overheard and said, "First time with beer, huh? Oona says it's like opera—you either hate it or like it."

"Actually, I don't like it or hate it. I think I may, one day in the far future, like it. As for opera, I'll let you know—if Neel ever takes me to one." Was it the beer that was making her open up with such impudence? Or was it the hurt that an opera was just another event, like Al's wedding tomorrow, to which he clearly never planned on taking her? She hadn't even known about the invitation until Al reminded them of the celebration slated for eleven o'clock the next morning.

"We can give you a ride," Sanjay had offered. "It's on our way."

"Not unless you exchanged your Mercedes for a minivan. Aren't you picking up Shanti and Bob?" Neel reminded him.

"Arre, see what happens when people forget to turn up for my barbecue? The wedding should be fun," Sanjay turned toward Leila. "Italians are like Indians. They believe in big spreads."

Now Neel said, "If it's opera you want, say the word and you're there." He clicked his fingers as if he were a magician.

She couldn't goad Neel about the wedding, but she could about the opera. Deep down she didn't really want to go to an opera, so his answer couldn't hurt her.

"You make promises you can't keep," Leila said, aware that she was talking more slowly than normal. "I can say *Aida* all I want just now, we'll still be standing here."

"You better watch out for her," Sanjay warned, "or you'll end up like me. Opera, ballet, symphony. I didn't know Oona liked all that painful standing-on-toes business. Not to mention the neckache from playing the violin."

"We can get season tickets together," Oona said, ignoring Sanjay.

"Thanks, but I think we'll do this on our own." Neel smiled at Leila.

Leila shook her head. It felt a little heavy and her right temple was beginning to throb. She wanted to go to bed, but she also wanted to make her point. "No, season tickets. So in case you can't go, I'll still have company."

"A few months of marriage and you have him down pat," a voice behind them marveled.

"As Patrick said, she's the smart one here," Neel said. "You've also had enough beer for one night," he whispered to Leila. "Let's go, shall we?"

· TWENTY-FOUR ·

NEEL WOKE AT HIS REGULAR HOUR and went straight to his study. The silent house, the desk with his things arranged exactly to his taste gave him the illusion that he was alone in the condo, that nothing had changed.

He picked up the new issue of *Stanford Magazine* and, ignoring the articles, searched the alumni section for news of Savannah. He'd been doing it for years, wondering where she was, who she was with. There was nothing about her and he closed the magazine, not entirely disappointed.

Was he thinking about her because of the wedding? He hadn't wanted to go, but Al Aspromante was too nice a guy to refuse. Al was incredibly excited, acting as if he hadn't been married before. As if the first set of wedding pictures, the best one framed, did not exist.

Al made forgetting look so easy. And here he was, sitting at a desk that still held all the letters Savannah had ever written him. He bent down to open the drawer, then shut it. Why bring up white wedding memories?

Thank God Al's wedding was going to be in the backyard. Short and to the point, Al had said. Then he'd added, laughing, that it was a good thing his parents were dead. Not only was he divorced, his second wedding was not being held in a church.

Would he have told Leila about the wedding if the others hadn't brought it up? Her sudden appearance yesterday had unnerved him, but then she had proceeded to surprise him by extricating herself nicely from the lie he had made up to account for her absence. He thought back to the chilly, smoke-swirled evening, how his anxiety had come up with a series of disastrous scenarios. She would not be able to keep up with the quick repartee. She would have nothing to say since she wasn't a part of this—his—world. She would cling to him like a lizard on a wall. But she had only approached him the one time, to hold her shawl while she played volleyball. Every other time he had been the one seeking her out—to ensure she didn't embarrass them both. It was only toward the end that he had begun to relax, breathing without fear that she was, after all, able to hold her own with the others. All in all, the evening hadn't been too bad.

But no, he thought now, he wouldn't be taking her today if Al hadn't reminded everyone. There was no point acting like a couple when it wasn't absolutely necessary.

He glanced at the clock. If she wasn't up in five minutes, he'd have to get her. Too bad he'd insisted she take the aspirins last night. There was, however, a small chance that she would still be hungover, in which case he could keep to his previous plans and go by himself.

Leila felt the light glow a faint red beneath her eyelids. Her dreams were always at their thickest and most vibrant in the mornings and now the warmth on her face pulled her awake. The first thing she saw was Neel, standing at the foot of the bed. And from that tall point the room began to take shape. The half-open door. The small circle that blazed like a lesser sun on the wall. Neel must have opened the blinds, letting in the day. He didn't move and she sat up in bed slowly, wondering what he wanted from her.

"How're you feeling?" Neel asked.

Leila pushed the hair from her face. "Fine." The word was more question than answer.

"You can thank those two aspirins," he said, and turned toward the closet door.

The two round pills she had taken with a large glass of water were like keys that opened the many doors of last night. The sand in her shoes, the white faces that reddened near the fire, the beer. Neel had warned her that she might wake up with a bad headache. But her head wasn't in pain; it just felt as if her brains weren't working at their usual pace.

What was he doing here, in the bedroom? Why hadn't he gone flying? And why was he holding out the blue T-shirt she knew was expensive because she had seen the same one in a store the other day?

"I let you sleep in, but we should leave in about forty-five minutes tops if we are to make it to the wedding on time," Neel said, and went into the bathroom.

He was getting ready for the wedding. His disappearing back, the offhand words, tightened Leila's heart with sadness and anger. Was he doing it again? Or was she *allowing* him to do it to her?

She remembered the time on the plane, when she looked away from his lying face and down at the rich, expansive beauty of this new country with its limitless possibilities. She had promised herself that she would wait to see how she would act. And today she had the chance to act in a way not possible in India. To be invited to a wedding the day before and to attend it. Even if her husband hadn't told her about it.

Or was she being unfair to Neel? Her mind grappled with the bits of hope that fluttered outside Pandora's chest. He *had* given her the pills last night and he *had* woken her up.

She would go. And she would enjoy herself, just like yesterday.

Wishing Neel had given her more time, she opened the suitcase that held her new sarees. The silks still smelled of India, a mixture of musk, incense, and a sharpness that recalled spices.

A wedding invitation generated so much excitement back home. Kila got to wear the one dress that was kept aside just for such occasions. Indy and she often exchanged sarees. Even Amma, who usually only cared that her clothes and face be clean, would get dolled up. The three girls would watch as Amma opened the Godrej almirah that held her good, going-out sarees. Then the chosen one, along with its matching blouse, was given over to one of them to iron. Kila especially loved the tin box that held Amma's meager collection of jewels. She was too young to know that the four extra bangles Amma slipped onto her wrists were paltry compared to the dozens worn by other women who loved to make unnecessary movements just to hear the rich jingle of gold against gold. The ridged bottle of Tata's eau de cologne, kept safely in the back of the almirah, was carefully opened and suddenly the whole room smelled of flowers. That scent was augmented by the short garland of star jasmine Amma wrapped around her bun. It was the sign that she was ready, pleased with the way her pallao lay across her chest, contented that the sindhoor was thick and red on her hair parting.

Leila's fingers rifled through the shiny layers in the suitcase, looking for a morning saree. Most of the new ones were meant for evening receptions, their colors dark and rich. Midnight blue, violet, burnt orange; she was beginning to worry she wouldn't find one when the bright colors of the Sunday-Monday saree peeked out from under the magenta one Smita had given her. It was perfect. Pink or yellow, it didn't matter.

She spread the saree on the bed, relieved that because she hadn't worn it, only the creases needed to be ironed. The blouse had been neatly pressed by the tailor and the petticoat, too, was in its original folds. Neel was still in the shower, so after ironing, she rushed to the other bathroom, anxious not to keep him waiting.

"You're not going in that," Neel pointed to the saree when she walked in, a little shy because the blouse and petticoat left her stomach completely exposed.

She picked up the saree quickly and held it against her torso.

"You don't like the color? I can change it to yellow." She turned the material over to the other side.

"This isn't a saree type of wedding. It's casual. I wouldn't be surprised if Al got married in jeans. I'm only wearing a sports coat because it might be chilly out there."

"So casual means you wear normal clothes?"

"It means the women will wear pants, not skirts or dresses." Frustration sharpened his words. "You can wear what you did to Oona's for dinner that night." Oona would probably come in an elegant ensemble that would fit in by standing out in just the right way.

"It's dirty," she said. Was this his way of putting up an obstacle?

"Then wear another pair. Just keep it simple."

"This saree *is* simple. It has a thin border with hardly any gold thread."

"Look, I'm just trying to help, all right? The wedding's in the backyard. No one's going to come in their Sunday best."

"Then it's a good thing I'm going in my Monday best," Leila said, and turned away as she starting draping the saree around her waist. Why did his idea of help seem so mean-spirited? And was she refusing to listen out of hurt or ignorance? She didn't know which other pair of pants to choose; she only understood Indian casual, which this saree represented. Back home she might wear it to see a new film, never to attend a wedding.

"You'll be the only one dressed up," Neel tried again. "Won't you feel odd?"

"I'll feel odder not being myself," Leila said.

Neel watched the saree wrap her into an Egyptian mummy. The

open doors of the closet just behind her contained rows of pants, tops, sweaters. Why was she insisting on being so Indian? If he were a typical old-fashioned husband, he could force her to listen to him. But his very modernness, his desire not to be her husband, left him dumb.

Leila's fingers moved automatically as she arranged the pallao. She had lost any pleasure in the ritual of getting ready. Neel was picking out his jacket. He wasn't the sort of husband who would kneel down and arrange the pleats so they fanned open with every step. Just as he wasn't the type of husband whom she could ask to explain the term "American casual."

It was only when she reached for the stick-on pottu that the excitement of going to her first American wedding returned. She had stopped wearing pottus at Neel's suggestion, agreeing that they didn't suit Western clothes.

The small dot nestled between her eyebrows. It was as if she were seeing it for the first time. No wonder Cynthia had been curious about it. In the past she hadn't noticed it because it was as much a part of her face as her lips and nose. But now, after so long an absence, the tiny circle stole attention away from every other feature. She raised her hand to remove it, then paused. The red felt changed color as she moved her head, but its meaning remained the same. The symbol of womanhood. This wasn't just her first wedding in America, it was her first wedding as a married woman.

They were in such a hurry and Neel's face was so stern that she didn't feel comfortable bringing up the issue of a present. It was only when he stopped the car that she asked, "This is where we are going to buy the present?"

"They don't want gifts," Neel said curtly. "And anyway, you wouldn't find a store here. It's a residential neighborhood. That's the house where they're getting married." He started climbing the stairs up to the door.

Somehow, even though he had told her it was going to be a backyard wedding, she had thought it would be in a church. She had never attended a Catholic wedding in India and was looking forward to a Julie Andrews–Christopher Plummer setting.

The backyard was rocky. The only sign that a wedding was going to take place was an archway decorated with roses. Everything else was stark and ordinary. Exactly like the guests, who looked as though they might be shopping in Safeway, except that they were here, wearing the type of pants Neel had said would be perfect for a casual wedding.

Her embarrassment was so complete that she forgot to pay attention and tripped on a flagstone.

Neel caught her arm.

"All right?" he asked.

She knew what he meant, but could not stop herself from confessing, "You were right," the words miserable and so softly spoken he had to bend to hear them.

"I did tell you . . ." He shrugged.

"I'm so sorry," she said, though what she really wanted to say was, *Take me home. I'll change. I'll even wear the dirty pants that aren't really dirty. I only wore them once.*

"Too late for that now," Neel said crisply, increasing his stride, eager to distance himself from her billowing pink presence. The breeze that blew down the leaves also whipped up her saree and she was struggling to keep it in place. The only help he was willing to provide was to usher her to one of the cast-iron chairs Al and Julia must use on warm days.

Leila tried to keep up, aware that her bright saree and hurricane arms gave her the appearance and movements of a clown.

"Thanks," she murmured as she sat down. Tears hovered in her voice, shimmered in the eyes that took in the unfussy, pastel clothes of the others.

Leila recognized many of the women from the previous night and wished with all her heart that she could be free like them. But the wind meant that she had to hold on to her pallao and her shawl, as well as her pleats, which kept opening and closing like an accordion gone mad. Her hair, too, was blowing all over her face and she marveled at the womens' short cuts that didn't get disheveled.

It was happening all over again. At home she was the outsider, the single girl who drew looks of "What, not yet?" and "Poor thing." Here, too, she was sitting at the edge, watching the others negotiate the terrain with ease, balancing wineglasses on rocky outcrops. She was so dwarfed by her misery that it was only when Oona was within touching distance that she noticed her.

"I'm so jealous of you, Leila. How I wish I could wear a saree."

Leila wished she could yank off the offending pink and hand it to Oona. Instead, she stilled the flyaway silk and said, "Not on a day like this, you don't."

"Not on any day." Sanjay laughed. "When my mother saw how tall Oona is, the first thing she said was 'How is that girl ever going to wear the saree I bought her?'"

"I tried, but there was so little material to tuck in, I was sure I would unravel at any moment. But you look absolutely stunning."

Leila was just about to shoot back with "Absolutely ridiculous" when Shanti joined them with "So this is where you all are hiding," a pale green Kashmiri shawl providing the only other Indian touch that Leila could see.

"Just trying to keep from blowing away," Leila said, aware that her saree had long ceased to be graceful. She could not stop thinking how out of place she looked, could not stop mentioning her gaffe.

"It's starting," Neel came to get them.

"Challo. We'd better go before Al accuses us of being the Indian Mafia." Sanjay said, laughing.

Neel stood beside Leila, his earlier irritation increased by Sanjay. Why was it that Sanjay always turned more Indian when Leila was around? He would never say "Challo" in the hospital. And thank God Leila had better control of that damned saree. She had wrapped her shawl tightly around her body so only the bottom half flapped against his legs.

Leila felt that the nightmare she had anticipated for yesterday's barbecue was happening today. Her every expectation was being proved wrong. The clean-cut man she had assumed was Al's son from his first marriage turned out to be the preacher. The bride wasn't even carrying a bouquet; and her sleeveless dress looked like a nightgown. The off-white material came to her calves, the only adornment the ruffles at the neck. Al's nod to being the groom was a tie, though contrary to what Neel had said, he was in slacks, not jeans.

People stood around in whatever space they could find. The wind kept snatching the preacher's words so Leila only heard half of what he said. She even missed Al saying "I do," but had full view of the kiss that went on for minutes, it seemed to her. Their second time around clearly had a happy beginning.

The big Italian spread that Sanjay had looked forward to was in the dining room. Leila went straight to a corner, trying to secret herself. But her bright pink couldn't be hidden and a number of the women she had envied came over to touch the saree, to marvel at its slipperiness, to tell her she looked lovely.

In India, compliments, if given, were usually backhanded. "Oh, where did you get this saree?" "Did I not see it in Saree Niketan?" which meant that it was good enough for them to buy. But no one would come right out and say, like these women, "It's so beautiful."

Were they being nice to her because they guessed she felt foolish? Little by little their smiling eyes and words relaxed Leila. It didn't seem possible that so many would pity her.

The heat roared out of the radiators and she hung the shawl over the back of her chair. The warmth was like India, and now that she didn't have to fight the wind, the saree draped around her perfectly, the pleats fanned out in flawless alignment. It might have been overkill to wear it, as Indy would say, but pants at a wedding would have left her feeling strange on the inside.

She held on to the glass of wine someone had offered when she came in. She was too afraid to drink any, given yesterday's experience, but didn't want to part with it. It made her feel like everyone else.

"Thank you so much for joining us today," Al said. Leila had been watching him make the rounds with Julia and now looked up into his blue eyes, which were set off by his white hair and deeper blue shirt.

"Can we get a picture with you?" Julia asked. Up close Leila noticed her dress was silk, embroidered with tiny white flowers.

People had been taking pictures with the disposable cameras meant just for that purpose.

"Neel," Al called out. "Can you do us the honor?"

Neel extricated himself from a group near the fireplace and came over.

"As Sanjay would say, 'Don't say cheese.'" Neel pressed a button and the flash went off.

"I feel like the mouse that got the cheese," Al joked. "Snapped with the two most beautiful women in the room. Thank you, my dear." He lifted Leila's hand and kissed it.

Leila just smiled, not sure what else to do. She wanted to say that his accent—and the gesture—reminded her of actors in films from the fifties, but thought he might feel she was aging him.

"How about one with the two of you?" Julia asked, and held out her hand for the camera.

The question froze Leila as she stepped toward her chair. She glanced in Neel's direction. Surely he would refuse. But no, he came beside her and even put an arm around her.

"Well, my dear," Al said, "you are giving your husband a run for his money. He used to be the best dressed one amongst us, you know. But not anymore."

The flash went off, and as before, Leila was momentarily blinded.

"You'll just have to get used to being second-best, Neel," Julia teased.

"Not for lack of trying." Neel laughed. "I did my best to get Leila to change into pants, but she refused to listen to me."

"A feminist!" Julia raised her fist in the air.

"I just know when I'm right," Leila said, and looked Neel in the eye.

Out of nowhere Neel felt her rightness, her ability to be comfortable just being herself, and wished he had it too. Then he thought how ridiculous he would feel in a kurta—and the feeling disappeared.

"Is that your second glass?" Hadn't she learned her lesson from the previous night?

"No, I haven't had any. It's just keeping me company."

"From what I could see, you've had lots of company."

"People are so nice here."

"Does that include me?" The question surprised both of them. Neel tried to hide it with a smile but knew it was too late.

"Only if you get me some food," Leila said. "I'm starving, but I can't figure out which items are vegetarian." His very question—this, from someone who preferred telling her things—allowed her to be honest and ask for help.

"I probably won't be able to either," Neel said. "But I can ask around."

When he returned with a plate piled with food, Leila had begun sipping the wine. Shanti and Oona had drawn up chairs beside her, telling her she was clever to have found the warmest spot in the house.

"Glad to see you're putting him to work," Shanti said.

"Oh, this was Neel's idea." Leila began eating.

"Nice," Shanti approved.

"Precisely," Leila said between mouthfuls. "How did you guess? It's Neel trying to be nice."

"And succeeding." Neel raised his glass. "To the Three Graces."

· TWENTY-FIVE ·

LEILA CONSIDERED "FALL BACK" a strange phenomenon, not just because India kept the same time year in and out, but because it was deceptive. It gave everyone an extra hour on the day the clocks moved backward, but for the rest of the winter it progressively did away with evenings, short afternoons quickly sunsetting into dark nights.

This night was even darker, with wind and rain drumming against the windows like a novice tabla player, all noise and no rhythm. It was like the monsoons, except that back home the wide-open windows brought in the rich smell of wet earth and the rain was warm, not stinging cold.

In the opposite building she could see the blue glare of a TV and just make out the contour on the couch. Another woman alone at night. Neel had gone flying. This morning she had hoped that maybe the two outings they had spent together would lure him away from his usual destination. But he had acted as usual. And so had she. She hadn't asked any questions and he hadn't told her any lies.

The woman in the other building switched off the TV and left the room. She had a life, as Rekha would say. Leila suddenly thought of Anu. Was Anu, too, looking out at the rain, thinking it was better to be with someone than to be alone?

The loud sound of the lock turning startled her. The air filled with the organic scent of rain, damp cotton, and masculinity. Neel walked carefully, trying to hold his coat and umbrella so they didn't drip all over the wooden floor.

"What are you doing?" he asked Leila.

What are you *doing home?* she countered silently. "I'm watching the rain," she answered.

"Rough night out there. Too dangerous to fly."

Not sure what to make of his unexpected presence, she stared outside, knowing that he had gone to place the umbrella in the bathtub.

"I'm starved," he announced, as he came back into the room. "Am I too late for dinner?"

"I haven't made anything. I was just going to cook something easy." The words came out like an apology and she immediately wanted to retract them. The response had been instinctive, the same any Indian wife would have said. But they were not husband and wife. He was a cheater, and she didn't want to continue being the subservient wife.

"Anything's fine by me." Tonight he had dropped off Caroline without suggesting dinner. He was surprised at how anxious he had been to escape her neediness.

Caroline had insisted on the trip to Sonoma, wanting to go even though it was foggy and on the cusp of rain. But it wasn't just the weather that made him reluctant. The poolside encounter had been a close call. Leila hadn't mentioned it, and he hoped she was too naive to suspect anything—unlike Sanjay, whose eyes had asked Neel what was going on, though he hadn't voiced his question. Neel regretted his semi-drunk confession at last year's Christmas party. He hoped everyone—especially Mr. Never-Stray-When-You-Are-Married Sanjay—had bought his explanation about the slides.

In the plane, Neel had handed the scarf to Caroline. "Please make sure that from now on you don't leave anything behind." He tried to soften the words, but they came out like an order.

"She saw it, is that it?"

"As a matter of fact, Jake found it and gave it to Lee thinking it was hers." Neel worried that Jake would discover that Jason didn't have a girlfriend. He didn't want them to see him as a husband who cheated on his wife. They wouldn't understand he had been forced to marry Leila, that he hadn't touched her, that continuing with Caroline technically wasn't cheating.

For Caroline, jealousy now took on a name: Lee. That's what Neel called his wife. The wife who had attended the barbecue. Who had gone to Reno. Caroline jammed the scarf into her purse. For a brief moment she hated him.

An anger Neel didn't quite understand made him say, "I have a feeling this storm isn't going away. I think we should give up the idea of that mud bath and dinner." He had suggested it because Caroline kept saying how awful it had been to leave Reno when all she wanted was to be with him. He was used to thinking of the plane as his refuge, not as a seesaw between two women.

Caroline burst out crying. Tears annoyed Neel. She sniffed and the sound grated on him like an instrument on glass. He handed her a tissue.

"I'm late." Caroline sobbed, because she wanted it to be true. It was a sure way of keeping Neel.

Fear, steel-cold and sharp, sliced into Neel's stomach. He thought he might throw up.

"How late?" He hoped, ordered her to say a day.

"Three days."

"I thought you were on the pill? Did you go off it?" he shouted. He'd kill her if she had. He was so careful he even paid for the pills.

"Oh Neel, of course I've been taking them. It's probably nothing. I shouldn't even have told you. I must be late because I've been so upset recently. Haven't you noticed how stressed I've been?" She wanted his anger to go away, wanted the evening they had planned to unfold. Why couldn't he kiss and comfort her?

"Let's hope that's what it is." He hadn't noticed anything unusual about her, too preoccupied with juggling the various compartments of his life. Now it had entered the plane, his haven. He felt like a dying man who sees his whole life before him, except that he was seeing the future: Caroline giving up her job to take care of the bulge beneath her sweater, the entire office knowing who caused that swell, Tattappa outraged . . . He knew that every time they had sex, no matter the precaution, there was always the chance a sperm would defy the odds.

He put another tissue into her trembling hand. Her nose was bright red, and a light pink highlighted the wrinkles around her eyes. Three years. Three years together, and he didn't even know her real age.

His marriage—and this—were both getting out of control. Should he make an appointment with a shrink? Sanjay had surprised Neel by admitting going to see a psychiatrist before his wedding. Neel had not expected Sanjay to be so American. And though Neel considered himself better adjusted, he couldn't divulge the various strata of his life to anyone, much less a stranger.

"Let's go back," he said, and this time he meant it.

IN THE BLACK AND WHITE KITCHEN, Leila cooked the meal she wanted to eat. It went against all of Amma's teachings, who prepared only those dishes Appa enjoyed. Leila knew this dinner was not heavy enough to be considered man's food. Amma used to make it the evenings Appa wasn't home, and her three daughters had always regarded it as a special treat.

Leila chopped onions, garlic, ginger, and green chili, and while they browned, cut potatoes into paper-thin slices. When the potatoes were semi-cooked, she added chunks of fresh tomatoes, a dash of Worcestershire sauce, salt and pepper, and let it simmer.

Amma had begun using the sauce only when Leila explained that yes, it was made by two Englishmen, but they had been trying to reproduce an Indian curry.

Sitting at the table, separated by the dish with no name, Neel thought, she looks so quiet. He remembered the night they had talked effortlessly, recalled her ease at the wedding and realized afresh that he didn't know much about her.

"How is your friend from Berkeley?"

"She's fine." Her mind on Caroline, Leila had to think for a moment before replying.

"Have you seen the campus yet?"

"No." Why was he talking to her? He never asked her anything personal. Except about ads and interviews.

"I can take you there one day if you like," Neel heard himself offering. They were married and slept in the same bed, and yet he had never done something as simple as drop her off somewhere.

"That's okay. Rekha usually comes to San Francisco."

"Have you seen her recently?"

"Yes. I did some translation for her."

"Really? For the university or for her personally?"

"For a woman at a shelter in San Francisco."

"And?"

"This woman could not speak English, so I went." She deliberately didn't tell him that she had signed on as a volunteer. Or that she was scheduled to start teaching at the YWCA as soon as they had need for her.

"Was it a bad case?"

"Not good, not bad." She, too, could talk the way he did.

"I see. How is your driving coming along?"

"I changed instructors," she informed him.

"Why? Wasn't he good?"

"He was a good driver, I'm sure, but he didn't treat me nicely.

Kept making comments about immigrants and how California isn't like it used to be."

"That's racist. You should have reported him."

"I did. It really shocked him. First I stopped the car while I was driving on Van Ness and told him not to shout at me and to take me back to the school. Then I spoke to his manager and so next week I will have a woman instructor."

"Good for you." Neel hadn't realized she had that much spunk. "Any news from your family?"

"Everyone is fine."

"How's your sister, the one who got into Mills?"

"She's good," she said, and added, "She may be getting married soon."

"What do you mean, may be?"

"Right now she is corresponding with a man who studies at Cambridge. They will see each other in a few months and then decide."

Neel remembered his first sighting of Leila and how he had been pleased by her looks and command of the English language. "What does he do at Harvard?"

"It's Cambridge, England. He studies economics. If it does work out, I'd like to go for the wedding."

"Sure, sure," Neel agreed, noticing the "I" and not "we." The Sunday of their meeting he had looked at her bent head and thought she would be a clinging wife. Now she was thinking of going to India by herself.

It was as if he were seeing her for the first time. Her black hair flowed over her shoulders, easily touchable. Her white caftan cast an upward glow, turning her skin into sunlit honey. Her face was bare of makeup, brown skin molded to the high cheekbones, and the eyes that Tattappa admired were outlined with long, dark lashes. Tattappa had said her eyes were made for dancing. Mummy had wanted to be a dancer, but she didn't have the right-shaped eyes. What kind of eyes do you need? Almond eyes, she had said. It was so funny, he ran to tell Tattappa. "Tattappa, Mummy wants almonds instead of eyes." Now he had a wife with the eyes his mother wanted.

Leila felt Neel staring and wondered if there was a smudge on her face. She pulled her hair into a bun and then excused herself. In spite of the cold, she was feeling hot and increasingly uncomfortable.

"What were you planning to do tonight?" Neel asked when she returned to the table.

"I was going to watch Zubin Mehta."

"Ah, Sanjay and Oona just went to hear him. They were raving about his conducting."

The phone rang. She didn't move. She waited for him to spring up from the chair like a suddenly released jack-in-the-box and run to the study. He always picked up the phone in the little room that was so clearly his she hardly ever entered it.

Once in a while she played out a scenario that began with the phone pealing and Neel racing to get it, shutting the door with a bang. In her mind's eye she gave them a few minutes before picking up the extension in the kitchen. Then she would hear for herself the voice that had brought its accent from France. Would the other woman be whispering sweet somethings into Neel's eager ear? In her fantasy, Leila interrupted their illicit words. She never said, "I'm sorry." Instead she interjected, "Oh, I thought you were finished." That was a clever line. If she said it, perhaps their affair would be finished.

This time, however, Neel reached for the extension on the kitchen wall.

"Oona, what a pleasant surprise! We were just talking about you."

Leila listened to his smooth voice easily speaking the white lies that would bring a smile to Oona's face. His plate was empty, as was the dish containing the curry. The fork lay beside the plate, unused. Neel had copied her and used his fingers, tearing the tortilla and scooping the vegetable with it.

"I know, I know, it's the perfect night to sit around the fireplace playing board games. But I'm afraid we'll have to beg out. It's just too wet. Another time, perhaps."

Neel patted his stomach as he returned to the table. "Dinner was very good, thank you. That was Oona. She called to see if we wanted to go over and play Scrabble, Monopoly, and some other games I've never heard of. I hope you don't mind, but I told her we couldn't."

"That's okay. I wanted to watch TV." She wasn't about to change her plans just because he had changed his and come home.

"I was wondering"—Neel laughed, surprised that he was so unsure of himself; it felt like he was on a first date with Leila—"would you like to play a game of Scrabble? It's been years since I've played, but it is a fun game."

Competing emotions staked their claim in her. Anger, sadness, scorn. And most astonishingly, happiness. She wished she could say, "No, thank you," just like that, with no reason. Instead she said, "Okay." This was what she had longed to hear when she first arrived in San Francisco. But Neel had hardly been home and never stayed long enough to talk, much less make words on a board. Now, on an evening she was to spend on her own, he was proposing they pick letters and play for points.

"Have you played it before?"

Irritation punched out her answer. "Yes, of course I have."

Twenty minutes later, Leila leaned against the sofa and contemplated the letters in front of her. I E N T R P and S. Should she shock him with PENIS? She decided on the safer route and adding an S to his GOAL, made SPRINT.

"You aren't beating me," Neel complained, "you're killing me. Why didn't you warn me how good you are?" But in fact, he enjoyed her prowess. She was clever and imaginative and had already made use of two triple-word scores.

"You didn't ask. You thought I didn't know how to play," Leila pointed out. The 100-point difference in their score gave her an insouciance she had never known.

"Why can't there be an earthquake when I need one?" Neel sighed. "Just a tiny one that shifts the board so we have to call it a draw? Or maybe I should pour you a beer and addle your brains."

Leila giggled.

"What are you laughing at?" Neel demanded. "I'm just about to make my comeback. Watch this." He put down ZEBRA.

"I'm not laughing at you. It's Zubin Mehta. Doesn't he look like a monkey?"

Arms going this way and that, face contorted, Mehta did look funny, and Neel began laughing. "He gets paid a lot of money to do that, you know. We should be more respectful."

"Oh, I do respect him. It's just all that gesticulating and jumping around seems so at odds with the serious business of conducting. Incidentally, AD is not a word. It's an abbreviation."

"Since when have abbreviations not been considered words?"

"Since Scrabble was invented. So I'm afraid ZEBRA is out. No triple letter for your zed."

"It's zee in America," Neel corrected her. "People don't understand when you say zed."

"I've already used it. They thought I was British."

"Ah, the good old British who left us our accents and nothing else."

"I wouldn't say that. What about trains, a divided subcontinent, and a ridiculous regard for white skin?" Leila said.

"I think they're still using the same maroon bogeys from before

Independence." Neel laughed. "God, those things are old and filthy."

"I must have traveled in one of those because it had an English toilet. No seat, and no one seemed to know how to use it, but there it was, very upright and very dirty."

"Yuk." Neel shivered.

"Do you value white skin?" he asked curiously a moment later. Perhaps if she had been much fairer she would have been married earlier.

Leila thought of long white legs.

"Skin is like the cover of a book . . ." she began.

". . . and only the inside matters," Neel finished impatiently. "That's all well and true, but I think many Indians feel intimidated, inferior to whites."

She hadn't felt that way and so far had no reason to.

"Is that how you feel?" It was the first personal question she had asked him in the States.

Neel sighed. "Well, I don't like it when a policeman pulls me over but not the car that's going faster. Or when a salesperson goes past me to help a white customer."

"But why does that make you feel inferior?"

"How would it make you feel?"

"Like it's more their country than mine. Do you think Sanjay and Shanti feel inferior?" She knew the answer, but asked him anyway.

"Don't know." Neel laughed. "How did we get on this topic anyway?"

"Blame the British," Leila said. "And now I have to thank them for adopting a Hindi word." She put down COOLIE. "All my vowels in one fell swoop," she said with satisfaction.

"Hey, I was going to make CLAY in that spot. Now what am I going to do?"

"Save it for another game," Leila said blithely. "That was my final word."

"One hundred and fifty–point difference!" Neel looked at their scores. "Would I feel this bad if I'd lost by ten points?"

"Absolutely. Just ask the silver medalist at the Olympics."

"Thanks a lot. I guess losers put things away?"

"Yes." Leila stood up. "And I shall go celebrate with a long shower."

As she felt the water heat her body, she considered the evening. This was the closest Neel had come to behaving like a husband. And at home there was no audience to play to, unlike at the barbecue and the wedding.

Why had she responded to him? Was this how she wanted to act?

Steam swirled around her as she turned this way and that under the jet of water. She loved taking showers. Back home they couldn't afford a geyser so it was always a bucket of cold water. When she finally stepped out, she could hear Neel in their bedroom.

"I'm almost done," she called, slipping on her robe.

He surprised her by walking in.

"I can't see a thing." He peered into the foggy mirror.

"Why do you need to see yourself brushing your teeth?" Leila asked.

"Because I want to make sure I'm still here?" He grinned.

"In that case, let me give you something else to look at," and with her index finger she wrote across the mirror: "I won!"

Neel laughed. "I never knew you were so competitive."

"Just victorious."

"I could have won, you know. Had a chance to use a triple-word score, but I didn't know how you'd react if I made coitus."

"I was going to make penis. Only I didn't want to embarrass you."

The shower had softened Leila's skin. Neel noticed that her cheeks were pink and damp twists of hair drifted around her face. She wasn't wearing a bra and he could see the dark rounds of her nipples. Was her waist as small as in Ooty? His parent-picked wife wasn't bad at all. She was Tattappa's choice, too. But—she was a virgin. She would not know how to respond to a caress or a kiss. If she was a typical Indian girl, she had never kissed anyone. He hadn't either, till he came to Stanford. Before his first time he had read Masters and Johnson, and tried to pretend he had lots of experience.

Leila braided her hair in the bedroom, then got into bed. It was another cold and fog-obscured night, but she was warm. She now knew what a penis looked like and exactly what coitus involved. American libraries didn't have plastic covers on books.

She heard the whine of his electric toothbrush, the steady rain of urine followed by three spurts. Flush. She curled into her corner of the bed as his heavy steps echoed in the largely empty bedroom.

Neel's eyes quickly adjusted to the dark. She was off in her corner, probably asleep. Or was she? Maybe they could talk a little. This was something else they had never done before.

"Lee," he whispered.

She wasn't going to acknowledge this name he had given her.

"Lee," he tried again, then sighed, settling into the mattress. It was a virgin, like her. He had bought it a few weeks before the India trip.

Leila wondered what would have happened if she had answered him. She looked at the moon, a bright fingernail floating in the sky. "It is the same moon in America," Indy had said. But in India Neel had not liked her. Tonight was the first time she had felt his enjoyment at being with her. This was the feeling she had wanted to bring home from Ooty. Not love, that would have been too quick, but enjoyment. Now Leila heard his breathing grow steady and the small movements of getting comfortable in bed ceased. She felt his body come closer and suddenly her neck stiffened. Didn't he know he was on her braid? She tried to move, but her head was held in place by his weight. She couldn't even try to free the braid because her back was to him. She couldn't sleep like this.

"Neel."

No answer.

"Neel," a little louder.

He moved and suddenly she was free.

"You were lying on my hair." Leila started to braid her hair again.

He wondered how it would feel to have that hair tent his face. His hands touched the shiny strands, lingering, sliding over her face. She didn't say anything and his fingers cupped the smooth moulds of her face. She had almost made penis, he remembered. He had wanted to make coitus. He kissed her.

A roller coaster started in Leila's stomach. She didn't respond initially, almost catatonic, her heart thudding to the anxious knowledge that the auspicious night had finally arrived. Then she was suddenly aware that once again she was pinned on the bed. This time her caftan had got caught between them. She shifted, moved her hand to adjust the material, and didn't see his face descending. Her hand hit his nose.

"I'm sorry, I'm sorry," Leila apologized.

"Shh, it's okay. Okay?"

He was asking her permission. Something held her back. Why now? Should she spurn him as he had her? His body was warm, his weight a pleasant thing to bear. Even as she struggled to come to grips with thoughts of anger, she started to melt. This was what she had wanted and dreamed of since the morning he had come to see her. Now he was approaching her, about to reveal the mystery of sex to her. As she continued to lie beneath him, the months of rejection, the fury and shame came together in a ball and she flung it aside, aware only that he wanted her. His desire for her was a strange and satisfying triumph.

Warmth and wetness surged through her and she felt desire loosen her limbs. Even though she knew he had been with another woman, she felt victorious. He was with her now. His shifting weight pressed against *her* breast, *her* stomach.

Neel kept kissing her, and with every kiss, her response grew deeper and longer. She didn't speak at all, just "Uh-huh" when he asked, "You safe?" Her heart stopped when he sat up. But he only unbuttoned his shirt and flung it on the floor. She caught him back in her arms. When he swung her on top, she lost that inebriated feeling and buried her face in his neck.

"Yes," he said softly, "kiss me," and she did, covering his neck with her mouth. She was boneless, her blood so hot she couldn't feel the cold air though her caftan had long ago been taken off.

She never stopped him, just kept pace. Maybe she wasn't a virgin. Neel looked down at her face, surprised at his disappointment, wanting to read her eyes, but they were closed.

Leila was wary when he parted her legs. She held her breath, wondering if it would hurt. She lay still, waiting to become a wife.

Neel felt her sudden tenseness, and almost stopped. Did she not want this? Then he knew. She was scared. He was her first. A tenderness, a desire to make sure she not feel any pain slowed him down.

"Did I hurt you?" he whispered.

She didn't say anything, just pressed the hand that had reached out and clasped hers. *Caesar plowed her and she cropped.* The line from Shakespeare surfaced and suddenly made sense.

She lay awake for a long time, listening to his racing heart, which slowed down only when his breathing was even. How could he sleep? She could not stop thinking of all that they had done.

· TWENTY-SIX ·

THE NEXT MORNING, Leila wanted to run and look at herself in the mirror. That's what Amber did after she slept with the king. Would she look as different as she felt?

Neel was asleep, their bodies facing each other, making a slight V in the mattress. In all her yesterdays she would have risen, taken a shower, and started her day without expecting anything from him. Now she closed her eyes, wanting him to be the first to awaken, talk, maybe even make love. They had fallen asleep without putting on their clothes. She had never slept in the nude before and was amazed how warm she felt.

Neel opened his eyes, not quite awake from the deep sleep that had been cluttered with dreams. He felt someone watching him and it all came back. Lee. Last night. She was smiling at him, her face so close he could almost count each of those incredible lashes. Not sure how to respond, he looked at the clock.

"Oh shit, oh my God, it's eight!"

"We slept in." Leila's voice was a little hoarse.

"I've gotta go." He pushed back the covers and tried not to feel embarrassed as he walked to the bathroom. When he was young he had developed a bad case of acne on his ass and typically made sure to keep it covered.

"I'll make it up to you, Leila," he called out above the hum of the razor. "Be home early tonight."

In ten minutes he was at the front door. By then Leila had brushed her teeth and changed.

"Neel."

He turned, hand on the knob.

"Have a good day." Leila came up and kissed his cheek.

A cable in a Muni bus had separated itself from the tangle of wires overhead and traffic was backed up for blocks. Neel felt impotent behind the wheel. At least in India one could honk and make noise. There was enough turmoil in his life without traffic making him late. His first operation was scheduled for 8:45 a.m. He had never been late.

The passengers in the next car were looking out of their windows, faces tilted to the sky. The Blue Angels were flying, making lots of noise with their precision patterns in the air.

Caroline! He hadn't thought of her until now. All this time he had only wondered how to avoid Leila so he could carry on with Caroline. Now he hoped he didn't have to see her. Maybe her period had come. He didn't want to think—even briefly—that she might be pregnant.

Sanjay was someone else he didn't want to run into. Mr. Pure-as-driven-snow Sanjay had probably only been with one woman, and that too without any mess. Neel knew that Sanjay would expect him to dump Caroline. Most days he, too, wanted out of their seedy, needy relationship.

Then he recalled Leila kissing him good-bye. Why had she done that? What did she expect?

The driver fixed the cable and, like the others around him, Neel stepped on the gas.

Leila felt like an American wife. She had desperately wanted moments like these and they were finally happening. She couldn't sit still, couldn't stop smiling, couldn't stop thinking about last night. She went back to bed, and in her mind saw Neel reaching for her. She could still smell him. Helen Keller had said she could smell the musk of a young man in any room she entered. Leila, too, could breathe the essence of Neel. Not his aftershave, but the maleness beneath it that recalled strong brown skin, sweat, and that which kept trickling out all morning.

She wanted to hear his voice but didn't call in case Madam Fake answered. She was no longer jealous of the woman, she just didn't want to have any reminder of Neel's past. He was hers now.

She was about to start on dinner when the phone rang. If it was one of those annoying telemarketers who always mispronounced their surname she would not hang up. She would say that both Mr. and Mrs. Sarath were on an extended honeymoon.

It was Neel. She loved the deep sound of his voice, that he was calling her Leila. There was a birthday party for Patrick and he had to show his face. He'd be home a half hour late, maximum.

She had been wanting him to come home to her ever since she arrived in San Francisco.

Once the clock sounded seven, she began to grow nervous. He'd said half an hour, but it could be any time now. In the past, cooking had always calmed her. The routine of chopping, stirring, frying, tasting, had been familiar, a balm to anxiety. Today she had wanted to cook an erotic meal, wondering if he, too, would get the moist suggestiveness of eggplant, the obvious sex appeal of zucchini. Now she understood why a woman she once saw on TV had said filling up the car was erotic. Everything reminded her of sex. She kept checking the pots, opening the oven, running to the bathroom to ensure she looked nice. She was wearing blue jeans and a new olive green sweater. When she'd tried it on last week, another customer in the changing room had told her she looked fabulous.

The door opened. She didn't run to him, but stayed in front of the stove. Her fingers trembled as she felt him crossing the floor toward the kitchen. She wanted to go up to him like in the morning, but was too shy. He could probably smell the brownies, maybe even the spaghetti that was almost done.

"Hi. I got you some cake." Neel proffered the small package, grateful to have something to hold between them. He'd been busy at the hospital, but not so occupied that he didn't think back to last night or the evening ahead. How was she going to be? And he? He hadn't planned to make love to her. It had just happened. Midway through the day he figured he'd just let this evening happen, too.

It didn't seem to be happening, he thought. She had barely turned around and didn't meet his eyes.

"It's chocolate?" He tried a second serve. It was like playing on a clay court. You didn't know how the ball was going to land or if your partner was going to hit it back to you.

"My favorite," Leila said, finding her voice. She didn't tell him about the brownies. It was so sweet—literally—of him to bring something for her.

"Let's share it," she suggested.

"Before dinner?"

"Why not? We can do whatever we want." She handed him a fork.

"You know, I've always wanted to eat dessert first, so yes, why not?"

Neel lingered over the meal, concentrating on the food so he could avoid her eyes. He had been nervous to open the front door, aware that his "I'll make it up to you" had been empty words, something to fill in the gap between waking and leaving. He wanted to say, "I wasn't thinking last night. I shouldn't have slept with you, and now I don't know what to do." But he couldn't bring himself to form those words.

After dinner, he took the easy route and suggested a movie. They wouldn't have to talk and it would take up at least two hours.

"I'll make popcorn, if you get the movie," Leila said.

"Don't you want to see one of the new movies in the theater?"

"It's so much nicer at home," Leila said.

"You'd better come with me, then. I don't know what you've seen." This was just one in the long list of things he didn't know about her.

"You mean the bits and pieces of movies I've seen. When they showed *Annie Hall*, it lasted forty-five minutes only. Indy and I wanted our money back, but the man laughed in our faces."

"I haven't seen *Annie Hall* either. Shall I get it?"

The movie proved a good choice. They both had to concentrate on the dialogue, and when it was over, he didn't have to fake being tired. He could barely answer Leila's question: "Why did the censor board cut so much in India?"

By the time Leila showered and brushed her teeth, he was already asleep.

The next day, Neel awoke to the predicament that he had switched days with Dr. Stael. It would be churlish to fly without inviting Leila. Though right now his plane didn't feel like a sanctuary.

"Do you need to buy some more clothes?" he asked during breakfast, thinking he could drop her off and not have to worry about finding things to do, at least in the morning.

"I have enough."

"Even for interviews?"

"Yes. The saleslady told me I just need one good suit for that and I bought a blue one."

"Great. Well—" Neel took a bite of toast. It was so crunchy a section broke off and landed on the floor.

"Oops, sorry."

Leila laughed. "Remember how Sanjay wanted to toast us?"

"Ah, Sanjay, I'm sure his little patients appreciate his sense of humor." Neel stood up. "I think—" he started, as Leila said, "Do you think—"

There was an awkward silence as each waited for the other to continue.

"Ladies first," Neel said.

"Since you are free today, I thought maybe we could go to the Golden Gate Park? But you were going to—"

He was faced with the first request she had ever made. "Oh, nothing," he said. The tune-up he was going to get done was something he'd concocted. It could easily wait another month. "I guess. Sure," he said. "What do you want to see there?"

An hour later, Neel turned to Leila in the car. "Are you sure there are supposed to be buffaloes here?"

"That's what it says in the guidebook."

"Well, I'm relieved to see the enclosure. I thought they might be roaming free."

"Like the pigs and cows and dogs back home. That's why I wanted to see them, actually. I miss those animals running all over the roads—streets. Is there any place you want to see?"

"Nope. This is my first time in the park and unlike you, I didn't read the guidebook."

"You've never been here?"

"I also haven't seen Alcatraz or Coit Tower. I keep thinking there will be time for all that."

"Then maybe we should park the car and walk," Leila suggested.

The green grass was as inviting as a red carpet. It was a weekday, but there were people everywhere. A group of women were stretching to tai chi. Several young boys flicked a Frisbee. Workers were erecting a stage and fences for the upcoming dog show. Couples lay together under the trees. Leila was happy to be part of this large family.

The children, couples, parents, reminded Neel that he was a

husband. It seemed to him that Leila was even walking closer to him as their steps continued past the Steinhart Aquarium.

"Want to go in?" Neel remembered the two-headed snake he had read about.

"It's such a glorious day," Leila said. "Let's stay outside." She didn't want to lose his company to display cabinets and darkened rooms where they would have to speak in whispers, if at all. In the Botanical Garden in Ooty he had kept his distance, taking photographs she had never seen.

They had walked a little farther when Neel saw a sign near the elaborate metal gates. "How about the Shakespeare Garden? Isn't that what you used to teach?"

Leila had somehow missed the garden when looking at the map. But when they went in, she was disappointed. Like its location, the garden seemed an afterthought. No bust of Shakespeare, just a few flowers and a large sundial.

She walked toward the back wall.

"Watch it," Neel said sharply. But it was too late. Concentrating on what lay ahead, Leila hadn't seen the sprinkler and didn't hear its sputtering approach. Neel sidestepped, but a passing arch of cold water doused her left side.

"Should we go back?" Neel looked at her wet sleeve.

"It's just a little damp," Leila said.

Four metal plaques were fixed to the wall. Leila approached one end. It was etched with lines from various plays.

"Are there more quotes on your side?" she asked.

"*Root of hemlock digged i' th' dark,*" he read the unfamiliar words slowly. "*Liver of blaspheming Jew.*"

"One of the witches in *Macbeth*," Leila said immediately.

"Impressive," Neel heard himself say. "But which scene and act?"

"Toward the end I think, so Act Four?"

"Very good."

"It always bothered me that Shakespeare could be so racist."

"Well, no racism that I can see in this one," Neel said as he read on: *"And in his blood that on the ground lay spill'd, A purple flower sprung up, check'red with white.* A little macabre, isn't it?"

"I don't think that's a play," Leila said slowly, trying to recall where she had read those lines. *"Venus and Adonis?"*

"Yes. I thought Shakespeare only wrote plays?"

"No, he also wrote long poems."

"Here's your last one, and if you get it right, I'll never quiz you on Shakespeare again," Neel said. *"What's in a name—"*

"Romeo and Juliet," Leila interrupted.

"How did you know? I didn't even get a chance to finish it."

"Everyone knows that one," she dismissed him.

"I guess that's what makes me special. I'm not everyone," Neel joked, though he was feeling a little intimidated.

"But you have the complete set of Shakespeare," Leila said.

"Doesn't mean I've read it. It's another one of those 'I'll do later' items."

Neel was still thinking of Shakespeare as he brushed his teeth that night. After dinner, Leila had pulled down the copy he had picked up from some going-out-of-business bookstore in Palo Alto and said it was no wonder he hadn't read a word. His edition contained the complete plays, poems, and sonnets, but no notes. Neel listened to her go on about various editions, though he didn't really understand the differences. When she recommended a particular one, he asked her to buy it.

He had just started flossing when the bathroom door opened and Leila's face appeared in the mirror.

"I'm almost done," Neel said.

"Okay if I brush my teeth?" Leila asked.

"Sure." He was standing directly in front of the sink. The

Anne Cherian

effect of her sudden appearance traveled to his fingers, and when he turned on the faucet for her, water gushed into the sink and sprayed them.

"Oops, sorry. We seem to have trouble with water today," he tried to make light of his nervousness.

"Not with water. With you. This morning in the Shakespeare Garden you didn't give me enough warning and now you deliberately got my sleeve wet."

"I did not," he defended himself and then laughed when he saw her smiling. "I did save you from falling at Al's wedding," he reminded her.

"You could have really saved me by insisting I wear pants," Leila joked. "I feel so overdressed every time I think of it."

"I remember it quite differently. You were acting like a queen, with long lines of admirers waiting to compliment you. The same ones who told me I didn't look good anymore." Neel wiped his face and left.

He was propped up under the covers, a book resting on his knees, when she came to the bedroom. But instead of turning the pages, he was turning over the events of the past days in his mind. They still hadn't talked about Sunday night. He had wanted to bring it up, but there had never been the right opportunity. Time had gone by quickly, effortlessly. During lunch at a Chinese restaurant she had surprised him—again—by knowing how to use chopsticks. She tried teaching him, only to give up and call him a hopeless case when he speared an eggplant after numerous unsuccessful efforts to pick it up the right way. "You can't give up so easily," she said.

They wandered through Chinatown and he enjoyed watching her face become a visual "Oh" when he informed her that those brown things hanging in the windows were horse penises.

"They're ox tongue," Neel relented, laughing and continuing, "I can't believe you believed me."

But she defended her naïveté, saying, "The Chinese eat chicken feet, so why not every part of the horse? As if ox tongue is any better."

Before he could respond, she darted into a store.

"You want something?" he asked.

But she was just happy to handle the various items, she said, reminding him that back home products were kept behind a counter and had to be pointed at if one wanted a closer look. Everything was touchable here, she said. Including her, Neel thought. He had never seen her look so animated before.

He kept forgetting that she represented an arranged marriage and his family's interference. He could not understand how he could enjoy himself with her when he had started out not even wanting to talk to her.

He watched her enter the bedroom. She walked so softly, her movements gentle and unhurried. Now she, too, was getting a book to read. They were like an old married couple, reading before going to bed. She told him she was filling the gaps in her reading of American literature. She had only taken one course in college and was systematically going through Melville and Hawthorne, books she checked out of the library. She settled into her side of the bed.

Neel, who had planned and plotted his life—making a list at a young age—felt out of control.

He closed the book.

"Everything okay?" Neel didn't know he had sighed until Leila spoke.

"Yes," he lied. "I'm just tired."

"You missed some toothpaste," Leila's finger dabbed the fleshy left corner of his lips.

Their eyes met and her hand remained suspended. He was suddenly aware that he was staring. Look away, look away, he told himself, but he couldn't. He concentrated on the strand of hair that was entangled in her eyelashes. Did it hurt her?

She moved closer, bringing with her that perfume he still couldn't place.

"We shouldn't. I mean, we can't," Neel said, finding his words.

"Why?"

"Because, well, because," and he remembered, "we don't have any condoms."

"Can't you use something else?"

The question hung in the air between them for a second and then found his genitals. She knew so little. His partners in the past had been well prepared, some even carrying their own condoms. He had always been uncomfortable about being one in a long line, worried as to how he compared to the others who had come before him. With Leila, he didn't have to worry. He was the first and only one, and her lack of experience engulfed him with desire. She didn't have a diaphragm that had stopped the semen of other men. She didn't take the pill to make her safe for anyone. "Can't you use something else?" she had asked, as if he had all the answers.

He remembered the package Ashok had given him. "Wait, I'll be right back." He went to find the travel bag.

He didn't want to think as he unzipped the black case and found the packet of condoms. His hands and legs seemed to have taken over anyway. One opened the square, silky package and the other took him back to bed.

· TWENTY-SEVEN ·

WEDNESDAY DAWNED AS DULL and rainy as Caroline's mood. She was anxious to get to work and see Neel. The weather was supposed to clear, but the gray skies didn't look like they were about to disappear any time soon. It would be a good night for staying in. Her short period had come and gone and there was no need for Neel to stay away. She had even turned down dinner with her brother to be with Neel.

She wished the day would hurry into evening. They always had dinner on Wednesdays and she wanted tonight to be special. Candles, champagne, chocolate: the three Cs she always splurged on with her lovers in times of uncertainty.

She wanted Neel to forget the outside world, and most of all she wanted him to forget that awful day on the plane. She should never have told him she was late. She had never seen him so angry, and it was the first time he had cancelled a trip with her.

Neel lingered on at the hospital, not wanting to leave the safe haven of the antiseptic building. He had forgotten about the dinner until Caroline paged him. It had forced him to cancel plans with Leila. Claiming she missed Indian food, she had suggested they go to New Delhi. Neel had balked, then noticed the smile in her eyes. "It's a restaurant that just got a great review," she said, and he was looking forward to it.

The streets were crowded with evening traffic and the slow, creaking cable car caused further delay. Ordinarily, Neel would have been like the man in the next car, constantly changing lanes in a futile attempt to get ahead. Stuck behind the San Francisco trademark filled with leaning, beaming tourists, Neel thought of Caroline's neat apartment, the full-size bed, the shelf on which she placed her collection of miniature Teddy bears, and the lamp she sometimes draped with a scarf.

Her period—along with his anger and the confusing developments with Leila—had kept him away until now. He had even managed to avoid her until today. She had been so understanding, apologetic, anxious to get back to their evenings.

As he walked up the stairs, an elderly couple passed him and the man said, "Evening. Haven't seen you in a while." Were people watching him? What the hell was he doing here, anyway?

He was just about to turn back when Caroline opened the door. She must have heard his footsteps.

"Sweetie, come sit by the fire. Can I get you something to drink?" When he hadn't arrived by six thirty she'd started worrying. He *had* to come; she had to romance him back to the old days.

This evening she'd waited nervously, moving from chair to sofa to chair, afraid the phone would ring and it would be Neel cancelling on her or her brother asking if she'd decided to forgo the show and have dinner with him. Caroline had lied about the tickets. What else could she do? Tell Dan that things were rocky with Neel? She needed to be with Neel, even though this was the only evening Dan would be in town. She couldn't tell Dan the truth, that she couldn't postpone dinner with Neel because, well, he was married and their time together was limited. Dan would insist she break it off—even without meeting Neel. It was so easy for other people to tell her to leave Neel; and the reasons didn't matter. He's Indian, he's married, he's stringing you along. They didn't understand that Neel was the best man she had ever gone out with and now he was her only hope. She had invested too much not to fight for him, for them.

And now Neel was here and they had the whole evening together.

"Nothing right now, thank you." Neel stared into the fake fire. The cement logs looked real, but the flames gave out more light than warmth. "A Stone Age TV," Leila had called the leaping, addictive reds and yellows of the fire he had lit during their Scrabble game.

Caroline surreptitiously touched the red silk underwear she had bought yesterday. "Let me give you a massage." She came up behind him.

Neel submitted to her touch and closed his eyes against the glare of the flames. He was in a position most men dreamed of. If only his college friends could see him now. Here he was, being ministered to by a beautiful white woman who a hundred years ago would never have considered him a man, much less a lover.

Caroline loosened his shirt and rubbed the cold from her hands before touching his neck. She crouched behind him, happy to be there. Flesh against flesh, she worked to untie the knots in his back. She desperately wanted to take them back to the days when nothing stood in the way of her confidence.

"Mmm, that's better. Can I have that something to drink now?" He didn't bother offering to help, just stayed where he was, the strain almost completely gone from his body.

"Champagne?" he raised an eyebrow. "How extravagant."

"You're worth it." Caroline smiled. "To us." She raised her glass. She was so nervous, she misjudged and banged Neel's glass. Golden liquid spilled onto the carpet.

"Your good carpet." Neel dabbed at the spot with a napkin.

"Just leave it," Caroline insisted. "I'll get it later." Tonight she didn't care about the small Persian prayer rug Neel had bought for her at an auction.

"You sure?"

"Yes. To us," she said again, and this time was more careful.

Neel regarded her with half-closed eyes. She looked like the angel on top of the office Christmas tree. Except that he could reach out and touch her. At one time he would have done just that, rejoicing in her body and how she responded to him.

"Can we have some music now?"

"Of course. Anything you want."

Neel fiddled with the knob. Their first night together, she had seduced him. It was she who had taken command, he who had followed her to the bedroom, tail wagging like a puppy. Things had changed so much since then.

"Do you think you can strip to this?"

Caroline stood up immediately, relieved that he wanted her, but uncomfortable and almost shy. This was and was not the evening she had envisioned when lighting the candles and putting the champagne on ice. She wasn't used to him being the initiator. The music was slow but she tried to marry herself to its rhythm as she removed her jeans and the striped silk shirt.

Neel was beginning to enjoy himself. Men paid money to see this. He poured himself some more champagne, not taking his eyes off her. All she had on were bikini panties. The red glowed against her skin and he knew, puffy and soft beneath the silk, was hair the same color as on her head.

"Stop," he ordered. He didn't want her naked.

As if his words were a leash, she stopped. She approached him slowly, not just to delay the delight but also to try and take some control. She kneeled in front of him, knowing exactly how she would gain complete mastery.

Leila's black hair floated in front of Neel's eyes. He recalled the pleasant aroma of her skin, her teeth nipping at his neck, her taste. How surprised he'd been by her eagerness, her willingness to explore and lead.

The longer he looked at Caroline, the less he wanted her. He stood up, knowing he was doing the right thing. He had started something with Leila. And he had to figure out where that was going.

Disappointment gripped Caroline so hard that for a moment she couldn't say anything, couldn't think. Then the doorbell rang. Dan. It had to be Dan.

"Stay, please stay," Caroline said softly. "Let's ignore it. Just some kids playing around." The evening had been like an obstacle course, starting with whether or not Neel would even show up. Now they were at the final hurdle. If he stayed into the night, Caroline would know she had won him back. All she had to do was make sure he didn't leave now.

"I'll tell them off on my way out." Neel walked toward the door.

"No, Neel, please—" Caroline said, quickly putting on her discarded clothes. What hold did the unwanted wife have on him? Sex had always worked in the past.

"It's just kids," he said. "I promise I won't let them get a peek at you."

Neel was surprised by the burly figure outside the door. "What do you want?"

The blue eyes narrowed in surprise. "This Caroline Kempner's apartment?" the man asked, even as he checked the number on the door.

"Yes," Neel answered.

"I'm her bro—Sis," he broke off, as Caroline came into view behind Neel. "I came to drop this off," he indicated a package, his voice loud and jovial. "Then I heard the music and—" His voice trailed off as he noticed the candles, the champagne glasses, Caroline tucking in her shirt, and Neel.

"Dan." Caroline reached up and kissed his cheeks, fingers trembling on his broad shoulders. "Neel, this is my brother Daniel. Dan, this is Neel. Dan's in town for just this evening and I wasn't sure we'd be able to meet."

"Well, little sister, I was free. You were the one with tickets for a show. I thought you couldn't cancel them."

Neel wished he had left ten minutes ago, wished he had never come over. It was clear that Caroline didn't want him to meet her brother. Otherwise why tell so many lies? He felt his face grow hot. Sanjay used to joke that Indians were embarrassment-free because they didn't blush, but Neel could feel the blood pour into his cheeks.

"Actually, I was on my way out." Neel reached for his coat.

"No, you're not." Caroline inserted herself between Neel and the door. "Please stay, Neel. Dan, now that you're here, why don't you join us for dinner?"

"I don't want to interrupt your plans."

Caroline was still blocking his way and Dan hadn't made any move to leave. He was glaring at his sister, his voice devoid of any warmth. Was he that angry about her lie? Suddenly Neel knew why Caroline had not wanted to answer the door, why she hadn't invited them both to dinner.

"I'm taking off," Neel said and stepped around Caroline.

"You don't have to, not on my account," Dan said.

"Neel, please don't go." Caroline had tears in her eyes, her hand on his sleeve. "I'm sure Dan would like to get to know you. Wouldn't you, Dan?"

"Sure I would. But he said he's leaving. Another time, then. Neal, did you say?"

"Neel. Well, Suneel."

"That's a new one. Suneel," Dan tested the name. "Mexican, is it?"

"Indian. Suneel Sarath." Not sure why he felt impelled to present his credentials, Neel added, "I'm a doctor at the hospital Caroline works at."

"We don't get too many Indians our way. First time I saw any was in New York City. Taxi drivers. With those things on their heads. What do you call them?"

"Turbans," Neel said crisply.

"How come you aren't wearing one?" Dan asked.

"Different religion." Neel wished he could end the conversation and leave.

"Those drivers," Dan shook his head, "couldn't speak much English. Your English is pretty good."

"So is yours," Neel said quietly.

The men stared at each other.

Dan was the first to speak. "Thank you for being so understanding about tonight. We don't get to see Caroline too much, what with her being in California and all. Now I can give the folks back home a full report."

This time there was no mistaking the meaning. Neel had met this type before. They believed themselves to be superior simply because their families had been in America for generations. The sort who saw a Sikh and thought he should "go home," conveniently forgetting that once their families, too, had been immigrants.

Now Neel ignored the brother and spoke directly to Caroline. "Thanks for the champagne," then deliberately added, "and the massage." Yes, he was taking the prudent route and leaving, but he could give that lump something to think about.

Caroline stepped toward him, but he didn't break stride. The last thing he heard was Dan saying, "Let the man go, Caroline."

· TWENTY-EIGHT ·

LEILA'S SUSPICIONS STARTED WHEN Neel phoned to say he was working late, could she change their dinner reservations to the next day.

For two hours she tried to convince herself she was being neurotic. That was a Rekhaism. But finally she grew tired of playing the daisy game—he's working late, he's with Caroline—and called the hospital. A polite, efficient American voice informed her that Dr. Sarath had left at his usual time.

How could he go back to Madam Fake after sleeping with her?

She was in bed when he finally came home, his body bringing a cold front to the warm sheets. What was it about Caroline that he could not keep away from? Had he filed her in his heart like he had her picture? Shanti and Oona didn't like her. What did Neel like about her? Was it because she was white? Did he want a mixed marriage so he would not be intimidated by whites? Was he as color-obsessed as the street urchins in Ooty who rushed up to foreigners shouting, "I touched them, I touched them!" Did occupation, status, breeding, all the things that mattered in India not concern him as long as his wife was white?

In the morning he smiled and chatted while dressing for work. He was acting the way he had on the trip back from Reno. Was this how he behaved when he had just been with Caroline?

"Did you change our dinner reservations?" he asked from the front door.

"No. I just cancelled them. What if you are busy tonight also?"

"Go ahead and make them. No cancellations this time," Neel said as he left. He hardly knew what he was saying, his mind still preoccupied with the unseemly events from the previous night. He shouldn't have given in to Caroline yesterday. There was much to regret about the evening, but at least he had had the sense to leave her apartment. He had spent part of the night driving aimlessly up and down the hilly streets. He had considered stopping at one of the many pubs on Geary, but didn't want to be around anyone. He felt raw and exposed, in need of the camouflage offered by his car. By the time he finally got home, he had stopped wishing for another evening, another ending, and was relieved that he could slip into sleep without talking to Leila.

Leila heard the front door slam on his words. Once again he was telling her what to do. He did what he wanted, but like everybody else, never asked what she desired. Leila had allowed her family to prod and primp her and where was she now? Sitting in a room, alone. But Amma wasn't in America; she couldn't push Leila to make the dinner reservation. Her stern voice and unblinking stare couldn't force her into one of the sarees she had insisted on buying when Leila would have preferred more salwar kameezes.

Leila ran to the cupboard and took down the suitcase that held the trousseau sarees. Neel might leave her, but she was not going to return to India. No one wanted her there: not Amma, and certainly no man, except perhaps a widower eager to find a mother for his children. In America she might be able to marry for love, make a new life for herself. Two American men had told her she was beautiful.

The sarees fell onto the bed and she inched into the folds with the scissors' sharp steel edge. Crimson, blue, violet. The silk cut easily, making a loud tearing sound. Amma had gift-wrapped her in this purple one for Raj. In this expensive magenta one, Jayadeep had run his eyes up and down her body, only to say no and send

Amma scurrying for other men. Even in America, the rejections mocked her. Not good enough for any man, the sarees shouted. She cut them all up, not even pausing when she came to the peacock green one. How Amma and she had fought over it. The scissors ripped the silk. Suneel, Neel. Cheater, liar, fornicator! The sarees lay ruined at her feet.

Only then did she cry, noiselessly, and it felt like a quiet dying. Exhausted, she barely had the strength to sit amid the ruins of her splendid wardrobe. She was amazed that she could even see, her eyes felt so empty—like the vacant eyes of unfinished statues.

Amma would be shocked at the waste, but Leila was glad to have gotten rid of that part of her life. She was as fed up with men and their promises as Rekha. Rekha was more Indian than she realized. She obviously wanted to get married, and was so eager to get a husband she was willing to date a married man. Both Rekha and she were parts of a triangle and knew what it was like to be on the acute side of love. She would call Rekha. Rekha would understand without pitying her, the way people in India would. She could give Leila some advice, listen to her. Tell her if there was any hope left.

She dialed the number quickly, the anger, hurt, and despair buzzing inside her like a hundred bees. After four long rings the answering machine came on and Leila listened to the whine of the tape, too discouraged to hang up. As she was about to replace the receiver, she heard a click, then Rekha said, "Hello. I just walked in. Are you still there?" the words rushed and breathless.

"I'm here. It's Leila."

"The palm reader," Rekha teased. "You'll be pleased to know that I am making something of my life."

"That's good." Leila wasn't sure what she meant.

"I just came back from seeing Tim. He wants to get back together. Swears he's going to divorce his wife."

"See? I told you everything would work out." Indy, Oona, Rekha—they were the lucky ones. She had called Rekha thinking it would be easier to talk to a fellow sufferer.

"No, you didn't say that. And I didn't say I'd go back to him."

"Then what?"

"I told him thanks but no thanks. I don't trust him. He may divorce his wife, but what if he cheats on me when we're married? Once a cheater, always a cheater. I've decided to make something better of my life. Hold on a sec. That's another call coming through."

Leila waited. Rekha was probably talking to Tim. From the little Rekha had told her about him, she knew he wasn't the sort to give up easily. She and Rekha were not in the same situation at all. As the silence continued, Leila felt increasingly stupid for calling. Rekha was leaving Tim, not the other way around.

"Sorry about that. One of my classmates. I think he has a crush on me." Rekha laughed. "But you didn't call to hear the vagaries of my non-love life. What's up?"

Cornered, Leila began a stammering account of the events over the past months.

"This is your friend, right?" Rekha clarified.

Belatedly, Leila realized that Rekha might guess she was actually talking about herself. "Yes, yes, it is a friend. You told me to tell you if I heard any stories, remember?"

"You mean to say he married her even though he was in love with another woman?"

Voiced like that it sounded hopeless. "Maybe he didn't love the American woman that much. He probably also didn't want to hurt his family by bringing home a foreigner."

"But it's his life. If he married your friend to please his family, then he should stick to his decision. It sounds to me like he wants to eat his cake and have it too. Has she confronted him?"

"No."

"Then how does she know he's still seeing the other woman?"

"She saw them together."

"That's nothing. People can be friends."

For a moment Leila felt hope. Then she said, "Indian men don't have women friends their wives don't know about unless they have something to hide."

"Oh, the poor thing. I feel so sorry for her. This guy sounds like he never gave their marriage a chance. This poor woman walked into a situation she had no idea existed. Do you think she'll talk to me?"

"No, no. She doesn't even know I'm talking to you. But you said to tell you if I know of any woman who is being abused. It is abuse, isn't it? Even though the husband is not beating her or demanding more dowry." That was the abuse Leila understood. Stories of girls with belt-striped backs, their arms dotted with cigarette burns.

"Sure it's abuse. Emotional abuse. Sometimes I think it's worse than physical abuse. Is the husband sleeping with both of them?"

"I don't know." Leila hesitated. "Yes, I think so."

"I guess some men like to hop between beds. But why does she sleep with him?"

"I don't know," Leila repeated. "Maybe she thinks she will keep him that way."

"That's an old mistresses' tale. Men only stay if they want to. Sex helps, but it's not the deciding factor. Is this guy educated?"

"Oh yes." Pride lifted Leila's answer. "He has some very high degrees. He studied in America."

"I wonder if he knows what he's doing. More to the point, does your friend know what *she* is doing?"

"She is trying to make her marriage work. It's what her parents would expect."

Leila's answer was pat. How could she confess that she was

beginning to like Neel? That she enjoyed talking to him, feeling his skin against hers? In the early days of the marriage she had dismissed the consideration he had shown his grandfather as showing off, as not wanting to be with her. Now she was the beneficiary, feeling warm on a cold night because he wanted to know if seventy on the thermostat was fine with her.

"Sounds just like Anu. But it takes two to make a marriage. Now that she knows, what is she going to do about him?"

"I don't know. I mean, she doesn't know." Leila quickly corrected herself before asking, "Do you have any suggestions?" Leila already knew what she wanted. She wanted him to forget Caroline and love her. But that had to come from him. She could learn his ways, know how to please him. But the love, the desire that would make him turn to her again and again, was out of her control.

"I'd kill the slimy bastard and make it look like an accident. Then I'd collect the insurance and live a comfortable life."

"You would really do that?" The old images of earthquakes and car accidents unfurled in front of Leila's eyes. She had never thought of money, though. Or life afterwards.

"No, of course I wouldn't do that," Rekha said. "I guess I don't have any great advice. She's got to do what she feels comfortable with. I know I'd rather live alone than with someone like that. I would never be able to trust him. Killing him is only a fantasy. I'm so tired of the stories I keep hearing at the shelter that just once I'd like to see the shoe on the other foot. Like Anu beating up her husband for a change."

"I think my friend would agree with you. She says that no matter what men do, it always comes out okay for them."

"Not always. At some point they have to pay their dues. Maybe not now, but in one, five, maybe even twenty years, they'll suffer. Isn't that what you call karma?"

Leila laughed. "You're beginning to know a lot about Indians. Soon you will know more than I."

"I doubt it. I'm not Indian and I'm not married to one, either."

"Neel is an American citizen," Leila said lightly. "And if I want, I can become one, too."

She had wanted to, had made strides in that direction, but always got held back by the rigid rules of India. She had changed her country, her name, her status, but she couldn't change herself.

· TWENTY-NINE ·

AS THEY WALKED INTO THE Indian restaurant, Leila felt as if she were cocooned in a shawl of disbelief.

She had taken a late walk in the evening, convinced that he would be with Caroline again. But Neel had been waiting for her when she returned, and instead of being annoyed that she hadn't cooked dinner or made reservations, he suggested they keep the original plan to eat out.

She still didn't trust that he really wanted to go out with *her*, and couldn't understand why he was suddenly making the effort to spend time with her. The combination of Neel's insistence—he phoned the restaurant—and her casual attitude gave her a power she had never before possessed. It prompted her to ask if she could drive to the restaurant. He hesitated, then handed over the keys without a word. Out of the corner of her eye she saw him sitting very quietly, only his feet betraying his nervousness. Every time she braked, he, too, pressed down. His restraint when she almost collided with a suddenly stalled car made her relent and forgive him enough so that by the time they pulled into the parking garage, she was talking to him.

"That wasn't too bad, was it?" she asked archly.

"No, you're a decent driver."

"I'd say thank you except you sound so surprised."

"You continue to surprise me." He smiled.

"And you did me by parting with the keys to your beloved Porsche," she shot back, swallowing the rest of her thoughts.

"It's just a car," Neel shrugged.

"So I can take it any time I want?"

"Oh, no. I've created a Frankenstein."

"Wrong sex," Leila mocked. "And Frankenstein was the student who created the monster."

"Yes, Teacher. Let's hope that review was right about the food. I'm starving," Neel said, as he pushed open the heavy wooden door.

The restaurant was dimly lit, with a bar that opened into the dining area. The afternoon buffet stand was tucked into a corner, but the aroma lingered and Neel's first thought was he'd have to dry-clean his jacket. The obligatory "authentic" Hindi film music played in the background. Neel recognized the melodramatic highs and lows, but could not place the singer or the film. At least the decor was less kitschy than most other Indian restaurants, with their penchant for garish garnishes of gold and silver.

"How sexist," Leila remarked. "All the pictures on the wall are of Maharajahs."

"I didn't know you were a feminist." Neel raised his eyebrows.

"You don't know a lot—" Leila began, and stopped as Sanjay slapped Neel on the back.

"I spy, I spy! Arre, caught the lovebirds out on the town."

"And I don't spy Oona," Neel rejoined. "Did we catch you eating out without your wife?"

"Now tell me, why would I do that? She's not feeling well, so I told her I'd take care of dinner. Take care, take out, one and the same thing." Sanjay winked at Leila.

"Is Oona sick or—" Leila paused, wondering if Sanjay was going to confirm her suspicion that Oona might be pregnant.

"She's very tired. She just finished working on a big case."

"Maybe you can come over for dinner sometime next week?" Leila offered.

"Leila Didi, you catch on fast. I was definitely fishing for an invitation!"

"Let us know a good time and we'd love to have you over," Neel said. "I'll make tandoori chicken."

"You know how to cook?" Leila was surprised as much by this revelation as by his seconding the invitation.

"How do you think I managed before I married you?"

"Neel can barbecue, but cook?" Sanjay laughed. "He used to open up a can of vegetables, throw in some curry powder, and tell everyone it was Indian food. He did such a good job convincing them that they used to think my genuine, streets-of-Calcutta samosas were some strange kind of wonton."

"If you like samosas, I can make my mother's recipe when you come."

"Looking forward, Didi, looking forward. Just keep Neel out of the kitchen." Sanjay laughed, and went to collect his order.

"It was nice to run into Sanjay. Makes me feel I belong here."

"I don't think this music belongs in the restaurant. That singer sounds as if he's in pain," Neel complained.

"He is. He's singing about losing the woman he loves."

"I'm afraid it all sounds the same to me. Just like the films. Predictable. Boring."

"I bet you haven't seen a Hindi film since you came to America," Leila challenged, irritated by his attitude. "They've changed, you know. They still make the Bollywood masala films, but there are very good art ones, too." Janni had taken her to see one of them. Why was she thinking of Janni here, in another country, sitting at a restaurant with her husband? Was it because Janni, too, had given her up?

"I'll have to take your word for it. I myself prefer French films."

The word "French" leapt out at her. Leila recalled the scene at the hotel in Reno. Neel bending down over the blond head. The silk scarf. Neel pronouncing Caroline's name the French way. Was he taking her out to dinner to tell her about the secretary?

"I didn't know you speak French," she bit out the words.

"I don't. But I can still appreciate the translation."

"I suppose some people prefer secondhand experience to immediate gratification." Her words were still bitter.

"Does it really matter?" Neel was taken aback by her tone. "You like one thing, I like another. I like chicken, you don't."

"I don't know if I don't like it. I've never eaten chicken."

"Would you like to try?"

"Why not?" Leila felt reckless.

"Really? Just like that, you are going to eat chicken?"

"Isn't that how you began eating it? One day, like any other day, you just gave up being a vegetarian." Just like he had given up his name, his upbringing, his word when he married her.

They were still not talking when the waiter brought their order: Tandoori chicken, chicken tikka masala, saag paneer, alloo gobi, raita, naan, and rice.

"Some champagne," Neel ordered. It wasn't like her to be waspish. Or was she moody because it was the wrong time of the month? He knew so little about her. Yet when he made the dinner reservations he'd assumed she would be grateful, and that they would have an easy time together.

When the champagne arrived, Neel raised his glass. "To celebrate the new you," he toasted Leila, and was relieved to see her smile.

Leila took a sip and then looked down at her plate. "It's quite tasty," she pushed aside her chicken piece, "but I don't really like the idea of eating flesh. And I don't know why they have to give it names like breast, thigh, legs."

"When you put it that way, it sounds cannibalistic. Let's pretend you never said that. Words, begone!" Neel moved his hand in a circle like a magician. "Now, where were we?"

"In Katmandu," Leila responded, a little dizzy from the champagne and his playfulness. "I just climbed Mount Everest and you were begging for my autograph." It was a game she had devised with Indy. A fun and easy passing of the time that also helped them learn geography.

"No way. I had just returned from climbing Nanga Parbat. Everest might be higher, but I went up the naked mountain." He stressed the last two words.

The phallic symbol, the gloriously naked mountain, rose between them, and Leila grew hot. She saw them in bed, Neel reaching for her, his hands like butterfly wings all over her body. They had done some of the things she had yearned for in India—seen movies and walked in the park, though he hadn't held her hand. But he had slipped back into his old ways and now, when she was preparing to give him up, he was being flirtatious.

"Here," Leila pretended to autograph her napkin and handed it to him.

Neel tucked it into his pocket. "I didn't know that the girl who poured out the coffee so seriously that morning could be so bubbly."

"Never judge a girl by her face," Leila mandated. He had known all along, then, that she had served coffee, not tea, the day he came to see her. "I don't think I'm bubbly," she continued. "It's such a vacant word. I'd rather you thought I had a bone of whimsy. Like this one," she pointed to her elbow.

Neel touched her arm. "Did you inherit it or get it some other way?"

Leila's heart beat faster. She loved the touch of his hand. "Some other way. Like I tell people who compliment my accent, I bought it in India. Cheap."

"This doesn't look cheap to me." His hand stroked the knobbly triangle.

"It was on sale. Two for the price of one," she babbled on, undone by his caress. "Like the Sunday-Monday saree," she continued, unaccountably glad that she hadn't cut that one to pieces.

"And what am I to make of a woman who wears such a tricky saree?"

"You can't make me into anything," Leila intentionally misunderstood his meaning. "I'm already formed."

"Except for the lines in your right hand," Neel reminded her.

"How do you know about that?"

"Every Indian is born knowing that. It is the epitome of contrary Indian philosophy. It allows you to have control over karma."

They were the last customers. Neel pointed to a yawning waiter and said, "I guess we should leave before they throw us out."

"I want some rat shit before we go," Leila said the words deliberately.

"I beg your pardon? Did I hear you say rat shit?"

Leila's giggles were laced with champagne. "It's those pastel-colored anise seeds. That's what we call them. I saw some in a bowl when we walked in."

"Well, if you want rat shit, you must have it." Neel spooned some on to her palm.

They left the restaurant and walked along slowly, past the cafés and shops.

Leila saw the lump of humanity on the pavement as they turned the corner. It still amazed her that America, too, had beggars. But unlike in India they were clothed, even shod, and spoke English. She felt sorry for this man, who was stretched out behind a placard that read ANYTHING HELPS. GOD BLESS YOU.

God *had* blessed her. She was taking a late night stroll with her husband, their bodies so close that their arms occasionally brushed each other. Every part of her was alive to his slightest movement and she knew that tonight he would reach for her in bed. She wanted to share some of that blessing. She opened her purse and gave the grizzled man a five-dollar bill.

"Thank you, beautiful lady. Good night, good night."

She was glowing, pleased at her good deed, when Neel said, "You shouldn't have done that. He'll only spend it on beer. Or cigarettes."

"How do you know that?" Leila looked back. The man had not moved.

"Because they're all losers. They don't want to do an honest day's work. They hang around here, preying on people's consciences, and then hurry to the nearest liquor store to feed their habit."

"Maybe that's all he has to live for."

"Oh, come on. He can do better than that. He can clean himself up, become a waiter, something, instead of just sitting around all day."

"Maybe he is doing the best he can. And it can't be easy, to sit and wait for charity. You've never been disappointed in life, have you? I'm glad I made him a little happy."

"Sorry. Forget I said that. You're right. I don't know a thing about him."

"Except that he has less than you." Leila would not give up.

"Peace offering?" Neel handed her the car keys.

"Peace accepted, but you can keep the offering. Driving here was enough for me," she confessed.

"Ah, now the truth will out. I may not know everything about you, but I do know you have never driven across the Golden Gate Bridge. Let's correct that."

· THIRTY ·

"BEAUTIFUL DAY, ISN'T IT?" Oona said brightly. "Back east it's freezing this time of year and here all we need is a light sweater."

Leila looked up at the blue sky. Americans followed the daily forecast with as much obsession as Indian farmers awaiting the monsoons. She had noticed that the temperature was making repeated appearances in her letters home, but she still couldn't make it a topic of face-to-face conversation.

"You look different," Oona said.

"Probably fatter because, unlike you, I feel the cold. Wool pants and a parka," Leila pointed out.

"It's not the clothes. It's your face."

Leila knew that some women glowed when they were pregnant. From an excess of blood in their faces, she remembered reading. Did making love have a similar effect? "I'm tired," she said. How could Neel, up so late at night, function well at the hospital?

"Neel keeping you busy?" Oona laughed at the look on Leila's face. "Don't bother answering. That was a Sanjay question. You don't mind going to Union Square?" she asked, her voice serious again.

Leila didn't care where they went. She was still so new that everything was stimulating. She loved the sheer variety in America. It wasn't just the cars that Sanjay had talked about at dinner. The skin colors, too, ranged from a dead white to a dark that could melt into midnight. The perfumes changed with every passerby; even the dogs could be waist-high or tiny enough to fit in a pocket. She was finally beginning to understand those books that spoke of

America as the land where dreams come true. It felt like a country that took in everyone and allowed them to live a life of their own.

"Well, are you ready for my surprise?" Oona asked.

"If I were ready, it wouldn't be a surprise." Leila said logically. She had never seen Oona this happy.

"You make a good point, Mrs. Sarath." Oona laughed. "We need to go into Macy's."

Leila took a deep breath as they walked in, taking in the racks of clothes, the decided steps of people who knew what they wanted and where they were going, their hair and tailored outfits just so. It still thrilled her that she could walk in wearing one outfit and leave in another. No long discussions with the tailor, no return for repeated fittings. Just a quick look in the mirror, and if the image was pleasing, a credit card followed by a signature.

Oona stopped in front of two female mannequins and whispered, "I know it's way too early, but I thought I'd buy a few things today."

Leila looked at the bright-colored pants and loose, striped sweaters. The outfits weren't particularly nice, but then she was still learning about Western fashion.

"You don't understand, do you? This is the maternity section. I'm pregnant."

"Congratulations." Leila smiled. She tried to stifle the pain of her own situation, tried to hold on to the fact she, too, had a husband and could become pregnant.

But there was the rub. Her marriage was filled with a roster of unanswered questions, the niggling feeling that things weren't quite right. The Oonas of the world exuded a confidence that came from limited failures. Their cheerful smiles were the result of men who called them "the love of my life" and first-attempt pregnancies. Even though Leila had the longed-for "Mrs." label, she still could not duck away when jealousy tapped her shoulder.

"That is such good news," she continued now, wanting to feel nothing but happiness for Oona. Why was it that another's good fortune only made her more aware of her own unstable life?

"I wanted to get something to prove that I'm pregnant until I begin to show."

"When are you going to have the baby?"

"In about seven months. Sanjay says it's unfair of me to hold our baby hostage for so long. He's already begun talking to it. Though I think he's a little shy about it, because he does it in Bengali." Sanjay had also told her they would have to perform special poojas, and Oona had felt estranged and frustrated. No matter how hard she tried, inevitably there was some tradition that escaped her—a gesture, habit, that ineffable understanding that gives life to what it means to be an Indian.

At the café, Oona ordered milk without even looking at the menu. Pregnancy had filled her with both delight and conversation. Sanjay's parents were thrilled and his mother wanted to come for the birth. "I really, really, hope she comes," Oona wiped away a milky mustache. Her own mother had promised them a crib. Her sister was sending a stuffed bear, which Sanjay wanted to exchange for a cardinal because they were from Stanford, not UC Berkeley. Her godmother planned to begin knitting immediately . . .

Leila didn't know she had fainted until she heard Oona's voice, thin and faraway. "Should we get a doctor? Her husband is a doctor."

She opened her eyes to see Oona and the waiter staring down at her, their faces at waist-level. For a second she was disoriented and then it all came flooding back: the café, Oona's pregnancy, her own struggles against jealousy and sadness. That was why she had fainted. Her body could only take so much emotion before falling apart.

She sat back up on the chair and smiled at the concerned faces. Oona looked whiter than usual, as if aware she was responsible for Leila's fainting spell.

"Would you like some tea?" the waiter asked.

She didn't want tea. She felt cold and queasy, not sick, but not entirely well either. Once seated again, she could not move. Her legs were so heavy it was an effort just to bring them around in front. *Pair bhari ho gaya*—the phrase appeared in front of her like a wagging finger. Heera used to say that every time she got pregnant, "My legs have gone heavy." As a young girl, Leila used to be amazed that a body part could get heavy one day, just like that, and would look curiously at Heera's hairy legs. When she was older, she giggled at the hidden implication, but it wasn't until now that she understood it. She was pregnant.

Was she going to be like Amma, who never suffered from morning sickness? Amma had fainted once with each pregnancy. She said the brief fainting spell confirmed the impending birth as surely as if a goddess had told her so.

"Leila, are you all right? Shall I take you to the hospital?" Oona thought Leila looked sicker by the minute.

"No, thank you. I'm all right, really. I just need to lie down." Leila was wondering how she hadn't noticed the skipped period.

Oona was doubtful the whole drive back.

"You should have let me call Neel. Your poor husband is going to be very, very upset."

"I just fainted. It's happened before in India," Leila lied.

"Really? That makes me feel a little better, but I'm still going to call Neel."

As soon as they entered the house, Oona picked up the phone, and Leila could do nothing but listen.

Oona smiled at Leila. "Your husband was remarkably calm. He asked me to make sure you stay in bed till he gets here. So let's get you to the bedroom. He's leaving right away, and I don't think he'll be too happy to find you standing up."

Leila felt unexpectedly warmed by Neel's reaction. It was nice to have people look after her. When she was sick, Amma used to let her eat rasam and rice in bed, while Indy and Kila hovered around, hushed and curious. ET never left her side, her tail curved around a body that fitted its furself against her. "Furrson and person purr-fectly content," Leila used to say. Oona tucked her under the covers, and Leila even forgot to be ashamed of the meager furniture in the bedroom.

"Now, is there anything you'd like me to get for you? Tea? I'd offer chicken soup, except I know you're a vegetarian."

Tea had caffeine and was bad for the baby. She would have to stop drinking her daily cup. Thank God she had given up fasting once a week. "I'm fine, thank you. I'm really okay."

She placed a hand on her middle and smiled at Oona. There was no need to be jealous.

"Do you want a girl or a boy?" she asked Oona.

"I just want a baby. Healthy and happy will do for me."

"And Sanjay?"

"He surprised me. I thought all Indian men wanted boys. To carry on their names and all. But no, my husband wants a girl."

Leila wondered if Neel would have a preference.

"I guess Sanjay wants a baby that looks like you."

"Oh, I don't know about that. He wants a girl so he can name her 'India.' He's getting a kick out of imagining introducing her as 'My daughter, Miss India.'"

The talk of babies still swirled around the room when Leila heard the front door open. She felt her secret was spread across her face. Would Neel guess? She hadn't thought of how she would tell him the good news. They were going to be a family. Under all that anger and hurt, that careless attitude, had hidden the hope first ignited when she put on the green saree.

"How are you?"

She had anticipated a furrowed face, but Neel's voice was even, his eyes normal. "I'm fine. Oona was just worried. I told her it's happened before. When I don't eat. I didn't eat anything this morning." Another lie.

He adjusted the bedspread and then checked her pulse. "Can I get you something now?"

She shook her head. "I think I'll just stay here for a while."

"Okay. But I think you should take some fluids once you are up to it. A sandwich in a little while would be good." Neel turned to Oona. "She's going to be all right. Thanks for alerting me. I can't have you all thinking I look after my wife so badly that she faints."

Leila curled her toes and clenched her hands into fists. She hated it when Neel was American suave. As always, he had managed to transform a strained moment into one that showed him in a good light. Just like in Reno. Oona was smiling and telling him he was a wonderful husband.

Leila didn't say anything. She listened as Neel went on smoothly, "All seems well, so I'll head back to the hospital." Oona's call had interrupted a conversation with a French intern that Neel wanted to finish. Jacques Olivier had recently found out that Caroline spoke French and approached Neel. "You are seeing her, yes? A little excitement on the side?" When the intern saw the look on Neel's face, he backpedaled, "Okay, sorry, my mistake. But perhaps you can tell me if she is available." It made Neel feel more than a little paranoid that people were watching him. First the couple outside Caroline's apartment and now Jacques at the hospital. He had to set him straight.

Leila watched them leave together. Was she imagining things, or did Neel seem impatient as Oona returned to collect the bag she had forgotten? What was so important at the hospital that he couldn't stay for even half an hour with her?

· THIRTY-ONE ·

CAROLINE GAVE HERSELF A LITTLE TIME to think about her decision. She didn't want it to be spontaneous, emotional or vindictive. This was one of the most important phone calls she would make in her life and she had to be calm and sure of herself. She replayed the scene over and over again: sitting at the dining-room table, sipping a glass of Merlot; voice soft, no hint of a stammer, words that flowed easily; fingernails painted, every inch the lady, out to get her man.

She didn't know how else to reach Neel. He refused to answer her pages and avoided her at the hospital. She hadn't even been able to tell him she had kicked Dan out of her apartment.

She had never seen Dan so angry.

"Are you out of your mind? Going out with him!"

"He is a doctor—" Caroline started, only to have Dan continue, "I don't care what he is. He isn't one of us. If Pop knew . . ."

"Pop wants me to be happy."

"Yes, but with one of our own. Not with that—that doctor."

"That doctor is better educated and makes more money than any of you," Caroline said.

"So? He's colored."

"He's Indian, Dan. And I mean to marry him."

"And when is that going to happen?"

"When—" Caroline stopped. Dan would be even more crazy if he found out that she had to wait for Neel to get a divorce.

"See, you can't tell me because deep down, you know I'm right."

Deep down Caroline knew she wasn't getting younger, that

finding a man, any man, was difficult, and that Neel had status and education. He treated her well and she would have a good life with him. But she didn't say any of that to Dan. There was no point. She might as well agree with him, for now. Then, after they were married, she would take Neel home. As she kept telling Natalie, it would be too late for the family to interfere.

She allowed Dan to believe that he had made her see sense. Happier, he took her out to dinner and told her that he wouldn't say a word to Pop.

She couldn't tell Neel what had really transpired. He would definitely break up with her. No, she would tell Neel that she had chosen him over her family, that she had made Dan leave.

Neel hadn't done that for her. He was still living with the wife his family had chosen. When Caroline chased him to Reno, begging him to take their relationship public, he had said it wasn't the right time.

He was just avoiding her. As she sat at her desk, watching the "hold" button on the phone blink on and off, repeating in slow motion the beat of her heart, she realized that she might lose Neel. That was when she decided to phone the wife.

When the time came, her hands shook so much she had difficulty opening the bottle of wine. She drank a full glass. Only when she felt ready for anything did she reach for the phone. She knew that Neel wasn't home.

The ringing filled the apartment and she pressed the receiver against her ear. Two, three rings. Her heart pounded, and she didn't know whether she was afraid it would be picked up or disappointed if it wasn't. Just when she was thinking of giving up, a brief silence replaced the ringing and a soft voice answered.

"Hello?"

Caroline forgot her careful preparations. "Is this, is this Dr. Neel Sarath's house?"

"Yes."

"Are you Mrs. Sarath?"

"Yes."

"You don't know me, but I think you should know about me."

There was no response at the other end of the line.

"My name is Caroline Kempner. I work at the hospital and I've known Dr. Sarath—Neel—for five years." As she said "Neel," she grew confident.

"I know your name. You are the secretary."

"Yes." Caroline was momentarily nonplussed. "I don't just know Neel professionally. We have a personal relationship." Was it the Merlot that was making her heart beat so loudly she could hardly hear the wife, or was it her own fear? She had never imagined she would be so frightened of his unwanted wife.

"I understand. I saw you at Reno."

"Then you know."

"About the slides. You brought them to my husband. He thought you were, how did he put it? Bucking for a raise."

Damn that Neel. He had lied about her, about them. She remembered the humiliation of waiting for him, being sent back to San Francisco like a piece of baggage. The warm effects of the wine vanished, replaced by an angry cold that chilled her to the tips of her fingers. Once and for all she was going to fix the odds. Neel had been hers for years and would soon be hers forever.

"There were no slides. I went to Reno to see Neel because we had quarreled. We are lovers."

"I see."

"I hope you do see. That's why I'm calling you. Neel and I have been lovers for over three years. It isn't as if we are just having an affair," Caroline explained. "He met me long before the trip to India last summer. In fact, he was all set to marry me when his grandfather got sick and he ended up marrying you."

"I see."

The monotonous, almost monosyllabic answers annoyed Caroline. She had anticipated anger, denial, tears, shouting. Not this patient, almost indifferent response.

"Did you hear what I just said? Neel never wanted to marry you. His grandfather wanted the marriage. Neel married you only because he doesn't want someone's death on his conscience. We kept in touch the whole time he was in India."

Caroline paused, but again there was no sound from the other end.

"Are you still there?"

"Yes."

"Well, anyway, I just thought you should know. I mean, I would want to know if I were you. When Neel returned from India with you, I was furious with him. But he told me he was going to get a divorce as soon as his grandfather dies. We thought that would happen in a few months. Neel may be married to you, but he has been seeing me the whole time. We see each other at work and then he comes to my home in the evenings. Even the first day back from India, he came to see me. He loves me and we plan to get married."

"Is Neel with you?"

"No." Caroline hesitated before continuing. "But I thought you should know what's going on."

"I know now."

Caroline replaced the phone in its cradle and looked at the lipstick marks on the wineglass. The conversation had been easier than she had imagined. No hysteria, just quiet acceptance. That was good. It would make things easier, especially when the divorce was in the works. The phone call proved that the wife was a meek little thing who would sign the papers exactly where she was told to by Neel.

She had thought the call would leave her relieved, lighter, give her the feeling of a woman in charge. She continued sitting in her chair, neither pleased nor displeased, waiting for the sound of Neel's finger ringing the doorbell. She had left him a message asking him to come over tonight. He hadn't said yes, but he hadn't said no, either.

· THIRTY-TWO ·

AFTER CAROLINE'S CALL, Neel had phoned. There was a crisis in the hospital . . . Leila barely listened to the hurried, lying words, but she understood that he would stay the night, returning the next morning or afternoon.

Any hope, any happiness she had given birth to in that short space between Oona's calling the hospital and Neel's getting here were gone. She had thought that Neel had put her first. But he had only made an inconvenient stop before rushing back to be with Caroline.

At first she was relieved not to have to see him, to have time to think. But all she did was go over that phone call, Reno, the scarf—each memory leaving her more and more humiliated.

She still didn't know what to do. After crying in bed all night she had come to stand by the window, the rush-hour activity below giving her something to look at.

Leila gazed down on the street and remembered that night so long ago when she had wondered why Neel was leaving her alone in the condo to go shopping. She leaned against the window, the wood pressed hard into her cheek. She was tired, so tired, unable to sleep since that blond voice had broken into her quiet evening, the fake accent confirming everything she had long suspected.

Tonight I can write the saddest lines. No, she rewrote Neruda, *Today I can write the freest lines.* She was free from suspicion, free in the sense that the worst had happened. But that didn't mean she wasn't sad, alone, unable to appreciate anything. Even the baby.

Last night's rain had brightened everything and the slants of sunshine on the wood floor contained no dancing motes of dust. Alcatraz was framed by the window, the island so close it must have frustrated prisoners. To the left was the Golden Gate Bridge.

The orange columns hung above the white-topped waters as if dangled by the hands of an aesthetic God. Beyond was India, a daikon root jutting into the sea. An ancient country with ancient traditions, it had given her this marriage but neglected to offer a solution should that marriage fail. She had been provided a husband and an airline ticket; though no one had said, "You must make this work," that order had been implicit. There was no place for her back home. Kila now slept in her bed, and her job was already taken by another spinster, teaching, until she too married and left.

Leila felt as ancient as the mariner, except there was no one in whom she could confide. She had tried to talk to Rekha, but something—Amma's voice, perhaps—had stopped her from making a complete confession.

There were two phones in the house, a luxury by Indian standards. She could pick up the extension in the kitchen and dial home, easily traversing the thousands of miles in a minute. Another luxury. But there the luxuries stopped. Amma would be pleased and surprised to hear her voice and Kila would clamor to get on the phone, if only to talk to America. She could not say, "Amma, I've suspected for a while that Neel is having an affair. But now I know for sure. His lover told me everything yesterday." Amma knew Neel as Suneel, and the terms "affair" and "lover" were not in her vocabulary. Once she was made to understand them, Leila knew what her mother's response would be. She would tell Leila to stay with Neel and forgive him. Amma had been raised on stories of mythical women who forgave their husbands everything. According to Amma, Rama and Sita lived happily ever after in the *Ramayana*.

Amma would expect Leila to be so good to Neel that he would forget Caroline. It was her responsibility to see that it never happened again. The surest way to do that was to have children. Amma would convince Leila her pregnancy had come at the right time. It was only in America that people warned couples a baby didn't solve marital problems.

And how could she burden poor Indy, just on the brink of marriage herself? Indy would insist that Leila leave him. That would ruin the family, but Indy would not care. Indy was not the oldest, trained to look out for the others, hammered into docility by Amma's words. Leila Begood. Leila was perfectly aware that her failure doomed her sisters' futures. Besides, she didn't want Indy to imagine all men were like Neel.

And if she did find the courage to phone Rekha? The other girl's perspective was tainted by her own experience with Tim, and by America. These days she was advocating the role of the vengeful suffragette, as if that solved the problem. "Kill Neel," she'd blithely say. And then she'd want to use Leila in her thesis.

Leila found herself in standing water between Amma's wishes and her own desire not to be with a man who kept a lover. Yet both choices, stay or go, were mad. Was she going to be like Asha, her old friend in India?

Poor Asha was married to an unemployed schoolteacher who still lived with his parents. Two days before the wedding, Leila had stood beside Asha on the rooftop terrace, looking out at the people hurrying home from work. "I will stay with him until my sisters marry," Asha said, her voice beaten down, so different from the shrill shouting and begging that had gone on for weeks as she pleaded with her parents to cancel the marriage. The man was bald, with pronounced buck teeth, and he spoke no English. Asha knew that everyone was tittering about the match. "Don't think like that," Leila consoled her. "It may all work out. At least he really wants to marry you." Asha's mother had bragged that the boy had gone straight from their house to the Temple to pray for the marriage. This was unusual because mostly it was the girl who prayed to be accepted. "I wish he didn't want to marry me," Asha said. "Anyway, by the time my sisters marry, I will be used to him and maybe I'll just stay." Amma had recently written that Asha was pregnant for the third time.

Leila couldn't bear to think about her own baby. For so many years she had performed the penance of fasting once a week to have a husband and children. Be careful what you wish for, she remembered the old Gypsy saying. Perhaps the Gypsies had learned that in India before taking it west.

She was still at her vigil by the window when Neel came in.

Neel had taken advantage of a brief lull in the early morning to catch up on sleep, and it had left him refreshed in spite of a hectic night.

"Is everything all right?" He wondered if she had received bad news from India. She looked so pensive and defeated. Like a beautiful Madonna, hair floating around her face. The silk caftan outlined her breasts, and the tiny concave waist curved out into her hips. What would she do if he went to her now, in full view of anyone looking in? This openness was an unexpected bonus of marriage. No assignations or appointments. No fear of being caught; everything was legal. Perhaps that old rogue Picasso was right after all. "You are wrong not to be married," were his last words to his doctor. "It's useful."

"Yes, everything is okay," Leila answered automatically. "Why do you ask?"

"No reason." He glanced at the coffee table. A blue aerogram. "Is that from your mother?"

"No, it's from your family."

"Is Grandfather all right?" he asked quickly.

"I didn't read this one. But last week your mother said he was the same." Neel didn't really care about his sweet old grandfather. He wanted the old man to die so he could marry his lover.

"Oh, good. I worry about him." Neel was so surprised to be sharing his feelings he didn't notice the look on her face. "You know how they never take care of themselves in India. Grandfather has this ridiculous village mentality that when his time has come, he will just give up the fight." It was a relief to speak with someone who really understood. Americans would put this down to Indian spirituality, conjuring an old man who looked and acted like a brown Jesus Christ. But Tattappa, born in a village without a hospital, had never learned to trust the medical profession. He was proud of Neel's accomplishments, but didn't think *he* needed a doctor.

They were in the kitchen when Leila blurted out, "There is something I have to tell you."

"Is it about Tattappa?" Neel looked at the phone. "Mummy called?"

"Your grandfather is fine," Leila repeated. "But I did get a phone call. From Caroline."

"Caroline?" Neel's relief was short-lived. "Did she want me to call her back?" He kept his voice casual, but he was thinking ahead to when he would tell Caroline never to call the house again. This was reason enough to end their relationship. End what? There had been nothing between them for a while.

"No. She called to speak to me."

"What about?" But even as he asked the question, Neel knew the answer. Caroline had threatened him in Reno, but he never thought she would follow through and contact Leila.

"She said the two of you are having an affair. That you never wanted to marry me. You did it to please Tattappa. That you are going to divorce me as soon as Tattappa dies." The words kept tumbling out. Leila couldn't bear to look at his face and stared at the telephone.

"She said all that?" Neel asked incredulously.

"Yes." She didn't elaborate. It was up to Neel. I have dared to disturb his universe and now he has to account for it, she thought.

Neel stood still, staring at the floor, before abruptly looking up. Their eyes met and held. Leila didn't blink and it was Neel who closed his, turned his face toward the ceiling, and sighed.

"I had no idea it had gone this far." He shook his head and felt the pieces come together, like the colored glass pattern in a kaleidoscope. He knew what to tell Leila. Tomorrow he would deal with Caroline. Once and for all.

"I never told you this, but oh, about three years ago I went out with her. Just for a little while. When I realized it wasn't going anywhere, I broke it off. Apparently she still hasn't got over it. I'm really sorry she called you. I'll have to talk to her, tell her never to do it again." He paused. When Leila didn't respond, he continued, "I could take action against her because this constitutes sexual harassment—and I will if you want me to, but it may create a number of problems. An immigrant man's word against an American woman. It's also hard to prove and might end up ruining my medical career. But I'll do it if you insist." He talked quickly, his voice growing louder with each word.

Leila considered them, and him. She didn't speak for a few moments, just thought about his logical, reasonable answer. He didn't have to tell her that he had once gone out with Caroline. He had been honest about that. But the serpentine French accent, and Neel's odd behavior in the past months, had stirred up many suspicions and questions.

"She said you went to see her the night we arrived." Leila remembered the long wait and how she had shivered in the cold apartment while searching through his files, Caroline's picture falling to the floor.

"What?" Neel wondered what else Caroline had divulged. "I went shopping. I knew the fridge was empty and it took me a while to find a place that was open. I wanted to get you some fruit. Remember the mangoes?"

"You were gone so long I got scared and looked through your desk. I found her picture there."

So the quiet mouse had squeaked as early as day one. He wasn't sure whether to be furious or intrigued by her chutzpah. Leila must have known about Savannah, too, all these months. He had thrown away her letters just last week. "Her picture? Maybe she gave it to me years ago. She could have put it there herself. I really don't know."

"Why did she come to see you in Reno?"

"I told you. I'd left some slides behind and she brought them for me. Don't you believe me?"

"She said you had quarreled."

"We did. In Reno. I told her she should not have come up. It didn't look right. You and I were—are—newly married, and people might think it strange to see her with me. I didn't bring her over to meet you because I don't like to mix my professional and personal life. I was going to tell you all this, but I had no idea how you would take it."

"Who sent you those flowers that first night?" Everything had to be explained if she was going to stay with him and hope again.

Neel hesitated. "Caroline did. I think it was her way of trying to get back with me. I'm sorry I didn't tell you. But looking back, I don't think I could have done anything different. You had just arrived. How could I possibly expect you to understand?"

"But how did she get inside?"

"Leila, this feels like the Inquisition. How did she get in? Very simple. There's a duplicate key in the office. For emergencies, if I lose my set. Most people leave it with a friend or a neighbor. Since I'm at the hospital so much, mine is there."

"I called the hospital that night you wanted me to postpone our dinner reservations because you were working late. This woman said you had left at your usual time."

"She must be the new girl they've just hired. Why would I lie about something you can check up on? As you did."

"The scarf in the plane. Who does it belong to?"

"I honestly don't know."

"It's not Caroline's?"

"Only if she left it there years ago."

"Is there any other woman I should know about?" Leila thought of Savannah's letters.

"No one who is important now. I'm married to you, and that's what is important." He didn't know he felt like this until the words came out. He was comfortable with Leila in a way he had never been with Savannah. Oh, he had admired and loved Savannah, but always felt he was trying to live up to her. Leila and he were more evenly matched. And Leila's parents loved him for the same reason that Savannah's had hated him. That he was Indian. Sanjay was right about the comfort of shared experiences. Sanjay was already worried that when he grew older he might be repelled by the very differences that attracted him to Oona now; that they might make him long for the Bangla girl he had always expected to marry.

"There is just one more question."

"Thank God." Neel smiled. "I'm not sure how I'll hold up if you question me for another hour."

He was being smooth again. For a moment she had stripped him of his American veneer, but now it was back.

"Did you marry me to please Tattappa?"

This, then, was the most important question, Neel realized. She had accepted and seemed relieved by his other explanations.

"Marrying you certainly pleased him. He is very fond of you. He thought you were very much like his wife, my grandmother, whom I never met. She died before I was born." Neel tried to gain time, weighing possible answers as he kept talking. "I had not gone to India with the idea of getting married. But once you were suggested, I agreed to see you. My mother had arranged for a number of other girls, but you were the only one who interested me. When I met you, I thought you would do well in America. That was important to me. I didn't want to marry someone who couldn't speak English and would constantly carp to return to India." Neel was relieved that most of what he was telling Leila was the truth.

Leila relaxed, the pressure-cooker tenseness vanishing. Indy was right. Neel *had* seen something he liked in her during that walk in the garden. He had intimated as much at the restaurant in Ooty. Of all the scenarios she had thought possible, this was the one she had not dared to hope for. Everything was going to be all right. There was no need to disappoint Amma, no need to feel jealous of Caroline, no need to have a limited life here with Neel, or live manless for the rest of her life.

She smiled. "I definitely don't want to go back to India. I love living here."

"You do?" Neel had never thought to ask her. "Well, I'm relieved."

"I never want to go back. Even if you were having an affair, I would not have gone back." Here she would be like millions of other disappointed women; not a pitiable symbol living out her days as the object of pointed fingers.

"There's no need to think of that. Everything all cleared and out in the open now?"

"There's just one thing."

"Uh-oh. It's the 'just one thing' that usually is the clincher. What is it you want to know now?"

"It's not a question. I have to tell you something."

"Well? Tell me."

"I'm pregnant," she said, expecting to see a smile, a look of excitement on his face.

For a brief moment Neel thought he was back on the airplane, and Caroline was saying, "I'm late." Then he shuffled his feet, gazed at the walls that were not pressing against him, and wondered why he was having a difficult time breathing.

"Pregnant?" Nothing had prepared him for this. Not Caroline. Not Cindy, a three-week encounter in Stanford who claimed he was the father of the baby she aborted. Not India, where babies are considered a gift from God. Neel didn't believe in God. He believed in choices.

Leila placed her hand on her stomach. "Yes."

"Are you sure?"

"Yes. Our baby will be born a few weeks after Oona and Sanjay's."

"You talk as if everything has been decided. Don't you think we should discuss this?"

"What is there to discuss?"

"Whether we should have the baby." Neel knew the word "abortion" was not in her vocabulary. Well-raised Indian girls got pregnant and had babies. It was one of the reasons why the population kept multiplying. "We just got married, we are getting to know each other, we're both young, why complicate things?" He knew these were American arguments and would not move Indian logic, which had a simple equation: Marriage = Pregnancy = Babies. He, too, had been raised to believe that. But America had shown him that a person could actually control his or her fate.

Leila sat very still. Once again he was turning everything upside down, making her feel she was wrong for wanting something so natural, so simple, that even the poorest Indians have it: the right to a baby and a husband who is happy to move onto the higher plane of fatherhood.

Neel kept going. "I know that I'm not ready yet. For one thing, this condo isn't the right place for a child. No yard, no family room. But aside from those considerations, children take money. I'd like to wait a few years, maybe more, until our cash flow is better. I guess what I'm saying is, I'm not prepared for diapers, crying, and all the other paraphernalia that comes with children."

As he spoke, the burgeoning being inside her took shape and Leila saw plump brown fingers curl around her thumb, large dark irises looking up at her, a black dot hidden on its back to protect against the jealous eye of others.

"I'm ready," Leila said, and the words came from deep within her, feral and fighting.

"You may be, but it takes more than that. I think you should think about it."

"I don't need to think. I want to have the baby. Why didn't you use a condom?"

"It was just that first time and I asked if you were safe."

"I wasn't sure what you meant."

"What do you mean, you didn't understand? Now you tell me. God!" He put his hands on his head.

"What will your parents say?" Leila hurled.

"My parents have nothing to do with this. They don't need to know anything. This is our decision." That threat wasn't going to work. His family had interfered enough in his life.

"I don't understand you. Why don't you want to have a child?"

"I told you, I'm not ready for one yet. I don't understand *you*. Why do you have to have it? You don't even want to consider other options."

"I don't see abortion as an option."

"Why not? It's not even a fetus yet. It's a mass of cells. Just because you're pregnant doesn't mean you have to have a child. It isn't as if you're in a village where you have no recourse."

"With or without you, I'm having my baby." Leila stood up. "You do what you like." She turned and left the room.

· THIRTY-THREE ·

THE CONDO WAS NOT BIG ENOUGH to accommodate two disparate minds. The atmosphere was as bleak and charged as the wild moors in *Wuthering Heights*, Leila thought. They ate the rice and egg curry quickly, the only sound the chime of metal prongs against porcelain. Self-righteous but uncomfortable, Leila tried to convince herself that this dinner was no different from previous silent meals. But she knew this time the tension between them was not due to a blond-haired woman but a baby.

Neel pushed the white oval containing a pale yellow yolk from one side of the plate to the other. Had she made the curry deliberately? Trying to remind him that eggs were unhatched chickens? She was just like Mummy, stubborn and stupid. Seemingly pliable on the outside, but unshakable once her mind was made up. From the very beginning, pouring coffee with her bent head, she had confounded him.

Sequestered in the study, he thought about Caroline. In the past, any disturbance had been balmed by her touch. Now she was the cause of his problems. Why had she called Leila? No discussion. No warning. Was it her idiotic, desperate attempt to get him back? Into what? A family that wanted to throw him out the door? Too bad he hadn't told the brother, "Listen, you loser, I never planned on marrying your sister." During one of their predictable fights last year when she brought up marriage and he resisted, she had suddenly turned on him and said, "I swear, Neel, if you ever dump me, I'll kill you. That's how much I love you."

"I'm frightened," Neel mocked, though he was mildly alarmed by her words. Part of him, however, was pleased that she loved him so much. "Want to die now?" His tongue circled one pink nipple. "Let me show you the weapon I'm going to use," he said, as he guided her hand between his legs. Those days of passion were gone. He had already given her up without realizing it.

He felt relaxed with Leila. Enjoyed discussing movies with her. Was even learning from her wide knowledge of literature. He was proud that everyone seemed to like her. Sanjay had told him three times at least how the sudden marriage had worried him. One of their Chinese-American colleagues had made an arranged marriage with a woman from Hong Kong and it wasn't working out. Sanjay feared the same might happen to Neel. Having met Leila, he not only understood but gave his complete approval. Then penny-saving Patrick, who never invited anyone anywhere, had surprised him by suggesting they come to dinner. "My wife really enjoyed talking to Leila at the barbecue. And since she's mad about India, she has all these questions. So warn your wife, okay?"

Lying in bed, Leila hoped the baby could not feel her anger. Larger than any fetus, the anger had lodged itself in her stomach, spreading throughout her body, making it impossible to sleep. Images from the past would not stop flashing through her mind: Neel with Caroline beside that heart-shaped pool; Neel leaving the day she fainted; her pregnant friends' happiness. Their husbands' pride and excitement. Oona's face. Kila as a baby trying to walk and ending up on the floor. The absoluteness with which Neel said he didn't want the baby. She couldn't, wouldn't, give in to Neel. It was wrong to throw away a gift from God. She didn't care what she needed to do, she was going to become a mother.

Neel's body was a dead weight in the bed, relaxed into the middle of the mattress. His closeness, the smell of his aftershave, the soft noises that weren't even snores were repugnant to her. She turned on her side, her stiff back to him.

She was still awake when the phone rang. She didn't move. Let Neel get it. It was probably Caroline. Leila glanced at the clock. Two fifteen was no time to call, but Caroline lived outside of time and morality. Women who steal other women's husbands don't care what they do or when they do it.

Neel jumped up and ran for the phone.

His voice filled the apartment.

"Mummy?"

Leila knew immediately that something had happened to Tattappa. No one called from India just to say hello. It was too expensive and people were more used to pens than phones. Leila turned on switches as she walked toward the study. It was always better to receive bad news in the light.

"Tattappa, how are you?" Leila watched as Neel strained to hear his grandfather's words.

"Tattappa, I can barely hear you." He was back on the basketball court, trying to hear what his grandfather was advising from the other end. Before he left for Stanford they had walked all over town, stopping to let a truck piled with steel cables pass by. "We are like that," Tattappa pointed to the long poles tied with a red flag to warn people of the danger. "Our bond is strong and dependable. No one can break it."

"What? Leila? Yes, she is here with me. She sends you her greetings." Even now Tattappa was thinking of him, wanting Neel to be happy with Leila. How could he be angry with someone who loved him so much?

The phone was a smooth, high-tech seashell, containing the sound of the ocean. Standing where she was, Leila could hear the crackling noise of the long distance. Neel motioned her closer and she came beside him, her arms hugging her body, trying to shake their fight from her bones.

"Yes, yes, everything is okay. What? What?" Tattappa's weak voice was replaced by a sound like a distant electric saw.

"We got cut off." Neel shared his worry and disappointment with Leila.

"Why don't you try calling back?" Leila said hesitantly.

Neel began dialing. Twenty tries later, he admitted defeat. The famous Indian telephone system had failed him again.

In the silence the kitchen clock ticked on its minutes—2:50 a.m. Just a little more than half an hour and yet so much had changed.

"Shall I make some hot milk?" Leila asked.

They took their mugs to the dining-room table and sat facing each other.

"It's the first time Tattappa has ever spoken to me on the phone. Why do you think he called?" This was something only another Indian could answer.

"To tell you something," Leila said, then decided to speak the truth. "I think he wanted to say good-bye."

"Maybe he will get better soon," Neel resisted. "I remember playing basketball with him. He must have been sixty at least but he was pretty tricky on the court."

"My sister and I used to see him in the market sometimes. We thought he was so nice because he bought sweets for the beggar children."

"He never told me he did that." Neel shook his head. "He'd say he was going to check up on his shops."

"Your grandfather owned shops?" Leila realized she had used the past tense and hastily added, "Which ones?"

"A saree shop and a small cycle-repair shop."

"Which saree shop?" Leila was curious.

"Nirmala. He sold it a few years ago."

"I didn't know he owned Nirmala. We got quite a few sarees there and on the last day the shopkeeper gave us one for free. We thought it was because we had bought so many."

"It was probably Tattappa's doing. He really likes you."

"But we never even talked to each other."

"Tattappa always says you can tell a lot about a person without speaking to them. The New Age people in the United States say that everyone has an aura. I guess Tattappa would agree, except he'd say, 'Jus-tuh from the face-uh wonly.'"

They both laughed at Neel's imitation.

"For years I begged Amma not to say 'ohniun' instead of 'onion.' It used to embarrass me, but she couldn't hear the difference. Then an Irish professor visited our college and he spoke with this strange accent. Everyone thought it was cute and I realized there shouldn't be double standards," Leila said.

"When I was about ten, I tried to teach Tattappa to pronounce 'physics' correctly. He'd listen, nod, and then the next time it would be 'pijiks' again. I finally gave up." Old, interfering Tattappa. Had he been checking up on Neel? Had he somehow known about the pregnancy?

The phone rang and Neel picked it up before the first ring stopped.

"Mummy? I'll leave immediately."

"He's taken a turn for the worse," Neel told Leila. "He's sleeping but can still talk. I hope I'm in time."

"I'll help you pack." Leila retreated to the bedroom.

What sympathy could she offer a husband she was only just getting to know? A suitcase and a voice without any fight in it.

· THIRTY-FOUR ·

"TATTAPPA HAS BEEN ASKING for you all the time," Father said when Neel entered the house.

Neel smelled death as he approached his grandfather. Old people acquired an old age smell that changed when death drew near. Neel did not have to examine Tattappa to know that he had a few more days at most to live.

"Tattappa, you called?"

Tattappa squeezed Neel's hand and a small smile appeared on his face. Neel had learned those words from Mark, and for a while always answered Tattappa with that phrase.

"The boy," Tattappa said slowly.

"The boy," Neel repeated gently, relieved that Tattappa's mind was still alert. "What did you call me for?"

"Suneel, I was worried. You—Leila." Tattappa paused, the words he wanted to say trapped inside his decaying body.

"Yes, Leila. Did you want her to come, too?" Leila's accompanying him had not crossed his mind. She, too, hadn't suggested it, Neel now realized. Was it because she was angry with him?

"No. You. You. I am sorry." Again Tattappa stopped, his convex chest cavity heaving up and down, up and down, from the effort to talk.

"Tattappa, you are a wonderful grandfather. You have nothing to be sorry about." Neel blinked away the beginnings of tears.

Tattappa squeezed Neel's hand again and the dulling eyes, practically blind without the thick glasses, looked grateful.

320

"The marriage. I knew you did not want it."

The confession came between them as nothing had before. Not Neel's decision to study in the States, nor his announcement to live there.

"I did the best for you." The last words were barely gasped out.

"I know, Tattappa."

"Tell me"—the words urgent and hoarse—"did I do wrong?"

Neel wondered that a man so proud could now be so humble. He was trying to form an answer when he noticed that Tattappa's eyes had closed, his breathing the regular one of sleep. Neel stayed beside the bed, tormented. Tattappa had wittingly forced the match, was admitting that he could have got Neel out of it. Neel had always known the motive: love. Even at his angriest, he had never doubted that. Could love be wrong?

What would Tattappa say to these past months? To the furtive meetings with Caroline, the cool treatment of Leila, the pregnancy Neel did not want?

"Suneel, come, eat something." His mother hovered near the door, her body as hushed as her voice.

He didn't want to leave Tattappa, had no desire to sit at the table, but if he didn't go, Mummy would worry. She was upset enough already.

Staring into the sweet, milky tea, Neel heard Aunty Vimla and Ashok come into the house.

"I am sure Tattappa also wants to see my Ashok." Aunty Vimla's voice was clear and strident.

"He is sleeping just now," Mummy said. "He just spoke with Suneel."

Aunty Vimla and Suneel clashed eyes. Neel waited to hear her say that he had tired Tattappa. But even she did not dare.

"Ashok has something important to tell to Tattappa." Aunty Vimla arranged herself in the chair and placed her hands on the table. "Ashok is going to have a baby." She said it with such pride in her son's ability, such surety that only Ashok could do this great deed. "You can to congratulate your cousin," Aunty Vimla urged Neel.

Neel wanted to clap Ashok on the back and say, "*Guinness Book of Records*, man. The only male I know to have a baby."

But no one would get it. Just as they had not understood the desire to choose his own wife.

What should he tell Tattappa? That he had done wrong to knowingly force Neel into an arrangement because he, Tattappa, thought he knew what was best? Neel could not imagine having that much certainty for another. He had always only been certain for himself. Especially when he was young and created the list to live by. Yet it had been challenged these past years. Savannah, Caroline, Leila—the women paraded in front of him. One was unattainable; one so needy; one his by law. But America had taught him that laws could be challenged and changed. Tattappa would never think that way. His was a simplicity that dictated a marriage lasted unto death. How could he tell Tattappa that even during the wedding ceremony he had been plotting a divorce? That he still wanted it?

For a brief moment he imagined never seeing Leila again. Having his old life back. And instead of relief, he felt—ambivalence. He remembered that Leila had packed his suitcase and because there was no time to shop, had looked around the house for small gifts. Mummy would like the soaps, Father the big nail clippers.

Leila. She was probably wondering how Tattappa was doing. He should call, tell her that he had arrived safely.

Without much hope of getting through, he was surprised to hear the phone ring. Fully expecting her voice at the other end, he hung up when the answering machine kicked on.

"Leila is okay?" Mummy asked.

"She wasn't there," Neel said, uncomfortably aware that Aunty Vimla was listening.

"Your Leila goes out at night?" Aunty Vimla's voice was high with shock.

"It's morning there," Neel corrected.

"Oh yes, yes, in Ahmerica everything is upside down." Aunty Vimla went back to slurping her tea.

Where could Leila be, Neel puzzled, as he put down the phone an hour later. After the second failed attempt, he was determined to reach her and decided to try every half hour.

Father came out of Tattappa's room and Mummy immediately poured a cup of tea, asking, "Then?"

The question was as familiar as the mole on Mummy's jaw, the curly black hairs on Father's large Buddha ears. This was how they always greeted each other. When Father returned from work, Mummy from the Temple, it had always been that question. Not the "Darling" Neel used to long for, but a simple, open "Then?" He knew, too, that now the word meant, "How are you doing? How is Tattappa?"

"Okay. Tattappa is still sleeping," Father sat down. "Ah, good, Ashok, you are here."

"Ashok is going to have a baby," Aunty Vimla preened. "We only got the confirmation this evening and hurried over."

"Tattappa will be happy," Father said. "Good, good." He drained his tea and returned to his vigil.

Neel was walking toward the phone when Father's voice urgently called him:

"Suneel, Tattappa is awake."

Father had switched on the light and the naked bulb gave Tattappa the jaundiced veneer Neel had seen on newborn babies. He lay in the same position, but this time there was a question in his eyes. The nap had not made him forget their conversation.

He wanted to know if Neel was okay. He had held on for that answer.

Neel looked down at the hollowed cheeks, the lips that had caved in because the dentures no longer fit. He could not let Tattappa die unhappy.

"Tattappa, you are going to become a great-grandfather."

"Ashok's Smita is in the family way," Father said.

"Tattappa, it is your Leila. My Leila," Neel corrected himself. "She is going to have a baby. That is why she did not come with me."

"So"—with an effort, Tattappa clasped Neel's hand in both of his—"so. It is as I hoped." And with that he closed his eyes, his fingers lax around Neel's hand.

Aunty Vimla's bulky shadow grew into the room, Ashok following meekly behind.

"Appa, Ashok has some good news for you," Aunty Vimla said loudly.

"He knows," Father said when Tattappa didn't open his eyes. "I already told him. Also our Suneel is going to become a father."

"You?" Aunty Vimla shot Neel a glance. "You are going to have a baby?"

"No, I'm not," Neel paused to better absorb her softening face. "Leila is."

And with that he hurried to the phone. This time Leila picked it up on the second ring.

"Where were you?" He couldn't stop the question. He had felt a bit of a fool calling so often.

She had been in the condo the whole time. Vacuuming, cleaning the bathroom, having a bath. She had just been out of sound reach every time he phoned.

"I was wondering," he said instead of the more personal "worried."

She had said she would have the baby on her own, and for the past two hours Neel thought she had left to do just that. Anything was possible. He knew that.

"How are you feeling?" he asked, trying to find a way to tell her about the conversation with Tattappa. "Everyone is asking about you, but I told them you could not come because of the baby." He pressed the phone closer to his ear, but couldn't hear anything.

"Leila, are you there?"

"Yes, I'm here." She had always been there for him. Didn't he know that?

"I'm glad. I thought we got cut off. Listen, if you are feeling better, why don't you call up some real estate agents. See houses with gardens. Remember what Sanjay said," he tried to inject some humor, knowing there was no turning back now, "babies are like dogs. They need gardens."

The next day, Tattappa died, and hardly had Aunty Vimla started crying hysterically when relatives, friends, neighbors, flocked to the house. Neel went out to the verandah for a few moments' respite from the copious tears and preparations.

A band of barefoot children ran past on the street, the oldest boy expertly rolling an old bicycle tire with a stick. Ashok's child would do this one day. His own would have roller blades, intricate models, computer games, all the toys Neel himself never had.

He had taught his friend Mark how to play cricket in the empty field across from the house. Tattappa used to worry so about the American boy, thinking he looked sickly because he was too colorless or because he was too red from the sun.

Neel sat down on the cane chair that had been on the verandah ever since he could remember. Tattappa never wanted a new one, re-caning this one every few years. Old-made chairs were superior to the new ones, he always said.

As Neel rocked back and forth, he looked out at the scene Tattappa had watched daily. Morning and evening, Tattappa sat in his chair, nodding, greeting the passersby. He had loved this house, this land, this street. He never wanted to leave, except to visit his village. This was as far as he wished to travel. He never even wanted any of the gadgets other families requested from their sons living abroad. Tattappa had always been happy with local things.

They were the same flesh and blood, yet so different. Neel had felt fenced in by the railings on the verandah; Tattappa proudly called them a fine decoration. Neel couldn't wait to escape; there were days when Tattappa never left the house.

Neel stood up, then sat down again. He tried to find Tattappa's contentment. Tried to feel how it would be to live on one street for the rest of his life. To be content without asking for more. No, he didn't have it.

A mosquito buzzed by. Without thinking, Neel crushed it in midair. Tattappa had taught him that and he still knew how to do it. He was Tattappa's boy after all.

· THIRTY-FIVE ·

NEEL WAS GONE FOR A WEEK, and after that first call, Leila spoke with him every day.

The day after he arrived, Tattappa had died, and as Neel said, suddenly he wasn't a grandson anymore. Knowing that Neel would not be able to stay till the thirteenth day, the family had broken tradition and celebrated Tattappa's long life by feeding the poor just two days after his death. Aunty Vimla had objected, but, Neel told Leila, everyone seemed to understand he had to return to San Francisco. A society had started building houses for beggars and Neel contributed money in his grandfather's name.

Almost daily one or another of Neel's colleagues called to offer their sympathies and she wrote down their names, occasionally having short conversations with them. She no longer feared that every ring meant Caroline. The new development in her own life had done away with the other woman's significance.

Oona and Sanjay came over one evening, bringing a card and flowers. They didn't stay long because Oona needed to rest.

For the first time, Leila felt she was a part of their life—and their love. She had planned to wait until Neel returned to tell them about the baby, but wanted to share the good news now. "I'm pregnant, too," she said. "We can rest together."

She waited for Oona to get excited, but instead the other woman looked down at her feet and Sanjay put his arm around her.

"We lost the baby," Sanjay said.

"I'm so sorry." Leila could hardly say the words. Had she willed it to happen? Could jealousy go so far? Regret brought tears to her eyes.

"I'm okay," Oona insisted. "I've got this great guy here and we'll try again. The doctor says one out of five pregnancies end in a miscarriage."

"Let's not dwell on all that," Sanjay said. "I'm still waiting to eat those samosas you promised me," he reminded Leila.

"I haven't forgotten the invitation. Let's make a date after Neel returns."

Rekha was the only one who didn't know the best of news and the worst of news. Leila wanted to forget that afternoon of confession when sadness had transformed her into a shameless talker. She phoned, hoping to get off easy and leave a message. But Rekha was home, and even before Leila could tell her about Tattappa and the baby, she began bemoaning her thesis. Or lack of thesis.

"It seems like Anu was the only Indian woman who's come to the shelter. Will your friend talk to me?"

"No, like I told you, she won't talk." To change the subject, Leila told her Neel was in India and that she was just beginning to feel the first changes from pregnancy—she no longer tolerated the smell of garlic, and craved sour things.

Rekha was genuinely excited about the baby, but was soon back to her main concern.

Her insistence annoyed Leila and before she could think, she asked, "Why do you want to pry into people's lives?"

"That's what journalists do. That's how we change things."

"I thought you were going to write meaningful stories."

"I do think my story will help others. It's not a vapid Prince Charles piece."

"But it will only help those who can read it. And most of the women who need to read it won't be able to, right? So, instead of looking for sad stories, why don't you do a thesis on arranged marriages?"

"I don't get it."

"Demythologize them. Most Americans think arranged marriages are exotic, bizarre. They forget that it's part of their heritage as well. Mail-order brides came by the boatloads from England. And besides, arranged marriages aren't so different from love marriages. Show their similarities." Leila knew she sounded didactic, but Rekha was being so narrow-minded.

"But they *are* very different."

"Yes and no. Many men and women who make these supposed love marriages use the same methods Indian parents use. You were just talking about Prince Charles. I know the papers kept saying it was the love match of the century, but my friends and I thought it was an arranged marriage. He had to choose someone from his own background and get approval from his parents."

"Hmmm. That puts the fairy tale in a whole different light."

Leila was pleased to give Rekha a new perspective. She was just like Cynthia and Harold, seeing things as an outsider instead of as a participant. It was that thought that made her continue. "It wasn't just Charles and Diana who had an arranged marriage. You have one too."

"What do you mean?" Rekha was astonished.

"I know you aren't married, but when anyone, you, the man on the street, is born into a family, it is like an arranged marriage. You didn't choose your parents or siblings. And yet you have to get along with them. Just like an arranged marriage."

"But in love marriages couples get to know each other before taking the plunge," Rekha insisted.

"If they get to know each other so well, how come there are so many divorces?"

"Bad luck, I guess." Rekha didn't want to talk about it anymore and Leila dropped the subject. Besides, she felt a little hypocritical, since she too had thought of divorce.

Shanti also visited, bringing a packet of jalebis. "They're sinful," she said of the orange-colored sweet shaped like a pretzel. "But they're syrup-dripping good. You've moved the sofa. It's cozier. I like it," she added approvingly.

"A little something to do while Neel is in India." She was pleased Shanti liked the new arrangement and hoped Neel would, too. She had also ordered an armchair that was to be delivered the next day. Neel had mentioned he wanted one and she had gone to some open houses to see how Americans decorated their rooms. Somehow she knew he would like the deep maroon leather with brass studs that lined the arms like a marching band.

"How have you been managing? Need me to take you to the grocery store?"

"Thanks, but I drive these days." Leila smiled. "See, I'm saying thanks correctly."

"I knew you'd get it. Not to dwell on funerals and death, but how is Neel coping?"

"He's okay, though he has a cold. They settled his grandfather's affairs and he's coming home the day after tomorrow." Her response bore the timbre of sadness, but there was joy at its root. She was now the custodian of Neel's answers. His colleagues called her to offer their condolences, they asked her for information about him. At such moments she felt guilty that the main effect of Tattappa's death was to bring her happiness.

"Good," Shanti said. "Then I'll get to see him before I leave."

"You are going somewhere?"

"New Zealand. A project came up and I jumped at the chance."

In her India days, she would have been rife with jealousy at

Shanti's chance to see a new country. Then even Ceylon, the tear-drop of India, was an exciting destination precisely because it was foreign. Now New Zealand held no magic for her whatsoever. Had she really looked longingly at the two islands when Ashok had suggested it for their honeymoon? Her life was here now, with Neel and the baby. "When did all this happen?"

"Very suddenly, actually. The editor who was going fell ill and they called me. I said yes before they could change their minds."

"You didn't consult with Bob?"

"You are so old-fashioned, Leila. I like it," Shanti added quickly, "but it is very much of the old world. I didn't 'consult with Bob,' as you put it, because he was in surgery and I'm capable of making up my own mind. It's funny, isn't it? In India we run around pleasing others and forget to make ourselves happy. Here everyone is a little too 'me' conscious."

"I guess a mixture of the two would be best," Leila said judiciously. "Shall we have some chai?"

"You read my mind. I'd love some. I'd better eat a jalebi now so it won't take away from the taste of the tea." Shanti nibbled and talked at the same time. "So, any thoughts on work, or are you still enjoying being a domestic goddess?"

"Still thinking about what to do." Leila didn't want to tell Shanti about the children's books. Just yesterday an agent had written saying he liked the story, did she have any more? Since then her fantasies revolved around getting published. She imagined telling Neel, "I'm going to have two types of babies, one of the flesh, and another that is intellectual." She'd dedicate the first book to her old and new family. She handed Shanti a mug of tea.

"What are you interested in doing?"

"Anything with words. Editing would be great. I'm going to be volunteering at the Y, starting next month. They have children who need extra tutoring in English and it will keep me busy a few evenings every week."

"Good for you. If I see any editing opportunities, I'll let you know. This tea is wonderful, Leila. It's different. What did you put in it?"

"Almonds. It's my short-cut version of *kahva*, the almond tea they make in Kashmir. Only mine isn't authentic." The almonds were on the counter as a reminder to be eaten daily—Amma used to say they helped to grow the baby's bones—and she had crushed some into the brew almost as an afterthought.

"This is light-years away from the awful tea they serve at the cafeteria. Bob and I had lunch there today."

Just a few weeks ago, Leila would immediately have imagined Neel having tea with Caroline in the same cafeteria, despairing that, unlike Bob, he never invited Leila to meet him at work. Now her eyes played out a different scenario: The secretary sat alone, while she, Leila, was the lucky Mrs. Sarath.

This morning she had sorted through Neel's closet, wanting to rid the condo of Caroline. She had deliberately not asked Neel about his late nights, because part of her suspected that he hadn't told her the whole truth. He had not broken up with Caroline years ago. He must have been seeing her those times he worked late because he had suddenly started coming home early after they first made love. She had to forgive him his past, even his recent past, if she was to stay with him. One by one she put her hand into suit pockets, expecting to see some remnant of his days and nights with Madam Fake, but always her fingers came up empty. At the last double-breasted gray suit she breathed easy, taking in the smell of her absent husband, who was present in the baby she carried.

"Why aren't you having any chai? Don't tell me you too are allergic to nuts?"

"As far as I know, I don't have any allergies. I'm having this." Leila raised her glass of orange juice.

"Since when does an Indian give up tea for juice? Are you pregnant? You do have a glow about you."

"An orange-colored glow?"

"Very funny. Come on, tell me."

Leila relented. "Yes, I am pregnant."

"Aren't you the sly one." Shanti raised her cup of tea. "To your baby. Tell me, is Neel thrilled? Is he ready to be a father?" So, she thought, the secretary fling is over and Dr. Suneel is settling down to being the good Indian husband.

"I hope so," Leila said.

She had spoken to him two hours ago. Indy's proposal was proceeding well and he had promised Amma to bring Leila for the wedding, unless it was around the baby's due date. Everyone knew she had not attended the funeral because it was too early in the pregnancy. The whole town, then, was aware of her good fortune. There would be no more talk of "poor Leila." The next time she saw them, there would be a baby in her arms.

Shanti left, and the empty apartment made Leila wish that Neel were already home. She wondered if he had spoken with Indy and on the spur of the moment decided to call her sister. As the long-distance buzz was replaced by a steady ringing, Leila thought how far she had come to being this person who easily picks up a phone and dials a country halfway around the world.

Indy answered, and it was as if they had never been parted. Words raced between them—interrupting; completing each other's sentences; changing topics quickly to make the most use of this expensive talking time. Amma and Appa had taken Kila to the Temple, so Indy didn't have to share the phone.

Indy said she could hardly wait to become an aunty. "I hope it's a girl. I'm not sure I'll know what to do with a little boy."

Leila asked when Srinivasan was coming to India. "Soon. I'm not sure when. Akka, I'm so nervous to meet him. How did you manage to keep so calm? I wish you were here to help me."

Leila promised Indy everything was going to be all right. "I just sent you some frizz control in the mail. Use it when he comes to see you, okay?"

Leila asked after their friends, including the woman who had taken her place at the college. But nothing much had happened the last few months, no marriages or engagements.

"There is something," Indy's voice faltered. "Janni died."

Leila was immediately transported to the crowded excitement of that first year in college. Sarees had replaced school uniforms. Some of the bolder girls wore lipstick. Classroom seats were not assigned and Leila always took the last row, eating, talking, sometimes even playing cat's cradle. In the big lecture halls the one teacher sitting up front didn't have the eyes or the energy to maintain discipline, and "bad" girls like Leila took advantage of that. There was no homework and hardly any tests. But what Leila liked best was the long bus ride to the college.

Liked it because she had met Janni in those aisles, sat beside him, squished, on the long seat at the back of the bus. And when he started passing her notes, she felt like a heroine in a Bollywood movie. On the big screen, couples took just one minute to fall in love. Now she had the same experience, writing his name a hundred times on paper that she threw away in case Amma's eagle eyes spied it. For months she had been content with the sporadic encounters. Then that day when the note was a question: *Will you come see a film with me?* The words kept echoing in her mind, her stomach too excited to eat lunch. She could think of nothing else during class except the hope that he wouldn't change his mind.

He hadn't, but someone must have seen them entering the cinema, because Appa came to get her even before the interval.

They didn't speak the whole way home. Amma met them at the gate and immediately took Leila to her room.

"So you went to your friend Saranjeet's house today? Such lies from my own daughter. No more college for you from now on. You are not to be trusted. Shaming our whole family. Stay here and don't move until I tell you."

For two weeks Leila lay in bed, her only companion an irate Amma. Indy wasn't allowed to comfort her. "I will not have you spoiling your sister," Amma shouted. "A Muslim boy. You want to be seen with a Muslim boy? Did you know that they can have three-four wives? His sister Yasmin is now the third wife to an old man. Is that what you want in your life?"

Each day was the same. Amma lectured and Leila listened through her tears. Her repeated sobs —"I'm sorry, Amma, I won't do it again"—weren't acknowledged. It was as if her tears had baptized her and she went from being the girl who always challenged Amma ("Why can't I cut my hair? I cut one inch yesterday and you didn't notice.") to being just another daughter squashed under her parents' will. Amma was unstoppable. Leila was too old to be beaten, so Amma used her only weapon: words. And when she left the room, the door was locked so Leila could not escape. When Amma returned, the berating started again as if nothing had been said earlier.

There was no need for Leila to finish college. A proposal had just come from a farmer, an older man who wouldn't care if he heard about Leila's shameless behavior. Appa was checking into it. By next month, Leila would be married. No more going out with a Muslim boy. Letting the whole world know by seeing a film together. What kind of daughter had she raised? And this Muslim boy? Did Leila think he really liked her? Hah! He was already seeing another girl. Saving her a place on the bus.

All this time Leila had been comforting herself with the thought that Janni, too, was suffering. That he was looking for her on the bus. Maybe standing around the college gate hoping to pass a note. Now Amma even took Janni away from her. Leila felt she had nothing to live for. How long could she listen? How long did Amma expect her to pay for this? She didn't want to marry an old farmer.

Now, almost half a lifetime later, Leila allowed herself to open up—fully—to that evening when the crows cawed so frantically, as if they sensed the approaching change and had to hurry to the safety of their nests. They gnawed at the calm of the evening, black sounds for a black event.

She emptied the bottle of pills, each white pellet innocent until massed together and swallowed with a glass of tap water. Her last thought was that Amma would be relieved, one less daughter to marry, Leila's bad behavior burned along with her body.

Afterwards, Indy told her how she had come into the room and tried to wake Leila for dinner. Then she screamed for Amma and Appa. The hushed, rushed taxi ride to the hospital, the extra money given to the driver so he would forget what he had seen.

Trying to get to the other side, Leila knew none of this.

Her hearing was the first of her senses to return to life. Voices, sobs, silence. A voice again, and this time she recognized it as Amma's. "My oldest child, my first baby. I could not have lived if she had died." Another voice, also broken. Indy. "Amma, she is going to be okay." Amma again, "We must go to the Temple tomorrow. I shall to scrub the floor in thanks."

A door whined as it was pushed ajar. A light was switched on and Leila opened her eyes. A nurse bent down, wagging her index finger in Leila's face. "Next time you better not eat chicken. See, eating flesh can be very dangerous." In a flash Leila knew what had happened. She had not succeeded and someone, Appa, probably, was telling people the suicide attempt had been food poisoning.

The old farmer was forgotten. They sent her away to Appa's village with Indy, two weeks during which Indy kept her sister in constant sight, afraid she might try something again. Leila had been tempted. But every time she wanted to throw herself in the river, she thought of Amma's words. "My oldest child, my first baby. I could not have lived if she had died."

When the rejections started coming, the incident was not brought up. But in the back of everyone's mind was the fear that people knew about Janni, that the suicide attempt had leaked out of the hospital. Had the gossip been started by the questioning nurse who knew it wasn't food poisoning? Perhaps Appa's insistence that his cousin be the doctor alerted suspicious minds. Was that why the men kept saying no? Were they afraid that Leila was unstable? Or did they think she had compromised her virtue and was too cheap for them?

Leila held the phone tight against her ear and stared at the dishwasher. Janni had wanted to be a mechanic and own his own TV shop. She would never see him again, the man who had bought her a movie ticket and made her think of passages in Mills & Boon books.

"How did he die?"

"A motorcycle accident."

Leila touched her mangalsutra and asked, "Was he married?"

"Yes, he had two children."

Leila didn't want to know any more.

> *Thou hast committed—*
> *Fornication? But that*
> *Was in another country, and besides,*
> *The wench is dead.*

She herself had died so many deaths over Janni. It had changed her whole life. Amma had made sure she paid for her mistake.

Just like the time she caught Leila turning down the waistband of her skirt so the hem would hang above the knee, the way other girls wore it. But Victorian, thrifty Amma wanted the skirt to look decent and last a long time. Then, too, she had stamped Leila down, insisting on checking her skirt every morning. Though Leila wore skirts and pants now, Amma would say it was okay because of Neel. He was the do-no-wrong son-in-law. But compared to Neel's dalliance, her brief tryst with Janni was so innocent.

"Poor children," Leila said, looking down at her stomach.

"Death comes in threes," Indy reminded her, but Leila didn't want to talk of Janni and dying anymore.

Babies also came in threes; she, Indy, Kila. Maybe the one she was carrying was the first of a trio.

THIRTY-SIX

NEEL RETURNED ON FRIDAY NIGHT wearing Tattappa's watch. The timepiece had yellowed with age and the thin, brown leather strap was tight around his wrist. Leila noticed it immediately but didn't say anything. She was happy to see him, happy to set the table with the meal she had prepared.

She had spent the whole evening making the dinner, excited that Neel was coming home. She had counted the days of his absence in terms of meals eaten alone. Four more breakfasts without Neel, three more dinners alone, until the final, solitary lunch today.

First she cleaned the whole condo, including the windows and the floors. Leila did not like the long-handled American mops, and squatted on the kitchen linoleum like Heera, using a cloth to swab it. She scrubbed the bathroom sink till it sparkled, thinking that soon Neel's toothbrush would be back in its place.

Only when everything was ready did she take a shower, lingering under the hot water. She had called the airline and timed everything down to the minute. Half an hour for Neel to get through Customs and another half hour to get a taxi home, where she would be waiting.

She had been saving the sample of perfume for months, hoping for just such an opportunity. She wanted to smell like America for Neel. She hoped he would like her new outfit. The yellow top enriched her own coloring and the slim cut of the jeans suited her. It still thrilled her that her legs were not wrapped into one by a saree. She had thought nothing of baring her midriff the first time she wore a saree, but had felt almost naked that day in Macy's when her legs stood apart like the metal divider in Kila's geometry box.

Neel had lost weight in the last week and there were new lines on his face. His words sounded gruff, interrupted by long spells of coughing. He was hungry, and Leila watched as he served himself some more rosemary risotto. She was used to thinking of rosemary as the herb of remembrance in *Hamlet* or a girl's name, not something used in cooking. The recipe for the courgettes and bottleneck squash called for just salt and pepper, but she had sprinkled on a little cayenne. It pleased her that she was beginning to experiment with American recipes. She had done the same with the green salad, adding the sharp-tasting baby bok choy to the bland butter lettuce.

That night, Neel walked into the bathroom as Leila brushed her teeth. Since his departure for India she had gotten used to leaving the door open and now felt shy to be doing something so personal in front of him. But he didn't seem to notice and began squeezing paste onto his brush. Their eyes met in the mirror, two bodies side by side, sharing a sink. And so much more, Leila thought happily.

Leila felt conspicuously different in her new nightie and fragrant Joy perfume. She watched as Neel switched off the lights and came to bed.

He sneezed and she asked, "Are you okay?"

"I'm just bushed." He yawned, then sneezed again. "The dinner was great, Leila. Maybe a good night's sleep will help my cold."

"Good night," Leila said. She wished he had not come back so tired and sick. She rolled over to be closer to him, but by the time she touched his hand, he was already snoring. She started to pull her fingers away, but his tightened. Leila smiled. Even in his sleep he was holding her. She was still smiling when she fell asleep.

The next day, his cold had gotten worse. His eyes and nose were red. Leila made the special tea Amma always brewed when they got sore throats and coughs. She boiled equal parts of milk and water and then spooned in the black tea leaves along with carda-mom, cinnamon, cloves, ginger, and sugar. She let it steep for a few minutes and then poured Neel a cup.

She wanted him to get well quickly. He had turned off his pager. It was to be just the two of them spending the weekend together before he returned to work Monday morning.

"I'm feeling a little better," Neel thanked her after breakfast. "I'd like to get out, do something. Is there anything you need? I've been gone a while."

"I have to go to the Indian store," Leila said, pleased but hesitant. She wanted Indian almonds. She knew Neel preferred the health food store, which carried many of the same ingredients. He still talked about seeing a mouse in the corner of the Indian one and how the owner had very nonchalantly said, "Oh, they're back again."

"The Indian store is too far away," Neel said immediately. He had just returned from the heat and overpowering odors of India and didn't want to be immersed in them again.

"Shanti says there's a new one just ten minutes from here." Leila jumped at her chance. "She brought me some jalebis from there."

They even found parking right outside the store, which Neel proclaimed a miracle. Leila simply thought it fit the day. Every-thing was turning out wonderfully.

They walked down aisles of freshly ground spices and products brought especially from India. Vajradanti toothpowder, Horlicks, incense. It was so reminiscent of the shops she used to frequent with Amma that Leila felt she might run into a former classmate at any moment. She wished she would. Then she could say casually, "Hello. This is my husband Neel." The word wasn't just a label anymore.

Neel walked alongside as she filled the blue basket with lentils and spices. With nothing else to do, he began to read the names. Garam masala. Ajwain. Panch poran. The array of pickles sent him back to college days when all the boys brought back bottles of lemon, mango, chili, bitter gourd, even meat and fish pickle. One of the doctors at the hospital who had spent a year in Bombay joked, "If you stand still long enough in India they'll pickle you." Neel had laughed, but pickles supplemented the meager diet of dorm food and he had even spread the spicy mixture on bread. A hot mango pickle sandwich was a popular midnight snack, with boys competing to eat the spiciest one, bragging that this was the way to become a real man and put hair on one's chest.

"Shall we get some whole mango pickle?" He suddenly wanted to taste his memory.

It was his chosen bottle, knocking around the other necessities, that made Leila say as she reached for the almonds, "It's for the baby."

"As long as I don't have to," Neel responded.

"Do you think the baby could be allergic to them, too?" she worried immediately.

"I doubt that. Eat whatever you want. Is there anything else you crave? Some other type of pickle?"

"Vadu manga is fine." She pointed to the tiny mangoes floating in the red chili sauce. "When I was small I used to frighten my friends by saying it was like a shrunken head, only it was a shrunken mango."

The woman who rang up their purchases was in a chatty mood. She spoke with the customer just ahead of them for such a long time Leila was afraid Neel would want to leave without the groceries.

"You handle it," Neel whispered. "My Hindi isn't very good anyway."

So Leila took care of the transaction, while Neel waited by the door.

"She's the owner," Leila shared the information.

"Really? She had better bone up on English if she wants to make a success of her store."

"I think she's already a success. Imagine running a store in a foreign country." The woman was so different from Anu, who was intimidated by her husband and her new country. Leila admired the woman's ability to take on such a large and confusing endeavor.

When they got home, the phone was ringing. Thinking it might be India, Leila grabbed it before Neel could free his hands.

"Hello?" There was no response and she said again, louder, "Hello?" A buzzing replaced the silence and Leila said, "I don't think it was India. Someone just hung up. It happened yesterday also."

"Wrong number, I guess," Neel said casually.

FIVE MILES AWAY, Caroline lit a cigarette. She'd taken up smoking in the past week, back to the one-packet-a-day habit she had given up since moving out west. It gave her something to do as she worried about Neel, their future, his odd behavior, and now his silence. He hadn't even told her about his grandfather's death. It was also from the hospital grapevine that she learned he was coming back to work on Monday. Hoping he might return early, she had called his pager. When she realized he must have turned it off, she called the house all morning. Each time the wife—soon to be ex-wife—answered.

Neel *had* to call her. There was so much to discuss. Maybe they could fly up to Sonoma to celebrate. She stubbed out the cigarette and reached for another one. Her fingers trembled. She hadn't eaten all day and it was mid-afternoon. If only she knew where Neel was. Was he home? On his way to see her? In case he was, she showered. She didn't want him to see her fat-faced again, like the other time he had returned from India and she cried so much they had to put his shirt in the dryer.

She came out of the bathroom, clean and smokeless, and immediately noticed the blinking green light on the answering machine. One call. Hope cranking up her heartbeats, she played it. It was Neel: "Caroline, it's Neel. I'll try and call you later. Don't call me." He was home. He wanted to talk to her! Sure that he would call before the night was over, she kept the phone beside her.

Neel bided his time, waiting for an opportunity to phone Caroline again. He didn't want her calling here again. Leila might begin to suspect that the hang-ups were Caroline clicking off because he hadn't answered the phone. He was quiet during dinner, allowing Leila to believe his cold was the reason. He ate quickly, eyeing his watch, hoping Caroline was not getting impatient. Leila chattered on, and he nodded to the tone of her voice, not the words. He was busy conducting his next conversation with Caroline.

"Wonderful quesadilla." Neel pushed away his empty plate. "You're becoming a real gourmet cook, galloping through all the Western countries. But you will make Indian food occasionally, right?"

"I thought you might like a change after being in India. Indian food tomorrow," she promised.

"Great. Listen, do you mind if I leave you to do the dishes? I need to make some calls to get ready for Monday. I left in such a hurry." This was going to be his last Caroline-inspired lie.

He sat down at the desk, reluctant to pick up the phone. If only he could put the entire episode, especially the last incident, to sleep. Close off that furtive part of his life so he could start dealing with the instant family in the other room. He hoped Caroline would take it well, that she would not create additional problems. Did she really think he would stay with her after she had told Leila everything?

He stared at the black phone and realized, through the throbbing of his temples, that he couldn't remember her number. It had been a while since he had called her and he had long erased her name from the auto menu. If only the pounding would go away. The cold had accosted his head and made thinking clearly difficult.

He dialed slowly, then with greater sureness as his memory returned.

Caroline answered on the first ring, as if she had been sitting there, waiting for his call.

"Neel, sweetie, you're back. I'm so sorry to hear about your grandfather."

"Thanks. You called earlier today, didn't you?" This was how he had planned to launch into the breakup. Put her on the defensive.

Caroline hesitated briefly. "Yes. I hung up."

"I told you never to call here." Neel considered bringing up that other call to Leila, but decided it would take too long. He wanted to do this as quickly as possible.

"But sweetie, I wanted to talk to you. I didn't know when you'd be back." She couldn't keep the reproach out of her voice.

"Monday. Didn't they tell you at the hospital?"

"They did, but I was talking about us."

There was a pause, and Caroline held the receiver tightly, her heart surging in loud, erratic thumps. Please, please, let him say he is coming over right now.

Neel was just about to start talking when she said, "Sweetie, I haven't seen you since my brother . . . I haven't had a chance to tell you. I was so angry that I kicked him out. I told him that I didn't like the way he treated you and if he couldn't be nice to you, the man I love, I didn't want to have anything to do with him. Ever."

Her words penetrated the miasma surrounding his brain and found that small vice of vanity he had thought was buried. For one glorious second his head cleared and he felt vindicated, victorious. She had chosen him.

Then his senses righted themselves and he realized that this was too much, too late. Indeed, it was something he had never really wanted from her. "You shouldn't have. You didn't have to do that."

"Of course I had to. He got the whole family involved so now I've cut them out of my life. I only want to be with you."

This was what he had wanted to hear from Savannah. Instead, she had ended things the day after he flew to see her. It still puzzled Neel that she hadn't broken up with him at Stanford. Why had she made him spend money on a plane ticket and a hotel room?

"Neel, when can I see you? We have so much to talk about."

He was pondering how exactly to answer when she suggested, "Tomorrow?"

Tomorrow was Sunday. He hadn't made any plans with Leila. Should he meet Caroline? The two options sifted slowly through the painful currents in his head. He was going to end it. That was certain. At least he wouldn't feel like a total heel if he did it in person.

"Let's go to a café," he said. She wouldn't be able to make a huge fuss in a public place. He could take the risk, knowing it was the last one.

"But we haven't flown in so long." They would start fresh, she'd make him forget that last tearful trip.

"I've got this cold," he said truthfully.

"Please? I've so looked forward to it. I love going up with you. Please, Neel?"

For a moment he thought longingly of the plane. It was his refuge, his time away from stresses. How he loved arching through a clear blue sky, feeling himself in control of his life, the rich, clean city spread out beneath him. But of course he couldn't take her up anymore. Those days had ended. Forever. "I just remembered," he lied, taking the easy way out. "Jake's using the plane. I'll pick you up at ten o'clock."

THIRTY-SEVEN

LEILA DIDN'T CARE WHAT THEY DID on Sunday as long as they were together. She slipped out of bed before Neel awoke, brought in the fat, rolled-up newspaper, and started the sambar.

When Neel came into the kitchen, he thought he was in his mother's house. The instant dosa mix was rising in the large bowl and the sizzling sambar spat small brown dots all over the white stove. He had asked for Indian food yesterday, but now wondered if the smell of asafetida would ever leave the kitchen.

"You're up," Leila said happily.

Caroline used to use those same words for another reason.

"Good morning," he said, and pulled out the sports section, relieved that his headache was gone. "Have you had breakfast?"

"I was waiting for you." Leila heated the iron tava Amma had insisted she bring to America and spread a spoonful of dough in a thin layer, similar to the crepes suzette she had watched chefs make on TV. "There's no potato curry, just sambar. I hope you don't mind."

"Not at all. I'm not too hungry," he warned. "I don't have much of an appetite in the morning."

"I know, but you need to eat, at least a little. It's good for your cold." She put a dosa on his plate and ladled on some sambar.

When the second dosa was ready, she took her place opposite him. She imagined a baby jumping up and down on the high-chair, playing with the salt and pepper shakers while she fed it tiny

347

pieces of dosa. When Kila was little, Leila used to give her small bites from the softest part of dosas.

"I hope the baby looks like you," she said, feeling a sudden rush of affection for him. She had been one among three sisters and after his accident Appa had not been a strong presence in the house. Neel's very maleness had been exciting and intimidating in the beginning. Now it was only thrilling. The spread of muscles across his back, the size of his ankles, the way he turned the steering wheel with one hand. His hands. She had always been partial to large hands and his almost covered the dinner-size plate that held the dosa.

"Maybe it will have your hands," she said. She used to tell Indy, "If a man doesn't have big hands, there will be nothing to hold on to during romantic walks." Today, she could see them going on such a walk. She would show him the Presidio, that special spot where she found blackberries, the aisle of trees permanently changed by the way the wind blew.

"The baby already knows exactly what he or she is going to look and be like. That was decided the minute the egg and sperm met." But she had been so sweet that Neel relented and added, "However, I do think a girl with my hands might have trouble getting a date."

"Date? I can't imagine any daughter of mine dating."

"You won't have to. She'll do it for you." Neel laughed. "I think a girl would be nice, though. Most of my cousins were boys, so a girl will pose a challenge for me."

"Two females with PMS. Yes, that will be a challenge."

"I guess we'll have to have a boy just to even things out."

He sneezed and she said, "If you are not feeling better, maybe we shouldn't do anything today. In the Bible even God rested on Sunday." After ten years of attending Catholic School—to which Amma had sent her reluctantly and only because it was the best school in their town—she knew the major stories.

"I guess God could afford to rest because He had taken care of all His obligations. I'm afraid I have to go flying this morning. I completely forgot about a date I'd made with Jake. It's to teach him to fly a loop," he explained. "I'd ask you to come with us but I don't think it's a good idea in your condition. Incidentally, this dosa is very good."

Would she realize the lengthy explanations covered up lies? He had wondered what reason would get him out of the house alone for a few hours. He had come up with this—the tidiest of all possible lies—late last night. Jake was a salesman who was hardly ever in the city. That trip to Reno had been the first time Neel had seen him in a year. And Leila had heard Jake asking Neel to teach him the loop.

Leila smiled at the compliment, though she was disappointed by the rest. Still, he *wanted* to take her flying. It was on the tip of her tongue to ask him to cancel, but he didn't suggest it and she didn't want to be pushy. Besides, a part of her admired him. He was an honorable man, keeping his promise even with a bad cold.

"Would you like to take some tea with you?" she asked.

"Sure, if it's not too much trouble. Though we may not have a thermos." He wouldn't be able to take it to the café, and would have to remember to pour the tea out before returning home.

"I found one with your camping stuff in the closet."

"I'll bring it down. Now I think I'll take a long, hot shower. That should wake me up."

His empty chair was replaced by the hum of the hot water pipes. The kettle began to gurgle and she listened to the noises as if they were a symphony conducted by Zubin Mehta. These were the sounds she had longed to hear, the everyday workings of a home and its occupants.

The phone joined the chorus and she picked it up knowing Neel would not be able to hear it. If it was an important call—maybe

India—she would go right into the bathroom and get him. She would not be shy and knock on the door.

It was Jake and she hoped immediately he had called to cancel the lesson.

"I'm going up to Reno next weekend and I had such fun the last time, I was wondering if you and Neel wanted to join me again."

"I don't know. Why don't you ask Neel?"

"Want to put him on the phone?"

"He's in the shower. But you can ask him when you see him. Aren't you flying with him?"

"Not with me, he's not. I'm off to New York in a few hours. Why don't you think about the Reno trip and let me know? Just leave a message with my answering service."

Hair wet, Neel strode into the kitchen holding a red thermos. "That shower did the trick. I'm feeling much better."

"Shall I make enough tea for Jake?" she tested him, taking the thermos.

"I'm not sure he drinks the stuff. He probably doesn't even know about masala chai, but sure, go ahead. How soon will it be ready?" He didn't want Caroline calling here again.

"Shouldn't take too long," Leila answered, feeling like a servant. He only wanted to be with Madam Fake. Why else would he lie to her? He probably wasn't even going flying. Caroline must be waiting for him at her home with her French accent, French cooking, French lingerie, French kissing.

She spooned in the dark, bitter tea leaves without thinking, and threw in the spices any which way. With every addition she felt more betrayed and belittled. Why was Neel continuing to do this to her? Why did he lie so much? How could he expect her to share him?

The brew grew darker, leeching color from the tea leaves. He had told Cynthia and Harold that he had fallen in love with her over a cup of tea. She had served him coffee that morning, but had believed his lies during dinner.

From the corner of her eye she saw the brown nest of almonds. Her wedding saree was scattered with almond designs embroidered in gold thread. Almonds were good luck, Amma had told her. Amma had told her many things. She had told her to keep the saree for the first baby. Amma had strung her own wedding saree into a long hammock, hanging it from a hook in the ceiling. She had placed Leila amidst the soft silk, letting the wind rock her to sleep. It was a tradition Leila had hoped to follow. Now she wished she had cut up her wedding saree that day when half her clothes went into the garbage.

"Is it ready yet?"

He was standing in the doorway, looking down at his watch, tapping his foot. His impatience was so loud it reminded her of the cars that waited for her at the crosswalk, engines throbbing as if they couldn't bear to be stationary.

"Almost," she said.

He looked handsome in the dark blue shirt she had bought him. "It's a welcome-back present," she had said. "I selected a blue one because your name, Neel, means 'blue' in Hindi." Lord Krishna was blue. He was her favorite God, the easiest one to recognize because of his coloring. Krishna, the great lover, was the only god with the ability to be with numerous women at one time. His power was so immense, he gave each woman the illusion that he was with her alone. She thought Neel had given up that erotic dance of ras-lila. She thought he had decided to stay with her—his wife—soon to be the mother of his child.

Her back was to him and he couldn't see what she was doing. She wasn't sure herself what she was doing when she reached for the jar of almonds. She put her hand in and brought out a handful.

The milk had formed a wrinkled layer over the cooling tea. As the almonds disappeared into the open mouth of the thermos, Leila saw Neel open his mouth to kiss Caroline. She saw his tongue swell, his throat grow so constricted that it was difficult to breathe.

He would not even be able to talk to Caroline. He would be too uncomfortable to roll around on the bed. He would come back to her, where he belonged.

· THIRTY-EIGHT ·

CAROLINE WOKE UP EARLY, anxious because she would be seeing Neel today, nervous because though he had agreed to meet, it was at her suggestion, and she didn't know what he was going to say. Would he bring up the call to his wife?

Fidgety, she phoned Natalie. They were always there for each other, and she need kindness, understanding, a sympathetic ear. She poured it all out, the phone call yesterday, that awful, terrifying pause on Neel's part and her insecurity about today. Natalie already knew about the aborted Sonoma trip as well as the romantic night Dan had interrupted. She had warned Caroline not to lie to Neel about throwing Dan out, told her that if things worked out between them, he would find out and be furious with her. As always, Caroline laughed it off, saying, "We'll be married by then." Natalie had countered, "And you think that solves everything, right? That's when it all begins, Caroline. In the scheme of marriage, a wedding is just the beginning."

Now Natalie listened, but instead of offering solace, she made Caroline even more nervous.

"He doesn't tell you his grandfather is dead. He doesn't tell you he's going to India. He doesn't call you when he returns, at least not until you call first, and you think he's coming over today to tell you he's going to divorce his wife?"

When Caroline tried to say that Neel must have had his reasons, Natalie laughed and said yes, it was a four-letter one: wife. "How come he didn't marry you when he had the chance?" Before

353

Caroline could come up with an explanation, Natalie added, "He didn't when he could, so why would he now?"

"Because we get along so well. We love each other." They did get along nicely and hardly ever fought, except when she brought up the "M" word. But even Natalie had to agree that that wasn't unusual. If women didn't prod men, they would live like clueless singles.

But Natalie wasn't convinced. "Look, I don't mean to rain on your parade, but how well do two people who only see each other one evening a week, who have to find out-of-the-way places to go to, and who act like strangers at work really know each other?"

"You're a big comfort," Caroline charged. "Did you wake up on the wrong side of life?"

"Sorry. I don't mean to sound so cynical. It's just that I've been there and I don't want you to get hurt."

"You're the one hurting me now," Caroline said quietly.

"Okay, sorry. I take back everything I said. Look, he's probably coming over full of honorable intentions."

"Yes, and I'm wearing a wedding gown."

"Seriously, though, he might be. People propose at the oddest times."

Caroline knew that Natalie was just trying to make up for her earlier sharpness. Neel had never wanted to meet at a café before, and both women had carefully avoided discussing the unusual suggestion.

"So," Natalie asked, "how are you going to handle it?"

"That's why I called you. Do I offer sympathy, or do I say, 'I've waited long enough, let's talk about us.' What do I do?"

"Whatever it is, don't start analyzing his every word and movement, okay? He's probably jet-lagged, an emotional wreck. So my advice is, don't make any waves, make it seem like just another get-together. What do you usually do?"

"You know—"

"Hey, I can't offer any advice there. I haven't had any in so long I'm practically a born-again virgin. You know him best, Caroline. You'll figure it out."

The trouble was, Caroline thought as she paced the bedroom, Natalie was right. She didn't know Neel, not the way some women know their boyfriends, not even the way she had known her fiancé. She knew some things about him, but they hadn't been connecting recently and she didn't know how to reach him.

She only knew that she wanted him to come over and say, "I love you and now we can get married."

She thought back to Natalie's question. Of course! He hadn't asked her to marry him before because he didn't want to hurt his grandfather. But now the grandfather was dead and there was nothing to stand between them.

It was going to be all right, it was going to be fine.

Then she looked at the clock and flew into another panic. He would be here any minute and she still hadn't decided which dress to wear. Neel had said she looked nice in dresses and all she had on was a black lace slip.

The bell. He was here. She'd greet him in the slip. It could mean she hadn't finished dressing—or that she was ready for him.

"Sweetie," she made to kiss him, keeping Natalie's advice in mind.

"Remember, I have a cold." Neel stepped aside. "Why get sick if you don't have to?"

Determined to start them off in the usual way, she said, "Then I'll kiss you with my mouth closed."

He turned his face at the last minute and she found herself pecking his cheek.

"It's not like you to be this careful," Caroline said, perplexed by his behavior.

"What kind of doctor would that make me?" Neel smiled, though Caroline could see he wasn't really joking.

Why was he acting so strange, hovering at the door, not kissing her back? Then it hit her. He was probably thinking of that last time with Dan.

"Sweetie, I want to apologize for my brother. I'm so sorry you had to go through that. But you won't have to ever again."

Neel looked away from that face, so white and blue and giving. He didn't want to be reminded of the last time when he had scurried away.

"Like I told you on the phone yesterday. I've cut off the whole family."

Neel felt himself weakening, felt her words turn the evening around. She had stood up for him, done what he should have. He had heard of women like this, but after Savannah had given up hope of meeting one. He never imagined that one day Caroline would make him her whole world.

Gratitude softened his voice. "Caroline," he began, then stopped.

"Sh . . ." She placed a finger on his lips. "You don't have to say anything. I know you would do the same for me."

He had come here to tell her the exact opposite. It was going all wrong. They were supposed to be at a café, with him saying his good-byes and then going home to Leila.

"I saw this new café just down the block," he tried to get them back on track. "We can walk there once you get ready."

"Come and talk to me while I finish dressing." Caroline turned without waiting for his response.

He hesitated at the inappropriateness of it all, but thought it would look . . . hypocritical to refuse. After all, they had been far more intimate than this.

He watched her swaying in front of him, her back even more

creamy against the black. The lace clung to her buttocks, the scalloped hem undulating between her legs. She turned to look at him from the doorway and suddenly he knew what she was up to. And having come prepared to let her down gently, he now understood that he was going to have to be even more careful. She couldn't read his mind, couldn't know that he had chosen Leila and that this was the last time they would see each other outside the hospital. He remembered how he had felt after Savannah and determined to spare her some of the pain.

Perfectly aware that she was reeling him in, each step toward the bedroom thundered in his head, keeping pace with the headache that had returned.

"My headache's getting worse," he said. "I really do need some tea. The caffeine should do the trick."

"I've got aspirin," Caroline offered.

"I'd rather get to that café and have tea."

"Why don't I make you some?"

First Leila, then Caroline—everyone wanted to *make* him tea. Leila had even kept him waiting while she doled in the spices.

"I can wait till you're ready," Neel insisted.

"It's just a cup of tea." Caroline kept her voice light.

"Why cook when you don't have to?" Neel countered. "I think I'll wait for you outside. I seem to be hampering your progress."

"Then help me," Caroline said quickly. He had never waited for her outside before. What was happening? Again she heard that pause on the phone, when he didn't speak and she'd suggested they meet today. But she hadn't meant meet for coffee. She had meant for them to get together and discuss their future. "Blue or yellow?" She held up two dresses. "Though maybe yellow is overkill for a blonde," she prattled on, willing her words to lure him back to the old days when he helped her undress rather than dress.

"Blue. Come on, Caroline, this is taking forever."

"I know why you're crabby. It's the headache. Water and an aspirin." Caroline put back the two dresses and this time marched quickly past him and into the kitchen.

"This is totally unnecessary, Caroline, really."

"Are you going to take it or do I have to make you take it? Remember the time I didn't want to try the retsina you brought over and you made me?"

She was being so cheerful and kind and—sexual. Yes, once, long ago, he had given her mouth-to-mouth retsina. Didn't she remember how uncomfortable it had been? That he had never tried it again?

Caroline took a sip of water and came toward him.

"No, Caroline, stop. Please."

But she didn't listen, and instead reached for his face.

Neel put his hands on her shoulders and pushed her away.

Caroline stumbled back, the water suddenly sour in her mouth. She couldn't seem to do anything right. She swallowed the water, heard it go down noisily, and wondered how long she could take this, standing almost naked in front of him. Tears gathered in her eyes but she forced them away. He had never liked weepy women. He had always liked her. He did, he did like her. Why else had he gone out with her for so long? He was tired. She was pushing him, asking too much too soon. She needed to give him space.

"Caroline, I'm sorry. Look, I meant to tell you yesterday, but I couldn't. I mean, I didn't think it was right to end things over the phone."

Caroline couldn't look away from his dark eyes. Her heart immediately accelerated and she felt as though she were about to throw up.

"I can't do this anymore. Not to you, not to me. It's over. I'm sorry."

Every word echoed in her head. She felt them course down her body and reach her toes, which curled into the cold floor. She didn't, couldn't believe them.

"What do you mean, it's over?" They hadn't fought, she hadn't made any demands, so what was he talking about?

She kept looking at that face, the color of a tree trunk, the lips that knew so much and could kiss so well.

It couldn't be ending. Not after all this waiting. No wonder Natalie didn't trust him. Natalie's married lover, too, had gone back to his wife. Five years of sneaking around and he had just ended it one day. Two years later, when they ran into each other at the supermarket, he told her he was divorced. He was already involved with another woman, younger, who could give him the family he wanted.

"I'm sorry," Neel said. "I'm sorry if I'm hurting you. I never meant it to be this way, but it is over. I'll leave now."

She couldn't let him walk out of the apartment, needed a way to keep him here, but the only words that left her mouth were, "Why? What did I do wrong?"

She could win him back. This wasn't like Natalie's situation. It was between the two of them because the wife had never mattered.

"Nothing. I don't know. It's over is all."

"But you said you'd marry me." She had hoped so much for that. Not a down-on-one-knee, ring-in-the-box proposal. Just a simple, "Will you marry me?"

"I never, ever said I'd marry you," he clarified, a little angry that she was putting him in this false situation.

"When you came back last summer, you said we'd get married when your grandfather died."

"You have a wild imagination. I believe my exact words were, 'We'll carry on as before.'"

"Then why can't we do that? You don't love this woman." She knew he had never dated an Indian, had heard the envy in his voice when he spoke of Sanjay's wife. She was her own best card.

"It wouldn't be fair to her."

"But what about me?"

"I never promised you anything. I treated you well. I even gave you a car."

"I never wanted that rotten old car. I want you. I've given up my whole family for you."

This time Neel did not accept the gift he had once so desperately yearned for. He had wanted to believe her story just to make up for the fact that he should have been the one booting off the brother, so he wouldn't have to look back on the evening with the same degree of humiliation. But he had always known it wasn't true.

"Then why didn't you tell your brother to leave when I was there? Why wait till I left?"

"Because . . ." Caroline hadn't prepared for this question. She had expected him to believe her and be happy.

"Because you didn't send him away." Neel took a deep breath. He hadn't just come to end things with her; he had come to end all the lies. "Your brother didn't even know about me, Caroline. Look, I'm not blaming you. My family knows nothing about you, either. This whole thing, this relationship, was never going anywhere."

"But we've been together so long."

"I'm sorry about that. It wasn't right of me."

"But you can make it right now."

"I can't, Caroline. At least not for you."

She read the rest of the sentence in his eyes.

"How can you want to be with her? She's so"—Caroline stopped herself from saying, "Indian."

"She's my wife," Neel said quickly. He didn't want her saying anything about Leila.

"But you told me you never wanted to marry her."

"That was in the summer. This is now."

"But what happened in that time?"

"She's pregnant." He hadn't planned on telling Caroline about the pregnancy, but their meeting was getting too long and complicated. Maybe now she would believe him.

My grandfather asked me to marry her, not sleep with her, he had told her when he'd rushed over to her apartment, leaving the wife in the condo. He'd been sleeping with both of them. When her period was a few days late, he'd had abortion written all over his face. But the young wife was allowed to keep her baby. She got everything: the doctor husband, the condo in Pacific Heights, the new car, the plane, the baby.

"You bastard, you lying, cheating, bastard!" Caroline screamed, wishing her words were arrows that would pierce him so he'd topple from the pain. "How dare you sleep with both of us? How dare you come here and tell me she's pregnant?"

"Caroline, calm down—"

"You're standing there and telling me what to do? You bastard!"

"Oh, and you're the good guy who just happened to call up my wife when I wasn't home?"

Natalie had warned her not to do it. She could hear Natalie say, "It doesn't matter how hard you fight, they always choose their wives in the end." She could see the vein throbbing in his forehead, how his nostrils flared with every word.

Caroline crumbled, and now could not control her sobs.

She raised her face toward him, tears clotting her eyelashes.

"Caroline, I'm sorry. I'm sorry if I led you to believe we would marry. You will never know how sorry I am. But it's over."

"What did I do wrong?" They all left her. She'd end up like Natalie, alone and bitter.

Neel shook his head. There was so much that was wrong. But he could not blame her. She had only been thinking of her future. In Reno, in calling up Leila. Even today. She could not know that it was his past that had brought him here.

When Savannah had disappeared into the folds of her family, he felt anger, sadness, and shame. "She didn't think I was good enough," he told Sanjay, wild with grief at what he could not have. Sanjay had staunchly maintained that Savannah was the one who wasn't good enough. "How did Oona do it, then?" Neel had not been able to stop that question. "I honestly don't know." Sanjay shook his head. "I was too busy trying to figure out how I had fallen for her. I always thought I'd go back and marry a nice Bangla girl."

But, he added, he had no choice. As he'd said on numerous occasions, he would have married Oona if she had been purple.

Neel had dismissed the claim as one of Sanjay's silly jokes. He had always envied the other man. But Sanjay wasn't being funny. He had fallen for Oona in spite of, not because of, her color. And just because she was white didn't mean theirs was a dream marriage. They had problems that couples in arranged marriages didn't have. A white wife did not guarantee happiness.

He'd been wrong all these months spent railing against his lack of choice. For years he'd wondered why it was he didn't have what Sanjay obviously had. Now he had it, too.

And just when he could say yes, he knew with absolute certainty that he no longer wanted that third item on his youthful list.

He didn't know how or why, but he felt his old skin slip off, giving his brownness a comfort he had never felt before.

And when that desire for a white wife left him, so did his anger. He hadn't realized how angry he had been. Angry at Caroline for not being the right white woman; angry at Leila for forcing him to become a husband and father.

There was no need to be angry with Caroline anymore. This

time when he looked at her face, he saw past the rabbitish eyes and the leaking nose and found—desperation. She wanted what he represented; just as he had wanted what she represented.

"You didn't do anything wrong. Please believe me when I say that. It just wasn't meant to be," he said gently.

"I'm never going to have anyone." She couldn't stop those fearful words.

"You will, Caroline." Neel said, "He just has to be right for you."

"Is your wife, this Lee, right for you?"

He remembered Tattappa's words, felt the watch strap tight on his wrist. "It is better to be with one's own kind," Tattappa had said.

"She is." The two words did not have the joy or freedom of "I do" but they carried the same commitment.

He was so much luckier than Caroline. She had grown up with dates every night of the week, the freedom to live away from the age of eighteen, and here she was, still alone. All those choices, and she hadn't been able to get her choice. Yet he, who halfway across the world had to keep his nights and days a secret from his family, now had, because of that family, a wife, and soon a baby.

Caroline had wanted all that with him. She wasn't asking for the impossible.

Jacques Olivier had assumed Neel was going out with Caroline, but that hadn't stopped him from inquiring if she was available. He was probably still interested in Caroline, still looking to find someone who would understand his French instead of being seduced by his accent.

He'd give it a few weeks and then encourage Jacques to follow up on his interest in Caroline.

It was that thought that followed him outside, not the tears and sadness of a time now passed. He had left her drinking the tea she'd wanted to make for him. This time she understood that he couldn't stay, that he would never again ring her doorbell.

He checked the clock in the car. He'd been here for almost two hours. Leila wasn't expecting him back quite yet. Perhaps he should have some of the tea Leila had made. She really was quite amazing. Instead of getting angry or asking him to change his plans, she had simply made him tea. For his cold.

He glanced around for the red thermos. Then he remembered she'd come running to the door and taken it from his hands, saying the milk was spoiled.

Too bad, he thought, as he started the car. The tea would have been nice.

· THIRTY-NINE ·

NEEL OPENED THE FRONT DOOR THINKING he'd have another hot shower to wash off the morning and then ask Leila to make him masala tea without milk.

"Leila, I'm back," he called out, and waited to hear her voice, footsteps, any indication that she was home. Guilty that he had spent the morning with Caroline, he wanted to get this first-encounter-after-the-lies over with.

"Leila?" he tried again, raising his voice and walking toward the kitchen, only to find it empty. Figuring she might be taking a late shower, he headed to the bathroom, but knew from the open door that she wasn't there, either.

He returned to the kitchen wondering what to make of her absence.

The newspaper was on the table and the dishes piled in the sink. The smell of frying dosa was still there, as was a small amount of leftover batter.

Then he noticed the aloe plant. It had tipped over and the green plastic container had split open, oozing soil onto the tile.

Everything was the same as when they were having breakfast—except for the plant. Had the wind blown it down? He scooped up the mud and placed the plant on a saucer. What had happened? Why hadn't Leila cleaned it up?

Where was she? When he hadn't reached her from India, he thought she had left him. But she had been in the condo the whole time.

Had she left him now? But why would she do that? She had no idea he was meeting Caroline and she had known for a week that he was prepared to become a father.

That was it, he thought with relief. Her pregnancy. She was probably feeling those strange urges and had gone out to buy something.

He sat on the squeaky new leather chair, trying to read the paper, listening for footsteps and the turn of a key. The printed words remained on the page, his mind still on Leila. If he hadn't lied to her, if she hadn't been so understanding about his going flying while sick, he wouldn't be feeling this jumpy and guilty. Thank God it was the last of Caroline.

Half an hour later, the same section of the paper on his lap, he suddenly thought that she might have left him a note. He'd said he'd be back around now, and it wasn't like her to take off without telling him. As he walked toward the fridge to check the board, he noticed the blinking red light on the answering machine. Hoping it was a memo from Leila, he pressed "play." He hadn't known about the memo feature, but she had read the instructions and shown him how it worked.

"Hi Neel. It's Jake. I spoke with your wife earlier about the trip to Reno. Turns out I got the dates mixed up. It's the following weekend. Leave me a message if you two can come. I'll pick it up from the Big Apple. See ya."

The happy, carefree American words sickened Neel. Of all the days in the year, Jake had to call this morning. He'd spoken to Leila and she had known there was to be no flying. Why hadn't she told him anything?

Had Jake phoned while he was in the shower? Neel tried to remember if there had been a change when he came downstairs. But he was so anxious to leave, so worried that Caroline would call, that he hadn't paid any attention to Leila. He had given her the thermos, waiting—interminably, it seemed to him, for the tea. All that while she hadn't said a word, just concentrated on making the brew. No, he suddenly remembered, she'd asked if Jake would like some tea. She had been testing him and he had continued the lie. Was that why she practically snatched the thermos from his hands? Just when he was at the front door, ready to step outside. Had she given him that much time to confess?

She had claimed the milk was sour. Neel wasn't so sure about that now. He checked the date on the carton; good for another four days. She had lied to him. So many lies between them, he thought, pressing his fingers to his temples where the fierce thud-thud of his headache was in full force. Since he wasn't giving Jake a lesson, Leila must have guessed he was with Caroline.

Where *was* she?

Neel paced the floor, trying to figure out what to do. Trying to figure out what Leila might have done. The problem was, he didn't know her well, had made so little attempt to get to know her.

She had that friend from Berkeley, he remembered. A journalist. What was her name? He strained his memory but nothing came to him. She'd kept that new friend to herself, and now Neel would never be able to get ahold of her if she'd gone there.

Maybe she had gone to see Shanti. They'd spent a lot of time together in Reno and it made sense that she would seek out a fellow Indian. He called up and wondered how he could ask about Leila without giving anything away.

Shanti, Bob reminded him, was in New Zealand. "She's left me for three whole weeks," Bob complained. "I can't wait to have her back."

Oona was the only other person Neel could think of. Sanjay had told him their two women were getting close, having tea, "and no doubt telling each other how impossible husbands can be." Sanjay had laughed. Neel responded with a smile, sure that

Leila would never discuss such things with Oona. But perhaps she did.

He picked up the phone, then replaced it. He couldn't call up and ask, "Is Leila there?" If she wasn't, he would be forced to tell Mr. Goody Two Shoes Sanjay all that had been going on. He didn't want Sanjay and Oona to lose respect for him, especially now, after he had finally cut off the past.

Neel suddenly remembered Leila telling him about Oona's miscarriage. He would call up, offer his condolences, and ask about Leila at the same time.

"Well, at least I know I can get pregnant," Oona rallied valiantly. "So we'll just keep on trying."

"Of course, of course." Neel was uncomfortable. "Is Sanjay there?"

Sanjay came on the line. "I tell you, Neel, it's very different when it's personal. We had to rush to the Emergency Room. I was with her the whole time but it wasn't my body having the D&C. I used to joke that I'm just the sperm donor. But I was right. We men aren't as brave as our women."

"Leila will agree with you. She says that the Adam and Eve story has been interpreted wrongly all these centuries. According to her, God created Adam, then decided He could do better, and so created Eve."

"Good one," Sanjay acknowledged with a laugh. "Leila told us the good news about you two. How is she doing? You taking good care of her?"

"Trying to," Neel answered. So Leila definitely wasn't there. Where *was* she? Had she really left him?

"Trying is not the same as doing. Arre, do I sound like your parents?"

"Yes, but also like a good friend who's been bugging me from day one to behave. Hey, Sanjay, hang on a second. I'm getting another call."

When he switched back to Sanjay, he said very quickly, "That was the hospital. Leila's there. I've got to go." He hung up even as he could hear Sanjay offer, "Can we help?"

Neel was halfway to the hospital when he realized he hadn't asked what had happened. All he heard was "hospital" and he panicked. Not sure in what condition he would find her, Neel made his way to the room the nurse at reception had given him.

Leila was lying on the bed, awake—and whole. She hadn't slit her wrists. Then, even as he relaxed, he realized he was in the maternity section. And Patrick was in attendance.

Had she tried to do something to the baby? His headache drummed inside his temples, but he could think clearly in spite of the pain.

"What happened?" Neel asked the other doctor. He couldn't bring himself to speak with Leila just yet.

"Why don't you tell Neel while I get us prepped," Patrick suggested easily.

Now he had to talk to her, look at the blue and white hospital gown from under which her legs splayed out into the stirrups.

Leila was taken aback by his appearance in the room. When the nurse suggested she call Dr. Sarath, Leila had resisted, giving in only because the woman seemed surprised. He might be gone the whole day, Leila said, then kept quiet when the kind nurse insisted a message on the answering machine would let the doctor know immediately upon his return home. Leila wasn't sure if he ever planned to return home. Still, she told the nurse to go ahead and call, and was relieved when they moved her to a private room before the woman could tell her if she had reached Neel.

Apparently, Neel had been reached and now here he was. Leila looked down at the white sheet. Her legs were apart, exposed. Should she expose Neel the same way?

"After you left to go flying," Leila said deliberately, "I felt a small pain, but I thought it was nothing. Then, when I was doing the dishes, it hurt so much I couldn't stand and I grabbed the counter. I was worried about the baby, so I came straight to the hospital."

The counter-clutching had happened an hour after he left. He had barely stepped outside the door when she hurriedly emptied the thermos, appalled at what she had almost done. Sanjay had said almonds could kill Neel. Then, as she watched the brown beads vanish into the drain, she wished they *were* going down Neel's throat. He should have stayed home, had another dosa, a cup of tea; but he was rushing back to Caroline. She could not fathom his decision. She had sensed a change in him this weekend, felt a closeness, a tie that went beyond the baby. Was he faking it?

She wanted to call up Caroline and tell her off, make up for that other time she had been unable to do anything but listen. But Neel was the one to blame. She should have said something before he left, when she had the chance. Instead, she'd wanted to kill him, then let him—the man she had forgiven enough to think of as a husband again, the father of her baby—walk away from her.

She remembered the baby with a rush of guilt. Could the baby feel her anger and panic? Would all these awful feelings cause a miscarriage? She had to protect the baby. It was hers. No one could take this tiny growing being away from her. Desperate for some calm, she had taken a long shower, forcing herself not to think of Neel up in the plane with Caroline. She tried to go about her day in the usual normal way, and so progressed to doing the dishes. That was when the first pain exploded.

Neel heard her say, "After you left to go flying," and felt a deluge of shame overwhelm him. "I shouldn't have gone this morning. I'm sorry. I'm here now. It won't happen again."

"Leila got a lot of sympathy, checking in by herself," Patrick said. "And once they knew she was your wife, they rolled out the red carpet for her. Called me from one of my patients. Only the best for Mrs. Sarath."

A nurse knocked on the door and Patrick excused himself, saying, "Probably that other patient. I'll be right back."

Leila still hadn't looked at Neel.

Neel knew he had to take the first step.

"You have every right to be angry," he said, and meant it. "I was taking care of some unfinished business. It's over now. It's just us."

She remembered Jake's invitation, his expectation that they were a happy couple who would want another trip to Reno. "If Jake hadn't phoned . . ." Leila let the sentence alone.

It dangled in the room, and Neel saw its completion as his chance at getting a new start.

"If Jake hadn't phoned, you would not have known where I went this morning. But the outcome would have been the same."

"What was the outcome?"

"I took care of that unfinished business," Neel repeated.

She wasn't going to let him off easy. "You already said that. What does it mean, though?"

Neel took a deep breath and said, "Those phone hang-ups this weekend were Caroline. She was trying to reach me because she thought I would marry her when Tattappa died. I never said that, but she refused to believe me. So I met her today to tell her once and for all not to bother me—us—again."

"Why should I believe you this time?"

"Because I am with you now."

"But you were with me before." In Reno, in their condo, he had spent every night with her, but still found time to be apart.

All relationships were like seesaws; Neel knew that. It was simply that with Leila he was used to being on the upper end. How could he bring them both to the same level? He had just started with "Leila," when Patrick, after a quick knock, entered the room.

"Okay, I'm back," he announced. "Leila clue you in as to why she came here this morning?"

"Yes." Neel answered.

"Everything checks out fine. The intern gave her a once-over, and I also examined her. But I want to do a sonogram, just to be on the safe side."

He sat down, touched some buttons, and then said, "I'm going to put this on your abdomen, Leila. It may be cold, and I'll need to move it around some. Try not to move too much, okay?"

Neel had been glad to turn his attention to Patrick, but now he looked down at Leila. She was crying.

"Leila," he moved quickly toward her. "Are you in pain?"

She shook her head.

"What's the matter?" His guilt rose afresh and now he would do anything to calm her. "I'm sorry I wasn't there with you this morning. I promise it won't happen again."

"Yeah, Leila, give your husband a break," Patrick interjected from behind wires. "We men are human, after all. And if you ever have to check in alone again, he'll have to answer to both of us."

"See?" Neel said. "It's going to be all right. I won't even go flying unless you can come up with me."

But Leila couldn't stop crying, and Neel, nonplussed by her unexpected behavior, plunged on. "I'll give up the plane. No more flying, all right?"

"I'm scared." Leila finally got the words out. She felt—insecure—in this room, unprepared for its gadgets and pretty wall pictures, and a doctor operating a machine she'd never seen before.

"You don't need to be scared anymore. I'm here for you."

"It's the baby." Leila sniffed and wiped her face with a tissue.

"Oona said one in five women have miscarriages." She didn't tell Neel that death always came in threes. Tattappa, Janni, and Oona's baby. What if babies counted as half? What if her jealousy caused her to lose the baby?

"But Patrick said you were fine. He's the best OB/GYN there is. Shh, don't cry." Neel held her hand.

"If I'm fine, why is he doing this, this sonogram?" It was the hard, cold machine with the wires that truly bothered her.

"Because you are my wife. You're getting special treatment. If you were Mrs. Anyone-off-the-Street, you'd be home by now."

"Neel's right. We reserve the best for our own. Which is why," Patrick paused as he looked at the screen, "I can tell you right now that your baby will have perfect Apgars. No doctor's baby is allowed home without those nice tens."

Leila had stopped crying and now looked puzzled.

"I'll explain later," Neel promised. "It's just a routine test done when the baby is born."

"Hey, you lovebirds, want to see what I see?" Patrick turned the monitor so it faced Neel and Leila.

A gray and white volcano came into view, the lines undulating, grainy. Patrick was peering at it, saying, "Good, good, everything looks fine. And see this? That's your baby."

"That dot?" Leila's voice was doubtful. She hadn't known what to expect, but it wasn't a dot.

Neel had seen the fetus immediately. The tiny pulsing cells grew bigger as he watched, then changed into a ball, and slam-dunking that ball was a hand, strong and lean and brown. Somehow Neel knew he was looking at the first picture of his son. "That dot is our baby's heartbeat," Neel said, his words a little choked. "It's a strong one."

"That's good, right?" Leila asked, relief making her cry again. But now she was crying from happiness. If the baby was fine, if the baby was not going to die on her, she could believe that the rest of her life would be fine as well. This was the way she had always lived her life. An old saree meant a husband, a green light meant he was home waiting for her, and a small beating dot meant being happy with that husband. And he was with her now, looking at their future together.

Neel wiped away the tears that seeped from the corner of her almond eyes and down her cheeks. "Yes, Leila, a strong heartbeat is good."

"So the baby is okay?"

"Yes, Leila, our baby is okay."

ACKNOWLEDGMENTS

THIS BOOK HAS BENEFITED from the eyes and intelligence of many individuals. Sunita Chander above all, for speaking the truth; Barbara Bundy, Julie Connery, Krysten Cogswell Elbers, Yanina Rovinski, Oona Aven, Anju Basu, Marie Stael von Holstein, Anne Stein, Suhl Chin, Soo Chin, Alex Gansa, Philippa Levine, Shadi Bartsch, Carol Muske-Dukes, Bonnie Yates, Margaret B. Yates, Sue Hausmann, Anu Chander, Russell Leong, Mary O'Sullivan, Kitty Felde, and Jason E. Carmichael for their gentle suggestions and who, by taking the time to read various drafts, gave me the courage to keep writing; Ranjan Dey for allowing me to use his restaurant, New Delhi, in the novel; Prakash Abraham and Gursharan Kaur for providing important information and Bharat Sarath, Arvind Krishnaswamy, and Savitha Varadan for double-checking those facts; Nori Kurashige and Jan Ozaki for catching typos; Vonetta Taylor for finding me the right fonts; and Arlene Tademaru for driving me places.

I RESERVE THE GREATEST THANKS for my wonderful agent, Bonnie Nadell, for returning that first call and staying on the line (you gave me so much more than the title of my novel); to Maria Guarnaschelli, my editor, for hearing the music in my novel; and to Ann Adelman, my copyeditor, for putting in those commas, etc.

CLOSER TO HOME, my brother Sunny came up with that crucial scene in the novel, and my brother Paul offered me a room to write.

A NOTE ABOUT THE AUTHOR

THIS IS ANNE CHERIAN'S first work of fiction. Cherian was born and raised in Jamshedpur, India. After receiving degrees from Bombay and Bangalore universities, Cherian moved to Berkeley, California. She received graduate degrees in comparative literature and journalism at the University of California, Berkeley. Cherian lives in Los Angeles and visits India regularly.